A PUP TO RESCUE THEIR HEARTS

ALISON ROBERTS

A SURGEON WITH A SECRET

ALISON ROBERTS

MILLS & BOON

First Published in Great Britain 2021
by Mills & Boon, an imprint of HarperCollins*Publishers*
1 London Bridge Street, London, SE1 9GF

A Pup to Rescue Their Hearts © 2021 by Alison Roberts

A Surgeon with a Secret © 2021 by Alison Roberts

ISBN: 978-0-263-29751-5

A PUP TO RESCUE
THEIR HEARTS

ALISON ROBERTS

MILLS & BOON

CHAPTER ONE

PAUSING ON HIS way to grab a coffee in the paediatric ward's staffroom was a deliberate action on the part of Dr Josh Stanmore. He'd spotted that new nurse coming towards him and, as Head of Department, he knew it was high time he introduced himself and made this new staff member feel welcome. He'd noticed her before, of course. Who wouldn't when that wildly curly, rich auburn hair would make her stand out in any crowd? The fact that she was undeniably gorgeous was not something that was consciously crossing Josh's mind right then, however. His motive was professional, not personal.

Even more unlikely to occur to him was the thought that this momentary, random interruption, in his quest to find a caffeine hit to help get him through the rest of a busy afternoon, would end up saving a life.

Maybe it was because he didn't want the newest addition to the paediatric staff of Gloucester General Hospital to feel intimidated by the HOD watching her approach that made him avert his gaze for a moment. To turn his head and glance through the windows of the

playroom that ran the width of this end of the ward. A playroom that was deserted for the moment because afternoon visiting hours were over and it was a rest time for all their patients.

Except…the playroom wasn't quite deserted, was it? Josh could see small, bare legs beside a large, pink bean bag. And an even smaller hand, lying palm upwards, with the fingers curled as if the child was asleep.

Or…unconscious?

With a muttered oath, Josh stepped swiftly through the door of the brightly decorated room, moving far enough to be able to see the rest of the child and instantly recognising that she wasn't one of the patients on this ward. This little girl wasn't wearing a plastic identification bracelet on her wrist and she was not wearing pyjamas or slippers. She had sparkly pink shoes on and a dark blue dress that was…*good grief*…almost the same shade as her lips.

It took Josh only another two strides before he could crouch beside the child. To check her mouth for any obvious obstruction to her airway and then slide his fingers down to her neck to feel for a pulse at the same time as assessing whether she was breathing or not.

She wasn't.

Josh had no idea how long this child had been unconscious. She wasn't breathing but she still had a palpable pulse so he wasn't too late. There was no time to go looking for equipment like a bag mask or a defibrillator. There was only one thing to do and Josh didn't hesitate. He pinched the little girl's nose shut as he pulled

in some air before covering her mouth with his own to try and deliver a lifesaving breath. And then another.

Breaths that failed to make that small chest rise.

He knew he had to call for assistance but fear was enough to make him take another few seconds to scoop this little girl into his arms and turn her face down with her head lower than her chest. He flattened his hand so that he could apply back blows that might be effective enough to dislodge whatever was blocking her airway.

She'd seen him standing near the door to the playroom and the fact that her path was about to cross for the first time with that of the man who was effectively her new boss had been enough to make Stephanie Hawksbury's heart skip a beat. For a moment she thought he might be waiting for her but then he ducked into the playroom and, by the time she got close enough to see through the windows, he was on his knees on the floor, playing with a child.

Wait…

Nobody played with a child by hitting them on the back like that. It took Stevie only another split second to process what was actually going on and the armload of toys she'd been returning to the playroom fell from her arms to scatter and bounce on the floor. She shoved the door open, dragging in a deep breath.

'What do you need me to do, Doctor?'

'Get the door.' His words were terse as he got to his feet with the child cradled in his arms. 'Treatment room…*stat*…'

Stevie held the door and then ran to get in front of

him so that she could hold the door of the well-equipped treatment room that was used for a wide range of procedures that included anything from inserting a new intravenous line to a full-on resuscitation attempt.

Like this one…

Josh Stanmore laid the small girl on the bed in the centre of the room. Stevie was already pushing the airway trolley closer. If he'd been delivering back blows, it was obvious that Josh thought this small patient was choking and it was very obvious that she was becoming hypoxic from lack of oxygen. The small face was as white as a sheet, making the contrast with her blue lips all the more shocking.

Stevie would get the defibrillator next, of course, because if the breathing had stopped completely, a cardiac arrest would not be far away. She also turned her head towards the large red button beside the door that could trigger a cardiac arrest alarm that would have a dedicated team rushing towards them to assist.

Josh must have seen the direction of her glance but he wasn't about to stop for anything just yet—perhaps because he knew he had all the equipment he needed in this room and that he also knew they had only a matter of minutes before irreversible brain damage could occur and they couldn't afford to lose even precious seconds. He didn't have a whole team of medics to direct but the intensity of the gaze that was currently fixed on Stevie suggested that he thought she was capable of providing whatever assistance he needed.

And, dammit…that was exactly what she going to

do. Whatever it took. There was no way she was going to let a child die in front of her like this.

'Start chest thrusts,' Josh ordered. 'I'm going to try direct vision to see the obstruction. If that doesn't work, we're going to need to do a surgical airway.'

Stevie positioned one hand on the centre of the child's chest and began pushing in the same way she would for compressions in CPR. Even if the child's heart was still beating, this was the protocol for a choking child because the action, like back blows, could potentially dislodge the obstruction.

From the corner of her eye, she saw Josh choosing a curved blade to snap onto the handle of the laryngoscope and clicking on the light to test it. He was also scanning the trolley.

'I can't see any Magill's forceps.'

'Second drawer down on the left.'

'Got it.'

'Shall I try another breath?'

'Yep.'

Josh was at the head of the bed and was pulling the stainless-steel trolley close. As Stevie positioned the mask over the child's mouth and nose and squeezed the bag to try and deliver air to her lungs, she saw Josh tug the tie loose on a sterile pack and roll it out to open it.

A cricothyroidotomy kit, with a large IV cannula, five-mil syringe, oxygen tubing and a three-way stopcock for a needle cricothyroidotomy. There were also scalpels and tubing if a far more invasive surgical airway was required. Stevie's heart sank at both the glint of the scalpel and what her fingers were telling her

as they tried to squeeze the bag. The air inside it was going nowhere.

'Still obstructed?'

'Yes.'

'Right…' Josh sounded perfectly calm. 'Let's see what's going on, shall we?'

He slid a rolled-up towel beneath the girl's shoulders to tilt her head into what was known as the 'sniffing' position. Holding the laryngoscope in his left hand, he gently inserted the blade into the right side of their patient's mouth and Stevie knew he would be displacing the tongue to the left, which could allow the bright light to show him any visible foreign body in her airway. His movements were careful and confident and, although she was holding her breath, Stevie realised she had complete faith in this doctor. He knew exactly what he was doing and he didn't appear to be at all intimidated by the fact that he was dealing with a life-or-death emergency and a ticking clock.

And he could see something… Stevie could only see the back of Josh's head but she could feel the intent focus of his entire body as he lifted the small-sized Magill's forceps he was holding in his right hand. Like an elongated and angled pair of scissors with blunt, circular ends, these forceps were specifically designed to be used in airways, to guide the placement of tubes or to remove foreign objects.

It was a delicate manoeuvre. Josh had tilted his head to be able to see what he was doing with the forceps and there was nothing Stevie could do for the moment other than watch. She saw the lines deepening around Josh's

eyes that told her this was no easy task. She heard the tiny sigh that suggested relief as he seemed to be winning and then she noticed the way he caught the corner of his bottom lip between his teeth as he held onto his concentration.

And then his breath came out in a growl of frustration.

'Lost it,' he muttered. 'It's so slippery...'

Stevie swallowed hard. The next step would be to insert a needle into this child's neck, which would buy them a little more time, but if that didn't work, they would have to create a way to get air into her lungs by cutting a larger hole. And the seconds were ticking past relentlessly. Had she made a mistake in not hitting the alarm button sooner?

As if he'd heard her thought, Josh flicked her an upward glance.

'This time,' he said quietly. 'Trust me—we've got this.'

She did trust him, Stevie thought. Even though she didn't know this man at all—hadn't even been properly introduced to him, in fact, in the few days since she'd started working here—she was ready to trust him even when it was a child's life hanging in the balance.

He moved even more carefully this time as he slipped the forceps down the little girl's throat, and the tension ramping up as he paused for a long moment to make sure he had a good grip on whatever the slippery object was, meant that Stevie could actually hear her own heartbeat thumping in her ears as she continued to hold her own breath.

It probably only took a few seconds for Josh to pull the forceps slowly clear but it felt like for ever because she had to know that they hadn't lost their grip. Relief surged through her body as she saw them emerge from the child's mouth with something between the ends and—in the same instant—she could see and hear the desperate gasp as the little girl sucked in her first breath in too long. Or had that sound come from her own lips and that was why Josh's glance flicked up again to meet hers?

If it was, he clearly understood. He held her gaze for no more than a heartbeat but she could see the relief in his own eyes and it was so genuine—and caring—that Stevie knew that this doctor was a person she could have the utmost respect for. That he was as trustworthy as her instincts had already decided. And that she liked him.

A lot.

'Let's get some oxygen on,' he said. 'I'm just going to have another look and make sure there's nothing else down there that I can see.'

'What was it?' Stevie looked at the sterile cloth on the trolley as she reached up to connect tubing to the overhead oxygen supply. 'Oh…a grape?'

'Yeah…' Josh was shining the light of his laryngoscope down the child's throat again. 'The message that you have to cut grapes for littlies still hasn't got out there well enough. I heard recently they're the third most common cause of food-related choking deaths in children. I can't see anything else down there.' He removed the blade of the laryngoscope, unhooked his stethoscope from around his neck and frowned as he

focused on the small girl's face while fitting the ear-pieces. 'Who is she, do you know?'

Stevie shook her head. 'I'm guessing she's a sibling of one of our patients. She probably came in during visiting hours.'

She held the mask, now with oxygen running, over the girl's mouth and nose. Josh's hand brushed her arm as he moved the disc of the stethoscope to listen to their patient's chest. Stevie could feel the twitch of movement under the mask she was holding in place.

'I think she's waking up...'

'Good...'

Stevie knew why there was still a note of caution in Josh's tone. The girl was breathing on her own but would she regain consciousness fully? Had she been without adequate oxygenation long enough for brain damage to have occurred?

They both turned their heads as the door of the treatment room opened. It was the first time that Stevie had seen the paediatric ward's nurse manager, Ruby, without a smile on her face.

'What's happening, Josh? What do you need?'

'We're under control, thanks, Ruby. I found this girl unconscious in the playroom—respiratory arrest due to a totally obstructed airway.'

'Oh, dear Lord...' Ruby closed her eyes in a long blink. 'I was just helping with the hunt for Amelia here. Her baby brother has come in for observation and her mother was feeding him while the registrar did the ad-mission. Dad went to the cafeteria to find a late lunch for them all and Mum assumed that Amelia had gone

with him. It's panic stations out there. I'll have to let them know where she is.'

Ruby moved far more swiftly back to the door than Stevie would have expected for a woman of her size and age and she'd no more than poked her head into the corridor to call out to someone than she was stepping aside to let other people into the room.

A young man, who was holding a baby. And a terrified-looking young woman with a pale tear-streaked face.

'Oh, my God...' she sobbed. *'Amelia...'*

The woman rushed towards the bed and, as she reached to touch her daughter, the little girl opened her eyes and burst into tears.

'Mumma...'

Stevie could feel the prickle of tears behind her own eyes. Happy tears, because the fact that Amelia was awake and speaking and knew who her mother was made it more than likely she had come through this life-threatening incident unscathed. It seemed the most natural thing in the world to look up and meet Josh's gaze yet again and, this time, it felt like an acknowledgement of a bond. The two of them had been the only people to share that very real fear, the tension of the fight, the relief of a successful outcome and now the joy of the world righting itself at least in this moment of time. A whole story that had taken only a couple of minutes but would be one that Stevie was never going to forget.

And, judging by the look in Dr Stanmore's eyes, he wasn't about to forget it, either.

'It's okay,' he reassured the crying mother. 'Amelia

here choked on a grape but we were lucky enough to find her in time.'

Amelia was in her mother's arms now. 'Oh, thank you, Doctor. I can't thank you enough…you and…?' She looked over her daughter's head, her eyebrows raised.

'Stephanie, isn't it?' Josh was smiling. 'I need to thank you as well.'

Oh, man…the warmth in those dark eyes was enough to be making something melt somewhere in the middle of Stevie's chest.

'I get called Stevie,' she told him. She tried to return his smile but she had a horrible feeling that, in the emotional aftermath of a crisis averted, her lips might be too wobbly to cooperate so she broke the eye contact to turn back to Amelia and her mother. 'I'm sure I'll see you both again very soon.' She stepped back, knowing that she was no longer needed in here and that she had a lot of duties to catch up on now.

'We'll need to keep Amelia with us for a little while,' Josh added. 'Ruby, could you sort an urgent consult with someone from ENT, please? It's just a precaution,' he told Amelia's mother. 'But I wouldn't be surprised if she's got a bit of a sore throat now.'

'But what happened? What did you say she choked on?'

Stevie held the door for Ruby and they both slipped out of the room while Josh filled the parents in on the details of the incident.

'We'll have to do a detailed report on this,' Ruby told Stevie. 'I need to get this consult organised right now

but could you come and see me in the office before your shift finishes, please?'

'Of course. I'll be there as soon as I can. I'm running a bit behind with obs on my patients now, though.'

'Emergencies tend to do that.' But Ruby was smiling. 'But well done, Stevie. I had a feeling the first day I met you that you were going to be an asset around here.'

Ruby's praise was as welcome as the warmth of Josh Stanmore's thanks had been and Stevie tackled the list of tasks associated with the four patients under her care on this shift with a growing confidence that her life was on a new track. A much, much better one than she'd been on for the last twelve years or so.

If only…

Between feeding and changing a baby whose mother had had to go home to her other children this afternoon, and taking a full set of observations, including an ECG on a four-year-old boy who had congenital heart disease currently complicated by a respiratory infection, Stevie snatched a moment to send a text.

Hey, Mattie…you home yet? Hope you had a better day at school xx

Thanks to one of the less pleasant duties of the day, getting a parent and a junior nurse to hold a wriggling, terrified toddler while Stevie got a blood sample, it was another half an hour before she noticed that her text had gone unanswered. It didn't surprise her but it did increase the background level of tension, especially as it would be another couple of hours before she could

get home and see for herself that the other half of her life—the personal and most important half—was at least getting closer to stepping on the same track as her professional one.

She had a horrible feeling that it wasn't...

'Stevie...'

She dropped the test tube she'd just finished labelling into a plastic bag and began pressing the seal together, turning at the sound of her name. This time she managed to find a smile for the paediatric consultant who was, by all accounts, not only the most important doctor but the most popular man in this hospital department.

'Hi, Dr Stanmore. How's Amelia?'

'Call me Josh,' he said, propping his elbow on the higher shelf in front of the reception desk. 'And Amelia's fine. She's been cleared by ENT and gone home with her dad, who's got instructions to bring her back if he has any worries about her coughing or with any change in her breathing or swallowing.'

'Oh, that's so good to hear.' Stevie's smile widened.

'I just wanted to thank you again.' Josh was watching Stevie's hands as she folded the lab test request to put into the pocket on the side of the plastic bag. 'I couldn't have dealt with that emergency without the kind of calm, experienced assistance you were able to provide.'

The glow of pride was giving Stevie that melting sensation again and, as her gaze lifted to meet a pair of eyes that were dark enough to make it difficult to distinguish the pupil, she could feel something else contributing to that tingling in her gut. Attraction was the

last thing she'd expected—or wanted—to ambush her like this but there was no mistaking that shaft of whatever it was a mixture of. Desire? Anticipation? Longing? *Hope...?*

'So...' Josh's smile was a bit lopsided now and one eyebrow had moved closer to the tumble of rather charmingly unkempt hair that was almost as curly as her own. 'I owe you a drink. What are you doing after work?'

'Sorry?' Stevie could feel her smile fading. That internal fizzing sensation was fading even faster.

'After work? Can I buy you a drink?' Josh's smile had also disappeared and that raised eyebrow now made him look a little puzzled. 'Doesn't have to be a wine. How 'bout a coffee?'

'You're...asking me out? For a drink?' Stevie spoke carefully. Slowly enunciating each syllable, which was the complete opposite of the way her brain was firing very rapid messages. Images of another attractive man. Another paediatric consultant, in fact. Echoes of a day that had changed her life for ever.

'Come for a drink with me, after work. And I'm not going to take "no" as an answer...'

'Just to say thanks for your help today.' Josh took his elbow off the shelf and straightened up. 'And to say welcome, of course. You're our newest staff member, after all.'

The new girl. Fresh meat...

'I do hope you're not hitting on me, Dr Stanmore.' Stevie dropped the plastic bag into the out tray for urgent lab tests and took a step back. 'I was just doing my

job in helping you with that emergency and a simple "thank you" is more than enough.' There were more echoes in the back of her head and what she could feel roiling in her gut now was nothing like the pleasurable tickle of attraction.

'I'm your HOD. It's my duty to make my new staff members feel as welcome as possible. You're not going to say "no" to your boss on your first day at work, are you, Stephanie?'

Stevie swallowed hard but the internal knot of something unpleasant, like anger, or possibly fear, was rapidly growing. She knew she shouldn't say anything more than offering a polite refusal of his invitation but, when she opened her mouth, something very different came out.

'Maybe in the old days it was generally accepted that a new nurse was fair game for every male in the vicinity.' Her tone was clipped. Controlled. Bordering on icy. 'I would hope we've all become a bit more enlightened these days when it comes to things like sexual harassment. Excuse *me*...' Stevie turned her back on her boss. 'I've got work to do.'

She didn't actually have to go into the supply room a little further down the corridor from the reception desk but it was the quickest way to escape the deathly silence behind her and the feeling of Josh Stanmore's gaze fixed on the back of her head as if it was the bullseye of a target. Stevie shoved open the door, let it swing shut behind her and then buried her face in her hands.

Oh... *God*... So much for her wonderful new start in life. She'd just ruined everything, hadn't she?

CHAPTER TWO

'I MEAN...WHAT'S her *problem*?' Josh tipped back the wooden chair he was sitting on so it was balancing on two legs. He tipped his head back as well, closing his eyes and letting his breath out in a long, weary sigh. 'I only offered to buy her a coffee, for heaven's sake, and she practically bit my head off. Even said something about sexual harassment, would you believe? I mean...*really*?'

'Hmm...' Nurse Manager Ruby's tone was noncommittal. She was still reading over what Josh had written in a section of her Critical Incident Report form. 'So your first attempt with the Magill's forceps failed?'

'Yes. It's remarkable how slippery a grape can be when it's coated with saliva. It was a delay in dealing with the obstructed airway of no more than twenty to thirty seconds and there's no sign of any injury from oxygen deprivation. She's a lucky kid.'

'She sure is,' Ruby agreed. 'We can be very grateful that you spotted her. Who knows how long it might have been before someone had found her if you hadn't happened to walk past and look through that window?'

'Oh…crazy new nurse would have found her at almost the same time. She was carrying a bunch of toys back to the playroom.' It was why he'd stopped, after all, because he'd wanted the chance to talk to her. Not that he would have done that if he'd had any idea how prickly she was.

Ruby's glance, over her half-moon reading glasses, was exasperated. 'So now she's crazy just because she didn't want to go on a date with you?'

'It wasn't a *date*.'

'What was it, then?'

Josh resisted the urge to roll his eyes. 'It was supposed to be a "thank you" for assisting me in an emergency. And a "welcome to GG's paediatric ward".'

'Ah…' Ruby nodded sagely. 'And the fact that she's young and gorgeous with that wild, red hair and those big, brown eyes had nothing to do with it? Tell me, Josh—if she was as old and ugly as me, would you have been so quick to offer to buy her a coffee?'

Josh grinned at Ruby. Okay, his most senior nurse was more than old enough to be his mother and she'd probably never had a particularly healthy BMI but she was not only one of the best nurses he'd ever worked with, she had a warmth that made it a real pleasure to be near her and a smile that could light up a room.

She was a wise old bird, too, and he had to admit there was some truth in what she was saying. He hadn't just been impressed with Stevie's professional skills this afternoon. At some level he'd also been perfectly well aware of exactly how attractive she was. He had *not* been hitting on her, however. He wouldn't think

of doing that when he didn't even know if someone was single.

The errant thought that immediately followed—that he would quite *like* to know if Stevie was single—was easy to squash. His relationship with that new staff member was never going to be anything other than purely professional from now on. She hadn't quite slapped his face in public but it kind of felt like she had and he wasn't about to offer her an opportunity to repeat the put-down.

He let his chair thump back to the floor in time to see the mischievous tilt to Ruby's lips, which was enough to make him smile himself.

'I'll never understand women,' he admitted. 'Is that all you need from me for now, Ruby?'

Her face was deadpan now. 'Wouldn't mind a coffee,' she said. 'Milk and two sugars, thanks.'

'Ha…' As he stood up, the sleeve of his white coat knocked some papers from the corner of Ruby's desk. 'Sorry…' Josh bent to pick up the glossy pamphlets and, as he put them back on the desk, the picture on the front—a back view of a man and a boy walking in a park—caught his attention.

'What's this about?'

'Oh…' Ruby glanced up. 'Someone from the social services team left those with me today. It's about the Big Brother programme where men volunteer to be a kind of role model to young boys who don't have a father figure at home. Someone safe, like an uncle or a big brother—for tweens and teens, mostly, when they're more likely to go off the rails or be giving their fam-

ily a hard time. We get quite a few solo mums through here and it's always good to be able to let them know what kind of community resources there are for getting support.'

She reached for a pen. 'I need to get you to sign this form before you rush off to get my coffee. Right there...'

He made two mugs of coffee in the staffroom and carried them back to Ruby's office a few minutes later. Her smile was a reward all by itself.

'You *did* get me a coffee. Always knew you were a good lad, Josh Stanmore.'

'You should have gone home a long time ago,' he told her. 'It's way past dinner time.'

'Oh, what's that?' Ruby tilted her head and looked up at the ceiling. 'Yeah...it's the pot calling the kettle black.' She closed her eyes as she took an appreciative sip of her hot drink.

'I'm going.' But Josh sat down on the wooden chair again. 'As soon as I've had this coffee, that is. I've been trying to get a chance to make it ever since that exciting little interruption we had this afternoon.'

Stevie would have gone home as least an hour ago, Josh thought. And then he gave himself a mental slap for even letting her enter his head. Needing distraction, he focused on the neat pile that those pamphlets were now in.

'Could have done with one of those,' he murmured.

'Oh?' Ruby was instantly alert. 'For a parent of one of our patients? You know something I don't know?'

'Doubt it. No... I was thinking of my own childhood. I got brought up by my grandmother. I could have

done with someone like a big brother.' Not that he was about to tell Ruby, but he'd been one of those problem kids. He could have easily gone completely off the rails. 'Instead, I buried myself in my room and spent far too much time watching medical documentaries and crime shows. I was determined to be the world's best forensic pathologist.'

Ruby laughed. 'And you end up working with kids who never stop letting you know how alive they are by their screaming and kicking, filling their pants and throwing up on you? What went wrong there?'

Josh shrugged. 'They smile sometimes. And give you cuddles. Guess I just love kids. Maybe they make *us* feel more alive.'

Ruby's face softened. 'You're not wrong there. You should have some of your own one of these days.'

'Nah...' Josh drained his mug. 'Not going to happen. I've got more than enough of them here at work.'

He could feel Ruby's gaze following him as he left her office, though. He could almost hear her thinking that it was a shame he was going to miss out on so much by not wanting to have a family of his own but he wasn't about to tell anyone the reasons why he was never going to become a father.

The idea of being a 'big brother' was a new concept, however. How different would that be, to have a relationship with a child who wasn't sick? A child who might be living a life that was a very long way from being in one of those perfect, nuclear families? Or any kind of 'real' family?

He'd been that child once. And maybe that was at

the core of the reasons he never wanted to try and create his own family but that was no excuse not to try and help another kid. It wasn't as if he didn't have plenty of spare time when he wasn't at work and he didn't even have a girlfriend making any demands on that spare time at the moment.

Charlotte from Radiology had crossed the line a few weeks ago when she'd given him the tearful ultimatum of either declaring his long-term commitment or admitting that their relationship was going nowhere. He'd been as kind as possible in making that admission but that particular scenario wasn't getting any easier to deal with due to familiarity. Why was it that women seemed to be so happy to sign up to a 'friendship with benefits' only to completely forget the clearly explained ground rules of a month or three later?

Oddly, he couldn't help wondering how Stevie would react to those ground rules and Josh found himself smiling wryly as he walked out of the front doors of Gloucester General Hospital. She wouldn't be reacting to any rules, would she? She'd be setting them all herself, like some sort of fierce headmistress in an exclusive school. Even more oddly, he had to admit that he admired that kind of ferocity enough for it to ramp up how attractive she was.

Josh shook his head, fishing in his pocket for his car keys. How immature was that? Hadn't he just been thinking he'd make a good role model as a big brother? This new nurse seemed to be creating unwanted ripples in his life—like a large stone being thrown into a

pond he happened to be standing in for some inexplicable reason. He needed to get out of water, obviously.

And stay out…

'Stay here for the moment, please, Mrs Hawkesbury. Someone will be in to talk to you very soon.'

'It's Ms. I'm not married.'

'My apologies. It's not easy to—'

'I need to see my son.' Stevie interrupted the junior police officer who looked like he should still be in a school uniform rather than the one he was wearing. *'Please…'*

To her horror, she could hear the wobble in her voice and realised she was so wound up that it was quite possible she might burst into tears at any moment. Fifteen minutes ago, Ruby had taken one look at her face after the phone call she'd received and told her to leave work early without even asking for any explanation after hearing that it was a family problem.

'Go,' she'd told Stevie. *'I'll cover for you.'*

Her nurse manager was one in a million, that was for sure, but she'd already known that. When she'd confessed that she'd been rather rude to the head of their department, Ruby had actually chuckled.

'Don't you worry about that,' she'd said. *'He knows how well you do your job and it won't hurt him one little bit to get turned down for once.'*

'Matthew's fine.' The baby police officer gave her a reassuring smile. 'We don't make a habit of locking eleven-year-old boys up around here. He's actually having a game of snooker in our staffroom with one of our

social workers, Tim. He'll bring him here as soon as you've had a chat with his boss, Angela. Ah…here she is. I'll leave you to it.'

Angela introduced herself as a liaison officer between the police and social services. '…and you're Stephanie, yes?'

'I prefer Stevie.'

Angela's smile was friendly. 'It's good to meet you, Stevie. Please, sit down.'

But Stevie remained standing. 'I need to know what's happening,' she said. 'I don't understand why he's been brought in here. He's a good kid. I know he'd *never* do something like shoplifting.'

'Please…'

The older woman's gesture towards the seat was a command Stevie couldn't ignore and, to be honest, it was a bit of a relief to sit down. Her legs still hadn't recovered from how fast she'd run from the hospital to this police station. She was still wearing her scrubs under her coat.

'You're living on Hastings Street, yes?'

Stevie took a breath. She knew that high-density, inner-city living wasn't ideal for kids but it wasn't as if she was renting an apartment in some dodgy estate where she knew she'd be putting her son in danger.

'It's close to the hospital,' she defended herself. 'For my job. I'm a paediatric nurse. And there was a good school—King's—within walking distance for Mattie. We only moved here a few weeks ago.'

Angela's nod was sympathetic. 'The incident occurred at the corner shop on your street. Matthew was

with a group of older boys and he was the only one the owner of the shop managed to catch. They were only stealing sweets but the owner's had trouble with this gang of lads for quite a while and he was fed up enough to call us in to try and give them a fright.'

A *gang*? Her serious, responsible boy was now part of a gang? Stevie shook her head. 'He was supposed to go straight home after school and get on with his home-work. I'm paying one of the neighbours to keep an eye on him until I get home from work.'

'That would be Mrs Johnston?'

'That's right… How did you know?'

'We took Matthew home to start with and he told us about the arrangement but Mrs Johnston wasn't there. She'd left a note on the door to say she was sorry but that her daughter was sick and she'd had to go and col-lect her grandchildren. Anyway…that was why we de-cided to bring him back to the station for a while. Until we could contact you and have a chat.'

To see for themselves whether she was a responsible parent? Whether Social Services might need to be in-volved? Stevie could feel her hackles rising.

'I've been a single mother for more than eleven years,' she said. 'And we've managed just fine. We've never been in any kind of trouble with the police or anyone else. *Ever*…'

Oh, help… She needed to take a deep breath. 'I'm not saying it's been easy. Moving to Gloucester is a new start for us but…it's harder than I thought it would be, to settle in a new city. I know Mattie's finding it a bit

difficult to get used to a new school. He's missing his old school friends.'

'Do you have any family nearby for support?'

Stevie shook her head. Her mother was hours away by train now. Twice as far as she'd been before she'd taken this huge step of starting a new life in this part of the country.

'Is Matthew's father involved?'

Stevie's head shake was a sharp dismissal of the idea. What would Angela think, she wondered, if she told her that the only involvement Mattie's father had ever had in his life had been to offer her enough money to get an abortion? She'd never told anyone that because she would never let her son know how unwanted he'd been by one of his parents. Despite how much the pregnancy had derailed the life she had planned for herself and how incredibly hard it had been at times, Mattie was the best thing that had ever happened for Stevie and she loved her little boy more than she'd known it was possible to love anyone.

Imagine if she'd been telling Angela about why he didn't have a father in his life when Mattie was brought into the room by Tim the social worker—which was exactly what happened only moments after that question had been asked.

Stevie got to her feet, her arm outstretched to gather her son to her side, but Mattie had his head down and looked as though he was almost shrinking into himself—as if he was trying to hide? Stevie dropped her arm. He certainly didn't look as if he would welcome a hug from his mother right now.

Tim introduced himself and then turned to Angela. 'We've had a good chat, me and Matthew. I don't think he's going to be getting himself into any more trouble.' He smiled at Stevie. 'It's been a bit of a shock, coming here in the squad car.'

Stevie couldn't smile back. It had been more than a bit of a shock having had to run here, wondering if this was another blow to the dream of the new and wonderful life—like that unfortunate encounter with the chief consultant of her paediatric ward the other day. Surely history couldn't repeat itself to the extent that she'd need to pack up yet again and find another new start?

'We've had a talk about other things Matthew could be doing after school before you get home from work. Did you know that King's Primary School offers an after-school programme that runs until six o'clock?'

Stevie nodded. She also knew how expensive it was.

'I happen to know there are spaces held there for special kids.' Tim's tone was casual but the glance Stevie received over Mattie's head suggested that he'd read her mind. That these 'special' spaces were funded by some kind of charity?

Stevie could feel herself bristling again. She'd never accepted charity.

'You'd quite like to try it out, wouldn't you, Matthew? If I can sort it out for you?'

Mattie still wasn't making eye contact with his mother but he nodded in response to Tim's query.

'I'll be in touch, then. Here's my card, if you want to talk anytime. And there's something else I thought might possibly be of interest.' Tim handed Stevie a pam-

phlet. 'We won't hold you up any more now, though.' He patted Mattie's shoulder. 'It's been a pleasure meeting you,' he said. 'But I don't want to see you back here anytime soon, okay?'

Stevie barely glanced at the pamphlet but she could see it had a picture of a man and a boy walking in some idyllic-looking park. She shoved it into her shoulder bag.

'Let's go, Mattie. It's time we went home.'

Her legs still felt strangely heavy as she got to her feet, however. Her heart was feeling a bit on the heavy side, as well. It didn't really feel like they were heading home at all, especially with how Mattie still had his head down as he was walking, scuffing his feet and refusing to respond to Stevie's attempts to talk to him with anything more than grunts.

'I'm not cross,' she told him. 'I'm guessing you only did what you did because you were trying to fit in. Or make friends…?'

Her suggestion earned a shrug, along with a sound that was equally noncommittal.

'We'll talk about it later, okay? After dinner. Don't know about you, but I'm absolutely starving.'

The elevator in their apartment block was out of order. Again. Stevie had already been on her feet for so long it was a real effort to climb flight after flight of stairs. At least she didn't have to worry about hauling a pram with her these days but she'd been wrong to think that life would magically get so much easier as Mattie got older. The challenges of being a single parent to a

tiny baby had been enormous but, in retrospect, they had been simple.

Mattie was now old enough and responsible enough to be able to keep himself clean and fed and entertained but the challenges were still there and seemed to be becoming far more complex.

At some point, preferably later this evening, they were going to have to talk about all this and she could only hope they could work together to find a new approach that might help. If she had to swallow her pride and accept assistance that could give her boy access to resources like an after-school programme that might provide both company and enjoyment then so be it.

At least she had Mattie's favourite food in the freezer and it wasn't bad parenting to allow a meal like fish fingers, chips and maybe a fried egg for a treat, was it—even if there wasn't going to be a green vegetable in sight?

This wasn't going well.

The lad had barely said anything during their introductory meeting so far.

'This was my mum's idea, not mine.' He got up from his chair and went to stare out the window. The room in this downtown building looked out over a busy road. 'I don't need a big brother.'

'She's coming today as well, yes?' Josh looked over the boy's head to where the social worker, Tim, was sitting on the other side of the room.

Tim nodded. 'She texted to say she's running a bit

late, but if Mattie was happy, we could go ahead and make a plan for what you're going to do next time.'

Josh was starting to wonder if there was going to be a next time. This serious young boy didn't look as if he was going to welcome a stranger into his life. Only eleven years old and he was clearly practised in protecting himself. How sad was that? Sad enough to remind Josh of things about his own childhood that he'd buried long ago, anyway. He got up, moving to stand beside the lad at the window. He didn't say anything—he just wanted to let him get used to him being close—but it seemed to have an instant effect of making the boy freeze.

It was the gasp of horror that made Josh realise that Mattie wasn't even aware of him standing there, however, and a split second later, the screech of brakes and then a squeal of tyres alerted him to what Mattie had been witnessing. A small dog had been hit by a car that was now accelerating away into heavy traffic, leaving the animal on the side of the road.

'No...' Mattie's face was white, which made his eyes look even darker and more horrified as he looked up at Josh. He was trying hard not to cry. 'It's...dead, isn't it?'

'No.' Josh glanced back through the window. 'Look...he's trying to get up now. Looks like he's hurt his leg, though. Shall we go and see if we can help?'

Mattie's nod was vehement and he caught his breath, poised to bolt towards the door. Josh caught Tim's gaze to check that it was okay to go outside with Mattie, seeing as they were only supposed to be having a family

meeting here at the organisation's headquarters today. Tim was nodding.

'Josh is a doctor, Mattie. I'm sure he'll be able to help that dog.'

There wasn't much they could do on the street, mind you, and there was nobody who seemed to be with the dog so Josh carried it back into the building. Tim found some towels and other things that Josh requested and Mattie crouched on the floor, staring intently at what Josh was doing as he examined the small, scruffy terrier.

'I don't think he's badly hurt,' Josh told him. 'But, can you see that?'

'What?'

'The shape of his leg?'

'It's different to the other leg, isn't it?'

'Well spotted.' Josh smiled at Mattie. 'And smart. That's one of the things they teach us to do at medical school when we're trying to find out what's wrong—to compare one side with the other to see if it's different. What do you reckon the problem is?'

'Is it broken?'

'I think so.' Josh's touch was very gentle but the dog yelped in pain.

Mattie reached out to stroke the wiry little head.

'Be careful. Even a friendly dog can bite if it's in pain or really scared.'

'He's not going to bite,' Mattie said. The dog whimpered but he had closed his eyes at the touch, as if it was comforting him.

'He hasn't got a collar,' Tim said. 'And he's pretty

dirty. I reckon he's a stray, which could mean that no-body's going to want to pay a big vet's bill.'

'I'll pay it,' Josh said. 'Is there a vet near here that you know of?'

'I'll look it up.' Tim picked up his phone.

'We'll need to make this little guy a bit more comfortable to take him to the vet,' Josh told Mattie. 'What I'll do is wrap a towel around his leg and then you can help me bandage it into a kind of splint.'

'There's a vet clinic just a couple of blocks away,' Tim reported a minute or two later.

'Right. I'll take him there now.' Josh used another towel to wrap and scoop up the dog.

'I'm coming too,' Mattie said. He was already beside the door, his face both anxious but determined.

Tim hesitated. Josh could see he knew he shouldn't be breaking the Big Brother protocol of a supervised first meeting but this was an emergency. It had also been enough to break through the obvious reluctance Mattie had had to connect with somebody new. If he was forced to stay behind, he might well retreat behind barriers that would be even harder to breach.

'Okay,' Tim said, finally. 'But you stay with Josh, Mattie. And don't leave the clinic. I'll bring your mum down as soon as she arrives.'

Mattie's gaze was fixed on the face of the little dog that was all that could be seen amongst the folds of the towel but then he glanced up at Josh and the expression on the boy's face just melted his heart. He would never let it show, in front of relatives or even his colleagues, but there were times Josh felt that desperate to help a

vulnerable baby or small child who was critically ill. Because of that, he knew how important it was to feel as if you could make a difference.

'This little guy's not too heavy,' he said quietly to Mattie. 'And I know he trusts you. Do you think you could carry him?'

He could almost see the inches of height Mattie gained as he straightened up and nodded solemnly. As Josh placed the injured dog carefully into the boy's arms, he caught his gaze again and that squeeze on his heart was there even more than before. This scruffy little dog had done more than provide a way for him to connect with this lad. By trusting Mattie to help with his care, Josh had taken a big step towards winning the trust of a child who reminded him of his much younger self.

And it felt like the best thing that had happened to Josh in longer than he could remember.

'Come on…' He held the door open for Mattie. 'Let's do this…'

It was the second time in little more than a week that Stevie had had the stress of racing through the inner-city streets of Gloucester with no idea of exactly what she was heading towards.

At least it wasn't a police station this time but the fact that it involved someone from Social Services was enough to generate anxiety—especially given that Stevie was now very late for the appointment to meet the mentor Mattie had been paired with at the Big Brother programme. She was hardly going to come across as a

shining example of great parenting when she couldn't even turn up on time and Stevie also had a horrible feeling that, even though she'd showered and completely changed her clothes, she might still be carrying the taint of the unpleasant incident of the vomiting child that had delayed her departure from work.

Even more worryingly, Tim the social worker was standing on the wide front step of the address she'd been given, clearly watching out for her.

'Has something happened? Where's Mattie?'

Oh, help…had he run away or something? He hadn't been that keen on the idea of coming here in the first place but, after that long talk they'd had about different things they could do to help him settle in a new home, he'd agreed to give it a go.

'He's just down the road, with his mentor, Josh. It's okay…' Tim added hurriedly as he saw Stevie's expression. 'I'll explain on the way to the vet clinic. I just wanted to tell you face to face rather than with a text message that might have worried you.'

By the time they arrived at the vet clinic, Stevie had been given the impression that the dog's accident might have been a good thing and provided a much faster route than normal for a relationship to develop between a boy who might be in need of a male role model and his mentor.

It was a bit of a shame that the match had been made with someone that had the same name as the man she was now doing her best to avoid in her new job but she could get past that if it was going to be a good thing for Mattie. Any interaction with Dr Stanmore had been

minimal since she'd been so rude to him and she hadn't even seen him in the distance today so it was easy to dismiss anything negative that the name stirred up.

Besides, she was focused on Mattie as they were shown into the consulting room at the clinic. She hadn't seen him look like this in a very long time—as if it was Christmas morning when he'd still been young enough to believe in the magic of Santa Claus, with the way his whole face was shining with excitement.

'Mum…look… I helped fix his broken leg. He's had X-rays and everything and I helped make the plaster cast. And Josh let me carry him all the way here and…he doesn't have a chip so Josh says maybe he doesn't even have a family and…can we take him home? Please…?'

Oh, my… Stevie opened her mouth and then closed it again. What on earth could she say? As soon as Mattie was told that there were strict rules in their apartment building that no pets were allowed, she was going to see that animation—joy, even—drain from his face. She glanced at Tim but he just gave her a sympathetic look. The vet could see she needed help, however.

'We can keep him overnight,' she said. 'There are some animal rescue sites on social media that we can put his photo on and, who knows, maybe we'll find he does have an owner so he won't need to go to the pound.'

'No…'

Mattie shook his head, turning away to look up at the man standing just behind him. A moment of silent communication that covered the shock of Stevie discover-

ing that the name of the mentor her son had been paired with was not just a coincidence. That he was none other than the most senior doctor in her department and the man she'd practically accused of sexually harassing her.

'I'll take him,' Josh Stanmore said. 'While we're looking for his owner, anyway.'

'Can I come and visit him, then?' Mattie's tone was a plea. 'Next time I see you?'

Next time? Oh, no… Stevie felt like the walls were starting to close in on her. Mattie wanted to see Josh again? Wanted to have a relationship with her boss? Surely Josh wouldn't be comfortable with that any more than she was?

But he was smiling at Mattie. 'I think that's up to your mum,' he said. 'That was the deal, remember? We were all going to meet today and talk about what happens next.'

Mattie nodded, turning back to fix his gaze on his mother.

'But you *said*, Mum…' His tone was accusing now. 'You told Tim that if I was happy we could plan what was going to happen next time.'

Across the top of his head, Josh was also staring at Stevie and it felt almost like the two of them were ganging up on her.

What was Josh even doing here? Surely he had enough to do with children in his working life? He might have a few at home as well as far as she knew but, in any case, a Big Brother match was inappropriate given her professional relationship with this man. It could also be extremely awkward. Imagine what Mattie

might tell Josh about her? It already felt as if her privacy had been severely breached here.

It couldn't possibly be allowed to happen, that was all there was to it, but this was going to have to be handled carefully. Things were fragile enough with Mattie to make disappointing him a big deal. This could turn out to be a turning point and Stevie needed time to think because the last thing she wanted was to make things worse. She knew her words were the classic parental cop-out but it was the best she could come up with under this kind of pressure.

'I'll have to think about it,' she said. 'We'll see.'

CHAPTER THREE

It had to happen, of course.

There was no way Josh could avoid seeing Stevie at work and, to be honest, he didn't want to avoid it. He'd been sharing his home for a couple of days now with a small, scruffy dog who had a plaster cast on its leg so it couldn't move very much, and Josh couldn't catch sight of the injured animal or carry it out to the garden for bathroom business without thinking of the boy who'd helped him rescue it.

A boy who reminded him of things that had shaped his own life. Like the loneliness. Like feeling that he didn't belong, or worse, that he wasn't wanted. That need to help others in order to make himself worthwhile. Good grief... Mattie even looked a bit like Josh had at that age, being a bit tall and lean for his age, with shaggy dark hair and brown eyes.

He wanted to know that Mattie was okay after the trauma of seeing that accident. He wanted to let him know that the dog was doing great and the only way he could do that was to speak to Mattie's mother.

He just hadn't expected that it would come in the

wake of more drama. Or that it would be Stevie who slipped into the treatment room as he stood there, unable to get on with the procedure he was there to perform. Unable to move, in fact, seeing as he was scrubbed and keeping his gloved hands from touching anything non-sterile. Fortunately, his small patient was sedated enough to be asleep on the bed in front of him and it was also fortunate that Stevie was clearly up to speed with what was going on. She had already pulled a gown over her scrubs and was reaching for a mask from the wall dispenser.

'Ruby said you need a hand for a lumbar puncture.'

'Mmm… This is Taylor. Her mum needed to step outside for a minute, along with Ruby and my registrar.'

'Yes.' Stevie didn't meet his eyes as she went to the other side of the bed. 'I found her inhaler but your registrar decided they needed to get her down to ED.'

'It was a rather dramatic onset of an asthma attack. She was a bit overwhelmed by all this.'

Stevie simply nodded, as if she knew exactly why Taylor's mother had been so upset. She bent down so that her face was close to that of the five-year-old girl. 'Hey, sweetheart,' she said softly. 'My name's Stevie.'

Oh…man… That note in Stevie's voice when she'd said 'sweetheart'. It was as though it had struck some weird kind of gong buried deep in Josh's chest. He could feel a reverberation of the single word that was giving him the strangest feeling of…what was it…*longing*? Or maybe it was sadness that he'd never heard anyone call *him* 'sweetheart' like that. As if they were so completely and utterly genuine.

Maybe that note had been what had pierced Taylor's sleepiness, although her words were slurred enough to suggest a good level of sedation as her eyes fluttered open. 'Where's Mummy?'

'She'll be back soon. She asked me to help look after you.' Stevie stroked wisps of blonde hair back from Taylor's face. 'I'm going to help you stay really, really still for Dr Josh, okay?'

''kay…'

'I can see you've got someone to cuddle. Is it a rabbit?''

'Is Bunny…' The girl's arms tightened around the stuffed toy she was clutching.

'You cuddle Bunny…' Stevie's murmur was reassuring. 'And I'm going to cuddle you…'

Taylor's eyes drifted shut again as Stevie moved her hands to a position where she could make sure the child couldn't move suddenly. She looked up at Josh.

'You happy with her position? Do you want the spine flexed any more than this?'

For a heartbeat, Josh was caught by Stevie's eyes. Mesmerised, even. Perhaps it was because her face was half-covered by a mask so it was her eyes that were more obvious. Or maybe it was because he hadn't noticed before that those eyes were such an extraordinary colour. A tawny kind of hazel with the same golden glints that were shining amongst the red in that wild hair of hers under the bright light above this table. As alive as the flicker of flames.

The moment was no more than a blink of time. 'Position's good,' Josh said crisply. 'We're all set up with

the skin preparation, sterile drapes and the tubes ready. Topical anaesthesia should be completely effective by now but I wasn't going to start subcutaneous anaesthesia without being sure she wasn't going to move.'

'Of course.'

Josh could see the way Stevie spread her fingers and increased the pressure where she was holding Taylor's shoulders and hips to maintain vertical alignment of the spine. It wasn't the first time that he'd realised she knew exactly what she was doing and it gave him absolute confidence to continue with this delicate procedure.

He drew an imaginary line between the iliac crests, knowing that where the line intersected with the spine would be approximately the space between the L3 and L4 discs. His small patient didn't seem to be aware of the fine needle he used to slowly infiltrate the area with local anaesthetic. It was such an automatic skill that Josh realised he was still a little too aware of who it was that was assisting him and he needed to remind himself that this was nothing other than a professional interaction.

'Taylor came in with a fever, headache and unusual drowsiness. She said her legs ached and she has a bit of a rash on one leg.'

'Oh…' Stevie's subtle nod was an understanding of why it was a priority to take a sample of cerebral spinal fluid to find out whether the symptoms were being caused by something as serious as meningitis. Then she tilted her head so that she could see Taylor's face while still holding her in position. 'That's no good, is

it, sweetheart? Not nice having sore legs.' She glanced back at Josh. 'Sound asleep,' she whispered.

Josh nodded. He was completely focused now as he reached for the lumbar puncture needle, holding it with the bevel pointing to the ceiling before carefully piercing the skin and then pausing to wait for any movement from his patient. Stevie had her head very close to Taylor's face. Josh couldn't hear what she was murmuring but it was obviously enough to distract the little girl from what he was doing because she barely even twitched. He advanced the needle, feeling the increased resistance of the spinous ligament and then further until he felt that resistance fade. He removed the stylet from inside the needle and was relieved to see the drops of fluid appear. He only needed to collect five to ten drops in the two sterile tubes so this would all be over very soon, having created minimal distress for his newest patient.

'Speaking of sore legs,' he said quietly, as he held the first tube in place to catch the drops, 'come and find me when you've got a spare moment later. I've got something to show you.'

He was making it look so easy but Stevie knew how much skill that took. Josh's confidence probably had a lot to do with the calm atmosphere in this treatment room as well. It was nothing like the tension they had worked under the first time they'd been in there together. This was so gentle that Taylor wasn't even waking up. So gentle that Stevie felt like it was a privilege to be this close to him and working alongside him like this.

Maybe she'd been stressing far too much in the last couple of days about how awkward it was going to be if—or more likely when—she had to interact with her HOD again. She hadn't detected anything negative in his expression when he'd seen who had been sent to assist him. If anything, Josh almost looked as if he was pleased to see her again after her days off. Which was why, when she saw him a couple of hours later, in the early afternoon, it felt easy to offer him a smile.

'Spare moment alert,' she said. 'It's my lunch break.' She held up a paper bag as proof.

Josh smiled back. A quick, easy grin that made his face light up, in fact. A smile that gave Stevie a curious burst of something…warmth, perhaps…that popped and spread somewhere deep inside her gut. Dark eyes always looked warm but there was something about the way Josh's eyes crinkled at the corners and one slightly out of line tooth provided the charm of an imperfection that took that smile to the next level.

'Perfect timing,' he told her. 'Follow me.'

He headed towards the smoke-stop door by the elevators that led to the stairwell. Oddly, it didn't occur to Stevie to hesitate in following him, even when he took the stairs two at a time to go past the highest level of this hospital block and onto the roof space. Built in a U shape, this wing of Gloucester General Hospital was directly opposite the one with the helipad and fast access to the emergency department on the ground floor. She'd never been up here before, of course, but what was surprising was that she hadn't heard about this space.

'It's a…a *vegetable* garden?' Stevie couldn't count

the number of raised beds that were awash with greenery. There were even fruit trees in huge planter boxes. People were working on the other side of the roof and seemed to be filling a container with freshly dug carrots.

'Isn't it great? The idea got started by some volunteers a few years back and it's kept growing…so to speak.' Josh was grinning again. 'I love coming up here for a few minutes when I get a break. There are seats—see? And a great view. If there wasn't so much forest or so many hills out there, I'd be able to see the village I live in.'

'That's why I wanted to come here,' Stevie said. 'My dream was to get out of a big city and live in one of those Cotswold villages. Inner-city Gloucester isn't ideal but at least we're out of London now. One step closer…'

Josh's sideways glance was curious but he didn't say anything other than to suggest a bench to sit on.

'Go ahead and have your lunch,' he added, after they'd both sat down. 'I know how precious any time to eat is around here.'

'Have you eaten already?'

Josh shook his head. 'It can wait.'

'Have one of these.' Stevie offered him the bag. 'Mousetraps are Mattie's favourite lunch but I made far too many of them yesterday.'

Josh took one of the baked triangles of toast and cheese and bit into it. Seconds later, his face lit up again. 'I'm with Mattie,' he said. 'These are *so* good.'

'Dead easy.' Stevie shrugged off the compliment.

Because she was actually trying to shrug off an even stronger dose of that warmth his smile had created earlier. 'It's just a bit of Vegemite on toast and then grated cheese and egg on top and you bake them in the oven until they're crispy. Have another one.' She held the bag out again but avoided meeting Josh's gaze. Instead, she looked around at the planter boxes. 'And thanks for showing me this. It's amazing.'

'Oh…' Josh paused as he reached towards the bag and then put his hand in his pocket instead. 'That's not what I wanted to show you. Here…' He had his phone in his hand now and he tapped the screen to reveal a photograph. 'I gave him a bath last night—as best I could while keeping the cast dry with a plastic bag, anyway. He looks like a different dog, doesn't he?'

Stevie looked at a much whiter, fluffier version of the little stray terrier she'd seen at the vet clinic. 'He certainly looks a lot happier.'

'He's loving my garden. I have someone from the village who helps me with housework and stuff and she's keeping an eye on Lucky during the day.'

'Lucky?'

'It was Mattie's idea for a name. Because he'd been lucky not to have been killed when that car hit him.' Josh hesitated for a moment. 'I thought he might like to see this picture. If you give me your number, I'll send it to you.' He tapped his screen again to open his contacts.

Silently Stevie took the phone and began to input her details. 'He'll love that,' she said quietly. 'He's been desperate for some news. Not that he's saying much.'

'How come?'

'He doesn't want to talk to me.' Stevie handed back the phone. 'He thinks I'm going to say he can't see you—or Lucky—again.'

'And are you?' Josh was holding her gaze.

'Well…it's not really appropriate, is it?'

'Why not?'

'We work together. And…' Stevie bit her lip but the genuine concern in Josh's expression overcame her hesitation. 'And I don't understand why you want to be doing it in the first place. You're a bit old to be a Big Brother, aren't you?'

'Fair call.' Josh nodded. 'I'm thirty-six,' he admitted. 'And that's the upper limit for being involved as a mentor but I'd never heard of the organisation until I saw a brochure that Ruby had. The more I thought about it, the more I liked the idea. Meeting Mattie only made me even more sure. He's such a great kid, Stevie. You can be very proud of what you've achieved as a parent.'

The praise was so heartfelt it almost brought the prickle of tears to Stevie's eyes.

'You should have seen how gentle he was with Lucky,' Josh continued quietly. 'He was quite prepared to risk getting bitten so he could look after him and so fierce in his determination to make sure that little dog was going to be okay.' The corner of his mouth curled upwards. 'Bit like his mum was when she was helping me deal with a totally obstructed airway once.'

Stevie ducked her head. More praise? It felt like Josh genuinely liked her. Admired her, even?

'I grew up without a dad,' Josh added softly. 'Without much of a family, in fact. I got adopted but then they

changed their minds down the track. I reckon I could have done with a "Big Brother" back then. Mattie told me that his dad died before he was born. That he just had you and his gran.'

Stevie bit her lip. That Josh had been adopted and then given up was such a personal thing to be sharing with someone who was pretty much a stranger and she could see way beneath those matter-of-fact words. She could see a small boy—who might actually look a bit like her Mattie, come to think of it—who was feeling lonely and unwanted. All she wanted to do was to reach back in time and hug that boy. To tell him that it was going to be okay. That he was going to grow up to be a rather extraordinary man, in fact.

Instead, she closed her eyes and let her breath out in a sigh because the most personal thing she'd carried around as a secret for so many years was suddenly overwhelming her. Why on earth it felt like Josh Stanmore was someone she could trust as the first person to share it with was too extraordinary to try and analyse but it probably had a lot to do with what he'd just told her about his childhood. Anyway, it was there and she felt…safe.

'Mattie's father didn't die before he was born,' she whispered. 'He just didn't want either of us. He did die in a car accident a few years later but, at the time, he just gave me more than enough money to get an abortion and find a job in another hospital—preferably as far away as I could get. It was only then that I found out he already had a wife. And kids. I don't ever want Mattie to know how unwanted he was by his dad. It

was easier to pretend he was already dead and just get on with being the best parent I could be all by myself.'

Josh was silent for so long that Stevie cringed. Her father, who'd also died a couple of years ago, had thought his daughter was ruining her life by the choices she was making at the time. That she was compounding her carelessness by stupidity. And even though she'd got past a lot of negative judgement from people over the years, she really didn't want more of the same from Josh.

She didn't get it. Instead, he caught her gaze and his face was very still and serious.

'So…you're brave as well as beautiful,' he said. 'But I think I already guessed that much.'

He thought she was beautiful? Oh…*my*… There was a flood of warmth deep inside her that clearly had nothing to do with the way this man smiled.

'And you make the best mousetraps ever,' Josh added, as if he was trying to lighten the atmosphere. Or give her an escape if she needed one? 'I'd better get back to work.'

As if to speed him along, his pager beeped. Josh read the message and Stevie heard the relief in the way he released his breath.

'Taylor's results from the lumbar puncture are back. She hasn't got meningitis.'

'Oh, thank goodness for that. Her mum will be so relieved.'

'She will—so I'd better scoot so I can pass on the good news.' Josh stood up but he was eyeing Stevie's

paper bag. 'I don't suppose I could take another one of those with me?'

Stevie grinned. 'Help yourself.'

Josh turned away, a triangle of toast in his hand, but Stevie found herself frowning. She was puzzled.

'Why did you bring me all the way up here to show me a photo?' she asked. 'You could have done that in the staffroom.'

Josh looked over his shoulder. 'I got the feeling that you're like me. That you wouldn't like having your private life gossiped about. Any secrets are safe with me, Stevie.'

The thought came instantly. Mattie would be safe with him, too. And nobody here would have to know anything about it, would they?

Stevie could feel a smile taking over her lips. 'I don't think I've shared a real secret since I had my first best friend at primary school.'

'I've never told anyone mine,' Josh said around a mouthful of mousetrap. 'I guess that means we're friends?'

Stevie had to laugh. 'I guess it does.'

Her smile faded as she watched him walk towards the stairwell door. Had he really chosen her as the first person to share an intimate secret with? She'd already known that Josh Stanmore was a brilliant doctor and totally dedicated to his young patients but she was aware of far deeper layers to this man now. He'd had a tough upbringing but he had reached a level of education and skill that made him a leader in his field. He'd seen her

son's best qualities within a short time of being with him and he was caring enough to want to follow up on that meeting, which made him perceptive and kind and…and possibly the most genuinely nice person that Stevie had ever met.

Mattie deserved to have someone like Josh in his life as a role model, she decided. And if she felt like it might be awkward because she worked with Josh, then maybe she just needed to get over herself.

It could work. At least she was quite sure of one thing she had learned about Josh Stanmore today.

She could trust him, which meant she was as safe with him as Mattie would be.

No. Make that two things. As impossible as it seemed, it really felt like Josh could see her for who she really was. That he not only understood what made her tick but that he approved of her.

Liked her…?

So, yeah… As unexpected as it was, it did seem like they were already friends. She sat amongst the vegetable gardens for a few more minutes, to eat the rest of her lunch, but when she got up to go back to work, Stevie found she was still a little puzzled. Josh had said he had someone to help him with his housework. Did that mean he lived alone?

Surely not… The man was gorgeous. He was also talented, confident, successful and had the ability to make a woman feel more than a little special. For the vast majority of women, that would be a totally irresistible combination.

Thank goodness she wasn't in that majority. That she was pretty much immune, even to charm and charisma on that kind of level.

'So…what can you see, Mattie?'

'You can still see where it was broken.'

'But can you see that new bone growth around the break?' Josh touched the smudged area on the illuminated X-ray in the vet's consulting room. 'Do you remember what that's called?'

'A…fracture…um…callus?'

'Wow…' Jill, the vet, sounded impressed. 'Have you been studying orthopaedics, Mattie?'

'Josh is teaching me.' Mattie seemed to grow an inch as he straightened. 'He's my Big Brother.' His face brightened. 'Did you know that the bones of dogs and cats are almost exactly the same as the arms and legs of people?'

It was Josh's turn to be impressed because there was no hint of amusement on Jill's face at being given a basic animal anatomy tip.

'I did know that,' she said. 'It's fascinating, isn't it? Do you know the name of the bone that Lucky broke?'

'He broke two,' Mattie said confidently. 'The tibia and…' He looked up at Josh. 'And the fibia?'

'Fibula,' he supplied.

'Oh, yeah… I remember now. And it was an oblique fracture.'

This time Jill did laugh. 'I think someone's after my job. What's the treatment plan now, Mattie?'

But Mattie shrugged, suddenly shy, and Josh was re-

minded of the first official sessions he'd had with Stevie's son after getting the surprising news that she had agreed that he could become Mattie's mentor. It was a good thing that nobody had come looking for Lucky yet because that was the connection Josh had been able to build on as they took the small dog for outings in the park, taking turns to carry him.

The dog wouldn't be ready to chase a ball anytime soon, either.

'I'm very happy with the way the bone is healing,' Jill told them, 'but Lucky needs to keep the cast on for another few weeks yet. He might have a bit of a limp for a while after that, too.' She glanced at Josh. 'You still planning to keep him?'

He could feel the sudden tension in the room as Mattie's body went very still.

'For now,' he said. 'There's obviously no one trying to find him and I've got used to having him around. I really like the little guy.'

Mattie said nothing more until they were out of the clinic and had tucked Lucky back into his crate in the back of Josh's Jeep. For the first time, he wasn't going to take Mattie back to Big Brother Headquarters to wait for Stevie to collect him. He was going to drop Mattie back home himself.

But Mattie wasn't looking too pleased about the new arrangement. He was scowling as he responded to Josh's reminder to put his seat belt on.

'What's up?'

'How long is "for now"?' Mattie demanded.

'Sorry, what?' Josh started the engine.

'You said you were only going to keep Lucky "for now". That means you're going to give him away later, doesn't it?'

Josh killed the engine. The depth of emotion in this lad's dark eyes wrapped itself straight around his heart like a vice.

'There's only one person I'd ever give Lucky to,' he told Mattie. 'And that's you, buddy. As long as no one turns up to claim him, he's kind of *our* dog, isn't he?'

The way Mattie struggled to swallow made it obvious how close to tears he'd been. He turned away to stare out the side window. 'We're not allowed dogs in our apartment,' he muttered.

'I know.' Josh started up the car again. 'But your mum told me that, one day, she wanted to live in one of the villages around here.'

Mattie was silent again, until they got close to his address. 'Can I really have Lucky, if Mum and I get to live in a proper house?'

'We'd have to talk to your mum about that but, if she said yes and nobody else has said that Lucky belongs to them, then I'd be more than happy for you to have Lucky. I know how well you'd look after him.'

Mattie thought about that as Josh parked the car. 'Mum said it's really expensive to get a house but, after she's been in her new job for a while, she's going to go and talk to the bank about getting a mortgage.'

'Hmm…' Josh needed to shut down this line of conversation. 'That sounds like a good plan.'

Stevie's financial situation was none of Josh's business, even if they were friends. And they *were* friends.

They'd shared secrets, hadn't they? And mousetraps. The unfortunate misunderstanding of that first meeting was forgiven and forgotten. They had an easy, enjoyable professional relationship and a connection that nobody else at Gloucester General knew anything about and Josh wasn't about to break the trust that had been put in him as Mattie's mentor.

Mattie was learning to trust him, too and the most surprising thing about that was how important it felt to Josh. Life changing, even. He was being gifted a position of huge influence in the life of a young boy— maybe even the kind of relationship he might have had as a father if he'd chosen to take that path in life.

He was never going to have a son of his own. There were too many children in the world who weren't getting the best of what life—and families—could offer. They were missing out. Like he had. Like Mattie was, even though he had the most amazing mother. What Josh hadn't expected was to feel like winning Mattie's trust was the best thing that had ever happened to him.

That he would do whatever it took not to let anything break a trust like that.

Not ever.

Oh, *help*...

She'd only expected Josh to drop Mattie off in front of the apartment block, not come up four flights of stairs with him. Should she ask him to come in? Offer him a coffee or something?

Stevie could feel the curse of the redhead sneaking up on her as spots of warmth bloomed on her cheeks.

This was awkward, which was a shame because it had become so easy to be around Josh at work in the last few weeks. Maybe it was awkward because it reminded her of the way she'd slapped him down so harshly when he'd offered *her* coffee...

And then it was suddenly, blindingly obvious.

He hadn't been hitting on her that day, at all. He'd just been being friendly. Welcoming. The way she felt she ought to be right now.

Mattie was pushing past her to get into the apartment. 'We took Lucky to the vet,' he told her. 'And it was so cool. I got to help with the X-ray. I had to wear this really heavy apron thing. Can I call Gran and tell her all about it?'

'Yes,' Stevie called after him. 'But hang your coat up first and don't leave your schoolbag there...' She turned to smile at Josh. 'Would you like a coffee or something?'

The beat of hesitation, and the flash of something she couldn't quite interpret in his eyes, told Stevie that Josh was also remembering that unfortunate first encounter at work. But...maybe that was amusement she could see in his face? A dismissal of something that would never have been an issue if they'd known what they knew now about each other.

And, weirdly, Stevie was aware of something that was almost disappointment. As if she'd prefer that he had been hitting on her and that, now that they knew each other better, he might think of doing it again...

Wow...maybe she wasn't quite as immune to this man's charisma as she'd thought she was.

Not that it would make any difference. Her initial worry that it would be inappropriate to be working with the man who had become a 'Big Brother' to her son had proved unfounded. What would, however, be completely unacceptable was anything *more* than a professional relationship or a friendship between them.

For a very intense moment, Stevie could imagine that she could see her own thoughts being mirrored in Josh's eyes and it felt as if the attraction was mutual. Almost in the same instant, however, Josh broke that eye contact and the moment evaporated.

'Tell Mattie I'll think up somewhere more interesting than the park for us to go to next week. And I'll see you at work, Stevie.'

It was definitely a relief to close the front door of her apartment and, for a long moment, Stevie stayed where she was. She didn't need to remind herself that this was all about Mattie. Or that she'd never hesitated to make sacrifices in her life that were necessary to put her precious child first. What was one more?

It wasn't as if she needed a man in her life because she was obviously coping perfectly well without one. And it wasn't as if Josh was feeling the same attraction. It was unfortunate that an almost forgotten part of her life—and her body—had chosen to wake up right now but it wasn't anything she couldn't handle. Lifting her chin, she turned away from the door. Towards her family.

'Is Gran still on the line, Mattie?' she called. 'I'd like to talk to her too.'

CHAPTER FOUR

It HAD BECOME something of a ritual, picking up the glossy real estate magazine from outside a nearby agency when she and Mattie went out to get groceries on a Thursday evening. After dinner and any chores were completed, they would both have an hour or so to treat themselves. Mattie would play his computer games. Stevie would find a picture-perfect Cotswold cottage for sale and clip the advertisement from the magazine to add to her collection. It was still a dream but it was starting to feel as if it wasn't a stupid dream because life was getting steadily better as she and Mattie settled into their new lives.

There were still things to worry about, of course—like the gang of local boys who'd persuaded Mattie to shoplift and got him into trouble with the police. He was managing to stay away from them but that was apparently causing problems. Not that Mattie was saying anything, but Stevie suspected he was getting bullied on a regular basis because of something Josh had told her today. That was another ritual that was adding pleasure to her life—meeting Josh amongst the veg-

etable gardens on the roof on the odd occasions their lunch breaks coincided.

'It was just a bit of name-calling going on from down the street when I walked home with him.'

'Like what?'

'He asked me to promise not to tell you. He's very protective of you, Stevie.'

'So you're not going to tell me?'

'Can't break a promise.'

But there had been reassurance in that gaze. If it was something that could compromise Mattie's safety, she could be sure that Josh would tell her anything she needed to know.

'Is there anything else I should know about?'

'Well...he misses his mates from his old school.'

'Yeah... I know that.'

'And he misses his grandma.'

'I know that too. I was going to get Mum to come and visit us but there's just not enough room in our apartment. Or hers, either. She moved into a tiny unit in a retirement village last year and there's only a two-seater couch as an extra bed.'

She'd hoped she wouldn't need to spell out that other accommodation was beyond her budget.

'He reckons he's old enough to go by himself. On the train.'

Stevie had shaken her head.

'He's too young to go that far by himself. What if he got off at the wrong station?'

'A bus, then? The driver could keep an eye on him. And maybe your mum could meet him at the other end.'

Stevie could almost hear the sound of Josh's voice as she remembered their conversation and she let her head rest on the back of her chair as she closed her eyes and let that awareness wash over her. Had he and Mattie already discussed this and come up with a plan during one of their weekly sessions? A flash of something that could have been jealousy rippled through Stevie at the thought of Mattie confiding in someone other than herself but, in virtually the same instant, she was both touched that Mattie was trying to protect her from worry about him and aware that she had to give Josh credit for being a big part of why their lives were so much better. Both her own and Mattie's.

His time with Mattie was the highlight of her son's week, even more important than the after-school programme he was now happily attending and, for Stevie, any time Josh's path crossed hers at work was definitely a highlight. She'd known that they would both be safe with him but now she was really starting to believe that. To feel completely safe. And she was over that brief flash of attraction to the man, despite how powerful it had been. They were friends, that was all. And they were both invested in Mattie's happiness.

It was a part of good parenting, wasn't it? Letting go a bit? Encouraging independence? Stevie went to the door of Mattie's small bedroom and watched him for a moment as he focused intently on the screen of the tablet he was holding.

'Hey, Matt?'

'Shh, Mum… I'm busy. Gotta open my parachute and find where I'm gonna land on the island.'

'Okay. We can talk later. I was just thinking that maybe you might like to go and visit Gran for a weekend soon and see your old friends. We could think about you going on the bus.'

'By my*self*?' The screen was forgotten.

'Would you like to do that?'

'*Yes...*' Even the sound of something crashing loudly in the game didn't make Mattie look down again. His face had the same kind of glow that Stevie had seen when she'd gone to that veterinary clinic that day to find him there...with Josh...

And there he was again. In her head. And somewhere deeper than that as well, because even thinking about him created an odd feeling of warmth. Comfort, almost. He was a thread that seemed to be weaving itself throughout every aspect of her life. Even giving Mattie the independence of a bus ride by himself had been Josh's idea. What would happen, Stevie wondered, if that thread got pulled out for whatever reason? Would her life unravel?

Was she trusting Josh too much?

Instinct told her that her trust was not misplaced but it was hard won after so many years of fiercely guarding her own independence as well as protecting her child. If it was just her that was in danger of getting hurt, it wouldn't matter nearly so much, but this was about Mattie and seeing that joy on his face was what mattered more than anything. Maybe it *was* okay that Josh was becoming such an important person in her son's life but there were others that shouldn't be ne-

glected and her mother—Mattie's only grandparent—
was top of that list.

'Let's video call Gran when you've finished your
game and see what she thinks about the idea.'

Mattie swiped his screen. 'I'm done. Let's call her
right now.'

There was always something a bit different about a Saturday morning ward round that Josh Stanmore thoroughly enjoyed. It was more relaxed, possibly because
elective surgery only happened on weekdays, consul-
tants were only called in when necessary and the prospect of an afternoon and evening off was a bonus. Less
pressure in general gave Josh extra time to spend with
the more junior members of his team. It also gave him
more time to spend with his patients.

Like thirteen-year-old Fraser who had been admitted
with diabetic ketoacidosis recently and was now learning about the impact a diagnosis of Type One diabetes
was going to have on his life. A quiet lad, and the old-
est of four children, Fraser had impressed Josh no end
by not only taking the news in his stride, coping with
being alone in hospital much of the time as his single
mother had to be home for his younger siblings but also
the way he was insisting on learning to test his blood
glucose levels and inject his insulin doses himself.

As Josh explained to his senior house officer, Fraser wouldn't be a candidate for an insulin pump until
he'd demonstrated how well he could control his blood
sugar levels, how consistent his motivation was, how
he could manage his diet and whether fluctuations in

levels were affecting his schoolwork, sports or day-to-day living. The first priority was to get him stable and well monitored.

'How's it going, Fraser?' Josh perched on the end of the bed.

'It's all good. My level was eight this morning.'

'Have you recorded that in your diary?'

'Yes.'

'When are you due for your insulin?'

'Right about now.' It wasn't Fraser who answered the query, however. It was his nurse who came behind the curtains with a stainless-steel kidney dish containing a syringe and alcohol wipe. She had a bright yellow, portable 'sharps' container in her other hand. 'Want to show the doctor how good you are at doing this, Fraser?'

Seeing Stevie on the ward on a Saturday took Josh by surprise and then he remembered that it was this weekend that Mattie had gone to visit his grandmother. Had Stevie made herself available to cover any gaps in the roster, perhaps? That wasn't what was his overwhelming reaction to seeing her, mind you. No…that was more like how much of a bonus it was that she was here, working in the same space at the same time as him.

So nice, in fact, that it was only now that Josh realised just how important his friendship with Stevie had become over the last weeks. How much he…*liked* her…and trusted her. This was the first time Josh had ever had a friendship with a woman that didn't include sex and, surprisingly, it had advantages he hadn't seen coming. Like knowing that it wasn't going to become

something that he needed to walk away from. Like how *safe* it felt.

Fraser clearly liked Stevie as well. It was Stevie that he was looking at for approval as he demonstrated and explained a now well-practised routine.

'So I've taken off both the caps and I dialled up two units so I can get the air out.' Fraser held the insulin pen up and squirted a fine stream of liquid into the air. 'Now I dial up my dose, which is one, and then I can inject it.'

He pinched his stomach, inserted the tiny needle, counting to six before he removed it. 'And that's it. Easy…' He was looking up at Stevie, whose smile told him exactly how well he'd done. How proud she was of him.

Just intercepting that look gave Josh a distinct squeeze in his chest that felt like…longing? As if he wanted to be the person that Stevie was proud of?

Whoa…where the hell had that thought come from?

Josh cleared his throat. 'Well done, Fraser. It's a brave thing to be learning to do by yourself.'

Fraser nodded slowly. 'I *was* scared at first,' he admitted. 'But then Stevie told me that was okay to be scared. And that you could only *be* brave if you did something that you were scared of. Because, if you aren't scared of it, you don't have to be brave, do you?'

For a heartbeat, Josh couldn't think of anything to say to that. Because he'd glanced up and caught Stevie's gaze as Fraser had been speaking. Because he could see that she knew exactly what it was like to be facing something that scared you and how hard it could be to deal with it. He'd told her that he thought she was

brave having chosen to face life as a single mother. That wasn't the only thing he'd said, either.

He'd told her that she was both brave *and* beautiful...

And, man...right now she looked more beautiful than any woman he'd ever seen. The highlights of that hair that could catch the light and flicker like firelight and those incredible eyes were there for everybody to see but there was so much more that Josh was aware of. Like her strength and determination. Her ability to defend herself and protect her son. The palpable amount of warmth and care she could offer her patients, like taking the time to have a philosophical discussion with a boy on the brink of adolescence about what it meant to be brave. If someone had told him that when he'd been just a kid, it might have made so many challenges more bearable. It might have made him a much stronger person, in fact.

It was Stevie who broke that brief eye contact. She held out the sharps container for Fraser to drop the needle into and then she shared a smile with her patient and Josh could feel the connection between them. The absolute trust. It was no wonder that Ruby was so impressed with her new member of the paediatric nursing staff. He was impressed himself, having no doubt that Stevie's encouragement and wise words had had a lot to do with how amazingly well Fraser was dealing with a major life change.

Stevie was dealing with one herself today, wasn't she? It had taken courage to let Mattie go off on an adventure by himself to visit his grandmother. Perhaps that was why she'd chosen to work today—so that she

had some distraction from knowing how far away her son was?

She was just as focused on one of his last patients to review this morning. Five-year-old Jackson had been treated for hydrocephalus as an infant but the shunt had failed and had been replaced a couple of days ago. Wearing his new, dinosaur, bicycle helmet, the cheerful boy was ready for discharge and a few adventures of his own but Josh took the time to make sure both Jackson's parents and his junior doctors were fully informed about the recent surgery.

Somehow, it wasn't a surprise to find Stevie in the staffroom later that morning with a neurology textbook open in front of her as she sipped her coffee. Ruby was at the sink, rinsing a plastic container, as Josh reached for a mug and poured himself some of the filter coffee that was always available.

'Saw you over at Cheltenham Central Hospital yesterday, when I was visiting a friend,' Ruby said. 'That's a flash new car you've got.'

'What?' Josh had no idea what she was talking about.

'Silvery thing. What is it? A Porsche? Maserati?'

Josh had to laugh. 'Are you kidding? You really think that's my style?'

'It might be a pretty good chick magnet,' Ruby murmured. She tilted her head towards where Stevie was sitting quietly reading. 'If, you know, nothing else was working. It's a bit strange, you being single for so long now. It's been months…' She was grinning as she finished drying her container and turned to leave, her voice rising again. 'Good to see that you've had a shave since

then, anyway. I don't hold with that designer stubble—
it's just laziness in my book.'

Josh shook his head. He still had no idea what Ruby
was on about, other than a reference to him and Stevie
being more than friends and that wasn't going to happen, was it? Not that he was about to tell Ruby of their
connection away from work. He sat down at the table
beside Stevie as Ruby left the staffroom.

'You checking up on what I was telling Jackson's
parents?'

'Of course not.' The spots of colour on Stevie's
cheeks made Josh wonder how long it was since he'd
seen a woman blush. 'I just wanted to know more. And
I couldn't remember what you'd said about the different sorts of shunts.'

It wasn't just that flush of colour on her face that
had captured Josh. He could actually sense her intelli-
gence and the hunger for new knowledge. It was going
to be a real pleasure to provide that, although, to be
honest, it would be a pleasure just to be sitting here,
this close to her.

'Jackson's got a ventriculoperitoneal shunt,' he told
her. 'It drains the CSF into his abdomen where it's ab-
sorbed into the bloodstream. It's the type of shunt that
has fewer risks than, say, a ventriculoatrial shunt that
drains it into the right atrium of the heart. Anything
else you want to know, just ask.'

'I'll read up on it all properly later.' Stevie glanced
at her watch. 'I'd better get back to it now. I think Fraser's mum is bringing his brothers and sister in to see
him after lunch so I'll need to clear the decks fast.' She

reached for a scrap of paper on the table in front of her to mark the chapter in the book but Josh had seen it first.

'What's this?'

'Just an advertisement I noticed in the paper.'

'It's a cottage in the next village to mine...' Josh picked up the ad and looked at it more closely. 'I saw the sign go up last week. Are you going to have a look at it? Look—there's an open home this afternoon.'

Stevie was taking her mug back to the sink. 'Maybe. I doubt that it's in my price range, though. An eighteenth-century Cotswold cottage with flagstone floors and a walled garden? It'll be worth a fortune.'

'Not necessarily. It obviously needs rethatching and probably even more work inside. Could be a bargain.'

Stevie took the clipping from his hand and closed the textbook around it, as if to finish the conversation, but Josh had seen the flash of something like hope in her eyes. This was her dream, to have a cottage like that, wasn't it? The force of the desire that she could achieve that dream was something else that took Josh by surprise.

'I could come with you,' he offered. 'I know a bit about renovating cottages like that. What time do you finish work?'

'Three o'clock.'

'That would give us just enough time to get there. You don't have to rush home, do you? With Mattie being away?'

She was surprised that he'd remembered. Josh could see that the surprise was about to morph into doubt, which would end up with her probably going home

alone to fret about Mattie so he tried to sound as if it was already a done deal.

'I'll be outside the front door at three p.m. Black Jeep, rather old and not very flash, despite what Ruby thinks. You can follow me to the village.' He drained his coffee and stood up. 'You'll be doing me a favour, actually. I'd love an excuse to go and have a look myself. That era of cottages is a bit of a passion of mine.'

It didn't matter that the thatch was covered in moss and so rotten in places the entire roof sagged a bit in the middle. Or that plastered interior walls were crumbling here and there, windows were broken, the kitchen was not much more than an ancient cooktop and a sink with a dripping tap and the small, walled garden hadn't been touched for years.

Stevie could see past all that. Already, in her mind's eye, she was sitting in front of a fire, looking up at restored, exposed beams with the smell of something delicious that was cooking slowly in an Aga that filled up a whole wall of the kitchen. She stood there for so long, for one last look, that the agent picked up his sign and gave them a wave before driving off.

Josh didn't seem to mind standing out here in the cold.

'You're in love with it, aren't you?'

Yes, Stevie could absolutely feel that deliciously intense combination of excitement and anticipation and... the *hope* that came with falling in love. She let her breath out in a happy sigh. 'It's perfect.'

Josh laughed. 'Dunno about that. But it could be

really nice. And, despite how bad that thatch looks, it seems weathertight for the moment so you wouldn't have a huge, urgent expense.'

'Mmm…' Stevie took a final glance over her shoulder. 'Did you see that fireplace?'

'An inglenook. I've got one of those. I've put a log burner into the space, which is really practical and looks great. Hey… I'm only five minutes down the road. Come and have a look. It might give you some ideas for your place.'

It was Stevie's turn to laugh. *Her* place? In her dreams.

But dreams were important, she thought as she followed Josh towards where they'd parked their cars down the street. Dreams were soul food. It was why she collected the pictures of gorgeous cottages—so that she could have a little bit of time to escape reality and dream of a future that was everything she could ever want. It was a bit like buying a lotto ticket. Or reading a romance story that had the perfect, happy ending. You knew that it happened to the lucky ones in real life so it wasn't just a fantasy to believe that it could happen to you, and for a few minutes while you indulged in that dream it *was* happening.

What better time to escape reality and dip into a dream just a bit further? If she went home now, she'd probably start worrying about Mattie. Her mother was taking great care of him but he'd gone off to see one of his old school friends this afternoon and he was having tea with his mate's family. She wouldn't even get a text message to reassure her for hours yet.

Had Josh known that? Was that why he had encouraged her to come out to this village to view a property she was unlikely to be able to afford? Why he was offering to give her even more ideas to play with? Her questioning glance was probably quite sharp, which might have been why Josh's eyebrows rose instantly, but then he smiled and Stevie knew that he knew exactly what she'd been thinking. And that she wasn't wrong. He wanted her to dream. To escape. And he was quite happy to go along with it. To be a part of her fantasy, even…

Something twisted deep in her heart right then. A combination of everything she knew about Josh Stanmore, mixed with the poignant feeling that someone cared that much about how she was feeling and, on top of that—like the most delicious icing on a cake—was the renewed awareness of just how gorgeous this man was, with those warm, dark eyes and that, oh, so contagious smile.

It was creeping up on her and she hadn't seen it coming so it hit her with enough force to steal her breath before she'd even finished taking it.

It wasn't just that cottage that Stevie was falling in love with, was it? However intense those feelings were for that ancient cottage, they paled in comparison to what she was feeling at this moment. And yet this man had never kissed her. Never even looked as though he wanted to kiss her so where on earth had this wash of overwhelming emotion sprung from?

Perhaps it could be traced back to the relief she'd seen in his eyes when he'd saved the life of that little

girl who'd come very close to choking to death. Or maybe it was the way he often made her feel so proud of her own work?

Was it the respect he'd shown when he'd made sure they were in the private space of the rooftop garden before talking about anything personal? Or was it because he'd won the trust of her son and herself and become such a special part of their lives?

Or maybe this had been enough on its own—that he was prepared to step into her dream and make it far more real than it could have ever been otherwise. Yeah… Stevie's steps slowed as they reached their vehicles. She could love someone just for that.

Mix that warm, fuzzy appreciation with the sheer masculine attraction this man exuded and the combination was a sexual timebomb. One that she could simply not allow to explode. But one that she didn't seem to have quite enough willpower to walk away from, either. Not that that was necessarily a problem, a small voice whispered in the back of her mind, because this extraordinary awareness was one-sided, wasn't it?

She should still go home, though. To her home, not his. Stevie opened her mouth to thank Josh for the offer and excuse herself but something quite different came out. 'I'd love to see your cottage,' she told him. 'I'll follow you again, shall I?'

Stevie was laughing again and it made Josh's grin widen even though he knew she was laughing at him. Or maybe she was just enjoying the exuberant welcome she was getting from Lucky as she stooped to pet the

little terrier as he shot outside the moment the front door was opened.

But she was shaking her head as she straightened. 'You're really calling this a *cottage*?'

'There's its name, right there, beside the door. "Weeping Elm Cottage". Named after that tree that takes up most of the front garden. It's a good thing there's a bit of a meadow out the back or there'd be no room for Lucky to have a run around. He's almost lost his limp now.'

'It's not a cottage. It's a mansion.'

'You haven't seen the estates that are tucked away in the forests around here. This is just a slightly bigger version of your cottage. Four bedrooms instead of two, that's all.' Josh held the door open for her. 'Come on in.'

He couldn't wait to see her face when he showed her his home. He wanted to see that spark of interest in her eyes that was intense enough to be more like passion as it lit up her whole face. It was intriguing to see it in something that had nothing to do with work. Or Mattie. What else did Stevie Hawksbury feel passionate about other than very old houses? What else could make her laugh because he would really love to hear that again.

His front door opened directly into his living room, with its whitewashed walls, rough-hewn beams, window seats beneath the multipaned windows, wide elm floorboards and the eye-catching centrepiece of a dramatic, stone-built inglenook fireplace. Lucky trotted ahead of them as if, he, too, was excited about showing Stevie their home.

Stevie's face didn't just light up, she looked almost

overwhelmed, standing very still—her eyes wide and her lips slightly parted—turning her head very slowly to take it all in. Josh couldn't take his eyes off her face. Especially that wayward, tight curl that had fallen across her forehead to almost tangle itself in her eyelashes. And the unconscious drift of her lips that made it look as though she was about to be kissed.

Good grief…that thought was enough to be stirring something in his gut that he hadn't seen coming. Something totally inappropriate given that definitive brush-off Stevie had given him the first day he'd met her. Fortunately, Josh caught a movement from the corner of his eye that made him turn his head.

'Off the sofa, Lucky,' he commanded. 'We've talked about this before, haven't we?'

Lucky jumping down was enough to break that stillness for Stevie. She was moving further away from him—towards the fireplace.

'This mantlepiece…' She stepped onto the flagstone hearth to reach up and touch the massive beam of wood that was embedded in the wall. 'It looks like a whole tree trunk. It's incredible. How old *is* your house?'

'Dates to about mid-eighteenth century, I believe. The wood burner doesn't look too out of place, though, does it?'

'It's gorgeous. And I love how you can stack the logs on either side like that. Did the flue from the log burner just go inside the original chimney?'

She was leaning in to peer up into the space and Josh didn't think to warn her not to touch the inside of the chimney. It hadn't occurred to him that there could

still be some ancient soot clinging to stonework until Stevie straightened and pushed that curl back off her face, leaving a huge, black streak in its place.

'Oh, no…'

'What? Have I got something on my face?' Stevie was touching her nose now, and then her cheek and then she saw her fingers and laughed.

'Don't move…' Josh walked past the fireplace to where the living room led into his kitchen. He grabbed a clean tea towel, ran it under the tap and went back to Stevie who used it to wipe her hands and then her face.

'Have I got it all?'

'Almost.'

Without thinking, Josh reached out and used the pad of his thumb to wipe a remnant of smudge from her cheek. Close to her mouth. So close, he could feel the corners of her lips. And how incredibly soft her skin was… It was his turn to stop in his tracks, suddenly overwhelmed with what he could feel. And see. The way Stevie's gaze was locked on his, the way those gloriously tawny eyes darkened and…oh, man…the way her lips had parted again. And this time, he just knew that she *was* waiting to be kissed.

That she *wanted* to be kissed.

It was obviously the day for not thinking things through. He hadn't warned her about the soot. He hadn't hesitated in touching her face but maybe, this time, he just didn't want to let anything stop him responding to an invitation that promised him something he might deeply regret missing out on if he didn't accept it.

By the time his head had dipped—oh, so slowly—far

enough for his lips to be hovering just above Stevie's there was no turning back. Not when she was coming up on her toes to close that final fraction of space between them. And certainly not when he could feel the soft, delicious responsiveness of her lips beneath his.

This was the kiss he'd been waiting for his entire life.

He just hadn't known it even existed.

He could feel Stevie melting in his arms as he deepened that kiss and time slowed to a point where it felt like this dance of touch and taste and sensation was as familiar as breathing. When it stopped being too much and became not enough but then instantly became too much again as Stevie pulled abruptly out of his arms.

Her breath was coming in short gasps but she still pressed her hand against her mouth. 'Oh, no…' Her tone was far less amused than his had been when he'd used those exact words when he'd seen the sooty smudges on her face. She sounded—and looked—horrified. 'That should *not* have happened.'

'No…' Josh's agreement was rather half-hearted despite knowing, deep down, that she was quite right. But it *had* happened and he wasn't exactly sorry. Clearly, he hadn't quite come to his senses again yet because what he actually wanted was for it to happen again.

And, judging by the fact that Stevie actually looked like she might be about to burst into tears—which was a bit scary given that he knew how strong a person she was—an opportunity to kiss her again wasn't going to happen any time soon.

CHAPTER FIVE

DON'T CRY, STEVIE ordered herself. *Don't you dare cry...*

But this felt a bit like that day she'd first met Josh all those weeks ago, when she'd gone to hide in that supply room and buried her face in her hands, convinced that she'd ruined what had held the promise of a wonderful new start in life.

There was nowhere to go to hide now. She couldn't even hide how she was feeling with the way Josh was holding her gaze like this. This wasn't the first time that Stevie had thought that he understood her way better than anyone else ever had and, coming in the wake of that astonishing kiss, she knew she really *was* in danger of bursting into tears.

'Hey...' His voice was soft. Gentle. 'It's not that bad, Stevie.' Josh was actually smiling as he put his arms around her to offer her a hug. 'It was just a kiss.'

Really?

It was impossible not to respond to the comfort of his arms around her body or to stop herself pressing her face into the soft wool of his jumper, in that dip below his shoulder that was just made for shielding someone

from the world. But...*just* a kiss? Stevie had never experienced a kiss like that. It still felt as if her world had tilted on its axis so sharply she'd been on the point of falling into space.

'It's a disaster.'

Her voice was muffled. Then she could feel as well as hear the amused sound Josh was making so she lifted her head to make sure he could hear her clearly.

'Mattie's going to hate me. Probably for ever.'

'Why?' Josh pulled back far enough to be able to see her face.

'You must realise what would happen if the Big Brother organisation found out I'd kissed my son's mentor. It probably breaks all the rules and he'd never be allowed to see you again and...and he's been happier just lately than he's been in a very long time.'

Josh was frowning. 'How on earth are they going to find out? Besides, I think it was me who kissed you, not the other way round.'

The implication of those words went straight over Stevie's head because she had too much else to think about. 'But *we* know. What if Mattie found out?'

'Mattie's not here,' Josh said calmly. 'The only person other than us who knows about that kiss is Lucky.'

Hearing his name, the little dog sat up, his head on one side, his tail wagging.

'It's about time for your dinner, isn't it?' Josh said. He looked down at Stevie and smiled. 'How 'bout I make us a cup of tea at the same time and we can talk about this like grown-ups. Like friends? It really isn't the end of the world.'

* * *

It really *wasn't* the end of the world.

It just felt like it.

But it wasn't until Stevie was curled up on one end of the soft, feather-filled cushions of Josh's sofa in front of the log burner he had fired up to show her what it was like when it was going, and they'd been sticking to neutral topics and had been chatting about renovating old houses and the cup of tea had been replaced by a particularly nice glass of wine, that she realised *why*.

It wasn't that she was upset by the fact that they had kissed at all.

What was actually devastating was that they couldn't let it go any further when every cell in Stevie's body was aching for more...

Josh was sitting at the other end of the couch and somehow Lucky had sneaked up to occupy the middle. The little dog was stretched out on his back now, looking for all the world as if he was sunbathing somewhere on a Mediterranean beach.

'He looks so happy,' Stevie said. 'And he's so cute. I can't believe his owners haven't come looking for him.'

'Animals get dumped for all sorts of reasons.' Josh swirled the last bit of wine in the bottom of his glass. 'So do people.' He drained the glass and reached for the bottle on the coffee table to refill it.

Stevie blinked at the dark undercurrent that three simple little words could generate.

'Sorry...' Josh sat back against the cushions and closed his eyes. After a long moment, however, he opened them again to look directly at Stevie. 'What

is it about you,' he asked quietly, 'that makes me say things I'd never say to anyone else? *Ever?*'

Stevie couldn't answer that. Even if she could have found the words, they probably wouldn't have come out given that squeeze in her chest that was taking her breath away. She'd never felt this close to anyone and it was far more than something purely physical. This felt like being touched on a far deeper level. One that was all about trust. And love…

'You did tell me,' she said softly, 'that you were adopted and then they changed their minds. I can't believe anyone would do something like that.'

'I got dumped the day I was born,' Josh said into the silence that followed Stevie's words. 'I believe I was in a foster home for a while and then I got adopted by an older couple—Colin and Judith Stanmore. They'd been trying to have their own children for twenty years by then and my mother was nearly forty.'

Stevie took a sip of her wine. Josh wasn't looking at her as he spoke quietly but she couldn't take her eyes off his face. Off those lines beside his eyes and lips that could deepen and light up his face when he smiled but, for now, just made him look serious enough to appear unbearably sad. Off the way he rubbed at the back of his neck when he was deciding whether to say something difficult.

'It was one of "those" stories,' Josh continued. 'You know, when people finally adopt a child and then this miracle happens and they discover that they can have their own child, after all. That happened when I was about three and my earliest memory was my parents

bringing him home from the hospital. I'd never seen them so happy. I was happy. Any photos from that time made us look like the perfect little family.'

'What happened?' Stevie encouraged softly. 'What changed?'

'Derek was their "real" son.' Josh took a long sip of his wine. 'Oh, I think they tried their best but it became a burden that I needed attention as well. I heard them, one night, talking about how it would be best to find me a new family but who would want me now that I wasn't a cute baby any more? And I was becoming so badly behaved.'

Stevie's breath came out in an incredulous huff. 'I wonder why that was?' she muttered, her heart breaking for the small boy who had been so desperate to be noticed. To be loved.

'The crunch came when Derek got sick one night. They both rushed him off to the hospital and I don't think it even occurred to them that they shouldn't have left me alone in the house. The police found me wandering down the street the next day, looking for them, and it was my grandmother who came to get me. My parents didn't want me back and she was so furious with them she took me home with her, even though she was well into her seventies and raising a child was the last thing she really wanted to do.'

Josh reached for the wine bottle to refill Stevie's glass this time. 'Sorry...not sure why I'm dumping this on you. Maybe it's a very long-winded way of explaining why I'm not about to abandon Lucky. Or why I felt drawn to get involved with the Big Brother programme,

perhaps. The first thing I thought when I looked at that brochure was how good it might have been to have someone like that in my life.'

'What happened later? Did your parents ever apologise?'

'Never saw them again. Grandma never spoke to them after that. She just did her duty and brought me up as best she could. She died while I was away at medical school. Her son and his family didn't come to her funeral or even contest her will, which was a surprise given that she'd left her house and everything to me.' Josh pulled in a deep breath. 'I think that was the final point of my journey in giving up on the idea of families. I decided that I didn't need one. Or want one.' He raised his glass. 'Friends, however, are entirely different. Here's to you and me, Stevie.'

She had to lean over Lucky to touch her glass to his.

So…she certainly knew why he lived alone now. But how sad was that—to never want a family because he'd been so unlucky with his own? And how heroic was it to have devoted his life to helping save the lives of other people's children, so that other families could stay together if at all possible?

'Oh…' Josh lowered his glass after taking a sip. 'I know where all that came from. I just wanted to reassure you that nothing's really changed, I guess. That I made a promise to the universe when I took on being Mattie's mentor that I would never do anything to break the trust he was giving me because…because I know how much damage that can do.'

Didn't he just? Enough damage that Josh was never

going to trust in family again. Enough that he was never going to do anything to hurt her son.

'Thank you.' Stevie's smile started out a bit wobbly but slowly grew. She had to blink a couple of times, too, just in case there was an errant tear hiding somewhere.

'That doesn't mean I can't be friends with Mattie's mum,' Josh added. 'But it does mean that you're in the same category. You've trusted me and I'm not going to break that trust.'

She believed him. In spite of that kiss that had just turned her world upside down she knew that Josh would never intentionally hurt her. Or maybe it was partly because of that kiss. Because nobody could kiss you that tenderly, as if you were the most important person in the universe, unless he genuinely cared.

Oh, man…

Stevie had never looked this gorgeous. Maybe it was because there were actual flames flickering in the background and those wild curls had been released from whatever ties tried to tame them during working hours and they were touching her shoulders and creating a kind of halo that picked up on every flicker of the burning wood in the fire in the rapidly fading daylight. He should get up and put a lamp on but he was enjoying watching her too much.

And *that* was probably because he still hadn't come to his senses completely. His brain had been doing its best—it had even dredged up ancient history that should have put paid to any fantasy moment—but his body

hadn't got with the programme yet. He could still feel what it had been like to touch Stevie. To taste her...

He still wanted more.

More distraction was needed. Something professional might help. Josh waved his hand at the massive bookshelf that lined the wall behind the sofa.

'I've got a small library of textbooks here, in case you hadn't noticed. If you ever want to read up on something—like hydrocephalus, perhaps—just let me know.'

Stevie nodded. 'I'd love to do some more training. I had a lot of catching up to do before I could get back to working in a proper hospital but I want to do more. I've lost a lot of years. Not that I regret it,' she added hastily. 'And working in aged care was the only sort of nursing with hours that fitted well enough around school and childcare but I'm loving getting back to paediatrics.'

'Is that where you worked before Mattie came along?'

Stevie nodded. 'It was always where I wanted to be. I couldn't believe my luck when I got a job at one of London's best paediatric hospitals. And I thought I'd met the perfect man on my first day at work. It was a dream come true.' She drank the last of her wine. 'Until it wasn't, of course.'

Josh heard the sigh of that broken dream. The broken trust. It made his own heart ache.

'I still thought it would be okay,' Stevie said softly. 'I thought he loved me. That we'd end up in that little house with a picket fence and we'd be that perfect little family. How naive was that?'

'You trusted the bastard,' Josh growled. 'Who was he? Some playboy medical student?'

'Um…' There was a gleam of amusement in Stevie's eyes. 'He was a consultant. Pretty much my boss, I guess.'

Josh could actually feel his stomach sinking like a stone. 'Oh… *God*… And then I go and hit on you the first day we met.'

Stevie dropped her gaze, giving her head a tiny shake. 'You weren't hitting on me,' she said. 'I just overreacted. You were trying to be welcoming to a new staff member. I get that now.'

'No…' Josh swallowed hard when the silence had gone on a little too long. 'I'm not going to lie to you, Stevie. I kind of *was* hitting on you.'

He heard the sharp intake of her breath as her gaze flicked up to meet his. He could also see her eyes darken again—the way they had just before he'd kissed her and, man…did that mess with his head, not to mention other parts of his anatomy?

One corner of his mouth tried to curl into an apologetic smile but it didn't quite work.

'I couldn't resist,' he admitted. 'There you were, the most gorgeous woman I'd ever seen, and you'd just demonstrated the fact that you were also highly intelligent, extremely good at your job and that you were strong and brave enough not to crack under the intense pressure of a life or death situation. You blew me away, Stevie.' It was his turn to shake his head. 'You still do.' This time, he did find a gentle smile. 'It was a good thing you knocked me back, though. You deserve someone who can give you far more than I could have.'

'Oh?' The look she was giving him had enough heat

to be melting something deep inside his gut. 'Such as...?'

'The possibility of a future,' Josh said. 'Commitment. The kind of thing I can never offer and, even though I've always made it clear that I can't right from the start of anything, I know I've hurt a lot of women by not being able to give them what they wanted.'

'That's not your fault.' Stevie was still staring at him. 'I understand why you feel the way you do and if you're always as honest about that as you've been with me, then you're not breaking any promises. Or trust. People only get hurt when they expect—or want—something that they thought existed that then gets taken away from them.'

There was something that Stevie wasn't saying. Josh couldn't decide what it was, exactly—was it too much to hope that she might be telling him that he wouldn't have hurt her by offering her a 'friendship with benefits' because she wouldn't have expected anything more than that? That she wasn't actually looking for a long-term commitment from any man because she had her life sorted perfectly well enough already? He had to clear his throat before he could say anything else and, even then, the words came out in a low kind of growl.

'What is it that *you* want, Stevie?'

'I want to know that Mattie's safe.' Her words were no more than a whisper.

'He is.' It was a vow. 'So are you.'

'We are good at keeping secrets, aren't we?'

'We are.' Josh held Stevie's gaze and it felt as if he was pulling her closer and closing that gap between

them. 'And that kiss can always be a secret if that's what you want.'

'What do *you* want?'

Josh could feel a smile trying to escape. 'It's kind of more what I *don't* want.'

'Which is?'

'To spend the rest of my life wondering—if just a kiss could be that mind blowing—what would it be like, even just once, to *really* make love to you?'

Oh…the way the electricity in the air between them reached a point where you could almost hear it sizzling. And the way Stevie's tongue appeared to touch her lip like that as she struggled to find any words in response. It was all Josh could do not to lean in and close that distance between them instantly. But this had to be her choice. Maybe he did lean a little, because Lucky stirred and slid off the couch to go and lie down with a disgruntled thump by the fireplace. Stevie didn't seem to have noticed.

'Just once?'

'Just us,' Josh murmured. 'Just tonight.'

Stevie's eyes closed for a heartbeat. 'A secret?'

'You said it yourself. We're good at secrets.' He was so close to her now. How the heck had that happened? When Stevie opened her eyes, she was going to see that he was close enough to kiss her.

Or maybe she felt it and moved herself. Because Josh was quite sure he hadn't leaned any closer but he could feel the warmth of her breath against his lips.

'I know what I want.' The words were no more than a sigh.

'What's that?'

'You...'

Josh had to take a very deliberate, slow breath to steady himself before he gave in to the overwhelming need to kiss Stevie again. To scoop her into his arms and carry her to his bed.

To give her everything he had to give her of himself.

Because if it was only going to be once, he was going to make sure that neither of them would ever forget this night.

CHAPTER SIX

'WHAT'S WITH THE hairy roof, Mum?'

'It's a thatched roof, Mattie. It's old and special.'

'Looks like it's going bald.'

'Yeah…it's going to need some fixing up. Let's go inside.'

'Why?'

'I told you. It's the last open home before it gets sold this week and I wanted you to see it.'

'Because you're going to buy it?'

'I hope so.'

Stevie lowered her voice as a couple went past them to go through the gate, not wanting anyone to hear any note of confidence in her voice, but it really did look as if things were coming together after weeks of effort. Her mother was providing a deposit from the 'rainy day' shares her father had put aside years ago and the bank was on board for a mortgage. Her limit for bidding in the auction was strict but she had to be in with a shout given how much work the cottage needed.

She clearly wasn't the only person seriously interested, however. Judging by the effusive welcome from

the smartly dressed estate agent waiting to greet the couple ahead of Stevie and Mattie at the front door, this wasn't their first visit to the property. Turning her head, she glanced at the late model European car parked behind her reliable but rather old hatchback and it felt like her dream might be developing some slippery patches as she tried to hang onto it but that just made Stevie even more determined. She'd won battles before and this was definitely worth fighting for.

'It's got a garden,' she told Mattie, brightly. 'Just a little one, but there's a village green not far down the road with plenty of room to ride a bike or kick a ball around.'

The mention of the garden seemed to have given Mattie a reason to get far more interested in this weekend outing. 'So this would be a *real* house, then? *Our* house?'

Stevie nodded and couldn't help her smile turning into a grin. Because she could see the way Mattie's face lit up with that kind of glow she had been seeing more and more recently—especially when he'd been out for his weekly session with Josh and Lucky. She could feel a very similar glow herself quite often these days and that also had a lot to do with having a session of her own with Josh.

Once would never have been enough, would it?

Not when the physical chemistry she and Josh seemed to have together was enough to stop the earth turning for a significant length of time. When even *thinking* about the touch of his fingers, or his tongue or of her touching him could make something in Stevie's gut ignite with a heat so intense it was painful.

'So this is the living room. Look at that fireplace.'

Stevie had had to learn the new skill of finding something else to focus on very fast when that heat threatened to melt any rational thought and she'd become very good at it because she'd had no other option. She had to work with Josh, after all, and going weak at the knees was simply not acceptable.

And she had to keep their secret from everybody. From her colleagues, including Ruby who had a well-honed radar for any shenanigans going on in her patch between staff members but, so far, she didn't seem to have picked up on any glances that lingered a little too long, that Stevie and Josh often shared a rooftop lunch, and that their rosters might have been juggled to give them the same days off more often than not.

It was a secret Stevie had to keep from her son, too, and, like most children, he had an uncanny ability to pick up on things that weren't being said. He was staring at her now, with a somewhat bewildered expression on his face.

'You really like this place, don't you, Mum?'

'I love it,' she whispered. 'But don't tell anybody.'

'Why not?' Mattie whispered back.

Stevie tilted her head towards where the real estate agent was talking to the couple in the kitchen. 'When people use an auction to sell a house, it's kind of a competition,' she explained. 'And it's better not to let the others know what you're thinking.'

Especially when it involved X-rated memories, like the one that came from nowhere as Stevie took her gaze away from that inglenook fireplace, thinking that

it needed a lot of work to look anything like the one in Josh's house, which led to a flashback to that first time together that was so vivid Stevie had to bite her lip quite hard to distract herself this time. They hadn't managed another night together since that weekend Mattie had been away but… *Oh, my…* Some of their afternoons when they both had a day off and Mattie was at school… Stevie could actually feel a blush warming her cheeks.

But Mattie clearly hadn't noticed anything amiss. He was smiling at her, in fact.

'What?' Stevie smiled back. 'What are you thinking?'

'About Josh.'

Stevie blinked. 'Oh?'

'It was something he said. About when we didn't have to live in that apartment any more. When we had a *proper* house?' His smile stretched into a grin. 'He said that Lucky could come and live with me.' The smile faded too fast then. 'But that was a long time ago. Do you think he might have changed his mind?'

'I wouldn't think so. Josh isn't the kind of man who would change his mind about something important.'

Stevie certainly knew that much about Josh—that he was completely trustworthy. And honest. When they'd both realised that not ever repeating that one-off, *amazing* night was going to drive them both completely insane, they'd both made a promise that it was never going to affect Mattie. And that if this overwhelming attraction between them fizzled out, they would make sure

it didn't destroy their friendship or do any damage to Josh's relationship with Mattie.

Okay…so maybe it was a bit more than friendship on Stevie's part but she was confident she could handle this 'friends with benefits' thing. The trick was to focus on the present and not try and imagine a future that involved any dreaming about things that might never happen because that was the way to avoid getting your heart broken. If a friendship with Josh was all that was ever going to happen between them, she would make the most of everything it brought into her life.

She was applying the same strategy to what this cottage represented as the potential home she was in love with. She was focusing on only what was happening now and the need to succeed in the auction this week. It was possible she might never be able to afford the kind of renovations that would make it perfect but just living here would be enough and she would make the most of everything that it could bring into both her life and Mattie's.

Mattie wasn't looking convinced by her optimism about whether Josh would keep his promise, however.

'Talk to Josh about it, next time you see him.'

'But that's not for days and days.'

'He doesn't live so far from here.' Stevie spoke without really thinking. 'Maybe we could go and say hello to Lucky on the way home.'

'Is that allowed? When it's not our usual day?'

'It's probably bending the rules a bit,' Stevie admitted.

'And how do you know where he lives?'

It was easy enough to shrug off the awkward question. 'Josh and I work together, remember? We're friends, too.'

It could be stepping over the boundaries they had clearly marked in the different ways their lives connected, though, so it might be a good idea to think it through a bit better. 'I can text him,' she told Mattie. 'And make sure he's home.'

The real estate agent and the other couple were coming back into the living room. 'Why don't you go upstairs and look at the bedrooms?' Stevie suggested. 'I need to ask a couple of questions about the auction.' To register her interest, in fact, though she was going to wait until she could speak to the agent alone.

'I don't know, darling.' The man was frowning. 'It needs an awful lot of work. Like totally gutting the place. And getting rid of that fireplace.'

'Ah…' The agent's smile was cautious. 'This is a Grade Two listed property.'

'What does that mean?' The blonde woman was a lot younger than Stevie. Was she his daughter or his girlfriend?

'It means it's legally protected from being demolished, extended or significantly altered without special permission.'

'It means a nightmare from what I've heard,' her partner added. 'You have to get permission for anything you want to do to the place like changing a tap and it can take months. Years, even.'

'Oh…' The woman pouted. 'But this place is so *cute*.'

The man sighed. 'All we want is a weekend bolthole

from London,' he told the agent. 'But if Autumn's got her heart set on this place, we'll have to at least think about it. As long as the price is right, of course.'

If he could afford a car like the one parked in the lane, he could probably buy this cottage without even worrying about a mortgage. Stevie could feel her optimism taking a huge dive. Enough to create fear, even. Then she overheard the man as he left, telling the agent that they had more properties to view, hope soared back again and the roller coaster was starting to do Stevie's head in.

She needed support, she decided, and she only had one really good friend available in her new life. One who, coincidentally, lived just down the road. What would happen if she just turned up on his doorstep, unannounced, with Mattie in tow? If nothing else, it would certainly let her know if she was right to trust him as much as she did.

And…she couldn't help the bubble of something else surfacing. The hope that she might see that there was something else she could trust? That what she and Josh had found together might actually be enough to change his mind one day. That he might come to believe— like she did—that family was really the most important thing you could find in life?

For a moment, Josh was stunned by the unexpectedness of finding Stevie and Mattie on his doorstep. It felt like planets were colliding when they weren't supposed to be even be in the same orbit.

But then Lucky launched himself at Mattie with a

joyous bark and Mattie dropped to a crouch to cuddle the little dog, which left Josh and Stevie looking at each other and he could see that she was apprehensive.

'We were just down the road,' she told him. 'At the last open house for that cottage. You know, the one I told you about at work?'

There was something more than apprehension in her eyes. A plea of some sort? Josh wasn't sure what it was but he *was* absolutely sure that he would oblige if it was at all possible. Because he wanted to see Stevie smile. Because *her* happiness made *him* happy. And suddenly that made it feel perfectly okay that she was on his doorstep. That she—and Mattie—could be part of any aspect of his life. Quite apart from a sexual relationship of a kind he'd never had in his life before, he and Stevie were friends and they'd both sworn that nothing was going to change that. If this was some kind of test of that friendship, he knew he could pass it with flying colours.

'Come in,' he invited. 'Tell me all about it. I'll make us a cup of tea. Mattie, bring Lucky back inside. You can go and play with him in the back garden, if you want. There's lots more space out there and you'll find a few tennis balls hiding in the grass. Lucky's very good at playing fetch and the vet says it's good for his leg to get a bit more exercise now.'

But Mattie didn't head straight for the meadow out the back. He followed the adults into the kitchen and Josh couldn't miss the significant look that Stevie gave her son, clearly encouraging him to say something.

'What's up, buddy?'

The squeeze that happened in his chest when Mattie looked up to meet his gaze had become very familiar for Josh. The connection he'd felt with this boy right from that first meeting had grown into something very solid that only became stronger whenever they spent time together. He cared very much about Mattie and very much wanted to be a part of his life for many years to come.

'You know what you said about Lucky that time? That if me and Mum got a proper house one day, Lucky could come and live with me?'

Josh nodded gravely. 'I do. And I remember saying that it would be up to your mum to say yes.'

Mattie turned that desperate gaze onto his mother. 'You will, won't you, Mum?'

'If we get the cottage, of course I will,' Stevie promised. 'But remember that it might not happen this time, Mattie. It could be that we'll have to keep looking for another house.'

'Like this one.' Mattie's smile was bright. 'I really like your house, Josh. Come on, Lucky, let's go outside.'

Josh reached for a teapot and some mugs. 'When's the auction?'

'Wednesday. One o'clock.'

'My afternoon off.' He winked at Stevie. 'I'll come with you, shall I? And then we can celebrate afterwards.'

'Oh, I hope so…'

The way Stevie's eyes were shining as they held his gaze gave Josh an even bigger squeeze than his connection with Mattie ever created. It was the thought of getting the house of her dreams that was making her

glow like that, of course, but maybe a part of it was the thought of just how they *could* celebrate afterwards when they had the rest of the afternoon to themselves. He made a mental note to put some champagne on ice.

It was all he could do not to reach for Stevie right now, in fact, and pull her into his arms. To lace his fingers through those delicious curls tumbling to her shoulders so that he could hold her head steady as he kissed her completely senseless.

And it was obvious that she knew exactly what he was thinking about. The way she caught the corner of her bottom lip between her teeth was a dead giveaway so it was probably just as well that Mattie chose that moment to come back into the kitchen.

'I'm hungry,' he announced.

'I've got biscuits.' Josh let his gaze hold Stevie's for just another heartbeat before he turned away. 'I might even be able to find a chocolate one.'

Mattie was silent for a moment. He looked at his mother and then at Josh.

'Is Mum your girlfriend?' he asked.

They both laughed. They both said 'no' at precisely the same time—as if the very idea was ridiculous.

'But she's your friend, isn't she?' Mattie persisted.

'Absolutely,' Josh agreed.

'And we work together,' Stevie added.

Mattie ignored his mother's comment. He was still watching Josh. 'And she's a girl.'

Josh laughed again as he held out the biscuit tin towards Mattie. 'Can't argue with that.'

He didn't dare catch Stevie's gaze. He had to slam

a mental door, as well, to stop a rush of pure sensation that was determined to remind him of exactly how feminine Stevie was and how much he loved every aspect of that gorgeous body of hers.

Mattie simply nodded, apparently satisfied. Then he took two biscuits and ran outside again with Lucky staying close.

Josh turned his attention to making the tea. 'Let's talk strategy for the auction,' he suggested. 'Are you going to be the first to bid, or hang back until it's slowing down and scare the competition off by making your bid then, as if you're just getting started?'

'I don't know,' Stevie said. 'But I'm worried about the people I saw there today. Older guy with a young blonde who want a weekend "bolthole" from London. I'm really hoping they'll find something they like better so they won't even be there.'

They were there.

Josh recognised the couple from Stevie's description. They were standing near the front of the crowded room the real estate firm was using for their auctions that day. He thought Stevie had a good chance of being successful, with both the pre-approved mortgage she had sourced and the help her mother was providing but she was looking nervous, which made him very pleased that he was here to offer some moral support. He liked the way she was standing so close to him, too—as if she really appreciated that he was here. Or maybe she was taking advantage of the freedom not to have to re-

sist that extraordinary magnetic attraction their bodies seemed to have for each other.

When the bidding started, however, she moved away to stand alone, as if she needed to focus on fighting for her personal dream. For herself and for her son. Josh could see just how much it meant to her by her focus and a tension that he was finding contagious. This was beyond important. This was the dream of a future that simply meant everything to her.

Stevie had been right in thinking that the couple up the front were her main competition. They came straight back with a new bid every time she raised her hand and it was getting closer and closer to the limit Josh knew could not be passed. The other couple were slowing down, taking that bit longer each time before outbidding Stevie so when she nodded to take the amount offered to her limit, Josh held his breath. He could feel his heart pounding against his ribs so heaven only knew how Stevie was feeling at this moment.

And then it happened. Another bid from the bolthole couple took the price several thousand pounds over her limit and Stevie went as white as a sheet. The urge to put his arms around her to offer her his strength was overwhelming but Josh couldn't move a muscle and his brain was racing past that first reaction.

He was thinking of Mattie. Of when he'd started to win the trust of a boy who had been struggling to find his feet in a new life. Of how Mattie had been almost in tears because he'd thought Josh might give Lucky away and how desperately he was hoping that he'd be

able to live with the little dog he loved so much when he and Stevie had their own house.

It had to be this house.

But the auctioneer had his gavel poised in the air. 'Going…going…'

In the split second before he could say 'gone', Josh could remember the look on Stevie's face when she'd fallen in love with this cottage. And he could feel the way it had made *him* feel at the time to see her glowing—as if he would be quite prepared to gift wrap the whole world and present it to her if it would make her look that happy all over again.

Because…because he loved her, dammit.

And she deserved to have her dream.

He didn't put his hand up in that pregnant pause before the auctioneer declared the cottage sold. He didn't even shout out the amount that was ten thousand pounds more than the last bid. He spoke loudly, to make sure he was heard, but calmly and confidently enough to advertise that he was just getting started here. And it worked. The bolthole couple was stunned into silence until the older man shook his head. Stevie looked just as stunned when the gavel came down with no further bids. There was no hint of joy on her face, though, as the crowd dispersed.

'Why did you *do* that?' Her voice was low. And fierce.

'I didn't want you to lose the cottage. You *or* Mattie.'

'So *you* bought it? You bought the house *I* wanted?'

'No… I made sure you could buy it.' Somehow this gift of assistance was going all wrong and Josh had

no idea how to fix it. Unless… Was it her pride that was hurt? Or had he threatened the independence she'd fought so hard for? 'It can just be a loan,' he added. 'With no pressure to pay it back anytime soon. It's only ten thousand pounds.'

'Only?'

'We'll work it out. Trust me.'

The agent was smiling as he walked towards Josh. 'Congratulations, sir…' He gestured to indicate a small side room where there was a table and some chairs. 'If you'd like to come with me, we've got a bit of paperwork to sort out here.'

It was only then that Josh realised there could be complications from his impulsive actions. Was he legally responsible for purchasing this property for himself now? It would have to be sorted before the paperwork got completed but there was something more important to sort out first.

'Just give us a minute, please,' he ordered the agent.

Then he grabbed Stevie's hand and took her with him into the privacy of that side room and pushed the door closed behind them.

'Think about it for a minute,' he urged her. 'I know it was a bit crazy but I had to try and help, because… because…' The words died on his tongue as he realised what he had been about to add.

Because I think I might be falling in love with you…

Whoa… Where had that come from?

It's okay, he told himself. *Of course I care about Stevie. We're friends, aren't we?*

'Because of Mattie,' he said aloud. 'We both know

how much he wants to live with Lucky. This way he can. And he'll be well away from that gang of boys who've been bullying him and…' Josh managed to find a smile because it felt like he'd reached a much safer space now. 'And we'll never be short of something to do on our Big Brother sessions. There's so much I can teach him about renovation stuff and using tools…it's enough to keep us busy for ever.'

His smile seemed to be reaching inside himself as much as out towards Stevie. He could see himself teaching Mattie to use a hammer or how to plaster a hole in a wall. He could see Stevie helping as well, and Lucky probably getting underfoot and in the way and they'd all pitch in to throw a meal together at the end of a day's work on the cottage. A barbecue, maybe? Or soup and toast in front of the fire.

Kind of like a family but so much safer because it was only about being friends. Because that was something that could be trusted to last so much longer. For ever, even, perhaps?

The shock of what Josh had done by placing the winning bid on the cottage was starting to wear off as Stevie stood there listening to him explaining why he'd done it.

And, creeping through the mist of what had felt like a direct attack on the independence she'd fought to maintain for so long, there was something else that Stevie could feel. A trickle of excitement. The promise of a kind of happiness that she'd always known was out there but had always seemed just out of reach for herself.

It wasn't just that she was about to sign the paper-

work that would make her the owner of the house of her dreams.

It was more that she could hear something in Josh's words that he probably had no idea he was saying. She could actually see him spending time with Mattie and working on what would be endless projects for years to come in that little house and garden. They'd be fixing things and painting and digging in the garden and she'd be there. Lucky would be there.

Just like a family.

And maybe…just maybe…that was the real reason Josh had done what he'd just done. He might not know it, and Stevie wouldn't dream of even hinting at it, but she couldn't help feeling that, deep down, Josh actually did want a family.

That tiny flash of fantasy had suggested something else as well. That maybe she had been wrong to be so convinced that she didn't need a man in her life. That she might actually be able to see a future that would be so much better if she had a soulmate to share it with. It couldn't be just any man, of course. The thought had only occurred to her because it was Josh she'd seen as a part of her life in this cottage.

It was only this man that she could trust enough to love. This man that—even if he never wanted more from her than friendship—felt like he was, indeed, her soulmate.

She found herself smiling back at him. 'Mattie's going to love that,' she said softly. 'So will I.'

Josh looked so relieved. 'It's what friends do,' he said.

Stevie took a deep breath and her smile widened,

although the edges of it might have wobbled a little. 'Let's get this paperwork sorted,' she said. 'Friends get to celebrate stuff like this, too, don't they?'

CHAPTER SEVEN

GLOUCESTER GENERAL HOSPITAL's rooftop vegetable garden had become 'their' spot.

A relatively private space. Sometimes the only space they could find time to snatch a moment of being close enough to touch when it had been too long since they'd been together away from work. Not that they did touch, of course—with anything more than perhaps some eye contact that went on a little too long—because the knowledge of any extra dimension to the friendship was also something that belonged only to them. A secret that nobody else needed to know and one that added a rather delicious frisson to their professional relationship.

If Ruby's bunions didn't make it preferable for her to put her feet up in the staffroom during her breaks, rather than climbing all those stairs and then trying to find somewhere at least a bit sheltered from a potentially chilly breeze, she might have guessed there was something more going on between Josh and Stevie but, then, it didn't happen often enough to have even caught the attention of the volunteers who cared for the gardens or any other staff members who ventured up here.

And if anyone had walked close enough to hear what they were saying, they would most likely have only heard a professional kind of discussion happening between the head of the paediatric department and that nurse with the amazing hair.

Like the one they were having at the moment.

'I feel so sorry for Toby's mum, Julia.' Stevie took a sip of the takeaway coffee she'd purchased, along with some sandwiches, in the staff cafeteria. 'Mattie used to climb on everything when he was a toddler. He could have easily fallen off the couch and broken his collarbone like Toby did.'

'Common injury,' Josh agreed. 'And, most of the time, it heals up without any complications.'

'But Toby's been left with an arm that barely functions, even after all that physiotherapy. He can't bend his elbow or flex his fingers or even hang on to a toy.'

'Brachial plexus injuries can be very damaging.'

'It's quite a common birth injury, isn't it? The nerve roots that go from the spinal cord to the arm and hand are between C5 and T1 so they get stretched and damaged if the head and shoulder get too far apart?'

Josh nodded. 'Regeneration of axons can be amazing in babies, though, so it pays to wait and track progress before doing anything invasive like a nerve graft or transfer.'

'What's the difference?' Stevie loved that she could ask any question of Josh and never feel like it was stupid. She was loving learning from him, as well. Partly because it meant they were never, ever going to run out of interesting things to talk about but also because it

gave her glimpses of an exciting future where she might be able to specialise in a new area of paediatric nursing.

'A nerve graft takes a section of nerve from somewhere else in the body, usually the leg, and it's used to replace the damaged nerve. A nerve transfer, which is what Toby's going to have, is a newer technique that can have a brilliant result. Instead of grafting in a section of another nerve, they redirect a nearby nerve so that it targets the muscles that can't function. There's a learning curve to getting the nerve to work properly but the end results can be outstanding.' Josh was smiling. 'Microsurgery is fascinating. I'm hoping I can go and watch the surgery.'

He was holding her gaze as well and Stevie knew he understood exactly how fascinated she also was.

'Maybe I could arrange for you to come and watch it too. It'll have to be in a theatre with a gallery given that there'll be a lot of people who want to be there.'

'Oh…do you think I'd be allowed?'

'Let me see what I can do.'

He was still smiling. Still holding her gaze but, suddenly, this was anything but professional. That attraction could spark between them like a lightning bolt and…well…it simply wasn't appropriate. Hospitals might be well known for passionate liaisons between staff members but very few would ever shut themselves into a linen cupboard—or even snatch a kiss in a rooftop garden.

It was Stevie who sucked in a deep breath and broke that eye contact. 'So who's going to do the surgery? Julia sounded quite confused after that family meet-

ing this morning. I think she was really intimidated by how many doctors were there.'

'Mmm…' Josh's smile had been amused as Stevie had taken charge of ending that meaningful moment between them. Now it twisted into something more like a frown. 'I'll go and have another chat with her before Toby goes home today. There were a lot of people in the meeting room. We had a consultant radiologist to go through the results of the MRI. Then there was the orthopaedic surgeon who looked after Toby when he was admitted with his fractured clavicle and the neurosurgeon that Toby got referred to.'

'But he's not doing the operation? Julia said something about it apparently being really lucky that some visiting expert was going to be available.'

Josh nodded again. 'Yeah. Some hot-shot paediatric plastic surgeon who did his advanced training in the States and is getting recognised as a leader in the field.'

'A *plastic* surgeon?'

Josh laughed. 'They do a lot more than superficial stuff. Rehabilitation plastic surgery is about function more than appearance. This guy—Lachlan McKendry, his name is—is getting well known for his success in microsurgery techniques.'

'And he's coming to work here?'

'Not exactly. He got headhunted from the States to join a private clinic in London, from what I've been told. He's got family here or something. Anyway, he also agreed to do a series of lectures and some advanced training in hospitals not too far from London and the Gloucester area got chosen first. So I guess Toby *is* re-

ally lucky. Our neurosurgeon, David, is excited about working with this guy.'

'And Julia thought the surgery might be as early as next week?'

'We're having another meeting later this afternoon when Mr McKendry will be here to get briefed. He may well want more detailed tests to happen first, like a CT myelography scan that uses a contrast to give a very detailed picture of the spinal cord and nerve roots.'

'He'll need sedation for that, too, I guess. Like he had for the MRI today?'

'Yes.' Josh checked his watch. 'I'd better go and see Julia. I'm sure Toby's awake enough to be discharged now.' He scrunched up the paper bag that had held his sandwiches and gestured towards Stevie's bag. 'You all done?'

'Yep. It wasn't the world's best sandwich.'

'Nothing's as good as your mousetraps for lunch.'

'I'll make some more.' Stevie got to her feet and brushed crumbs off her coat. 'I could send some with Mattie on Thursday for when you do your Big Brother thing.'

'Fabulous.' Josh was leading the way through the raised garden beds towards the door that led to the stairwell. 'Did he tell you where we're going this week?'

'No. I got the impression it was boy stuff that I didn't need to know about.'

Josh laughed. 'He's right. We're going to a hardware store to check out tools we're going to need. We might do a bit of internet surfing to find some instructional videos as well.'

'Boy stuff, huh?' Stevie had to pass close to Josh as he held the door open for her and she deliberately paused for just a heartbeat at a point where she was close enough to feel his body heat because it was too delicious to resist. And maybe she was having another one of those glimpses into a future that could hold something even more exciting than advanced qualifications in a nursing specialty. Even better than owning her own home and achieving an independence she'd dreamed of. She could almost hear an echo of Josh's voice in that glimpse as well, saying that teaching Mattie about renovation and tools would keep them busy for ever.

Don't go there...

The warning was hardwired into the same part of her brain. She knew better than to buy into the kind of dream that could set you up for a broken heart. Yes, it was there but she wasn't going to trust it.

Not yet...

And it was easy to diffuse. To turn it into something very different. Stevie flicked her gaze up to graze his. 'I'll have you know,' she said softly, 'that DIY is one of my many, many talents.'

She loved the way she could trust that Josh would always respond to her like this. That the level of attraction was always so easily—and equally—ignited. She saw the way the muscles in his neck moved as he swallowed. The way his eyes darkened to almost black as they locked onto hers. From behind her, as she moved past, she could hear the way he needed to clear his throat.

'He's pretty excited, isn't he? About the move?'

'Counting sleeps,' Stevie agreed.

'So am I,' Josh murmured as he caught up with her at the first landing, his hand brushing hers on the railing of the stairs. 'We're almost going to be neighbours.'

'Colleagues, friends *and* neighbours…' Stevie threw a smile over her shoulder as she sped up her descent to the next landing. She was laughing as her mouth ran away with the words that were coming from nowhere, perhaps fuelled by the heat that simply the brush of his hand had generated. 'What more could you possibly want?'

With the door swinging open and a lab technician carrying a coolbox coming into the stairwell, there was no chance of hearing any response Josh might have made to that impulsive question. Which was probably just as well, Stevie decided later that afternoon as she hurried away from work at the end of her shift. Josh's aversion to anything like permanence, or family, was just as hardwired into his brain as her own difficulty in trusting men had been.

Had he even answered her? Maybe he might have thought she was pushing boundaries that he'd made very clear a long time ago. It wasn't as if she'd seen him on the ward again this afternoon and had had the opportunity to share a glance or a smile and reassure herself that nothing had changed.

Stevie had walked to work that morning but the quickest route home was to cut diagonally through the car park to get to the main road. And maybe it was because she was thinking about Josh that made it so easy

to spot him even well up ahead, walking across her intended path towards the main hospital building.

'Hi,' she called. 'What are you doing out here?'

He didn't seem to have heard her. Or was he ignoring her? Stevie's smile faltered. It looked as if he was
just going to keep going, cross her path and not even
look at her. He was looking over his shoulder, in fact,
his attention seemingly caught by an extremely flash
car. A silver car, which rang a vague bell for Stevie but
she ignored it because she was more worried than ever
that she might have been skating on thin ice by putting
labels on their relationship when it was something they
never really talked about.

What was worse was that, when Josh did turn his
head, he seemed to look straight at Stevie and not even
blink as he focused on the hospital buildings ahead of
him. As if he didn't see her. Or didn't want to? What on
earth was going on? And what was he doing, wearing
a suit? Josh never wore suits. He often came to work in
jeans before he changed into his scrubs.

'Hey... *Josh?*'

She knew he had to be able to hear her but he was
still walking away. Stevie had the sudden, horrible realisation of what it might be like if whatever it was they
had between them at the moment fizzled out and she
was aware of a beat of fear. But, at the same time, the
Josh she knew would never treat anybody this rudely.
Bewilderment coated the fear and somehow became
anger.

'*Oi!*' she shouted. 'What's going on, Josh? Are you
seriously just going to walk away from me?'

That stopped him in his tracks. He turned to face Stevie as she kept marching towards him. But then her steps faltered and it felt as if the earth's axis was tipping slightly off kilter—but not in a good way, like it had the first time Josh had kissed her.

He looked weird. And kind of angry.

'What is it with people calling me *Josh*?' he demanded. 'It seems to happen everywhere I go around here. And who the hell are *you*?'

Stevie opened her mouth and then closed it again, her brain spinning as she took in the fact that this *wasn't* Josh. It was someone who looked astonishingly like him, however, but up close she could see the differences. This man was a little more solid, perhaps—his hair was shorter and he had some carefully managed designer stubble going on. Most of all, the way he was looking at her held nothing of the warmth she was so used to seeing in Josh's eyes now.

And that was when something clicked. Stevie could hear again a snatch of a conversation she'd overheard in the staffroom a few weeks ago between Ruby and Josh.

'Saw you over at Cheltenham Central Hospital...

'That's a flash new car you've got... Silvery thing...'

'Good to see that you've had a shave since then, anyway...'

Stevie opened her mouth again. And swallowed hard.

'My name's Stevie,' she told him. 'And I'm sorry I shouted at you like that but...but you look incredibly like a friend of mine. Someone who works here. I... thought he was ignoring me.'

'Ah…' His smile was polite. 'And this friend is called Josh, I take it?'

'Yes…'

'I'm Lachlan,' he told her. 'Lachlan McKendry. If you work here, perhaps you can help? I'm heading for a meeting in the paediatric department.'

'Oh…of course. I've heard about you. You're the famous plastic surgeon.'

The way his eyebrow quirked stole Stevie's breath away. He was *so* like Josh it was spooky. They said everybody had a doppelganger out there somewhere but this was impossible.

Unless…

Stevie knew that her intense stare was coming across as being rude. That this renowned paediatric surgeon had probably decided it would be better to go and find the department he was looking for by himself. Yes… he was turning on his heel as if he couldn't wait to get away from her.

'Wait…' Stevie sucked in a quick breath. 'I know this might sound totally crazy but…are you, by any chance, adopted?'

That stopped him for a second time. His expression was more dumbfounded than angry now.

'Not that it's any of your business,' he said slowly. 'But, no, I'm not.'

'Sorry…' Stevie bit her lip. 'It's just that you look so much like Josh, you could be brothers. Twins, even.'

That made him laugh but then he shook his head. 'Sounds like the stuff of fairy tales. If you'll excuse me, I don't want to be late for my meeting.'

His meeting.

With Josh and the other specialists involved in Toby's case, like the neurosurgeon, David and the orthopaedic surgeon and all their respective registrars.

Stevie could imagine how shocking it would be to come face to face with someone who looked so much like herself that it would be like looking into a slightly cracked mirror and it certainly wouldn't be something she wanted to happen in front of other people. And, even if her wild idea that these men could be closely related was no more than the remotest possibility, it was still a potential bomb that was about to be thrown into Josh's life.

The urge to protect him was as fierce as any Stevie had ever felt to protect Mattie. The kind of urge that could only be this strong when you loved someone enough for their welfare to be more important than your own. Not that Stevie was going to take any time to think about what was going on in her head—or her heart—and what it might mean for the future. She just knew that she wasn't about to let Josh face this without her being there to support him if he needed her.

'I know exactly where you need to be,' she told Lachlan McKendry. 'Follow me.'

They walked in silence as Stevie led Lachlan swiftly into Gloucester General Hospital, along corridors and up the stairs. She couldn't make small talk because there was too much going on in her head.

What if the almost impossible was somehow true? That Josh was about to discover he had a cousin, perhaps? Or a brother? It would force something on him

that he believed he had never needed and had no desire for now.

Family.

Real family. Not a chosen sort of family that she might dream that she and Mattie could become one day. This was flesh and blood kind of family. Someone that you had a genetic bond with. Someone who could drag a painful past that Josh had kept secret into a present that he couldn't escape.

This could turn his world upside down.

There would be time later to worry about how this might affect her and, more importantly, how it might affect Mattie, but right now she had to try and engineer a way that could provide the privacy she knew was essential for two men who could both be about to face something life-changing. It was only when Stevie noticed she had gone above the level for the paediatric department that she realised her subconscious had come up with the perfect plan. She pushed open the heavy doors that led out to the rooftop garden where she'd been, only hours ago, with Josh.

'What's going on?' Lachlan blinked as he looked around.

'Wait here.' Stevie injected the same kind of authority into her voice that she'd used with Mattie when he'd been too little to understand why he couldn't just run out onto a pedestrian crossing. 'Trust me, please... There's someone you have to meet before you do anything else. He's the head of the paediatric department so it's who you've come here to see, anyway, but...' Stevie's brief head shake acknowledged that this was too compli-

cated to try and explain. 'I'll be back in a few minutes and then you'll understand why this is so important.'

It wasn't simply that she had run down the stairs so fast that had Stevie's heart thumping hard as she tapped on Josh's office door a minute or two later.

'Josh?'

The note of urgency in her voice made him look up instantly but Stevie couldn't offer any kind of reassurance, like a smile. What was happening here wasn't just some strange coincidence. Stevie just knew it was huge and she knew that Josh could see that in her face because he was already getting to his feet and his forehead was creased with concern.

'What's wrong, Stevie?'

'Come with me. There's something you need to see.'

CHAPTER EIGHT

JOSH KNEW WHERE they were going as soon as they started heading upstairs and the fact that Stevie wanted them to be somewhere as private as possible was alarming, to say the least.

Had something happened to Mattie?

But Stevie's son seemed to be the last thing on her mind right then.

'Do you remember that day when Ruby thought you had a new car?' Stevie was racing up the stairs. 'A really flash one?'

'Yeah…something ridiculous like a Maserati.'

'And she said you'd needed a shave?' Stevie was out of breath as she reached the door at the top of the stairwell and she paused to look back at Josh. 'She was telling the truth.'

'What? I have no idea what you're talking about.'

'I know.' Stevie had her hands on the heavy door, ready to push it open, but she paused to catch his gaze. 'Whatever this is,' she said quietly, 'it's going to be okay…'

There was something in the depths of those glori-

ously hazel eyes that Josh had never seen before. It felt like a promise—that she would do whatever it took to *make* it okay?

No wonder Josh felt like he might be stepping far too close to the edge of a cliff as he followed her outside. And then he found himself staring at the man who was clearly waiting for them and he could actually *feel* his world being turned inside out.

'Josh? This is Lachlan McKendry. Lachlan, this is Josh Stanmore. Um… I thought it might be a good idea if you two had a bit of time before your meeting.'

Neither Josh nor Lachlan responded. They were both staring at each other.

Fascinated.

Spooked.

Josh could feel Stevie watching him. He could hear the concern in her voice in the way it faltered. 'Do you want me to stay?'

He turned towards her and, for a moment in this free-fall of what felt like a seismic change in his life, Josh knew that his friendship with Stevie was a safe haven if he needed one. Not that he could run away from this. And it was not something that anyone other than himself and the man in front of him could deal with, but knowing that he had someone he could trust who was in his corner was enough to give him the strength he needed.

He gave his head only a single shake. 'Thanks, Stevie.' He held her gaze long enough to let her know just how much he appreciated the fact that she'd given him a chance to deal with this privately, at least to begin with. Had she chosen this obscure part of Gloucester

General because she'd remembered that it was where he'd brought her to protect her own privacy? It felt like a lifetime ago but it was a reminder of how solid their friendship had become. How much trust there was between them.

'We'll talk soon,' he promised.

'Soon' turned out to be three days later, thanks to a day off for Stevie, a shift that didn't coincide and the understandable confusion laced with astonishment that meant Josh needed to spend any free time he had right now with Lachlan McKendry. Apart from a text message or two that assured Stevie he was fine and a promise that he wasn't going to let anything interfere with his time with Mattie, she had no idea how Josh was really coping until he dropped Mattie home after their Big Brother session on Thursday. Stevie knew then that she had been right to feel worried.

Josh looked as if he hadn't slept properly for days. As if he'd lost weight, too, and he even had a noticeable five o'clock shadow today, which made him look even more like Stevie remembered Lachlan had looked. The almost haunted look in Josh's eyes squeezed her heart so hard that it hurt and he was holding her gaze with an intensity that suggested he had been missing her company as much as she had been missing his.

'When did you last have a proper meal?' she asked.

'I'm not that hungry, to be honest.'

Stevie thought quickly. She already had Mattie's favourite fish fingers and chips dinner keeping warm in the oven but she could hardly offer some of that to Josh.

He clearly needed to eat something, though. And maybe he needed someone to talk to even more. He was still holding her gaze and, if they hadn't been able to hear Mattie in the background, she was quite sure he would be kissing her senseless. The desire for that to *be* happening was so strong that Stevie knew she had to, at least, have some time with Josh.

'There's an Italian restaurant down the road,' she told him. 'Cheap and cheerful but they do the best lasagne I've ever tasted and their fresh salad and garlic bread is to die for.' Yeah…he was hungry. Stevie could see the spark of interest in those dark eyes. 'How 'bout I meet you there in ten minutes? I just need to get my neighbour to keep an eye on Mattie. Someone has to make sure you have a decent meal. You're not on call tonight, are you?'

'No.' Josh was smiling now. Maybe he liked that she was taking charge and trying to look after him?

'Have a glass of wine while you're waiting, then.'

Stevie put her hand on his arm to encourage him to turn and, despite her body's protest that what she wanted to do more than anything was to pull him back and into her arms, she gave him a gentle shove on his back to make sure she didn't give in to that desire. And to make sure Josh didn't hang around to protest that he wasn't hungry.

'I'll see you there,' she said, closing the door behind him.

The carafe of red wine looked to be half-empty by the time Stevie arrived at the small, local restaurant and the

plate of pizza-style garlic bread only had crumbs left on the red, gingham napkin that matched the tablecloth.

'I was hungrier than I thought I was,' Josh admitted. 'Shall I order some more?'

Stevie nodded as he signalled the waiter. 'I'll have a glass of wine, too, please. And then I want to know what's going on.'

Josh shook his head as he poured her some wine from the carafe. 'I don't even know where to begin. It's crazy...'

'Start at the beginning. From when I left you on the roof. I haven't even *seen* you since then.' Stevie added a smile to counteract what could have been interpreted as a somewhat desperate undertone to her words. She couldn't let Josh know just how much she'd been missing him. That she might be starting to depend on his presence in her life?

Josh was smiling back. 'I'm sorry. And you're the only person I can really talk to about this—the only one who will get just how much of a shock it is.'

'So you *are* brothers?' Stevie tucked away those words of being the only person he could talk to about this. She knew they would feel like a verbal hug when she pulled them out again, later.

'The first thing I asked him was where and when he was born. Same place as me—in Cheltenham. Same year as me. Same day...'

'Oh, my God,' Stevie whispered. 'I knew it. You're *twins*...'

'Lachlan was as shocked as I was. He couldn't believe that his mother could have given one of her ba-

bies away. He decided that maybe I'd been stolen. That his mother had been told one of her twins had died or something to cover it up.' Josh stopped and took a deep breath. 'But the whole time we were talking about it we were watching each other, you know? And it was so weird. His voice is so like mine and we'd start speaking at the same time and we'd move at the same time and…it was like looking in a mirror.'

'Did you go to that meeting?'

'No. We had to postpone it. It's not as if the surgery is urgent and neither of us would have been able to focus, which would have made it a waste of time for everybody involved. Plus, I'm not ready for the grapevine to get hold of this information with all the gossip that'll happen. I don't think anybody saw us together but thank goodness you intercepted him before he turned up at the paediatric ward. Can you imagine how Ruby would have reacted?'

The fragrant, steamy triangles of fresh garlic bread straight from the pizza oven were placed in front of them, along with a big bowl of fresh salad and the lasagne they'd both ordered.

'She would have whisked him off to her office and interrogated him,' Stevie joked. 'Nicely but, oh, so thoroughly.'

'Exactly. So thank you for giving us the best private space we could have had—until Lachlan came to my place the next evening, that is, and, man, did we need the private space then.'

'Why?'

'He was wrecked.' Josh was silent for a moment as

he tasted his food. 'Oh, boy…this is good.' He ate in silence for another minute but then put his fork down. 'This is a hell of a lot harder for him than it is for me, I think. He didn't even know he was adopted.'

Stevie nodded as she added a scoop of salad onto her plate. 'He sounded quite sure he *wasn't*, when I suggested it.'

'He went home after we met and accused his mother of giving away his twin brother and demanded to know why. It sounds like it ended up being the most enormous row. She said she had no idea he was one of twins but, even if she'd known, she wouldn't have wanted two babies. She didn't even want one and she'd only agreed to the adoption to save her marriage. Lachlan said it made sense of a lot of stuff but it still did his head in. I think he found it a bit cathartic to talk about it, to be honest. We were up pretty much all night and there might have been a bit of whisky involved.'

Stevie blinked as Josh paused to eat a few more mouthfuls. The chance meeting between twin brothers who'd been separated as babies was astonishing enough. That they'd both had less than loving upbringings was not so much of a coincidence as a tragedy but it sounded as if a bonding process was well underway.

'She lives locally,' Josh added. 'The mother. Jocelyn or Josephine? I can't remember. Anyway, she's not actually that far from me. In one of those estates I was telling you about—with a huge mansion and its own forest? The McKendrys have family money from way back, which was why Lachlan's father was desperate for an heir, I guess, but he was also a cardiothoracic surgeon

in some exclusive private hospital in London—famous enough to have been given a knighthood. Lachlan said there was never any choice about the career he was going to have, right from when he got sent off to boarding school when he was only about six years old.'

Stevie shook her head. 'Unbelievable.'

'He kind of rebelled, by going into plastic surgery instead of cardiac or neurosurgery. And then he took off as soon as he could to do postgrad training and work in the States.'

'What's brought him back here?'

'He'd been headhunted by a children's hospital in London and came back last year because he said he was, finally, a bit homesick. He's been in demand for lecture tours and specialist training and so on since he got back but the Gloucester area is the first one he accepted and that was because he can still travel to London if he needs to and he's got some major family stuff he needs to sort out.'

'I guess his parents are getting older?'

'His father died more than a decade ago. It's his mother who's causing the problems and she sounds like a very difficult woman.'

'She sounds horrible. How could you adopt a baby like it was some kind of sticking plaster to hold a marriage together?'

Josh shrugged and his expression reminded Stevie of why he'd turned his back on the concept of marriage and family long ago. That those kinds of relationships couldn't be trusted. That they could do more harm than good, even.

'Seems like her carers don't like her much, either. They keep resigning.'

'She needs carers?'

'Full time.' Josh nodded. 'With medical training. I think he said she's got brittle diabetes. Or asthma. Maybe both—I've forgotten everything we said. It wasn't just Lachlan spilling an outline of his entire history—I was doing the same. It was like we had to catch up with as much as possible, as soon as possible.'

He reached for his wine glass and took a long sip, his gaze holding Stevie's over the rim.

'You're the only person I've ever said anything to about my background but... I don't know, it just felt so easy to talk to Lachlan. We'd only just met but I felt like I'd known him for ever.'

'You kind of have,' Stevie said softly. 'You shared a womb for nine months.'

But Josh shook his head. 'I don't think I buy into that "twin" stuff. Or even an automatic genetic connection.' He shook his head again, as if he didn't want to even think about it, turning his attention to his meal again.

'Anyway,' he said a minute or two later, 'Mrs Mc-Kendry's housekeeper threatened to walk out recently so Lachlan decided to kill two birds with one stone. He's basing himself at the family mansion while he divides his time between hospitals here and his work in London and he's planning to use the three-month stint to get some kind of permanent arrangement in place for his mother. Or his "ex" mother, as he was calling her by the time we talked.'

'So he's here for a while longer, then?'

'Yes. Another couple of months, at least. I think that day that Ruby clocked him was his first day at Cheltenham Central. He's going to start with us next week, to line up Toby's surgery and some lectures and demonstrations he's going to present on new suture techniques amongst other stuff. What gets done in Emergency or even elective surgery can have major repercussions down the track for anyone, but especially for paediatrics. I'm looking forward to learning the latest myself.'

Stevie ate the last forkful of her salad. 'No wonder you were both up all night. Sounds like you talked about everything.'

Josh nodded slowly. 'Seemed like that at the time. Now it feels like we've barely started.'

'I'd like to meet him again.'

Stevie tried not to advertise just how intrigued she was to discover more. And to see what changes it might mean for Josh's view of the world—and family?

Oh, no…she couldn't go there. Poor Josh had quite enough to deal with, without adding any hint of pressure from her for something that wasn't even on an agenda. She offered him a smile. 'I mean, if he's your twin I'm sure he's a nice guy.'

To her relief, Josh smiled back. He had a bit more colour in his cheeks as well so maybe he was feeling better after eating.

'I told him about you,' he said. 'After he asked if I'd ever been married. Or if I have a girlfriend.'

'Oh?' Stevie's heart skipped a beat. Had their friendship been promoted to the status of a relationship? She caught her bottom lip between her teeth at the same

moment her breath caught in her chest. The longing to hear Josh say that he considered her to be his girlfriend was powerful enough to override anything else.

But Josh's smile was fading. 'Turns out we both have the same aversion to permanence in that department,' he said. 'Weird, huh?'

One side of Stevie's mouth quirked into a wry smile but she had no words to find. The stab of something a lot deeper than disappointment was definitely sharp enough to remind her of what heartbreak was like. Enough to make it very clear that she had let herself get into a dangerous place where she could end up getting badly hurt. Was that why it was called 'falling' in love?

'So, what do you think?'

'Sorry, what?' Stevie had been so lost in her own thoughts she'd missed what Josh had been saying as he pushed his empty plate away.

'I was saying that Lachlan suggested a night out. Apparently there's a locum nurse who's living in and looking after his mother and Lachlan would like to take her out to a nice restaurant somewhere to give her an evening off. He wants us to come as well. I think he's as glad as I am that we didn't have to come face to face with each other for the first time in front of other people so he'd like to thank you properly.'

Josh was reaching across the table as he spoke to cover Stevie's hand with his own and she could feel the warmth of that touch spread from her fingers to her arm and then wash into every cell in her body to pool, deep in her belly.

'Sounds fun.' Somehow she managed to keep her tone light. 'Let me know when so I can sort a babysitter.'

'Next week, maybe? Or the week after that? We need to get Toby's surgery out of the way first, I think, but it would be better if it was before your settlement on the cottage, wouldn't it? You'll be busy getting things sorted and then moving and I guess it might be harder to find a babysitter until you know people in the village.'

Life was certainly about to change in the near future but Stevie's excitement about the move was suddenly tinged with apprehension about other changes that might be coming—for both herself and Josh. That stab of more than disappointment was still there, deepening into a kind of chill that was more than enough to smother that delicious heat. It felt cold enough to be something very like fear. She couldn't leave Mattie out of the equation, either. Josh might have promised never to hurt her son but who knew what was going to happen in the future, when such major changes had been triggered in Josh's own life?

'Speaking of babysitting…' Stevie scrunched up her napkin as she got to her feet. 'I'd better get back and let Mrs Johnston get home.'

It took another couple of weeks before Lachlan Mc-Kendry was ready to do the nerve transfer surgery that would hopefully restore shoulder and arm function to two-year-old Toby. More tests had been necessary, including a repeat electrical study of nerve function right before the surgery was scheduled.

The gallery of the operating theatre was full but no-

body had queried why Josh had someone from the paediatric nursing staff sitting right beside him in the front
row. Perhaps because it was now common knowledge
that it was Josh's brother who was the star performer
in this intricate surgery?

There were screens that allowed them a close-up look
at what was happening below and Josh had been watching in fascination from when the first felt pen marks
had been made on the child's back to mark anatomical
points for the meticulous dissection Lachlan was making to expose the nerves he was targeting.

'So, we're going to use distal branches of the spinal
accessory nerve to neurotise the suprascapular nerve,
which is the classic approach to repairing a damaged
brachial plexus network. I'm working slowly here, because there are a lot of small vessels and I don't want to
have to cauterise them when I'm this close to the nerve.
I hope none of you are expecting an early lunch today.'

The ripple of sound was too muted to be labelled
as laughter. It was more like an acknowledgement that
what they were witnessing was of far more interest than
lunch but it did make Josh glance sideways, because
anytime he thought about lunch there was always a
background thought of mousetraps. And of Stevie.

As if she could feel the touch of his gaze, she shifted
her head so that she could glance at Josh for a moment,
instead of the screen. There was a hint of a smile tug-
ging at one corner of her mouth and her eyes were glowing. She was loving this opportunity to get so close to
the action that she turned back to watch again almost

instantly but Josh let his gaze linger on her profile for a heartbeat longer.

He'd been right in thinking that Stevie was his safe haven. If anything, over the last few weeks she'd become such a rock he couldn't imagine not having her in his life. So many things had changed and what had helped him more than anything in coping with it all was talking to Stevie about it. He'd told her things he would never dream about saying to anyone else and her responses often made him feel not only understood but could give him a new perspective. Like that late-night phone conversation last week…

'I felt kind of jealous for a while, you know? Lachlan had everything money could buy. He never had to take a job in a bar or delivering pizzas to get through med school. He had a home where he was wanted. A father who was proud of every prize he got at school.'

'But was he any happier than you were, do you think?'

'No. I don't think he was…'

Lachlan was certainly in his element right now. His voice was calm and confident as he kept up a commentary for his audience.

'I'm going for the donor nerve first, because finding the suprascapular notch and nerve is a bit more challenging.' There was almost a smile to be heard in his voice now. 'But success is always sweeter after a challenge, isn't it?'

It wasn't the first time that Lachlan turned his head, signalling that he needed perspiration swabbed from his forehead and it made Josh frown. Was Lachlan under

more stress than it seemed? Could the challenges that had intruded on his personal life be having a background effect on his professional performance?

At least they were working towards getting used to the bombshell of discovering each other. Getting to know each other. And having the news hit the hospital grapevine hadn't been nearly as confronting as Josh had feared, because—apart from Stevie—nobody knew he was adopted and nobody could guess that he hadn't even known himself that he had a brother. People assumed he'd just kept his personal life private and they respected that. So far, nobody had even tried to find out why they had different surnames. Perhaps they were still too intrigued by the similarities between Josh and Lachlan to move on to what was different.

'Here we go…' Lachlan's voice was clear and confident. 'I'm opening up the trapezius muscle now. You'd expect the nerve to be in the muscle but it isn't. It's below the muscle, in the fatty layer. Again, I'm going slowly.'

He was being so careful—the way Josh was with any procedure he performed. There was no denying how similar he and Lachlan were. It seemed like every time they were together they discovered something else they shared, like a favourite colour or food or movie. And, sometimes, it was something on a physical level, like a gesture. Or the fact they both had the same, slightly crooked eye tooth. Things were adding up, that's for sure, and Josh was beginning to wonder if Stevie was right about a genetic connection. A 'twin' thing? She'd said something else about it the other day.

'You have family, Josh. It's not a matter of choice. This is real. Genetic. You have more in common with each other than you'll ever have with anyone else on earth. A bond that's there whether you want it or not. And it can be a bond that's more important than anything else—like the one I have with Mattie.'

But Stevie had built that bond from the moment she'd chosen to go through with her pregnancy and it had been strengthened every day since. Josh had no history with his brother at all. Could that bond still be significant? The idea of whether nature or nurture was dominant in shaping personalities and lives was a topic that had just become very personal for Josh but there was no denying they both shared the same passion for medicine.

Even as his thoughts strayed on one level, Josh was focused on the screen, watching every tiny, careful snip Lachlan was making to get through the muscle to find the nerve he needed.

'Some of you might be interested in reading about new advances in nerve and tendon transfers.' Lachlan seemed to have the same ability to be thinking on different levels because his hands never faltered in their task. 'It's an exciting field that's offering a lot of promise in restoring function for people with tetraplegia, for example. Giving them enough movement to be able to gain independence in feeding themselves, or driving a car. Ah…there we go. There's the suprascapular nerve. Can I have a vessel loop, please?'

Josh watched as the nerve was identified by the soft loop and then cut to leave the end ready to be joined to the functioning nerve. Yes…he did have a lot in com-

mon with Lachlan but their connection had reached a totally new level just last night when they'd stayed late at the hospital as Lachlan had explained the detail of today's surgery to Josh. As they'd stood outside, ready to go in their separate directions, Lachlan had paused.

'Do you think it made it easier, knowing all along that you'd been adopted?'

'I think it made it worse. I knew I was different. That I didn't belong, somehow, but I didn't know why until a "real" son came along and I wasn't wanted any more.'

But Lachlan had shaken his head. *'I never knew and I think that was worse because I didn't belong either but I never knew why. Until I met you.'*

Maybe it had been at that moment that Josh had begun to change his mind about the existence of a meaningful genetic connection between people. Something that would never change. That could be trusted, no matter what.

And, if he'd been wrong about that, maybe there were other assumptions about relationships he needed to revisit.

As he watched his brother perform the extraordinary task of joining tiny nerves together with sutures that were almost invisible to the naked eye, Josh felt himself letting go of some nameless tension. Even his body relaxed, to the point where he could feel his thigh touching Stevie's leg.

Could she feel that heat? It was burning through layers of fabric for Josh.

What would she say if she knew that his focus wasn't completely on the end of Toby's surgery now, he won-

dered, as his gaze drifted from the screen to Stevie's profile again. What if she knew he was thinking that she might need to revisit some of her own assumptions— like the one about genetic connections being 'real' because you had no choice about them?

Surely a chosen connection could be just as real? Like the one that had grown so strong between him and Stevie? It was more than he'd ever found with any other woman on earth.

Again, it seemed that Stevie could feel his gaze, in the same way he was so aware of the subtle touching of their legs. She barely moved her head but her gaze managed to find his. And hold it. And it seemed as though she was answering a question that he hadn't realised was showing in his eyes.

Telling him that she agreed with him about the connection they'd found.

Promising him that it could be trusted…

CHAPTER NINE

DESPITE BEING DETERMINED not to build any hopes high enough to mean her heart would shatter into many more pieces when things changed, it was impossible to ignore the significance of being invited out to dinner with Josh and his twin brother. By the time a date had been agreed on—at rather short notice, in the end—and a restaurant booked, the event suddenly took on an importance that was generating rather a lot of tension.

It felt like a *date*…

As if Josh was happy to go out in public with her as his partner. To introduce her properly to the only real family he had. To potentially be seen, in fact, by people who worked in at Gloucester General, in which case the grapevine would have a new rumour to disperse and embellish.

Stevie could have been distinctly apprehensive by the potential step forward this outing could represent in her relationship with Josh but she wasn't allowing herself to think about that. Living in the moment had worked very well when she'd decided she might as well make the most of one night with Josh Stanmore so that's what

she was doing again. Making the most of what could be a fantasy date.

When she heard that Lachlan had chosen one of the most prestigious restaurants in the region, her first re-action—apart from the nervousness that came from knowing that she was going to feel like a fish out of water—was to thank her lucky stars that she already had a suitable dress.

Nobody needed to know that it had been a fabulous find in a London charity shop a couple of years ago. A dress so gorgeous that Stevie had had to try it on, even though she'd known how unlikely it was that she would ever have an occasion that she would be able to wear it. And trying it on had been a mistake because there was no way she could leave it behind in the shop. Not when she'd discovered that such a rich shade of burgundy could look so amazing with the deep, auburn colour of her hair. Or that the combination of the cross-over bod-ice that exposed just enough of her shoulders, and the hem of the full skirt being so much higher at front than the back to reveal glimpses of her legs as she moved, made it the sexiest dress she'd ever tried on.

So she'd bought the dress and it had hung at the back of her wardrobe ever since. Sometimes, Stevie would notice it and stop a moment to touch it, loving the feel of the lace fabric and remembering how the silk lin-ing had slipped over her skin like a lover's touch. That feeling was still there as she put it on to actually wear out for the very first time, along with relief that it was still a perfect fit, but there was something a lot more intense that *had* changed. That slip of silk against her

skin didn't give her a fantasy moment of some imaginary lover. This time, it made her think only of Josh and how his touch made her feel.

How she knew, right down to her bones, that she would never find another lover who could make her feel like that.

Another man that she could trust enough to love as much as she loved Josh Stanmore.

Mattie's jaw dropped when he saw her come out of the bathroom when she'd finished getting into her dress and doing her hair and make-up.

'You look beautiful, Mum… Like a princess.'

'Thanks, hon.'

'Are you really going out to dinner with Josh?'

'I am.'

'Because you're his girlfriend?'

Oh…help… There was no mistaking that gleam of hope in her son's dark eyes. He really wanted her and Josh to be together, didn't he? For Josh to be part of his future as a lot more than a Big Brother mentor, and that sounded a note of alarm that Stevie knew she'd have to deal with properly at some point. But not right now because that could spoil this fantasy and the temptation to indulge in the pleasure of living the dream for just a few hours was too strong. It wasn't going to hurt anyone, especially Mattie, because she wouldn't let that happen.

Stevie found a smile that she hoped was both reassuring but casual enough that it would help let him down gently when that time came. 'Because I'm his friend,' she said. 'And I met his brother a little while ago. He's coming too, so it's not like a date or anything.'

'Josh has got a brother?' Mattie's eyes widened as he was completely distracted. 'I never knew that.'

'Josh didn't either.' Stevie bent to drop a kiss on Mattie's head. 'But it's a long story and it'll have to wait until you see Josh again because it's his story to tell, not mine. Now… I'm going to go and tell Mrs Johnson I'm ready to go. Are you all set for tonight?'

'Yeah… I'm going to talk to Gran and do some more packing. Are we really moving next week?'

'We are.'

'And Lucky's going to come and live with us straight away?'

'That's something else to talk about with Josh. He might want us to be properly settled in before Lucky comes.'

'Talk about it tonight,' Mattie instructed. 'Tell him I want Lucky to come on the first day we move in. I want him to sleep on the end of my bed.'

The scruffy little dog was the last thing on Stevie's mind, however, when she found herself sitting in Josh's car a short time later and they were on their way to what she could pretend was a date and it was… It was almost overwhelmingly exciting but terrifying at the same time.

'You're very quiet tonight.' Josh sounded sympathetic. 'I guess you're probably exhausted from all the packing you're doing on top of everything else.'

'Actually, I'm trying to remember the last time I got taken out to dinner. And I've never been to a Michelin-starred restaurant in my life.'

'You look like you go out to places like this all

the time. Your dress is gorgeous and that hairstyle is very elegant.'

'Thanks.' Stevie had to smile. 'It's just a messy bun. There's not much I *can* do with hair like mine. It has a personality all of its own.'

Josh laughed. 'Like you,' he said, turning to catch her gaze. 'I think you're both very well suited.' He was slowing the vehicle. 'I think we're here.'

'Wow…' Stevie took in the ivy-covered stone walls of the old manor house and the circular drive in front of it with a floodlit fountain in a central garden. 'It looks amazing.'

'Mmm…' Josh shook his head. 'Don't know how Lachlan swung it on such short notice. I'd heard that you needed a good percentage of royal blood or something to get a reservation here ever since it got its latest Michelin star.'

'Didn't you tell me that his father had been knighted? I'm guessing the name would be well known in these parts.' Stevie was watching Josh's face as he parked his car. 'Does it still bother you? That Lachlan grew up in such a different world?'

Again, Josh turned so that he could look at Stevie directly. 'You know what? I think I might have resented it a whole lot more if you hadn't put me straight.'

'Put you straight? How did I do that?'

'You made me realise that being so wealthy hasn't made Lachlan any happier than I am.'

Stevie felt a glow of pride that came from knowing that Josh had put such importance on something she'd said. She couldn't help the rebellious thought that fol-

lowed almost instantly—that he might have a similar epiphany if she told him how she really felt about him. If she suggested that they could build a future together…

'To be honest,' Josh added, as he reached to open his door, 'I'm a bit worried about him. I think he's really struggling to get his head around having been adopted, so finding out he's got a brother has been more a shock to him than it is to me. He's not saying much, but I reckon he's lost weight over the last few weeks and he seems to look more stressed than ever now.'

'Maybe tonight will help.' Stevie followed his example and climbed out of the car.

She could help a little, too, by not disturbing Josh with any overly personal confessions. He had quite enough going on in his life and this wasn't *really* a date, was it? She might have indulged in a bit of a fantasy but she was really only here because Lachlan wanted to show his appreciation of how she'd sheltered the first meeting of these brothers. She smiled brightly at Josh as he arrived beside her to walk inside the restaurant. 'If nothing else, I'm sure the food will be extraordinary.'

The maître d' was waiting to welcome them, but also had a message to say that Mr McKendry had rung and he was running a little late.

'He asked that you be served a glass of champagne at the table while you're waiting. Please…follow me.'

If the menu was anything to go by, the food was certainly going to be nothing like Stevie had ever tasted. She and Josh read the items on the parchment paper while they sipped the champagne.

'Seafood risotto with squid ink?' Stevie whispered.

'And venison with blackberry brandy? Who thinks up combinations like that?'

'Foodies love it.' Josh smiled. 'And I read somewhere that the Cotswolds are rural England's foodie capital, but you know what?' There was something in his eyes that was melting something deep inside Stevie. He leaned closer and his words were only for her ears. 'I'm no foodie. I'd be just as happy with some of your mousetraps. Ah…that looks like Lachlan arriving now.'

Stevie was still smiling as she watched Josh's brother hand his coat to someone and then turn to help his companion remove hers. Stevie blinked.

'I thought he was bringing his mother's nurse?'

'He is.' Josh was also watching the way his brother was slipping that coat free from the shoulders of the rather gorgeous young woman with wavy blonde, shoulder-length hair. 'They do look like a couple,' he murmured. 'I wonder if that's something else he's not saying much about.'

The new arrivals hadn't noticed they were being watched yet and, as Lachlan turned to look for where his brother was seated, he also didn't notice the way his companion was looking up at him but Stevie recognised that look all too well. There was definitely something going on there. Something that made them a very close couple.

Her mouth suddenly went dry enough to make her reach for her water glass. Maybe tonight had the promise of being something even more than an hour or two of fantasy? It happened at weddings, didn't it? People who might be thinking that getting married was the

last thing they wanted got unexpectedly coaxed into a very different direction. After thinking that they both shared a similar aversion to any kind of permanence in their relationships with women, if his brother really was in a meaningful relationship, could it change the shape of those boundaries he had in place around his own heart? Make a difference to how Josh felt about his own future, perhaps?

It was throwing him off balance a little, to be honest.

Josh hadn't expected Lachlan's mother's nurse to be such an attractive young woman. She had bright blue eyes in a classic combination with that blonde hair and she had a smile that was wide enough to be second only to Stevie's in the way it could light up a room.

'Call me Flick,' she'd told them the moment Lachlan had finished introducing her as Felicity. 'I've only ever been called Felicity by the taxman or the police.'

'What were the police after you for? No, don't tell me…' Lachlan was smiling. 'I think I'd rather leave that to my imagination for a while.'

Josh caught the ghost of a wink sent in his direction but it only added to that unsettled feeling. This was supposed to be an outing to thank both Flick and Stevie, wasn't it?

So why was it suddenly feeling like they were all on a double date?

That they were two couples seemed more obvious as they ordered their drinks and starters. Both Josh and Stevie chose stuffed Portobello mushrooms while Lachlan and Flick both ordered hay-smoked scallops.

It was a relief for Josh that the conversation turned in a more professional direction by the time those starters were served.

'How's that lad doing?' Lachlan asked Josh. 'From the brachial plexus repair?'

'Very well…' Josh was looking at Stevie, however, as he lifted another mouthful of the mushroom towards his mouth. He had been perfectly genuine in telling her how much he loved her mousetraps but these mushrooms were definitely to die for. Judging by the twinkle in her eyes, she was thinking along the same lines and it gave Josh an equally delicious frisson to know that they could have an entirely private moment like this when they were in such close company with other people.

'I've been trying to get back to see him again,' Lachlan added. 'But it's been full on.' He put down his fork, having barely tasted the scallops. 'Lectures here, surgeries there and I've had to dash up to London a couple of times as well.'

'Sounds stressful.' Josh could feel himself frowning. Was it all too much? Enough to be the reason why Lachlan was looking as if he'd lost weight? That he was too pale?

As if he could sense his brother's concern and wanted to brush it off, Lachlan was smiling brightly. 'At least I don't have to worry about anything on the home front.' He raised his glass in Flick's direction. 'You're doing a fabulous job,' he told her. 'I'm not at all surprised that London Locums considers you to be one their very best nurses. I will be grateful to you for ever. For everything…'

Flick dropped her gaze, seemingly embarrassed by the praise. Or was there some kind of hidden message there? A private moment, like the one he'd just had with Stevie? Whatever it was, it felt like distraction might be welcome.

'How long have you been doing locum nursing work, Flick?' Josh asked.

'Oh, years…' She looked up again to smile at him. 'I love the excitement of everything being new. Meeting new people, getting to know a new place. A new challenge…'

Lachlan made a sound that could have been suggesting that a 'challenge' might be an understatement in this case, but then became one of discomfort.

'It's a bit warm in here, isn't it?' He rubbed at a gleam of moisture on his forehead with his fingers, pushing it into his hairline, which made him look far less groomed than usual. Then he pushed back his chair. 'Excuse me for a moment. I just need a bit of fresh air.'

There was no mistaking the flash of real concern in Flick's eyes as Lachlan headed for a set of French doors near their table that led to a potager garden with strings of fairy lights woven into the low box hedges. She abandoned her own food and looked ready to go after him but Josh moved first.

'I'll go,' he said quietly.

The air was certainly a lot fresher outside but it didn't seem to be making an immediate difference to Lachlan, who was loosening his tie and undoing the top button of his shirt as Josh arrived by his side.

'You okay?'

'I'm fine.'

'You'd tell me if you weren't, wouldn't you?'

'Of course.' Lachlan's smile was a little too wide. 'You're my brother. Family, huh? *Real* family, that is…' He was staring in through the panes of the French doors to where Stevie and Flick were talking to each other. Because the fact that his mother's nurse was here was a reminder of the family he'd thought he'd had that *wasn't* real?

No…for a heartbeat there was something in Lachlan's gaze and his body language that Josh thought he could read only too well. It was enough to make him turn his own head to watch Stevie for a moment. To let himself feel that pull that was so strong it felt as if it could smash through any kind of barrier that was in the way.

It was so hard to imagine his life without Stevie in it now. Josh didn't *want* to imagine that. More than anything, he wanted to trust the extraordinary connection he'd found with Stevie. He would never have thought he'd actually be thinking in terms of a 'real' relationship but he couldn't deny that he was starting to. Something real enough that it could even lead to creating his own family?

But, then, he'd never expected to be presented with a real family member out of the blue, like this, either. The foundations of all those barriers Josh had built so many years ago appeared to be on rather shaky ground now. Was that something that Lachlan was also grappling with, perhaps? That might be contributing to the stress levels that were clearly affecting him?

'I think Flick's worried about you, too.'

'There's nothing to worry about,' Lachlan said. 'Not for you, and especially not for Flick. She's only here temporarily. Until I set up something permanent for my mother. Or put her in a home, perhaps. Which I might do any day now, the way things are going…'

'Maybe she would like to stay longer,' Josh suggested. 'I get the impression that you guys really like each other.'

He was speaking quietly, his gaze drawn back to Stevie, and it felt like he was saying his next words aloud for his own benefit—just to see what it felt like to explore this new, mind-bending idea.

'She might like the idea of something permanent herself,' he said. 'Maybe it's a shame if you don't hang on to something that's too good not to keep.'

Lachlan gave a huff of something like laughter as he pulled at his tie to take it off completely, except there was no amusement in the sound.

'Are you kidding? And here I was thinking that we were on the same page as far as women went. I mean, we both know that families aren't worth the effort and we both know why.'

'*We're* family now,' Josh said softly. He could understand exactly why Lachlan might be finding his feelings confusing. Overwhelming, even. Maybe it was something in common that could end up being the most important connection of all between them?

But Lachlan was turning away from the window. 'That's different,' he muttered. 'It's still time to move on the moment the girls get any ideas about anything

permanent. A "future".' He made quotation marks with his fingers around the word. 'It's an "F" word as far as I'm concerned. Breaks all the…the…'

Lachlan never finished that sentence because he simply crumpled like an abandoned puppet and all Josh could do was to step in and break his fall. He caught his brother in his arms just before he hit the flagstone terrace.

He tilted Lachlan's head back to make sure his airway was open. Then he felt for a pulse in his neck, at the same time listening and feeling to see whether Lachlan was breathing. He felt the rush of warm air from the restaurant as the French doors were opened behind him and then Stevie and Flick were both there.

'What can I do?' Stevie asked.

'Oh, my God…' Flick dropped to her knees beside Lachlan, her face as white as a sheet. *'No…'*

Josh caught Stevie's gaze. 'He's breathing,' he told her. 'And he's got a good, steady pulse. He may have just fainted for some reason but I think we'd better call an ambulance.'

The maître d' came through the doors in time to hear the end of his sentence. 'I've already taken care of that,' he said. 'They'll be here any minute.'

CHAPTER TEN

LACHLAN WAS CONSCIOUS by the time medical assistance arrived but his level of consciousness was down far enough to make him seem drowsy and his speech was a little incoherent so he'd been helped into the back of the ambulance to be assessed. The results from the ECG monitor, blood pressure check and oxygen saturation clip were normal enough not to cause concern.

'How much has he had to drink?' one of the paramedics asked.

'Not enough to do this,' Josh told them. 'I think there's something more going on here.'

'Gotta go home…' Lachlan tried to sit up. 'It's my mother… She's the one who's sick…'

'She's all right.' Flick was standing by the open back door of the ambulance. 'I just rang Mrs Tillman to tell her that I would be going to the hospital with you so I might be later than expected.'

But Lachlan was shaking his head. 'No need. I'm fine. And it's my mother you're employed to care for… not *me*… I don't need it… Can look after myself…'

Flick clearly tried to hide her reaction to his words but Josh could see they'd been hurtful.

'I'll go with Lachlan,' he told her. *Don't worry*, he tried to add silently. *He won't be alone.*

Flick nodded. 'I could take Stevie home, then.'

'No…that's in totally the opposite direction.' Josh turned to catch Stevie's gaze. He wanted to ask her to come with him as he accompanied his brother to Cheltenham Central, which would be the nearest hospital. He wanted her by his side as he waited to find out what, if anything, was wrong. But who knew how long that might take? She had to get home for Mattie.

'I'm going with Lachlan,' he said, to Stevie this time. 'I'll follow the ambulance in my car, so is it okay if I get a taxi to take you home?'

Stevie nodded. 'Of course.' She held his gaze. 'Call me later—when you know what's going on?'

'It might be late.'

This time she shook her head. 'I'll still be up,' she told him. 'It doesn't matter how late it is.'

She was going to wait up for him to call.

Josh was smiling, even after the taxi had left and he was in his own vehicle ready to follow the ambulance.

It didn't matter that Stevie wasn't coming with him to share the wait and any news—good or bad. She was going to be waiting up for him and that was enough.

Oddly, it *felt* like she would be holding his hand, anyway.

Josh arrived at Cheltenham Central to find Lachlan in an observation area attached to the emergency department.

'They want to keep me in overnight.' Lachlan looked almost as pale as the pillows he was lying back against.

'I'd make a fuss and discharge myself but I'm… I'm just so damned tired, I don't want to move.'

'What do they think caused the syncope?'

'They're waiting for the blood results to come back. Consultant here thinks it could just be some kind of virus. I'm running a bit of a temperature and it fits with my not feeling so good in the last week or two.'

'What sort of "not so good"?' Josh could feel his frown deepen as he perched his hip on the end of Lachlan's bed. 'I did think you've been looking really tired. And you've lost some weight, too, haven't you?'

'A bit…' Lachlan closed his eyes. 'I've had some abdominal pain on and off so I haven't been eating much.' He managed a smile. 'And, hey…thanks for being here. Who knows, if I find I need a new kidney or something it could be really useful having a twin.'

Josh grinned back but the smile faded as he held his brother's gaze. He could actually feel the connection between them moving up a notch at this moment. Several notches. Had he really believed that he never needed or wanted family? This was his brother. His *identical* brother. It could be him lying in that bed and, if it was, he'd want family beside him.

It was Lachlan who broke the silence that had fallen.

'I was blaming how I felt on the stress of all the insanity of the last few weeks. I felt like someone had taken my life and turned it inside out. And upside down. And stomped on it. I was blindsided by finding out I'd been adopted. That the woman I thought was my mother had never wanted me in the first place. But finding out I've got a brother…well…that's a good thing.'

Josh nodded. He needed to swallow hard.

'And Flick…she's a good thing, too. You freaked me out back there by suggesting that it could be something permanent, mind you.'

'I get that.' Josh sighed. 'I think I freaked myself out a bit as well. I'd actually started thinking—'

He didn't get a chance to confess that he was starting to change his own mind about that aversion to permanence, thanks to how he felt about Stevie, because the curtain around Lachlan's bed opened.

'Hope I'm not interrupting anything. I'm Graham— a consultant here.' The newcomer held his hand out to Josh. 'Wow… I've heard about you two but you really are identical, aren't you?'

'I'm the better-looking twin,' Lachlan said. 'You've probably heard that, as well.'

Josh could see that, behind the attempt at humour, Lachlan had become very still. He was looking at the paper the consultant was holding in his hands and Graham's smile had vanished by the time he spoke again.

'You've got something going on, Lachlan,' he said. 'Your blood count's all over the place. White blood count's way up and red cells and platelets are low enough to be concerning.'

Josh actually felt a chill ripple down his spine. He'd seen blood results like that come in on children all too often. He might have referred those patients to the oncology team instantly but he was often there as the parents were given the devastating news that their child had leukaemia.

Lachlan had joined the dots as quickly as Josh had.

He could see the shock in his eyes, even though he was doing his best to hide it.

'Not just a virus, then?'

Graham could see that both the doctors in front of him knew exactly how serious this could prove to be. 'We've already lined up some more tests for first thing tomorrow.'

'Do they include a bone-marrow biopsy?' Lachlan asked quietly.

Graham nodded. 'I've already been in touch with the team you'll be admitted under. The HOD of Haematology is a great guy. He's offered to come in and have a chat with you tonight, if you'd like.'

But Lachlan shook his head. 'I'm really tired,' he said. 'I think I'd rather get some sleep.'

Josh was still sitting on the end of the bed when the emergency department consultant left. The shock was still there but he knew how to keep it from showing in his voice.

'Can I get you anything?'

'No, thanks.' Lachlan didn't open his eyes as he spoke. 'You should get home. That dog of yours probably needs to get outside.'

'I can stay for a while.' Josh didn't want to leave his brother alone. His own mind was racing fast enough as it gathered the implications of what they'd been told. 'If you want to talk.'

But Lachlan turned away. 'Go home, Josh,' he muttered. 'I just need to sleep.'

'I'll be back tomorrow, then.' Josh hesitated as he turned towards the door, however. He was pretty sure

Lachlan was not about to go to sleep but his brother clearly wanted to be alone.

Because, like Josh, he'd spent his life having to deal with the tough stuff alone?

'Just call if you want to,' he added softly, his fingers curling around the phone in his pocket. 'Anytime.'

He had the phone in his hand by the time he got back to where he'd parked his car. It was almost a shock to realise that it was only a matter of a few hours since he'd had Stevie sitting in the passenger seat and they'd been on their way to a fabulous restaurant. Before his life had been derailed—*again*.

He wished she was sitting there right now. He wanted to tell her how afraid he was that Lachlan was seriously ill. And he could do that. She was, after all, waiting up for him to call but, if he started, where would he stop? Would he just let it all come rushing out? Tell her that he was scared that maybe he'd discovered he had a brother only to have to face losing him?

That he would tell her how much he'd wanted to have Stevie holding his hand for company and support tonight. That he wanted her to tell him that it was all going to be okay. That he wanted to feel her arms around him. To hear her say that, even if it wasn't all going to be okay, she'd be right there beside him.

That he would never need to be alone again.

But…what if she didn't say that? If she didn't feel that way? It wasn't as if they had a definitive diagnosis for Lachlan yet, either. That would come tomorrow, probably after a raft of more focused investigations, and he would be seeing Stevie at work so there would

be plenty of time to talk. Maybe the weather would be nice enough to have lunch on the roof? It was a shame they'd missed everything other than the starter at that posh restaurant.

Josh didn't put his phone away, though, even after he was sitting inside his car. He found Stevie's number and sent her a text.

No real news yet. Talk to you tomorrow when we get more test results. Maybe we could meet for lunch?

Her response was so quick she must have had her phone in her hand already.

Sure. See you tomorrow. Sleep well.

It was time Josh put his phone down and headed for home but he wasn't quite ready to move. He opened a browser and found a site that he relied on for accurate and up-to-date medical articles.

Adult onset leukaemia, he typed into the search bar. *Diagnosis, treatment and prognosis.*

Gloucester General's rooftop vegetable garden seemed to have become the background setting that marked milestones in Stevie Hawksbury's new life. It had been where the aftermath of that awkward first meeting with her boss had been smoothed over enough to be forgotten. Where they'd shared secrets and cemented the first foundation stones of their friendship in place.

It was where so many private conversations had

taken place in snatched minutes of shared lunches. It had been one of those conversations that had persuaded her that Mattie was old enough to travel alone to visit his grandma and she was still seeing the benefits of the independence and confidence that weekend had given him. Or maybe it was her son's relationship with his Big Brother mentor that was making it seem like Mattie was growing more mature and grounded day by day.

It had been the weekend of that independent trip that had been one of the biggest milestones of all— when she and Josh had made love for the first time. Another ripple from the stone that had been cast on the day that Josh had brought her up here to these gardens. She loved coming here. Except that, today, Stevie was barely aware of where they were. All she could think about was how pale and drawn Josh was looking when he arrived. All she wanted was to put her arms around him and hold him as tightly as she could.

All she did, however, was to pass him the plastic triangle that contained the sandwiches she'd bought at the cafeteria, although she let her hand brush his and their eye contact to linger for a heartbeat. She knew there was a group of junior doctors sitting not that far away, having also chosen to take their lunch break where they could find a bit of sunshine and, even though Josh had been happy to take her out to a famous local restaurant last night and it had felt almost like a date to start with, at least, Stevie was quite sure he wouldn't want rumours about them to start circulating around the hospital. Especially not today, when he looked tired enough for it to be too much effort to even open that plastic triangle.

'Did you stay with Lachlan all night?' she asked.

'No. He told me to go home. Said he needed to sleep but I think he just wanted to be alone. I was there this morning, though. I was with him when he got the results of his bone-marrow biopsy.'

Stevie had opened her own sandwich container but any appetite for lunch evaporated instantly on hearing those words. She felt fear, she realised. For Lachlan. But even more for Josh because she could see her fear reflected in his eyes and she could feel the painful cracking in her own heart. She didn't need to ask the question.

'It's AML,' he said quietly. 'Acute myeloid leukaemia.'

'Oh… God…' Stevie totally forgot about anyone who could see them. She put her hand over Josh's and held on.

'We both had our suspicions last night,' Josh continued. 'After the results of the blood count came through and we added up all the other symptoms, like extreme fatigue recently and odd bruising and a fever and so on. The ED consultant even said that the haematology consultant was prepared to come in and talk to Lachlan right there and then but the diagnosis wasn't official until the results of this morning's biopsy came through.' Josh closed his eyes as he rubbed his forehead. 'There should be less than five percent of blasts in bone marrow—they're the immature white blood cells. Lachlan's got more than twenty percent.'

Stevie swallowed hard. 'I'm so sorry,' she whispered. 'How's Lachlan coping?'

Josh seemed to squeeze his eyes even more tightly shut. As if he was staving off tears?

'The first thing he said was that I'd better get myself tested. That if there was a genetic component to being at risk then I might be next.'

The wash of fear that Stevie had felt only minutes ago came back so fiercely that she instinctively broke the skin contact between her hand and Josh's in case he could feel it too. But the words came out before she could stop them and it felt all too obvious that she was afraid.

'That's not true,' she breathed. And then she caught the corner of her lip between her teeth. 'Is it?'

Josh opened his eyes and turned towards Stevie. He wasn't smiling, but the crinkles at the corners of his eyes deepened, as if he appreciated that she was so concerned about him.

'Funnily enough, when I was sitting up all night, reading up on every type of leukaemia I could think of, I came across a fairly recent article about identical twins getting diagnosed with AML within days of each other. Concordant AML, it's called…'

'And…?' Stevie couldn't bear the pause.

'They were just kids.' But Josh found a lopsided smile. 'But they had a sibling who was an HLA match and they got a stem cell transplant, which has apparently cured them. They didn't even get any GVHD.'

'GVHD?'

'Graft versus host disease. It's a common complication with any kind of transplant that can be serious. It often goes away after a year or so but the better HLA

match you can get, the less risk there is of getting it in the first place. HLA is human leukocyte antigens.' He let his breath out in a long sigh. 'I think I reviewed my entire haematology course between about four and six this morning.'

The cracks in Stevie's heart deepened. She wished she'd been there for Josh. To bring him something to eat or just coffee. To talk things through. Just…to *be* there…

'I will get myself tested,' Josh added. 'Not to see if I've got anything abnormal going on in my blood. To see if I'm going to be the perfect match to donate my bone marrow for the transplant.' That crooked smile was back. 'And, if anybody should be the perfect match, it's got to be an identical twin.'

'That must have helped.' Stevie said. 'To tell Lachlan that.'

'I haven't told him yet.'

'How come?'

'It got mentioned, of course, but it's down the track and there's some rough stuff to get through before a stem cell transplant is going to be on the agenda. The focus right now is on getting more information about the subtype and staging and planning the chemotherapy regime that needs to start as soon as possible. Hopefully tomorrow. And…' The expression on Josh's face was a silent groan.

Stevie hadn't thought her heart could sink much further but she'd been wrong. 'And what?'

'There was other stuff happening. Between Lachlan and Flick. She was there this morning, as well. You

should have seen her face, Stevie.' Josh had to stop talking. He took a deep breath and then cleared his throat. 'She looked like the world was ending. Said she was so sorry but she couldn't do this again. And then she walked out of the room.'

'Again?'

'Lachlan told me later that her husband had died—a long time ago now—from pancreatic cancer. Six weeks from diagnosis to death and she never left his side. It broke her, he said. She's been running ever since.'

'But I saw the way she looked at him,' Stevie said softly. 'And we were talking while you were outside with Lachlan at the restaurant. I know she's in love with him.'

As much as *she* was in love with Josh...

'Well...she can't face this.'

Stevie was quite sure of what she knew about how Flick felt. How powerful did the shadow of her past have to be to make her walk out at a time like that? How devastating that must have been for Lachlan. And for Josh to be there and witness what could have been a sudden end to his brother's relationship.

'How did Lachlan take it?'

Josh was rubbing his forehead again with his middle finger, as if the touch might reduce the discomfort of his thoughts.

'He kind of shrugged it off. Said he didn't blame her, after what she'd been through. But you could see that it hurt. I told him I'd be sticking around but...you know what?'

Stevie didn't say anything. She just held his gaze.

'I hate myself for saying it but I get why she's running.'

'I know. I can't even imagine how hard this is for her. Or for you. But it's so lucky you've found each other—you and Lachlan.'

'Is it?' Josh broke the eye contact by closing his eyes. 'Yes, of course it is. I'm just… It gets me—here…' He put his hand on his chest. 'And I don't think I've felt like this about anyone since I was a little kid. I've never let myself feel like this because I know what happens. I know this isn't Lachlan's fault but the end result could be the same.' His voice was so quiet it felt like Josh was talking aloud to himself. 'There are no guarantees in life. You can't trust that anyone's going to hang around for ever. Or even for the important stuff.'

'Sometimes you can.' The cracks in Stevie's heart were wide enough to be breaking her heart, knowing that Josh had gone through his life not trusting enough to let himself love someone. Or to *be* loved by someone. 'I'm not going anywhere, Josh.'

'Thanks…' Josh was looking down at the plastic container he was still holding. 'And thanks for getting lunch but… I don't think I can eat right now. I need to get going, too. I've got to catch up on the ward round I missed this morning.'

'Take them with you. Try and find time to eat later. It's not going to help you or Lachlan if you don't look after yourself.'

Josh nodded, getting slowly to his feet.

'And I'll tell Mattie that you won't be able to make his Big Brother session this week.'

'No…don't do that.' Josh straightened, taking a deep breath. 'That's important, too.'

'He'll understand.'

Josh shook his head. 'He might seem like he's growing up really fast at the moment but he's still just a kid on the inside and I don't want to let him down. And, hey…it'll be good for me, too. We'll go somewhere nice with Lucky and forget about the rest of the world for a while.'

'Oh…that reminds me.' Stevie was on her feet now as well. She would find time to eat her sandwich later—although it didn't seem likely that she was going to feel hungry anytime soon. 'Mattie wanted me to talk to you about when Lucky's going to move in. He's got this idea that he wants him to sleep on the end of his bed the first night we're in the cottage but I said that it might need to wait until we're a bit more settled in.'

'Okay.' Josh was smiling. 'Sounds like he's excited about the move.'

'We both are. I should warn you that he knows you've got a brother you didn't know you had. He's probably going to have a million questions about that, too. Sorry…'

'I'll cope.' Josh's face had softened and he stood there for a moment, just holding Stevie's gaze. Looking for all the world as if he wanted to kiss her…

And, suddenly, it didn't matter who might be watching or what sort of rumours might circulate. Josh might believe that he didn't need anything more than a friendship from her but what he actually needed more than anything right now was to know that he had someone

who cared about him. Who was going to do everything they could to help him through whatever he was about to face.

Stevie closed the gap between them and put her arms up to offer him a hug and, to her relief, he didn't seem at all bothered that other people might see them. He leaned down and let himself be hugged and Stevie held him as tightly as she could. So tightly she could feel the beat of both their hearts. It felt like he was even letting go of some of the tension in his body, just for a heartbeat or two—but it was enough.

Hopefully, it was enough to let him know everything he needed to know.

CHAPTER ELEVEN

THE SKILLS OF being able to compartmentalise and focus purely on what was in that particular compartment had never been more valuable. And, man… Josh had needed to call on those skills in the last day or two.

He was using them now as he stood beside the trolley that contained all the patient notes for children who were currently inpatients. He was anxious to find out what had happened since he'd seen one of his young patients on this morning's ward round. Four-year-old Jayden had managed to stick the prong of a fork far enough into a wall plug to receive a significant electrical shock. His panicked mother had rushed him into Emergency and he'd then been admitted to hospital for treatment to burns on his fingers, hand and chest and observation for an irregular heartbeat that was potentially of concern.

Today Josh had requested both surgical and cardiology consults and he was scanning Jayden's notes to find out the latest results of any new investigations. He was relieved to note that today's observations were normal for temperature, blood pressure, oxygen satu-

ration and GCS. Blood test results were also normal. The daily dressing change for the burns had gone well and the current pain management was adequate. A note had been made that a plastic surgery consult should be arranged in case of possible grafting needed to one fingertip but even that didn't dent Josh's focus.

He was more interested in the results of the echocardiogram that had been done this afternoon and the new ECG in the series that had been requested. The irregular rhythm had been caused by premature beats in the atria of the heart but they seemed to be settling now and the cardiology team was confident the abnormality would resolve soon.

Josh breathed out a sigh of relief at this point and finally allowed a breach in the wall of the mental compartment he'd been in for some hours now that didn't allow anything other than a focus on his patients. He let his gaze drift back to the section in Jayden's notes where the surgical team had suggested a referral to a more specialist area. Lachlan's specialty. The longing that it could have been possible to call his brother in to review the case was so strong it was a physical pain in his chest and, as Josh slotted Jayden's notes back into the trolley, he closed his eyes and took a deep breath to try and counteract that pain.

He was lucky he had different compartments he could use right now, like his work and his responsibilities to a small, white dog who needed walks and food. Lachlan didn't have the luxury of any kind of distractions and, after the initial shock, the reality of his situation had sunk in with what threatened to be

a devastating effect. When Josh had gone to see him last night, Lachlan had pretty much ordered him not to continue his visits.

Josh kept his eyes closed for another moment as their conversation flashed through the back of his mind while he searched for the exact wording that had haunted a restless night and been forced under cover while he'd been working through an exceptionally busy day today.

'You don't have to be here. I know I'm not exactly good company.'

'I want to be here.'

'You managed without me in your life for thirty-six years, Josh. It won't be that hard to get used to it again.'

'I don't want to get used to it. You're my brother. The only family I've got.'

'You might have to get used to it.'

There'd been no amusement at all in Lachlan's huff of laughter.

'Take a leaf out of Flick's book. She's managed to walk away, no problem.'

'Has she? Has she actually gone?'

'Well...she's still here—in the district, at least. But only until we can find another locum nurse. My house-keeper, Mrs Tillman, is sorting that mess out for me. You're not going to believe this, but she says Josephine is upset about me. Crocodile tears, huh?'

'I doubt that. Sometimes it takes a shock for people to wake up and see what really matters.'

'Well... I've had a shock and...guess what? Nothing really matters. Go away, Josh. Get on with your own

life. Get over yourself and marry that nice girl with that astonishing hair.'

Lachlan had even found a smile, although it hadn't lasted long.

'Go. Be happy for both of us...'

It had been a knee-jerk reaction to the shock of a frightening diagnosis, which had been made all the more confronting by having already had his life turned upside down by recent developments. Josh wasn't about to give up on supporting his brother, however. In fact, perhaps he could go over to Cheltenham Central right now and still have time to be back in town to meet Mattie at the Big Brother Headquarters, as usual, at four-thirty p.m.

A twist of his wrist revealed the face of his watch but it was clearly incorrect. He reached into his pocket for his phone only to find that he'd forgotten to charge it last night and it was completely dead. Josh turned away from the trolley to look at the wall clock in the ward's reception area and it was then that he simply froze.

It was six p.m. How on earth could that possibly have happened? He'd never even been late to meet Mattie for their weekly session together on a Thursday, let alone completely forgotten about it. Stevie had suggested it could be cancelled, hadn't she? She'd known he had too much going at the moment but he'd refused. What had he said to her? Oh, yeah…that their time together was important, too. That Mattie might seem like he was growing up really fast but he was still just a kid on the inside. He'd also said that he didn't want to let him down.

Worse than that, Josh had promised Stevie long ago that he'd never do anything to hurt Mattie.

Oh… God… He had to try and put this right.

Right now…

Stevie knew who it was before she even opened the door of her apartment to find Josh standing there.

She also knew there had to be a very good reason that Josh had not shown up for his session with Mattie this afternoon but, no matter how good that reason was and how apologetic Josh was looking, it wasn't likely to be enough. Not this time.

'I'm *so* sorry,' he said. 'I completely lost track of time.'

That was it? No major emergency in the ward? No new development that had been serious enough for him to have had to rush to his brother's side? He'd just… *forgotten* about Mattie?

'He tried to walk home after he'd waited for you for more than an hour,' Stevie said. 'And you know what? That gang of boys he'd had trouble with when we first moved here were waiting for him when he got close to home.'

'Oh… God, *no*…' Josh's eyes looked even darker as his face paled. 'Is he hurt?'

'He's got a few bruises. Had his schoolbag stolen…' Stevie had to swallow hard before she could continue without her voice breaking. 'Mostly, he just got terrified.'

'Can I come in?' Josh's voice was raw. 'And talk to Mattie?'

Stevie wasn't at all sure she could cope with hav-

ing Josh too close right now. Her head was all over the place. Her heart felt like it was breaking.

'It's a mess in here,' she said. 'There's barely room to move with all the packing boxes and piles of stuff.' She turned her head away from him. 'Mattie? Can you come here for a minute?'

Mattie's bedroom door was the closest one to the front door. Even if he hadn't guessed who had come calling, he would have heard Josh's voice.

'Don't want to,' he responded. 'I'm busy.'

Playing an online game, Stevie suspected. The way he'd spent far too much time doing when they'd first moved to Gloucester.

'Please?' Stevie didn't raise her voice. Mattie knew the tone she was using well enough to understand that this was something important. And, a few seconds later, he appeared outside his bedroom door to stand in this narrow hallway. He didn't look at Josh, though. He was staring at his feet.

'I'm so sorry, Mattie,' Josh said again. 'I'll make it up to you, I promise.'

Mattie said nothing. He didn't look up, either.

'Tomorrow,' Josh offered. 'I've got a day off. How 'bout we go and check out your new village and see where the best places are going to be to walk Lucky?'

Mattie shrugged. 'Whatever…'

He stepped back into his room and pushed the door shut behind him. It wasn't quite a slam that would have required a response from Stevie but it was certainly firm enough to be a warning that he was done with communicating for now.

Josh looked at Stevie as if he was expecting her to fix this somehow but that wasn't going to happen, was it? This had become too big and Stevie was being pulled in two very different directions.

'Why didn't you call, Josh? Or send a text or something? I could have gone and walked home with him. Made sure he wasn't going to blame you for this.'

'My phone was dead. I meant to charge it last night but I fell asleep on the couch. I'd been trying to read up on all the latest clinical trials for AML. Look, I'm sorry I've upset Mattie. I'm beyond sorry that he ran into trouble. You know that, don't you?'

Of course she did. Like she'd known there would be a good reason behind what had happened. Too many good reasons but that didn't alter the fact that her son felt betrayed. Like he didn't matter enough. This was tearing her apart more than she'd thought it would. She knew what Josh was going through and she wanted to support him in whatever way he needed but…this was *Mattie* they were talking about. Her precious son. The boy she'd based her life around ever since he'd been conceived. The boy they'd both promised they would never do anything to hurt. Now Josh had let him down and Stevie hadn't been able to do anything to protect him.

'He's not just upset,' she said. 'He's really hurt, Josh. You're way more important than you probably realise in his life. You're far more like a father figure than a big brother for Mattie and he *trusted* you. You've let him down and…and you promised you'd never do that. That you'd never hurt him.'

Josh was rubbing his forehead in that characteristic gesture of trying to collect or redefine his thoughts.

'This is what happens, isn't it?' he muttered. 'You get close to people. When you trust them and you let them trust you. And then people get hurt.'

Stevie had the sensation of the walls closing in around her. There seemed to be a lot less oxygen in the air as well. This was it, wasn't it? The barrier that Josh had always used to keep himself safe. Was he about to reinstate it? With her and Mattie on the other side? She couldn't let that happen. It didn't matter if she got hurt but it sure as hell mattered if Mattie did.

'You can't just walk out on him,' she said slowly. 'You must know how much that would hurt him.'

'Of course I do.' But Josh shook his head. 'It was a mistake, wasn't it? I should never have got involved in the first place. He can't think of me as his dad, Stevie. I'm *not*.' He was turning away. 'You know perfectly well that I never wanted to be *anybody's* dad.'

The crack in Stevie's heart opened wide enough to be a potentially fatal wound. 'Just go,' she told him.

She couldn't cope with this while Josh was standing this close to her. The idea that he was about to push her out of his life was bad enough but that he thought his relationship with Mattie had been a mistake was beyond heartbreaking. How on earth was she ever going to explain this to Mattie? It had been easy to make sure he didn't know about the rejection from his biological father but this was on a very different level. The amount of damage this could do was scary. She would have to cope with what might be the hardest challenge she'd

ever faced but she needed time to think about how she was even going to start. And she needed to do it alone because Mattie wasn't about to listen to anything else that Josh might have to say.

She lifted her chin. 'I'll deal with this.' She bit the words out. 'I have to, because I don't get a choice about being a parent or not. I'm Mattie's mother and that's never going to change. I don't *want* it to change.' She pulled in a new breath. 'We don't need your help. We don't need *you*...'

Josh still looked as though he had no intention of going, so Stevie helped him out. She shut the door in his face.

She didn't try and open Mattie's door because she knew it would only make things worse if she forced him to talk to her before he was ready. She wasn't ready, either, so it was just as well she had a whole lot of packing to finish in the kitchen before she could even start cooking dinner.

Stevie did tap on Mattie's door, however. 'It's going to be okay, Mattie,' she called softly. 'I promise.' She bit her lip. 'I'll call you when dinner's ready.'

It took longer than she'd thought to finish wrapping all the glassware and plates in newspaper and stacking them into boxes. And then she heated up the oven and unwrapped a frying pan she'd already packed by mistake.

'There'll be no more fish fingers or chips or fried eggs once we've moved,' she told herself. 'It's going to be a new life and we're going to make it work.'

They had to and that was all there was to it.

This time, Stevie opened Mattie's door after she'd knocked on it.

'Dinner's ready,' she said. 'Come and wash your hands.'

There was no response to her instruction.

Because Mattie wasn't there…

In that moment of time, seconds before Stevie knew she would be frantically calling for her son and checking the bathroom and living room and Mrs Johnson's apartment and the stairwell of the building, she knew she wasn't going to find him.

She could sense the emptiness…

And that was when the fear stepped in…

CHAPTER TWELVE

THE CLOSING OF that door felt like a slap in the face.

A dismissal.

He wasn't wanted here, was he?

He took the stairs to get out of this apartment block because he needed the movement. Not that it stopped his brain raking through everything, mind you, but at least it felt like he was pushing through it by moving. It would be worse to be standing still inside an elevator, letting it smother him. Seeing that expression on Mattie's face when he'd turned away from Josh had taken him straight back to his own childhood. To when those feelings of being let down had been sharp enough to cut so deeply.

He hated that he'd let Mattie down. More than that, he admitted as he hit the street and headed to his car. He'd hurt him badly and Stevie had every right to be angry with him but it hadn't been intentional. He had way too much going on at the moment, that was all. And, because he'd needed to shut out the overwhelming worry about Lachlan so he could do his job, he'd ended

up shutting out too much—to the point of forgetting something even when he knew how important it was.

Josh sat in his car for a minute, looking up at the floor that was probably the one where Stevie and Mattie's apartment was. Should he go back? Try and explain?

No. He turned the key and started the engine. He had to get home. He didn't know if Lucky had even been let out this afternoon and the little dog's dinner was overdue as well. He added that concern to everything else and it was, possibly, the straw that was about to break the camel's back.

The mix of the level of worry he'd already been dealing with from the moment he'd known that his brother was sick along with the remorse that had sent him rushing to apologise to Mattie and Stevie was coagulating into a much harsher emotion.

Anger.

Not with Lachlan for being sick. Or Mattie for being hurt. Or even Stevie for pushing him away like that. He understood. Of course he understood. Josh knew exactly why this was all going so very wrong. He'd broken the rules. He'd let himself get too close to others and he'd let others get too close to him. And now people were getting hurt. Including himself. The way he'd been hurt—too often—when he'd been too young to defend himself. The way he'd vowed that he would never let happen again.

He left the outskirts of Gloucester behind and headed towards the outlying villages along winding roads and gave in to beating himself up.

Why on earth had he thought it was a good idea to

join the Big Brother organisation when it was painfully obvious he was going to get close to whatever kid he developed a relationship with? Especially one who had reminded him so much of himself as a kid?

He'd let himself get far too close to Stevie, as well. Had he really believed he could keep the kind of distance from her that he'd managed to hang on to in every one of his previous relationships with women? Stevie was nothing like any of those women. The connection they had was like nothing he'd even believed existed.

Lucky was overjoyed to see Josh as he arrived home and he was also desperate to get out into the garden. Josh got the little dog's dinner ready but wasn't tempted at all by the idea of eating anything himself. He went to pour himself a small whisky instead, but the sight of the bottle that he and Lachlan had all but emptied on that night they'd sat up talking till all hours gave Josh another kick in the guts.

Was this the worst thing of all right now?

That he'd found he had *family*? A brother? Not just any sibling either, but a twin. An identical twin, which was the closest kind of genetic relationship it was possible to have. They'd only known of each other's existence for a short time but already it was like catching glimpses of a part of himself he hadn't known was missing.

It was something precious.

And it was under threat. Breaking something deep inside him. Blowing holes in any carefully crafted defence systems and…and it *hurt*, dammit.

Lucky had finished his dinner and was trying to stay as close to Josh as possible as he paced around his house.

'I'm not going to let him do it,' he told the dog. 'I'm not going to let him push me away like that. He might not like the idea of needing someone any more than I do but that's just the way it is.' Whatever journey was waiting for his brother, he wasn't going to be taking it alone.

He punched in the rapid dial number on his phone and listened to it ring. And then he listened to Lachlan's voice telling him he wasn't available and inviting him to leave a message.

Josh hung up instead. Then he looked down at the little white dog. 'I'm going to the hospital,' he said. 'Want a ride in the car?'

His phone rang as he fastened his seat belt and he answered it without even glancing at the screen, assuming it was Lachlan returning his call.

But it wasn't his brother. It was Stevie.

'I was wrong, Josh.' They were her first words. 'We *do* need you...'

The fear in her voice broke his heart wide open. He might be getting glimpses of a part of himself that he hadn't known was missing when it came to his twin brother but it was at that moment that Josh realised Stevie was an even bigger part of his life that had been missing. He couldn't not love her. He couldn't allow her to be frightened, either. Not if there was anything he could do about that.

'I'm on my way,' he told Stevie. 'What's happened, darling?'

'It's Mattie.' He could hear the strangled sob in her voice. 'He's run away...'

* * *

Having Josh with her didn't make it any less terrifying for Stevie that Mattie had run away but as she stood beside his car, wrapped in his arms, she knew that it was the only thing that could have provided any kind of anchor in this totally unexpected and unbelievably scary maelstrom.

'This is my fault,' she told Josh. 'I knew he was upset but I just left him alone. I was packing crockery and pots and things in the kitchen because I thought the best thing I could do was to make sure we moved as soon as possible. That I got him away from that gang of boys that had scared him.' She took in a shaky breath. 'I was making so much noise it's no wonder I didn't hear him sneak out of the apartment.'

'We're going to find him,' Josh said, softly. 'And I don't think I'm going to let either of you out of my sight ever again.'

They were words that Stevie might have been dreaming of hearing but right now they just floated over her head and evaporated into the night.

'Let's go,' she said.

'Where, first?'

'I don't know.' Stevie climbed into the Jeep. 'Anywhere we can think of. I just need to be going *somewhere*. Doing *something*.'

The police had agreed that Stevie and Josh should go and search for Mattie. Mrs Johnson from next door would be keeping watch and would let them know if Mattie returned home. He hadn't been missing long enough to justify a full-scale police operation, espe-

cially since he was old enough to be able to hide effectively if that was what he intended to do. The police would keep an eye out in the area, of course, and they'd have a word with that gang of boys that were known to be causing a bit of havoc locally.

'Where would he go?' Josh wondered aloud. 'Who would he want to talk to if he was upset?'

'His gran,' Stevie said.

'Maybe he's headed for the station, where he caught the bus that time to go and see her. Do you know if he's called her?'

Stevie shook her head. 'She would have called me if he had. I don't want to tell her what's happened just yet. I don't want to worry her, in case it turns out to be nothing…'

Josh was heading for the central city but he glanced at the sign indicating the direction to take a motorway out of town. 'He wouldn't be trying to get to your new house, by any chance? Or mine—to see Lucky, maybe?'

Hearing his name, Lucky sat up on the back seat and wagged his tail but, again, Stevie shook her head.

'He doesn't even know the name of the village yet.' But she turned to look at Lucky again, reaching out to pat the little dog. 'He does love Lucky, though.'

'We're not that far from the vet clinic we went to a couple of times. He loved being there and helping with Lucky's care.'

'He did.' Stevie found a wobbly smile. 'That was the first time I'd seen him looking really happy since we'd moved here. Lucky—and you—made such a difference for us.'

Josh had slowed the car and then stopped. 'The park here. This is where we brought Lucky on our first official Big Brother session. When we had to take turns carrying him because he couldn't walk yet.'

They both got out of the car and walked a little way along the path. Josh was holding Stevie's hand and she was holding his so tightly he was losing sensation in his fingers.

'Mattie!' Stevie shouted. 'Are you here?'

'*Mattie...*' Josh echoed her call. 'Where are you, mate?'

They stood there, listening to the silence coming from the dark shadows in the park.

'He's not here,' Stevie whispered. 'I can feel it. Just like I could feel that he wasn't in the apartment. It's just too...empty...'

'I know.' Josh squeezed her hand.

Stevie rested her head against his shoulder to take a deep breath. 'Thank you,' she murmured.

'What for?'

'Being here.'

'Where else would I be?' Josh turned his head so that he could capture her gaze. 'I love you, Stevie. And I love Mattie.'

Oh...the look in his eyes. This wasn't the kind of love that came with a friendship. This was the soul-deep, one-of-a-kind love that could connect two people for a lifetime. The kind of love that Stevie had tried—and failed—not to have for Josh. But she could only focus on his last words. That he loved Mattie.

'He adores *you*,' she told Josh. She had to swallow

hard to fight back tears. 'When you asked who he'd want to talk to? That would be you, even more than his gran. Maybe he felt bad about not talking to you when you came to apologise for missing the session today. He might be trying to find you.'

'But he doesn't know where I live.'

'He knows where he's always found you, though. Every Thursday.'

'The Big Brother Headquarters.' Josh was looking over Stevie's head. 'It's just down the road. Come on...'

This part of the inner city was much quieter in the evenings and the wide street was almost deserted. Josh drove slowly and then pulled up close to the building they both recognised.

'Spooky place at this time of night,' he said. 'Surely he wouldn't come here?'

But there was a shadow on the wide step in front of the door. At first glance it looked like a rubbish bag. Or a pile of old clothing, perhaps, but on closer inspection it became obvious that it was a small person, hunched up, with their head cradled on their arms.

Stevie and Josh were out of the car at exactly the same moment. They even spoke at exactly the same time and in exactly the same tone of absolute relief.

'*Mattie...*'

For the longest time the three of them sat on that step together. Stevie was on one side of Mattie and Josh was on the other and they both had an arm around him.

A Mattie sandwich.

There was a street lamp nearby, which gave more

than enough light for them to be able to look at each other over the top of Mattie's head. To hold that eye contact long enough to be absolutely sure that there were promises being made. Maybe the exact wording of those promises would have to wait for a whispered conversation when they were alone in each other's arms but, for now, this was enough.

More than enough.

Stevie had never felt this happy. Ever.

'Oh,' she finally said aloud. 'We'd better let the police know they can stop looking for Mattie.'

'I left my phone in the car,' Josh said.

'I'll do it.' Stevie dialled the number she'd been given and it was a quick message to impart.

Mattie was looking up at her when she'd finished. 'Were the police really looking for me?'

'Of course they were. I had no idea where you were.' Stevie's voice wobbled. 'You scared me, Mattie.'

'Sorry, Mum…' Mattie ducked his head and reached to stroke Lucky, who was sitting quietly on his feet, pressed as close as he could get to his favourite person.

'Why did you run away, mate?' Josh's query was gentle.

'I heard you.' Mattie gulped in a huge breath. 'I heard you say that you weren't my dad…'

He still had his head down, focused on Lucky, so it was only Stevie who could see how genuine the apology in Josh's eyes was.

'I'm really sorry, Mattie,' he said. 'I know it's not much of an excuse but I'd had a bad day. A bad week,

in fact. Did you know that I've got a brother I didn't even know I had?'

'Yeah… Mum told me. How come you didn't know?'

'It's a bit of a long story that I'll tell you soon. Bottom line was that we got given to different families when we were born because our mum didn't want us. Or couldn't look after us, maybe. She can't have been as brave as your mum.'

Mattie finally looked up at Josh. 'That's really cool,' he said. 'To have a brother. *I'd* like a brother. Or a sister, even…' Then he sighed heavily. 'But Mum can't have another baby.'

'Oh?' Stevie blinked. 'Why not?'

'Because you don't even have a boyfriend, Mum.'

'Yes, she does.' Josh spoke quietly but with absolute conviction. 'Your mum has a boyfriend who loves her very, very much.'

'But you said,' Mattie insisted. 'You said you didn't want to be my dad. That you never want to be anybody's dad.'

Stevie held her breath as the silence stretched. She watched the way Josh tilted his head until it was almost touching Mattie's. As if this was a private conversation.

'I only said that because I was scared,' he said, very quietly. 'If I was going to be anybody's dad, in the whole wide world, I'd want it to be you.'

Mattie's voice was almost inaudible. 'Why?'

'Because I love you,' Josh responded. 'Like the way I love your mum. Which means it's never going to disappear. Ever…'

He looked up and the touch of that eye contact was

like a hug. A promise all on its own. Stevie had to blink away tears that were just part of this enormous happiness.

'Really?' Mattie was staring at Josh intently.

'Really.'

Mattie sucked in another big breath. He was leaning towards Josh now and he lowered his voice. This was also private.

'You *could* be my dad,' he whispered. 'If you married my mum.'

'I'd like that very much,' Josh whispered back. 'But only if that's what your mum wants too.'

Stevie didn't bother trying to stop her tears as she joined in the whispered conversation. 'I'd like that very much, too.'

And there it was again. That look of love that Stevie would never get used to seeing. A look that she knew she could absolutely trust. A love she could trust even more.

'Will you come and live with us then?' Mattie couldn't keep whispering. 'With us and Lucky in our new house?'

The corner of Josh's mouth curled into a smile. 'Do you think it might be better if you all came to live in my house? It's a wee bit bigger.'

'But what about *our* new house?'

'We can talk about that later,' Stevie told him. 'But I'm thinking that if we fixed it up and made it nice, maybe your gran would like to come and live closer to us.'

'Brilliant idea,' Josh agreed.

But Mattie was frowning. 'You said you were scared,' he said slowly. 'And that was why you said you didn't want to be anybody's dad. But you're a grown-up. What are you *scared* of?'

'Ah…' Josh spoke to Mattie as if he was a grown up himself. 'Losing things,' he told him. 'Especially people. This brother that I'm going to tell you all about? His name's Lachlan and…and he's pretty sick right now.'

'Is he going to die?'

Stevie lifted her arm from around Mattie to touch Josh as she saw him struggling to answer. And she filled the silence.

'We hope not,' she said. 'There's a special way that Josh might be able to help him get better. It's called a stem cell transplant but Josh can tell you all about that. He needs to talk to Lachlan about it first.'

'Yeah… I do.' Josh got to his feet. 'And there's no time like the present, is there? I reckon he's going to be really happy to hear that Mattie's going to have a dad because—' he was grinning at Mattie '—that means he's going to be an uncle, doesn't it?'

Mattie's eyes widened. 'He hasn't even met me.'

'So come with me.'

'Oh…' Stevie got to her feet. 'But it's you that Lachlan needs to see now. It's a private sort of family conversation you need to have.'

'Exactly.' Josh held out his hand. 'And you're family, too. *My* family.'

Stevie took hold of Josh's hand and took a step forward.

'Wait for me.' Mattie scooped Lucky into his arms as he jumped to his feet. 'I'm coming, too.'

The shared glance between Stevie and Josh was full of laughter this time. As if they'd leave him behind... He'd brought them together in the first place and somehow he'd created the space that had convinced them both that they could trust what they had together. For ever.

They all went towards the car. They had an important visit to make now and Stevie knew it was a big step into her future and, whatever that future held, if they were together it was all she could ever have hoped for.

Stevie made sure Mattie had clicked his seat belt into place in the back seat as Josh instructed Lucky to lie down on his blanket. She turned to get into the front seat but Josh caught her shoulder to turn her and then pulled her into his arms. He caught her gaze first.

'I love you,' he said softly.

'I know.' Stevie wanted to smile but this was too big. 'I love you, too...'

Josh caught her lips, then, in the softest, most eloquent kiss in the world. So tender it broke Stevie's heart—in a very good way...

'Ew...that's so gross...' Mattie had his face pressed against the window. 'Can we go now?'

They both laughed but then Josh touched her lips again with the briefest promise of a kiss. And then they caught each other's gaze and both spoke at exactly the same time. Whispered, in fact, so Mattie couldn't hear.

'Later...'

* * * * *

A SURGEON
WITH A SECRET

ALISON ROBERTS

MILLS & BOON

CHAPTER ONE

'No...' LACHLAN MCKENDRY put his hand over his eyes as he lowered his head. 'You can't do that...'

'I'm afraid that's what it's come to, lad. I really don't think I can take any more.'

'But you've been part of the household for as long as I can remember.' Lachlan was using his middle finger and thumb to massage his temples now. 'It will fall apart if you leave.'

'It's already fallen apart. Your mother has just fired her nurse. Again. That's three so far this year. And it's not as if she actually fires them. They walk out because she's so appallingly unpleasant to them. Impossible. She told this last one that she was an imbecile. Too stupid to live. That it was no wonder she had to work as a private nurse because nobody was ever going to marry someone who had a face like a camel. The poor girl was in floods of tears when she left this morning.'

'I can imagine. But, Mrs Tillman... *Please*... We can't lose you as well.'

Lachlan was aware of a rising anxiety. If his family's loyal housekeeper walked out, he didn't have the excuse

of living and working in New York any longer. He was in London now, by comparison a mere stone's throw from the Cotswolds and the huge, old manor house he'd grown up in. His father had died many years ago and he had no siblings to share the burden of his mother so this was his responsibility. His alone, and sadly, not one he relished, that was for sure.

Josephine McKendry was not only a prickly and difficult woman, she had health issues that were serious enough to need full-time care. She would be better off in a rest home that catered for people that could afford the best but his mother was fond of saying that there was only one way she was ever going to leave that house and that was feet first, in her coffin.

'She's told me I have to administer her insulin injections.' Mrs Tillman's voice was rising as fast as Lachlan's anxiety. 'Me... I can't even stick that temperature thing into the Christmas turkey without feeling rather faint myself.'

'Mother's perfectly capable of administering her own insulin.' Unless she was having an asthma attack, of course. Or a bit of angina...

'That's as it may be.' Mrs Tillman sniffed. 'But, as you well know, she's not about to do anything she doesn't *want* to do. And she thrives on the attention. She's just got bored with the last nurse, that's all. She was just too easy to intimidate, I think, but I'm not about to let her start on *me* and that's *that*.'

'That's absolutely fair enough...' Lachlan looked up as his secretary poked her head around the door of his consulting room. He shook his head and held up his

hand, indicating that he needed a few minutes before his next patient was ushered in. 'Listen… I'm going to call London Locums right now and see how soon they can provide a nurse for Mother. And I'll drive up this evening, as soon as I've finished my clinic. I'll get this sorted, I promise. But please, please don't leave, Tilly.' Using the housekeeper's old nickname was part of turning on the charm. It had always worked when he had been a kid, home from boarding school for the holidays and wanting a biscuit or some other forbidden treat from the kitchen. 'And…what about Jack?'

Mrs Tillman lived in a cottage on the estate with her husband, Jack, who had always been the head gardener on the property.

'He's not getting any younger, either. His back isn't as good as it was. Maybe it's time we both retired.'

'Oh…not just yet. *Please.* And…you know what? I think it's high time we talked about a raise in your salary, don't you? Yours and Jack's. So you can set yourselves up for a really comfortable retirement?'

There was a long moment's silence that stretched until Lachlan heard a very long sigh being released.

'You always did have me wrapped around your little finger, young man.' Mrs Tillman sniffed again. 'I'll have some dinner ready for you tonight but I'm not making any promises.'

Lachlan headed out of the room, having assured Mrs Tillman that she was an absolute angel. He then found a smile for his secretary and receptionist who was right outside his door, clearly on a return mission to see if

he was available yet. He leaned closer, to let her know that he was about to impart confidential information.

'I need a few more minutes, Sally,' he whispered. 'Bit of a personal emergency to sort out.'

'Oh…' Good grief…was Sally actually batting her eyelashes at him? 'No problem, Mr McKendry. It's not a patient waiting for you, though—it's someone from the PR department of your hospital.' She was smiling at him now. 'But I'm sure she'll understand if I say you've got an *emergency* to deal with.'

'Thank you so much. And could you find the number for a company called London Locums and then put me through? It's rather urgent.'

'I'm onto it.'

Sally sped back to her desk and Lachlan ducked back into his office for the private call that came through a commendably short time later. It was somewhat childish, but he noticed he had his fingers crossed as he picked up the phone on his desk with his other hand.

Felicity Stephens was standing in the middle of chaos when her phone rang and it was tempting to ignore the call and get on with unpacking her suitcases—and airing out her attic apartment, of course, because it was distinctly musty after her absence of several months.

Answering the beep of an alarm or a call that could be vital was hardwired into her brain, however.

'Flick? I hope I'm not disturbing you.'

'Not at all, Julia. I'm just staring at my suitcases, trying to summon the energy to unpack them.'

'Oh…' She could hear laughter on the other end of

the line. 'I've called at precisely the right moment, then. Don't unpack—I've got another job for you.'

'Really? I hope I've got time to sleep off the jet lag.'

'No. It's urgent. I have, in fact, a rather famous plastic surgeon on the other line right now, desperately hoping that you're going to say yes to what is a very urgent position.'

'How urgent?' Flick pushed waves of her hair back from her face. It felt lank and lifeless—a bit like she felt herself after the incredibly long flight back from Australia.

'To start as soon as you can get to the Cotswolds. Preferably this afternoon.'

Flick's laughter had a hollow ring. 'You've got to be kidding.'

'He'll pay double your normal salary. And it only needs to be until he can find someone permanent, although, from what I've heard about his mother, she's known as a bit of a dragon so it might not be an instant fix. She needs careful handling, apparently, which is why I thought of you. You do "difficult" cases better than anyone I know.'

'Ha…not necessarily by choice.' But Flick had to admit she was slightly intrigued. Plus, she'd never had the chance to explore the Cotswolds and wasn't that supposed to be one of the most beautiful parts of Britain? 'Who's the famous surgeon?'

'His name's Lachlan McKendry. I've known of him for a few years, now. I guess I took notice of the articles about him because he's…well…kind of cute.' Flick could almost hear Julia shaking her head at such ado-

lescent behaviour. 'Anyway, he grew up here—well, in the Cotswolds. Did his medical training in London but then went to the States for postgraduate degrees.

'He's a paediatric plastic surgeon who specialises in nerve reconstruction,' Julia continued. 'He's in demand at every international conference and he got headhunted to come back to London by The Richmond International Clinic, which is the private arm of St Bethel's Hospital in Richmond, but he's splitting his time between private and public work. It's his mother who needs the full-time care.'

'What's her medical history?'

Flick listened as Julia rapidly listed what added up to be a complex set of conditions that needed monitoring and frequent treatment. It certainly sounded like a challenge and that was almost as enticing as a completely new part of the world to explore.

'So...what can I tell him?' Julia spoke cautiously enough to advertise her hope that Flick could help her with this important client. 'He's on hold even though it sounds like he's probably got a waiting room full of patients. He's desperate.'

Flick eyed her suitcase. It still contained everything she needed for a temporary position. A bit of extra money would certainly come in handy after those expensive flights from the other side of the world and her car definitely needed a good run after being garaged for so long.

'Tell you what, Julia. I need a couple of hours to wash my hair and sort myself out and then I'll drive up and meet this dragon and *then* I'll decide. You can tell

this Mr McKendry that, as long as his mother isn't unbearably obnoxious, I'll hang around until he can find someone permanent.'

'Oh…bless you, Flick. You're the best.'

'Hey… I'm not making any promises.' But Flick's smile was wry. 'Text me the address. I'll aim to get there somewhere around six-thirty p.m.'

Jennifer, from the public relations department, was in her forties and immaculately groomed, as if she was ready to stand in front of cameras at a moment's notice to inform the public of anything important that involved either St Bethel's Hospital or the Richmond International Clinic. She opened her briefcase the moment she sat down in Lachlan's office and produced a sheaf of papers.

'There are a few things I need to check before we release the exciting news that you'll be available for the specialist postgraduate training scheme they've been begging you to do in the wider Gloucester area.'

'No problem.' But Lachlan glanced at his watch. He would prefer to escape from London before peak-hour traffic made it too tedious. Then something clicked. The timing of this crisis with his mother was actually quite serendipitous. 'In fact, it could be that I may have to spend more time in the area during this—what is it, a twelve-week programme? I may even stay there at times and commute back to London when I need to.'

'Yes, it's twelve weeks. Is there a reason for you wanting to base yourself away from London?'

'My mother lives not far from Gloucester. She's… ah…not very well at the moment.'

'Oh, I'm sorry to hear that.' But Jennifer clearly had other things on her mind as well. 'You won't have to pull out of upcoming obligations in London, though, will you? You're due to start filming for that documentary next week.'

'Ah…yes. They've been following young Dexter since he had his surgery for the brain tumour a couple of years ago. And I'm going to do a masseteric nerve transfer surgery to treat his facial paralysis.'

Jennifer nodded. 'They want to film the initial consultation with you, Mr McKendry, when you're explaining the surgery to him. And that'll be a good time to talk to them about having cameras and crew actually in the operating theatre. I'll come to that meeting as well. I've already spoken with Dexter's family and the neurosurgical team he's been under. Everyone's very excited about being part of the documentary.'

'It won't be a problem,' Lachlan assured her. 'It's in my diary already and I'll work around any current cases. If I could reduce my patient load over the duration of the postgraduate training course, though, that will offer more time to devote to the training. I can be available to operate as well as deliver lectures, which might be of even more benefit to the surgeons wanting to upskill.'

'Yes…' Jennifer was nodding enthusiastically. 'And it will be so valuable for inter-hospital relationships as well. I'll look at adjusting your rosters and outpatient clinics here myself, and then chase up any paperwork

that might need covering to give you clinical privileges in other hospitals. Or at least the big ones in the area—Gloucester General and Cheltenham Central. I'm sure they'll be delighted to get more of your expertise.'

'I'm happy to oblige,' Lachlan told her. 'Even a small change can make a big difference in paediatrics. A registrar in an emergency department learning a new suturing or wound closure technique—for a serious dog bite, for example—might mean that a child is less scarred and won't need further surgery later on.'

Jennifer was scribbling notes. 'I'll put together a press release after I've talked to all the hospital administrators who are keen to get on board with this programme.' Her glance up at Lachlan was impressed. 'You're going to be rather busy for the next few months. I've never known any of our doctors to be in demand quite like this.'

Lachlan shrugged. 'I like being busy. And the commute will be a good thing. I'm going to enjoy giving my new car a bit of a run on the motorways.'

If he did end up basing himself out of town to focus on finding a more permanent solution to the problem his mother was presenting, frequent trips to London would also give him a break from her and that would be a good thing for both of them. Better than good. Vital…

And…it was impossible to stop another thought flashing through the back of his head with the speed of light. Another small issue that he'd been putting off dealing with despite knowing that action was overdue. Being largely out of town for some time would present the perfect opportunity to bring an amicable end to his

current liaison with Shayna, the very cute physiotherapist he'd met a few weeks ago. Or was it nearly two months? Too long, anyway, given that she was getting too attached.

Good grief, she'd even asked if she could have her own space in the chest of drawers in his bedroom, despite having had the 'F' rules clearly spelled out from the beginning. A relationship for Lachlan was about Fun and that was all. No Full time. No Future. No Family.

Lachlan glanced at his watch again, letting his breath out in what might have been a small sigh of relief that split-second interruption had provided.

'Speaking of which,' he told Jennifer, 'I need to get going, but just email me any queries. Or leave a phone message and I'll call back as soon as I can.' As if his phone wanted to back up his promise, a text alert sounded. Lachlan glanced at the screen, standing up as Jennifer got out of her seat. It was a message from Julia at London Locums and he could see the initial lines of the text.

Felicity's on her way to meet your mother. Good luck. She's the best—

Lachlan didn't open the message to read the rest. Yes, Julia had said on the phone that this nurse would only be deciding whether or not to take the position after she'd met his mother but getting her there was the biggest hurdle to get over. He'd had many, many years of learning that he could get pretty much anything he wanted with a combination of charm and unlimited funds avail-

able. He could feel his lips curling into a smile that was already anticipating success in dealing with the initial step of solving the problem of his mother.

'You know what, Jennifer? I'm confident that I've already got arrangements in place that will make this all run as smoothly as possible. I might even be back by tomorrow morning and have some time to meet up. We can thrash out the final details of the training programme. Maybe you can give me some tips for working with that film crew as well.'

Jennifer gave him an unreadable look. 'I think you'll manage just fine, Mr McKendry. You seem to have everything well under control.'

Yes...

He *did* have things under control. The issue of dealing with an aging and difficult family member was nothing he couldn't handle and Lachlan McKendry had every intention of doing so with kindness and patience. Josephine McKendry was his mother, after all, and you only ever got one of them.

And how could you not feel happy when you could stay in the fast lane and pass everything else on the M4 as if they were barely moving? He settled a little deeper into the butter-soft leather seat of his brand-new, Dolomite Silver Porsche 911 Carrera. Zero to one hundred kilometres an hour in four point two seconds. Not that he'd tried that out yet, of course, but it would be fun...

The average time from London to Gloucester was a couple of hours but Lachlan wasn't going that far because the family estate was in a deeply forested pocket

amongst Cotswold villages. He'd be able to shave at least forty minutes off that kind of journey time. The inbuilt sat nav in his dashboard was already recalculating his arrival time as Heathrow Airport flashed past. He should be at his destination by about six-thirty p.m. Just in time for an aperitif before one of Tilly's delicious dinners.

A vocal instruction was enough to raise the volume level of the music coming from a sound system that was one of the best Lachlan had ever heard but he wanted something a bit more upbeat. Something that fitted in with his current optimism.

'Play "Living on a Prayer" by Bon Jovi' he instructed.

He could totally get on board with the chorus of that song. He was, literally, almost halfway there already.

This couldn't be right, surely…

Flick slowed her bright yellow Volkswagen Beetle as she turned past ornate, wrought-iron gates to find herself on a tree-lined driveway that was so long she couldn't even see a house. It looked like the entrance to a National Park. Or a residence of a minor Royal, perhaps? But, then, Julia had told her that Mrs McKendry wasn't a 'Mrs' at all. She was Lady Josephine because her now deceased husband had been knighted for his services to cardiothoracic surgery or something. She'd also said the family was seriously wealthy and that the house she was going to had probably had McKendrys living in it for centuries.

'You'll love it, Flick,' she'd added. 'A real taste of old-

fashioned, upper-class England. Bit different from what you grew up with in Australia, I'm guessing.'

A 'bit different' was already an understatement. Finally coming to the end of the driveway, Flick felt her jaw dropping as she took in the circular drive with a central garden and ornate fountain and the enormous house behind it. The beautiful stonework and countless lead-lighted windows, a slate roof that looked many hundreds of years old and the sense of history it evoked sent a shiver down her spine. The stories that would have seeped into those stones…

Flick had worked in many different places in the years she'd been with various medical locum agencies based in both Sydney and London. She'd worked with aeromedical retrieval services, in both private and public hospitals, general practice clinics, private homes and even on superyachts but she'd never felt like she was stepping back in time like this. She should be in a small carriage, being pulled by a couple of horses, she decided, as she parked her little yellow car nearest the door at the top of a wide sweep of steps. She should be wearing a long, boofy dress and any second now the doors would be flung open to reveal a butler ready to show her into…ooh…a drawing room, perhaps? Or a library? She stood at the bottom of the steps for a moment longer, staring up at the walls of the house as a smile stretched across her face.

She was still smiling as she turned at the sound of gravel being spat out from beneath fast-moving tyres but it faded as an expensive-looking silver car came to a stop that was abrupt enough and close enough to send

small pebbles to hit her boots and it was completely gone by the time the driver emerged from the car and walked towards her.

Wow…

It wasn't a coherent word in Lachlan's head. This was more like a sensation that had started in his eyes but was now trickling down to every cell in his body. A rather overwhelming sensation but that was entirely appropriate, given that he was actually walking towards what had to be the most gorgeous woman he'd ever seen in his life.

She had blonde hair that didn't quite touch her shoulders and it was parted in the middle. Not quite curly but wavy enough to make a delicious frame for a face that was, quite simply, perfect. Big blue eyes. A cute snub nose. A generous mouth that looked as if it was made for laughter.

The rest of her body was just as amazing. It only took the briefest of glances to take in slim legs covered in faded denim and tucked into knee-high boots, a soft white shirt that hung loose onto her hips. The denim waistcoat and a couple of unusual, silver chain necklaces told him instantly that this woman had her own style and personality. That she was…different…

It was only a fraction of time before he looked back at her face but there was no hint of a smile there. That didn't stop Lachlan from finding his own—the one that never failed.

'My day just got a whole lot better,' he told her. 'If

you're the Felicity Stephens that's come from London Locums, that is.'

She was staring at him.

'If you're who I think you are, I was told that you're a doctor?'

'That's right. I'm Lachlan McKendry. It's my—'

She interrupted him. 'A plastic surgeon, yes?'

'Also correct.' That direct stare was a little disconcerting now. 'Why do you ask?'

'Well, I'm wondering if it's in a professional capacity that you're assessing my body in quite such an obvious manner.' There was a definite hint of a smile on her face now, as she turned away from him. 'I'm quite happy with my boobs as they are, thanks.'

Oh…he wanted to say that he agreed wholeheartedly but he wasn't about to open his mouth again in a hurry. He'd never had a slap like that when he'd tried to turn on the charm. Okay…flirt a little. Who wouldn't when they met the most beautiful girl in the world? And maybe that was the problem. Looking like that, this locum nurse probably had to deal with being hit on all the time. No wonder he had annoyed her and that was the last thing he wanted to do.

He needed to fix this.

And fast.

Felicity Stephens was the key to his being in control of this current disturbance in his life and Lachlan couldn't afford to antagonise her. Taking the steps two at a time, he caught up with her just before she reached for the lion's head brass door knocker. He also caught her gaze.

'I'm so sorry, Felicity,' he said quietly. 'I *was* a little overexcited to see you—but it's because I've had a rather difficult day and I suspect you might very well be the answer to my prayers.'

She held his gaze, as if gauging whether his apology was genuine or not. Lachlan could almost feel himself lowering his guard—just enough that she would see a glimpse of a version of himself that nobody ever really got to see.

She blinked. 'And I probably overreacted,' she said. 'I could blame jet lag because I only got off a flight from Australia at lunchtime today. Or…' There was a flash of humour in those astonishingly blue eyes. 'It could be being called "Felicity" that got my back up. I'm Flick, except for official identification, like in my passport.'

Flick…

A name that was as different as she was. This woman was getting more intriguing by the minute but Lachlan didn't say anything. He just nodded as he pushed open the enormous front door of his childhood home.

'Please come in,' he invited. 'I'm quite sure that my mother is going to be just as delighted to meet you as I am.'

CHAPTER TWO

'WHO ARE *YOU*?' Lady Josephine McKendry looked a lot less than delighted when she was introduced to Flick.

'This is Felicity Stephens, Mother.' Lachlan straightened from having kissed his mother's cheek. 'One of the best nurses that London Locums has on their books, I've been told. We're lucky enough that she happens to be available and she's come to meet you. Oh, and she prefers to be called "Flick".'

Lady Josephine snorted rather inelegantly. 'That's the name for a fire engine, not a person. Didn't there used to be some dreadful children's song about that?' She rested a piercing gaze on Flick for a breath before turning back to the window beside her armchair. 'You can both go away. I'm not in the mood to be shown off to someone like some interesting medical specimen.' She seemed to be completely focused on the beautiful, formal garden that was fading into the dusk as part of the much wider view offered from the first floor of this house.

Flick caught Lachlan's gaze. She should give up now and just walk out because it was quite clear she wasn't

wanted. Needed, perhaps, but that wasn't her problem, was it? This was Lachlan McKendry's mother and he was here so he could look after her, even if it was more than a little inconvenient.

But something was stopping her.

Something that was complex enough to intrigue her.

The tension between this mother and son was palpable. It almost felt as if Josephine hated her child but what mother could ever do that? It also felt like her lack of warmth was something that was still hurtful to Lachlan even though he had to be a few years older than Flick, who was in her early thirties. You'd think that she would, at least, be proud of a son who had achieved so much at an early age. A son who was famous, admittedly very good looking and…sophisticated? Was that the word Flick needed to encompass the kind of charm—charisma, even—that this man exuded?

But that was something else that was intriguing. Because Flick knew that Lachlan's persona was a front. A shop window that gave nothing away about what could be on offer if you were allowed inside. She might not have guessed, despite having cultivated an image of her own that prevented anyone getting close to who she really was, except for that tiny moment in time— no more than a heartbeat, really—when he'd apologised for being such a blatant flirt and she'd seen something in his eyes that had had nothing to do with the over-confident, charming and superficial barrier he'd created.

She'd had a similar moment of insight when Lady Josephine had glared at her before turning away. Just

enough to know that this rather frail, older woman was frightened.

Of dying? That would be understandable, given her fragile health. She wasn't exactly geriatric, either. If Lachlan was in his mid-thirties, Lady Josephine might only be in her early seventies. Late sixties, even?

Or was it because of something even deeper than that? Dying alone, maybe, because of what had happened to cause such a rift between herself and her son?

Whatever. In spite of the bone-deep weariness that only jet lag could create and an emptiness that made Flick realise it had been far too long since she'd eaten anything substantial, she couldn't walk out on the puzzle these people presented. People who had everything, it would seem—the most gorgeous house she'd ever seen, in the most idyllic setting, and unlimited funds to keep it that way—but they were both miserable. No, that was the wrong word. They would probably both empathically deny that they were less than happy. Because they didn't want to recognise it themselves?

She took a step closer to Lady Josephine's chair. 'I don't need to be here for long,' she said calmly. 'But you might need some assistance until you can choose your own private nurse. Could I help you with your evening medications, perhaps?'

Lady Josephine sniffed. 'You're far too pretty to be looking after old, sick people,' she said. 'Stuck in the middle of nowhere.'

'I'll take that as a compliment,' Flick murmured. She didn't dare look at Lachlan because that would remind them both of that small altercation when they'd met.

Lady Josephine turned her head. 'Why aren't you married?' she demanded.

Flick's eyes widened. 'Are *you* married?'

'That's none of your damned business.'

Flick's smile was one-sided. 'Exactly.'

One side of Lady Josephine's mouth twitched, as if she was amused by the response, but she hadn't finished.

'Who was your last patient?'

'An elderly gentleman who lived in Sydney, Australia. His name was Stanley.'

'What was wrong with him?'

'He was unwell with quite a few underlying health issues. A bit like yourself, I believe.'

'What happened to him? Why did you leave?'

'He died,' Flick said quietly.

Lady Josephine snorted again. 'You didn't look after him very well, then, did you?'

'Mother...' Lachlan's protest was ignored by both the women.

'He was quite happy with my care,' Flick told his mother. 'Mind you, it was a bit hard to tell because he covered up how he was really feeling by being impossibly grumpy and demanding. Also a bit like yourself, I suspect, Lady Josephine.'

She could hear a stifled laugh from Lachlan's direction. More surprisingly, it was obvious that Lady Josephine was on the point of losing her own battle not to smile.

'You'll do,' she said, turning back to the window again. 'You're feisty. I rather like feisty.' She waved her

hand. 'Go over to that table over there and sort out the mess my housekeeper's made with all my medications. The stupid woman couldn't even bring herself to check my blood sugar level.'

'That sounds like a good place to start, then.' Again, Flick caught Lachlan's gaze as she walked past him to get to the table. Her glance was a warning not to take anything for granted, however. 'Low blood sugar can make anyone grumpy,' she murmured. 'I might as well make myself useful while I'm here.'

Lachlan's smile was unexpectedly genuine. 'Thanks. I'll go and make *myself* useful too, and see what Tilly's organised for our dinner. It'll be worth staying for, I promise.'

Tender roast beef and vegetables like crispy potatoes and soft, sweet triangles of pumpkin, Yorkshire puddings and a rich gravy made from pan drippings had always been Lachlan's absolute favourite meal. Tilly had set the table in the formal dining room but Lachlan had instinctively vetoed the choice.

'We'll eat here in the kitchen,' he told the housekeeper. 'It's so much more homely and…and I'm rather hoping to persuade this nurse to stay. I think she might even have Mother wrapped around her little finger already.'

Tilly chuckled. 'That'll be the day. Do you want to take her tray up or shall I?'

'I'll do it. If Flick's not done with the medications, I can give her a hand. Poor thing must be dead on her feet. She only flew in from Australia today.'

'Nothing that a bit of my good home cooking won't fix, I'm sure. And a good sleep. I've got the guest suite made up for her and that's a very comfortable bed.'

Mrs Tillman was not only the head gardener's wife and the housekeeper, she was cook, cleaner, secretary and mother figure and Lachlan had no hesitation in giving her a hug.

'You're the one person in my life that I've always been able to rely on, you know that?'

'Oh, get away with you.'

Mrs Tillman gave him a push and Lachlan was laughing as he turned to find that Flick had come into the kitchen. Oh, help...had she heard what he'd just said? And did it matter if she had? Yeah, it kind of did. For whatever reason—even if it was just to persuade Flick to stay in the house—it seemed of paramount importance to impress her, and revealing that his childhood housekeeper had been more important than anyone else in his life might seem...well...unimpressive? A bit pathetic, even?

But she was smiling. 'Something smells *amazing*,' she said. 'The last meal I had was the plastic kind you get on planes and I can't even remember how long ago that was now. I'm Flick, by the way...' She held out her hand. 'And I'm guessing you're Mrs Tillman?'

Tilly wiped her hand on her apron before taking Flick's and grasping it warmly. 'I am.' She turned back to the oven to take out a steaming tray. 'I expect Her Ladyship's probably been telling you how useless I am with needles or the sight of blood.'

Lachlan knew perfectly well that Flick had heard

even more disparaging comments about Tilly but there was no flicker of agreement on her face. Instead, she took another deep, appreciative sniff. 'She did say that she was ready for her dinner and I can see why she must be looking forward to it. Oh, wow…are those Yorkshire puddings? I tried to make them once and they came out like punctured tyres.'

Lachlan joined in the laughter and the kitchen suddenly seemed even more homely and welcoming than he'd remembered it being.

'Sit yourselves down,' Mrs Tillman ordered. 'I'll serve up, take a tray upstairs and then I'll be off home to my Jack. He'll be wanting his dinner, too. Lachlan, you can show Flick here where her rooms are, can't you?'

'It would be my pleasure.' Lachlan smiled at Flick. 'Tilly's made up the best suite in the house for you.'

'But…' Flick was frowning. 'I haven't decided whether I'm staying or not.'

'You can't drive back to London tonight. Not when you're jet-lagged and hungry. Besides—' he tried another smile—the one where he knew that those shutters came down for a blink of time '—I just happen to have a highly recommended bottle of Australian wine in the fridge and this seems like the perfect moment to open it.'

Flick's face stilled and she was holding their eye contact. Lachlan knew he should break it before it became far more significant than it actually was, but he couldn't. He was caught by something he could see in that blueness that was even darker in this shadowy old kitchen. Something he couldn't begin to define but it

was doing something weird to him. This had nothing to do with the overwhelming attraction he'd been aware of when he'd first set eyes on this woman. No…whatever this was, it was making him feel both sad and happy at the same time. What on earth was that about?

It was a moment that felt utterly silent, which was crazy because there was a background of busy clattering of plates and pans and cutlery. A moment that also felt a lot longer than it probably was. It was Flick who shifted her gaze first.

'Go on, then,' she said. There was a smile in her voice even if it didn't quite reach her lips. 'I reckon that's the best offer I've had all day.'

Lachlan hid the smile that wanted to appear as he headed for the fridge. He hadn't made his best offer yet, by any means. Whatever it took, he was going to try and make sure that Flick would decide to stay. Preferably for as long as possible. Not just because she was the most beautiful woman in existence. Maybe it was because she seemed to know exactly how to handle his mother, which was nothing short of a small miracle. Or maybe it was because, despite it being disturbing, it felt like that strange way she'd made him feel was somehow important.

Vital, even?

'This is, quite possibly, the most delicious dinner I've ever eaten in my life.' Flick eyed the piece of fluffy Yorkshire pudding, dipped in gravy, on the end of her fork as she tried to decide whether she had room for one last mouthful. With a sigh of defeat, she popped it in

her mouth, closing her eyes to savour this final morsel. She could feel the heat from the cream-coloured Aga stove at her back and the unevenness of the flagstone floor beneath her feet, she could smell the aromas of the wonderful food they were eating and still taste the smoothness of that wine that had accompanied the meal. But, most of all, she was aware of the man who was sitting at the end of this old, oak kitchen table. There was an energy about him that was disconcerting. Impossible to ignore.

She opened her eyes. 'I'm pretty sure that your mother's medication is all up to date, although I'll check again. But what kind of other assistance does she need in the evenings?'

Lachlan put down his fork and reached for his wine glass. 'She doesn't actually *need* any assistance at all,' he said. 'She's only sixty-three and she's perfectly capable of looking after herself—she just chooses not to when it comes to medication. After various crises, including diabetic ketoacidosis from not taking her insulin, a coma from taking too much and an asthma attack that could well have been fatal if Tilly hadn't found her, I decided that a full-time medical carer was essential. Actually, being in a rest home would have been more practical, given that I was living in New York at the time, but Mother absolutely refuses to leave this house.' His smile was wry.

'I sometimes wonder if it was my father she fell in love with or the family mansion that he'd inherited. He was quite a lot older than her—about eighteen years—

so it can't have been too much of a surprise that he died first.'

'How long ago was that?'

'Hmm…' Lachlan drained his wineglass and reached for the bottle on the table. He reached for Flick's glass but she shook her head.

'I'd be out for the count if I had any more.' And, no matter how tired she felt, she didn't want to sleep just yet because it was more compelling to listen to what Lachlan had to say. To find out more about what it was that made this man so…so *intriguing*…

He refilled his own glass. 'I was a senior registrar,' he told her. 'So it's quite a few years ago now. I'd just signed up for a rotation in cardiothoracic surgery, which pleased my father so much he booked his favourite table at the Ritz for a family celebration. He collapsed before his entrée arrived, with a massive heart attack.'

'Oh, *no*…'

'It was quite lucky we were in the city. It meant he was in hospital getting the best treatment almost within minutes. And it looked as though he was recovering but there was too much damage to his heart muscle. He had a cardiac rupture a week or so later and died instantly.'

Flick was silent for a moment, her brain retrieving something Lachlan had said. Or maybe the tone in which it had been said.

'Was that what made you change your mind about which specialty you wanted to follow?'

'What?' Lachlan looked astonished. 'Good grief, no. It was what gave me the freedom to do what I wanted to do. Up until then my destiny had been sealed. I went

off to boarding school in time for my sixth birthday and the headmaster introduced me to everyone as the boy who was going to become a famous surgeon just like his father.'

Flick's jaw dropped. 'You got sent to boarding school when you were *five*?'

Lachlan's gaze slid away from hers as if he'd revealed more than he'd intended to. He reached for his glass again.

'It wasn't so bad,' he said. 'I got to come home in the holidays. If I did well in my exams, my father was happy. If Father was happy, then so was Mother and, if they were both happy, I got to do whatever I liked.'

Flick's heart was being squeezed so hard it hurt, imagining that small boy who was being sent away from home. Who had learned to work hard at school to try and earn his parents' approval. Love, even…?

She kept her tone light, however. Instinct told her that Lachlan would not appreciate pity. 'So what was it that you liked to do?'

Lachlan shrugged. 'I helped Jack in the gardens. Persuaded Tilly to give me biscuits. I read a lot and… I guess I know every square inch of the patch of woodlands we own. It's the most beautiful place in the world. Not that I've set foot in it for years, mind you.'

'When did you head to New York?'

'As soon as I could. I changed that surgical rotation from cardiothoracic to plastics and then kept going with postgraduate study. I'd always been fascinated by plastic surgery. I know that makes most people think of something like breast augmentation but that is of no inter-

est to me whatsoever.' He caught Flick's gaze and held it. 'I see it as a way to repair things that can enhance someone's *life*. To improve a disabling disfigurement, perhaps. Or use the magic of microsurgery to restore function even more than appearance.'

His passion was unmistakable and Flick cringed as she remembered that flippant remark she'd made.

'Sorry,' she murmured.

Lachlan shrugged again. 'Doesn't matter. I shouldn't be boring you with my opinions. Or with the family history, either.'

'Knowing more about your mother is important.' Flick couldn't call Lady Josephine his 'mum' because it just didn't feel right. 'If I'm going to take the position here.'

She saw the flash of hope in Lachlan's eyes. 'What do you want to know?'

'Is it too far-fetched for me to be thinking that her grumpiness might be due to depression?'

'I wouldn't say that she's ever been a particularly happy woman,' Lachlan said slowly. 'But her life certainly changed a lot after Father died. I put a lot of that down to her late onset Type One diabetes and the angina on top of the asthma she's always had, but I guess her social life pretty much vanished over the same time period. She loved being a prominent surgeon's wife. A "Lady". A local celebrity, really. There were always public appearances and lots of parties and dancing. Mother used to be a patron of all sorts of things as well and that's all in the past.' He was frowning now. 'You could well be right. It might explain her lack of inter-

est in coping with her medications. And, if that's the case, it might make a real difference if it got treated.'

And there it was again. That flash of what looked like hope. This time, it didn't have anything to do with the idea that someone else might shoulder the burden of caring for the difficult person his mother had become. Rather, it was hope that there could be a way of helping Lady Josephine get more joy out of life. However dysfunctional Lachlan McKendry's relationship with his mother was, he cared about her.

The knowledge added another layer to that image of a lonely little boy being sent off to boarding school far too early and learning to earn his father's approval. Had that small child felt a mother's rejection when he'd needed his own love returned? No wonder he was hiding behind an image that would never invite pity. A charismatic, privileged playboy type of image that would normally have alienated Flick instantly. But she'd seen behind the shutters, hadn't she? Just for an instant or two but she knew there was a very different person there.

A person that was capable of touching something she'd believed had died in her a long time ago—the ability to feel an interest in a man that was genuine enough to generate physical attraction.

She could feel it now. A tingle, deep in her belly that stirred memories poignant enough to almost bring tears to her eyes. Which was ridiculous. She was just overtired, that was what it was.

'I really need to get some sleep,' she told Lachlan.

'Of course. I'll show you your room.' Lachlan was

on his feet instantly but then he paused. 'Have you…?' He shook his head. 'I don't want to put any pressure on you but…'

He wanted to know if she was going to stay and look after his mother. Of course he did. If she left in the morning, he'd have to stay and make other arrangements and he would probably need to adjust his schedule. She shouldn't stay, Flick thought. Not with that unexpected revelation her body had just provided, which was every bit as unprofessional as the way Lachlan had been trying to flirt with her when they'd met on the doorstep.

But there was a woman upstairs who was unhappy enough not to care whether she took the medications she needed to prolong her life or at least make it more comfortable. A son who cared deeply about his mother even if he'd never been loved enough as a child. And there was this amazing house surrounded by woodland that was, apparently, the most beautiful place in the world.

Maybe it was that glass of wine on top of a good dose of jet lag but Flick felt like she'd stepped into some kind of modern fairy tale. She was in a magic setting and there was the equivalent of a wicked queen upstairs. Tilly was a loyal servant and Lachlan…well, he could easily step into the role of a prince.

What did that make her?

A good fairy?

A potential princess?

Simply too tired to think clearly? Yep, that seemed to be what it was because Flick had to catch the edge of the table as she stood up, her weariness enough to make her unsteady on her feet.

She could see concern in Lachlan's eyes now, along with the question she hadn't answered.

'You know what?' She held his gaze. 'I *have* decided.'

She could see right into those dark eyes now. No shutters. He wanted her help. He needed it. How could she possibly refuse?

She couldn't.

'I'll stay,' she said. 'If that's what your mother wants.'

'I'm sure she will.' Lachlan was smiling. 'She said you were feisty. She likes you.' There was more than relief in his eyes now. Flick had the impression that *he* liked her as well.

The feeling was mutual, then. Not that there was any question of stepping over any professional boundaries. Something that, even this morning, would have been unthinkable on a personal level and now, with Lachlan McKendry about to employ her, was totally unacceptable on a professional level.

Flick let her breath out in a sigh of relief. Because there was no need to think about that familiar tingle and what it might mean. Every reason not to, in fact.

'Are you sure I don't need to check on your mother before I go to sleep?'

'She's got an alarm. Here...' Lachlan went to an old, pine dresser at the end of the kitchen and picked up a small electronic device, like a pager. 'You take this. She'll ring if she needs attention.'

And there she was. Employed as Lady Josephine's private nurse with absolutely no idea what was going to happen. But that was okay. Flick thrived on a challenge.

Facing up to them had been what had saved her many years ago—the only thing that had made life worth-while, even. She loved new places. Something differ-ent—and this was as different as it could get. If it wasn't a fairy tale, it was definitely a mystery and it certainly wasn't going to be boring.

CHAPTER THREE

BEING IN THE spotlight had never fazed Lachlan Mc-Kendry.

Perhaps it was because he'd grown up with parents who'd had more than their fair share of media attention. Or that he'd worked hard enough at school to attract attention for his academic achievements as much as his family connections and had then gone on to garner international acclaim for his skills. If he was really honest, however, he'd also always rather enjoyed the way it made people look at him as if he was someone special. Especially women.

Like the way he was being watched right now from more than one direction as his introductory part in Dexter Thompson's documentary was being filmed. Jennifer from PR was in the background, with a tablet device in her hands, watching his every move, and the stare from a young sound technician with a cheeky smile was unashamedly blatant. Even the documentary producer who would be interviewing Lachlan on his own very soon, to get his personal take on the case, was letting her gaze linger without bothering to hide her interest

as Lachlan continued with the physical examination of how severe Dexter's facial paralysis was.

'Can you raise your eyebrows for me? That's great… Now, close your eyes and keep them closed if you can.' Lachlan used his middle finger and thumb to pull the skin above and below the eyes to provide resistance. It was very obvious that Dexter had almost no control of half his face. 'Okay…puff out your cheeks for me. And—last one—show me your teeth…'

He had questions for Dexter about the irritation he got in one eye due to the impaired eyelid movement, the mouth ulcers he experienced frequently and the difficulties he had in eating and drinking because one side of his mouth couldn't function normally. Sometimes Dexter's only responses were a nod or shake of his head because his speech wasn't always clear, but when it came to admitting that he often drooled or lost pieces of food, his hesitation and the way he dropped his gaze spoke volumes about just how much this problem was affecting his life.

When he heard what could have been a soft sound of distress from Dexter's mother, Bridget, who was sitting beside him, Lachlan was concerned that he'd upset his young patient enough for them to need to stop filming for a while, but Dexter simply turned his head to catch his mother's gaze and then took a deep breath, looking back at Lachlan and clearly ready to continue. Lachlan thought it was his mother's presence that gave Dexter renewed confidence but he changed his mind when he glanced briefly in the same direction himself.

Bridget was one woman here, at least, who wasn't

remotely interested in looking at Lachlan as anyone other than the doctor who had the ability to help her son. She wasn't even looking at him at all, in fact, because her attention was firmly fixed on her son. There was an unmistakeable, quiet pride in her face but the overwhelming interpretation of that look was one of absolute love and that gave Lachlan an odd twist of emotion, not unlike the one he'd had when he'd first met Felicity Stephens—that very strange mix that was both sad and happy at exactly the same time.

The feeling was almost identical, in fact, and in that split second of awareness he decided that it was more sad than happy, which made it something to push aside as hard as necessary to make it disappear completely. There was something far more important to focus on, anyway. It was time to move on to explaining his part in Dexter's treatment.

'So this is a diagram of all the nerves in your face, Dexter.' The medical illustrations department of St Bethel's Hospital had done a great job of making this colourful, laminated poster. 'These yellow lines are the facial nerve and its branches.' He touched a point on the diagram. 'This is the main trunk and this bit here is what we call the motor nucleus.'

A cameraman had stepped forward to zoom in on the poster. Dexter was nodding, managing to look as if they hadn't already rehearsed this quickly beforehand, and Lachlan was keeping his language as simple as possible because he knew this programme would be mostly watched by people with no medical training.

'The good thing about an acoustic neuroma, which is

the kind of brain tumour you had taken out a couple of years ago, is that it's benign, which means it isn't cancer. That doesn't mean we can leave it there, of course, because it keeps growing and can cause complications like the loss of balance and build-up of fluid inside the skull that you experienced.'

Maybe when he was talking to the producer, he could go into more detail about how dangerous the tumour could be because of its proximity to the brainstem and the fatal outcome that could happen.

'A bad thing about an acoustic neuroma, though,' he continued, 'is that it grows very close to the facial nerve and the surgery to remove it can cause damage and swelling and lead to facial paralysis. Like yours. But another good thing is that you had your surgery less than two years ago, which means there's less scarring on the facial nerve and the chances are much better that the nerve transfer we're going to do will be successful.'

Dexter lifted his head, the camera changed direction from the poster to his face and Lachlan knew that the next shot would capture the hearts of any audience, as the lad instinctively returned Lachlan's smile.

At fifteen years old, Dexter should be beginning to explore the new world of relationships that teenagers found themselves in but the damage to his facial nerve gave him a disfigurement that made even smiling at a girl something to be avoided at all costs because only one side of his mouth could curl up, leaving the other side to seemingly droop further and the eye on the same side to be too wide open and staring, as it was now. Even

more poignantly, the unparalysed side of Dexter's face was shining with hope.

It wasn't just the future audience of this documentary whose hearts would be captured. Right now, Lachlan was aware of the catch in his own chest—the kind that had been what had drawn him in to this branch of medicine and kept him here, fascinated by every case and determined to make a real difference in the lives of children and young people just like Dexter. It was hard not to get too emotionally involved in a case like this but, unlike that confused feeling he wasn't even going to try and analyse, Lachlan knew exactly how to handle this kind of emotion. You used every ounce of skill you had to get the best possible outcome, and when it was a success there was immense satisfaction to be found and that was a form of happiness all in itself.

This time, Bridget had to reach for some tissues. 'It's been so hard,' she said quietly. 'Kids can be so cruel, can't they? The bullying and so on...' She wiped her eyes and gave Dexter an apologetic smile. 'Sorry,' she mouthed silently.

Maybe they would cut that bit out later because that was when the filming of that segment ended. Lachlan would spend a few minutes explaining the masseter nerve transfer surgery, have a brief conversation with the producer that was likely to focus on how life-changing the procedure could be for Dexter and then he had some time to himself for the first time in two, long days. He'd been busy tying up cases he'd been involved in, to help clear his schedule to allow time for the postgraduate training course, ever since he'd come back to

London the morning after Flick had agreed to take on the position as his mother's private nurse.

Dexter and his mother were getting ready to leave his consulting room and Lachlan saw Bridget pause to drop a wad of used tissues into the bin. The random thought that he was quite sure his own mother had never shed a tear on his behalf gave him another one of those strange twists of an emotion he didn't want to explore. At least it was fainter, this time, but it made him wonder what was going on in that Cotswold manor house.

He'd arranged for his mother's GP to visit yesterday to give her a thorough check-up and discuss her management with her new nurse, but what Lachlan really wanted to know was how Flick was coping with a difficult client. There was definitely anxiety there that she might pack her bags and walk out like so many others before her, despite the fact that Tilly had told him in last night's phone call that Flick was coping extraordinarily well. What was the phrase she'd used? Oh, yes… that she had Lady Josephine 'eating out of her hand'.

That would be something to see. The weird feeling came back a bit stronger then and Lachlan decided it must have something to do with concern for his mother. Guilt that he wasn't doing quite enough, perhaps? He needed to get back home and see how things were going.

No. He *wanted* to get back home, he realised. As soon as possible…

An appointment had been made for tomorrow for the electromyography tests that would map any nerve activity still functioning on the paralysed side of Dexter's face but Lachlan wouldn't have another part to

play until the actual day of the surgery and there were still some boxes for Jennifer to get ticked before the film crew could be allowed into the operating theatre.

'There hasn't been a date pencilled in for the surgery yet, has there?' he asked her.

'Not yet, no. Given the arrangements that need to be made, including input from the hospital's ethical committee regarding the filming and publicity, I can't see it happening before next week. Is that a problem?'

'Not at all. I was just thinking that it could be a good time to line up the first lectures for the training programme in the next few days. What was the session that Cheltenham Central wanted to start with? Suturing techniques?'

'Yes. With specific reference to dealing with dog bites.' Jennifer shook her head. 'Seems like they must get a lot of them.'

'They can leave devastating scarring on a young child. I have an entire lecture written on that topic that I delivered in the States. It won't take me long at all to make it more relevant with some UK statistics. Have you got suggested seminar times?'

'Yes.' Jennifer opened a new screen on her device. 'Okay…there's an open session available for tomorrow, actually, but that's far too soon. There's another one, the day after tomorrow, on Thursday. How does that sound?'

'I could do both.' Lachlan nodded in response to the producer, who had signalled that they were ready to start filming again. 'I'm planning to head back to the Cotswolds this evening,' he told Jennifer. 'I may as well

stay for a few days and get things really rolling. Can I leave that with you?'

'Absolutely. I'm sure they'll be delighted to get things started and short notice shouldn't be a problem because they're planning to film any sessions there for anyone who can't make themselves available. You're okay with that?'

Lachlan nodded. He was obviously going to have to get used to having cameras around more often.

'Do you want to make yourself available for surgeries as well?'

He nodded again.

'Mr McKendry? Are you ready?' The documentary crew was waiting for him.

'I am indeed,' he responded.

He was ready for anything. Including an incredibly busy schedule with all the extra commitments being arranged and spending a lot more time in his childhood home. He was, in fact, looking forward to being there more than he had done in...well...decades. Probably not since those first school holidays when he'd been released from boarding school and would be filled with hope that being back in his beloved woodland would instantly make his world much closer to perfect.

Lachlan had long ago given up believing in fairy tales where a magic wand could be waved or a magic place could provide an escape from reality. Hope had given way to acceptance of the way things were by the time he'd been about Dexter's age and that had been followed by a determination to create his own world.

One that he could control. One that could provide all the happiness he needed.

He sat back at his desk and tipped his head back a little, closing his eyes as he felt the brush of the sound technician's fingers as she clipped on his lapel microphone again.

The sooner this interview was finished and he could get on the road, the better. Maybe that was why he felt as if he was looking forward to heading home so much. Except that getting to the end of this protracted business of filming didn't explain the frisson of something that was rather more than simply anticipation of an escape. Something that he'd seen in Dexter's face only minutes ago. Something that he hadn't been aware of feeling himself in such a very, very long time.

It felt remarkably like hope…

There was something magic about this place.

The stunning view from the suite of rooms that Lady Josephine McKendry occupied in the north-facing upper rooms of the manor house would never get old, Felicity Stephens decided as she took a moment to soak it in. Close to the house, the pebbled pathways were straight lines between neatly trimmed box hedging. Then there were formal gardens and what looked like acres of lawn surrounded by the woodlands that Flick hadn't yet had time to explore, but she could feel the pull towards that fairy tale forest more strongly every time she looked out of these windows.

That echo of Lachlan's voice she heard every time she did so was also gaining strength.

'I guess I know every square inch of this patch of woodlands we own. It's the most beautiful place in the world...'

Was it weird that the pull of that timeless, mysterious woodland in combination with a remembered snatch of conversation could create a twist in her gut that felt like desire? Longing, anyway, although she wasn't sure what it was that was making its absence felt so poignantly. Maybe she was just finally becoming aware of the loneliness that came with her chosen lifestyle.

'What are you looking at, Felicity? You're not getting paid to stand around staring into space, I'll have you know.'

Flick had had two days of practice dealing with Lady Josephine's acerbic comments and had found a strategy that was working well. She simply ignored *what* was being said in favour of trying to interpret *why*.

'Do you need some help getting dressed, Lady Josephine?'

'Don't be ridiculous. I'm not a child.'

The older woman emerged from her en suite bathroom already dressed in what appeared to be her uniform of a tweed skirt, stockings and sensible shoes, a pastel-coloured twinset and a string of pearls. Except that the pearls were still in her hands.

'There's something wrong with the catch,' she said.

'Let me try.' Flick took the necklace, noting the slight tremble in Lady Josephine's hands that was probably why she hadn't been able to fasten the catch. It could also be an early sign of her blood sugar level dropping. Flick bit back a smile. She certainly couldn't rely on ir-

ritability being another sign, could she? 'Right…that's got it. Let's test your BGL again.'

'There's nothing wrong with it. I'm not dizzy. I don't have any pins and needles in my hands or feet. And my speech is perfectly coherent.' Lady Josephine walked into her sitting room to sit on an upright chair beside a small table. 'I've had my tablets and my insulin already. I would rather be left alone to get on with my crossword puzzle, thank you.'

'Sometimes it's a good idea to find out if blood sugar levels are falling before you have a full-blown hypogly-caemic episode and end up unconscious on the floor.' Flick wasn't about to be dismissed. She unzipped the small case that held the blood glucose meter, lancets, alcohol wipes and test strips. 'Besides, we talked about this yesterday when your doctor came to visit. It's the new plan designed to see if we can get better control of your diabetes.'

'A plan that's intended to prove I'm incompetent, you mean.' Lady Josephine glared at Flick. 'This is Lachlan's idea, isn't it? He had no right to arrange that doctor's visit behind my back. He wants to see me locked up in some old people's home, doesn't he?'

'Quite the opposite.' Flick held Lady Josephine's finger steady as she pressed the lancet to pierce the skin. Then she used the alcohol wipe again, to discard the first drop of blood that appeared, holding the test strip ready to catch the next drop. 'He wants you to get good control of all your medical issues so that you can get back to things you enjoy. Like walking? Tilly told me that you used to love walking your dog.'

'The dog died,' Lady Josephine snapped. 'And exercise gives me asthma these days, anyway. And angina.'

'It's actually been proven to help strengthen your cardiovascular system. In the long term, it will make it less likely that you'll get attacks of either asthma or angina.'

The chat she'd had with the GP at the end of his visit yesterday had been quite revealing.

'I'm not convinced she does get angina,' he'd told Flick. 'She's refused to have a stress test or even a twelve lead ECG done. It could be asthma but, to be honest, apart from one incident quite a while ago, it's never been severe enough to need anything more than the occasional use of her bronchodilator. I've never needed to put her on steroids. The diabetes is more of a problem but whether it's genuinely brittle or simply the result of poor control or a non-compliant patient is probably something we need to find out.'

Flick made a note of the current reading on the monitor.

'What is it?'

'Just a bit on the high side.'

'So I should have had more insulin. I told you that when we did the test before breakfast.'

'It's not high enough to be a problem,' Flick said. 'But we're going to test a lot more often for the next few days.' She held on to the monitor. Her next job today was to go through the saved data in the device and see if she could find any patterns. She was going to start a meticulous food diary for Lady Josephine, too. 'Did you understand everything the doctor was saying about it?'

'I'm not an imbecile.'

Flick smiled. 'When I was training, it took me a bit of time to get my head around things like the dawn phenomenon and the rebound effect that too much insulin can cause and—'

But Lady Josephine was holding up her hand. 'Do stop prattling. Why don't you make yourself useful, instead? Put that dressing gown away and then take that breakfast tray downstairs. Goodness knows what Mrs Tillman's doing but it's obviously not what she's *supposed* to be doing.'

Being a personal servant had never been part of Flick's job description but she wasn't going to let it bother her any more than an unpleasant personality she suspected was a defensive shield Lady Josephine had perfected.

Her dog would have loved her no matter what she was like with people.

How much of a loss had that been?

'I do think we should get some gentle exercise into your daily routine,' she said calmly, as she picked up the discarded dressing gown. 'I can come with you, in my professional capacity, and we can deal with anything that might happen in the way of asthma or angina. I'd love to see more of your gardens.'

'If I want your opinion, I'll ask for it.'

Flick could hear the snappy words coming through the bedroom door but they were easy to ignore as she looked for an appropriate place to hang the dressing gown. It was tempting to leave it on the end of the bed but more intriguing to have a peek into what seemed to be a dressing room beside the bathroom and, when

she did, her jaw dropped. Like two sides of a coin, this huge, walk-in wardrobe had an astonishing dividing line. On one side were all the dull skirts and twinsets, sensible shoes and dressy suits. On the other side, muted only slightly by plastic dust covers, was an astonishing number of dresses in every shade of the rainbow. *Ball gowns?*

Still blinking, Flick went back into the sitting room. She opened her mouth to ask about those dresses but Lady Josephine had opened the newspaper to the crossword puzzle page and gave the distinct impression that she would not appreciate being interrupted so Flick changed her mind and picked up the breakfast tray instead.

Timing, she reminded herself, could be everything.

Flick's fork made a loud clatter on the flagstones when she dropped it in surprise at Lachlan's unexpected entrance into the kitchen that evening.

'Sorry… I didn't mean to give you a fright.'

He stooped to pick up the fork at the same time that Flick reached for it, which meant they were suddenly rather too close to each other. At the same moment, they caught each other's gazes and, for a heartbeat, and then another, it seemed that they were both caught— unable to break that contact. He had given her a fright, Flick decided. That was why her heart was beating hard enough to probably be visible. She grabbed the fork and straightened.

'You shouldn't sneak up on me like that,' she told

him. 'Next time I might keep hold of my fork and use it to protect myself from intruders.'

He was grinning. 'I'll get you a clean one in that case. May as well cut the infection risk.' He turned away, but not before Flick had discovered it wasn't possible to not return a smile like that.

'I'll get myself one, too,' he said. 'That looks like one of Tilly's exceptionally good shepherd's pies and I'm hungry enough to eat a horse.' He opened a drawer and picked up some fresh cutlery and then got a plate from a cupboard. 'I'm sorry I didn't give you any warning that I was coming. It was a last-minute decision in a crazy-busy day. I'm involved in filming a documentary and it seems to take an inordinate amount of time to rehearse and then film and then do it again if necessary. I've been tripping over cables and having my nose powdered all day.'

Flick accepted the clean fork. She loved eating her dinner, alone at the table, in this gorgeous old kitchen. Mrs Tillman always left something delicious in the oven after taking Lady Josephine's tray to her room, and Flick would come and help herself after she'd written up her notes on her patient, showered and changed out of the tidy skirt, blouse and cardigan she was wearing as a uniform into casual jeans and a soft, comfortable sweatshirt.

The kitchen had instantly become her favourite room of the house and, because it was where she'd shared that dinner with Lachlan on her first night here, it was easy to feel like there was always an echo of him in the room. Having the real thing here, unexpectedly, was

taking a bit of getting used to. The kitchen seemed to have suddenly come to life in such a dramatic way that colours seemed brighter. There was more warmth coming from the Aga and even the smell and taste of the food was heightened.

Lachlan had heaped his plate with the savoury mince and its mashed potato topping. Then his chair scraped as he pushed it back on the flagstones and leapt up to stride towards the huge fridge. He had to hunt for a few seconds before coming back with a bottle of tomato sauce.

'Don't tell Tilly,' he said. 'She'd be horrified I still do this. She let me do it when I was a kid but told me never to do it in polite company.'

Flick laughed. 'Who said I was polite?' She reached for the bottle as Lachlan put it down. 'Might just try this myself. I always had a bucket of it to dip my chips into. Hot chips, not crisps,' she added.

'Oh, that's right. Australians are like Americans and call crisps "chips" as well, don't they?'

'Mmm…' Flick shook the bottle and then squeezed it. This was weird, but it felt as if she'd been sharing food with Lachlan McKendry all her life.

And, maybe it was because of that feeling of being so comfortable in his company that made it seem that they would never run out of things to talk about, especially when Flick was genuinely interested in everything Lachlan was telling her about. Like the documentary that was following children and teenagers who were facing big physical challenges.

'When will it be on TV?'

'Not for ages, I expect. They'll need to follow Dex-

ter for at least six months after his surgery to see how well he learns to use the new nerves and the amazing difference it will make to his face…and his life.'

Those last words were so quiet that it seemed that Lachlan hadn't intended them to be heard and there was something in his expression that actually gave Flick a lump in her throat.

'You know that, don't you? It will make that much difference.'

Lachlan's face was still now and his gaze was steady. 'It's what I do,' was all he said.

Oh…*wow*…

There was no arrogance in that statement or what it implied. None of the over-confident or superficial gloss that she had assumed went hand in hand with the charm that had put her off when she'd first met Lachlan. That kind of confidence could only come from knowing exactly how good he was at what he did and the unguarded depth Flick could see in those dark eyes made it equally obvious how much he cared about what he did. She'd already had a glimpse of the real person this man was but this…

This was impressive enough to wake up way more than any brain cells. Enough to send a chill down her spine to trickle into every other cell in her body. It was just…incredibly sexy, that was what it was.

And disturbing…because it was an attraction that went deeper than something purely physical.

Flick didn't want to be attracted to Lachlan. She especially didn't want to recognise a soul that was even more attractive than the body that carried it. She hadn't

expected to meet someone who could stir feelings like this again. She'd had years of being convinced that her ability to even fall in love had died along with the man she'd considered to be the love of her life. The one she'd chosen to marry and be the father of her children. Any dreams of creating her own family had also been buried back then and it had been a hard-won battle to come to terms with that and find peace with what her life had to offer.

It felt like that peace had just been broken. Like a stone thrown into a still pond, there had been an initial splash and now there were ripples forming. Tiny waves spreading that threatened to undermine the foundations of the new life Flick had created for herself in the last few years.

She didn't dare look directly at Lachlan as he told her that he had lectures and training sessions in the area and that he would be staying in the house for the next few days. Luckily, she had finished her dinner so she could excuse herself.

'I should go upstairs and see Lady Josephine,' she told him. 'We're doing more frequent BGL measurements and I want to collect her tray and see how much she's eaten. I'm keeping a food diary, which I'll track along with her glucose levels in the hope that we can get better control of her diabetes.'

This was good. Even mentioning Lachlan's mother was enough to create a very safe, professional boundary. Good grief…even acknowledging an attraction to her client's son was just as bad as the way Lachlan had

been flirting when he'd found her on his doorstep the other day.

'Sounds good.' Lachlan was reaching for another helping of the shepherd's pie. 'I've got some work I have to get done this evening before my first lecture in Cheltenham tomorrow but please tell her I'll pop in and see her in the morning before I leave.'

'Sure.'

Flick put her plate and cutlery into the dishwasher. She was finding her own control now and it was no problem to find a smile for Lachlan as she left the kitchen. She didn't need to worry about her peace being too disturbed. Ripples from even a boulder being thrown into calm water eventually subsided to leave stillness in their wake again.

She just needed to wait.

Oh…and it might be a good idea to avoid the disruption of anything else like that being thrown in her direction but if it happened again, at least it wouldn't take her by such surprise.

If she was alert, in fact, she might be able to deflect them before they even landed. Because she didn't want to feel those kinds of things. Not again. They were too intense. And, no matter how seductive they might be, they carried the very real danger of being too painful to make them worthwhile.

CHAPTER FOUR

As HE'D REMINDED Tilly when he'd come home to start sorting out the problem with his mother, this kitchen had always been the place Lachlan had found the most homely in the McKendry family's historic manor house. The only place ever that had the magic mix of warmth and welcome and safety, despite anything else that might be happening in the world, that only a real home could provide.

But it was also a place that Lachlan didn't feel like he'd ever quite belonged, no matter how much he would have liked to. Maybe that was because it had never been a place he was supposed to be in. It had been for the cook, when they'd had one, and any other servants employed in the house to help Tilly. He'd never eaten anything other than a treat like a slice of cake or biscuits fresh from the oven at this kitchen table when he'd been a child and the scenario would have been even more unlikely as an adult coming back to visit his parents. The idea of his mother eating in here was unimaginable but that had nothing to do with the reason he'd started

avoiding this room himself as he'd got old enough to make his own rules.

No… As Lachlan walked towards the kitchen, having driven up from London again, he was realising that he had probably unconsciously avoided this part of the house for so many years because it tapped into that happy/sad feeling that was so disturbing. A feeling that he'd been aware of more often in the last few days—ever since Felicity Stephens had crashed into his life, come to think of it. And, yes, 'crashed' was an appropriate word because it felt like something had been broken. The thing that had safely contained that feeling, perhaps?

Anyway…it occurred to him now that, if he wanted to fix whatever had been damaged enough to release unwelcome feelings, it might be necessary to find a way to identify exactly what it was, so he thought about it briefly as he passed the sweep of where the main staircase began in line with the doors to the formal drawing room. It was an unsuccessful process, however, because the feeling was too nebulous. Like a fragment of dream being chased after you'd woken up and the closest impression Lachlan could catch was that it felt like seeing the missing thing you'd been searching for forever at the precise moment it was vanishing from sight around a corner.

The happy part came from whatever it was that he'd caught sight of.

The sad part was because it vanished again, leaving a bereft certainty that it could never be captured.

He didn't bother turning his head to look through

the door into the formal dining room as he got to the point where the hallway narrowed as it led to the service areas of the house. He'd instinctively known that a meal with Flick at one end of the mahogany table that could seat twenty people would not have helped his quest in persuading her to stay and care for his mother. Tilly's fabulous meal in the comfort of the kitchen, along with that Australian wine, had been perfect—not only because Flick had decided to stay—and that shepherd's pie a couple of nights ago, even though it had been only the second meal he'd ever eaten either in the kitchen or with Flick, had made him feel as if he'd been doing it for ever.

As if…

As if there was a new dimension to what this heart of the house had to offer in the way of being homely.

'Perfect timing,' Flick said as he entered the kitchen. 'You have a knack of arriving when dinner is ready.'

Her welcoming smile only deepened the thought that was still lingering in Lachlan's head. That he'd missed something along the way. That this genuinely *was* home and it had been a mistake to avoid it for so long. He'd eaten out in a prestigious, local restaurant last night with some of the senior doctors from both the Cheltenham Central and Gloucester General hospitals who had invited Lachlan to lead the plastic surgery component of the postgraduate training course being offered and it had been a delicious meal, but he was actually looking forward to Tilly's cooking tonight even more. Like her roast chicken, perhaps?

Or…

'What is that?' He stared at the dish on the table.

'Asparagus quiche.' Flick already had a segment on her plate and she was adding some salad. 'Your mother requested a light dinner and agreed that keeping a food diary is a good incentive to make some healthy changes here and there.' There was a twinkle in those astonishingly blue eyes that made it impossible not to smile at her. 'Although what she actually said was more along the lines of, "I don't suppose I can stop you if you're so determined to be the food and calorie police".' Flick was grinning back at Lachlan. 'Grab a plate. It smells great.'

'Hmm.' Lachlan headed for the cupboard but paused to lift the lid of a crockery bread bin to release the scent of a freshly baked loaf. He was smiling as he put the breadboard, loaf, knife and a big pat of butter onto the table but then he paused again, his smile fading.

'You're…um…wearing a uniform.'

A smart uniform, he had to admit, with what seemed to be a very stylish kind of clinically white tunic with a side fastening of buttons and a softly curved V-neck that was outlined with a dark navy blue that matched her trousers.

'I always do,' Flick told him. 'I hadn't brought it with me when I came here because I packed in a hurry and I wasn't sure I was going to take the position anyway but I've had some of my stuff sent from London so I can look more professional. Your mother approves. I would normally get changed before dinner but I got too hungry.'

Lachlan approved as well because it seemed to signal that Flick was settling into the position and wasn't

about to disappear. For a moment, he was tempted to say something along the lines of how much he also approved of women in uniform but he bit that back, knowing how unwelcome it would be. He, too, needed to be professional, he reminded himself as he sat down at the end of the table. He couldn't help another glance at Flick, however, as he sliced off a thick wedge of the bread.

She had her hair scraped back into a ponytail that was clipped up to the back of her head but there were strands of those blonde waves that were clearly determined to escape and Flick pushed one of them back and tucked it behind her ear as if she was aware of his gaze. Not that she looked up from her plate but just watching that deft movement of her fingers and the odd notion that he could feel that touch himself was enough to make Lachlan search for a distraction.

'How's it going?' he asked. 'With my mother?'

'I think our plan to test her BGL more often and take precise notes of any food intake is paying off. Her levels have been steadier than they have been for a while.'

'That's great.'

'On the other side of the equation, though, I'm not making much progress in the plan to get her exercising more. She hasn't even come downstairs in the few days I've been here already and Tilly tells me she hasn't set foot outside the house in months. And, before that, it was only to take the dog out. I offered to go with her, in case it brings on her asthma or angina, but she…um… wasn't keen on that idea.'

'Bit your head off, huh?' Lachlan shook his head.

'Dogs and biting. It's what I've been talking about all day.'

'Oh?'

'I had a session at a private hospital in Gloucester and one at Cheltenham Central this afternoon. It's post-graduate surgical training that's intended to incorporate plastic surgery techniques into other areas of paediatrics where applicable.'

'But…dogs?'

'Children are the main victims of dog attacks and the injuries can be horrendous. It's not always possible to transfer them to a specialist paediatric trauma centre like my London base at St Bethel's Hospital and, sometimes, the wounds aren't serious enough to warrant that so advanced techniques in debridement and suturing are something all surgeons are keen on learning.'

'I can imagine.'

Flick was holding his gaze now, clearly interested in what he was telling her. Because this was a professional discussion and that gave her permission to let her guard down? Thank goodness he hadn't made some stupid, flirtatious remark about how good she looked in her uniform. As if it made any difference, anyway. Flick would still look gorgeous if she was wearing a sack.

Or nothing at all…

Hastily, Lachlan dropped his gaze to his meal and focused on his food, Until he could sense a growing tension in the air. At least he knew how to defuse that now.

'Dog bites are very challenging injuries for plastic surgeons,' he told Flick. 'And more than half the cases involve the face. A dog doesn't just bite, either—it tends

to clamp its jaws and then shake its head. A puncture wound can become a combination of crush, laceration and tear injuries, sometimes with a fracture to complicate things even further.'

Flick's eyes had widened. 'Maybe I won't suggest that we get your mother a new dog, then, to encourage her to exercise.'

Lachlan laughed. 'Our lovely old golden retrievers wouldn't have hurt a fly. Brie was the last one and she got to the grand old age of seventeen. I don't imagine her walks with my mother in recent times would have been exactly strenuous exercise.' He ate a last bite of his quiche. 'She used to be as fit as a fiddle. She was a competitive ballroom dancer in her youth.'

'Oh…that explains the dresses.'

'What dresses?'

'In her wardrobe. I was putting her dressing gown away and one side of the wardrobe is full of amazing-looking dresses. I thought they must be ballgowns but now that I think about it, they were too short for that and it makes sense. Wow…she must have done a lot of dancing.'

'She taught it. That was how she met my father. She came here to give him private lessons in the ballroom, apparently.'

Flick's jaw had dropped. 'You have a *ballroom*?'

'Have you not gone exploring?'

She shook her head but then one side of her mouth curled into a hint of a cheeky grin. 'I wanted to,' she admitted, 'but it felt a bit like snooping. And Tilly said

that most of the house is shut up because it's never used and it's too expensive to heat.'

The idea that he could give Flick something that she'd just admitted she wanted was enough to make Lachlan feel inordinately pleased with himself.

'Shut up, maybe, but it's not locked up. Have you had enough to eat?'

'Yes, thanks…why?'

'I'll give you the grand tour.' Lachlan got to his feet. 'Now?'

'Well, having a look at the gardens and the blue-bell woods might need to wait for daylight but we have plenty of lights in the house. Unless you've got something else you'd rather be doing?'

'Are you kidding? I'd love to.'

Oh…that *smile*… It didn't just light up a room. It made the entire world a brighter place. It made Lachlan believe that there was joy to be found in the most unexpected places. That simply being in Felicity Stephens' company was a delight and that she would be up for all kinds of adventure. Fun with a capital *F*.

He didn't take her upstairs because that was mainly just bedrooms and bathrooms other than his mother's larger suite that Flick was already familiar with. Going up to the old servants' quarters in the attics would be fun but probably too dusty and potentially badly lit. There was more than enough to show her on the ground floor, anyway, like the formal dining room not far from the kitchen and then the enormous drawing room that had the conservatory at the other end.

There was his father's study that looked as if it hadn't

been touched since his death, the library with its leather armchairs and walls of books that actually had the original ladders needed to get to the higher shelves, the gallery with McKendry portraits that went back several hundred years, and finally the ballroom with its magnificent parquet flooring, ornate plaster ceiling and the wall of arched windows that looked out onto the terrace and gardens like the formal drawing room. The chandeliers still glittered despite probably more than a decade of gathered dust and the look on Flick's face was one of absolute awe.

'I feel like I've got a part in some period drama.' She was almost whispering. 'I'm actually wearing a big, boofy dress and, any moment now, the orchestra is going to let rip with something like "The Blue Danube".'

'Classic.' Lachlan smiled.

He walked towards a cabinet near the main doors to the room. 'There was a state-of-the-art sound system installed in here just before my father died. I wonder if it still works after all this time.' He switched it on, watched the chosen disc with its classic waltz music slide into place and then adjusted the volume controls as the first notes of the violins came through the dozens of speakers that had been discreetly placed to provide surround sound that was so good it felt like the room had an invisible, full symphony orchestra in attendance. Seeing the delight on Flick's face, Lachlan turned the volume up a bit more before walking back to her. He twirled his hand, gave a bow and then straightened to offer his hand.

'May I have the pleasure of this dance, Mademoiselle?'

Flick just laughed. 'I can't dance to save myself,' she said.

'And I was required to learn when I was seven years old,' Lachlan responded. 'This will be a good test of how good I still am at leading.'

He could see her hesitating so he held her gaze and hoped that she would understand that this might not be professional but he wasn't hitting on her, he was offering her an insight into who he was. The things that had shaped him into the man he was today. He wanted her to know who he really was, he realised—as a person and not her employer. In the same way that he wanted to get to know who the real Felicity Stephens was and why she chose to live her life in the way she did, without any solid roots in a particular place or lifestyle, which was pretty much the opposite of what Lachlan had always been expected to embrace.

It was unlikely that Flick could read anything below the surface, of course, but whatever it was she saw in his eyes, it was enough to make her shake her head but keep smiling. Even better, it was enough to persuade her to take his hand.

'Okay…put your left hand on the top of my arm, keep hold of my right hand and here we go…' He kept his movements in slow motion as he directed her. 'Step back with your right foot, sideways with your left foot and then close the gap with your right foot.'

There was fierce concentration on Flick's face as she followed his instructions and she managed to reverse the movements of the basic box step to start by

going forward with her left foot. By the time they had repeated the move slowly a few times, it felt like she was getting the hang of it.

It also felt like the warmth of Flick's skin was starting to burn Lachlan's hands. He only had his hand loosely against her back but he was acutely aware of every movement of her muscles and that heat and her softness and it seemed to be seeping into every cell of his own body.

'You're doing great,' he told her. 'Let's see if we can actually do it in time with the music, shall we?'

It wasn't a huge increase in speed but it was enough to confuse Flick completely. She stepped on his toes, used the wrong feet, swore several times and finally started laughing helplessly.

Lachlan was still holding her hand. He still had his other hand on the small of her back but they weren't stepping in any direction. Flick felt like she was melting in his arms as she laughed but then she got control of herself and looked up at him.

'Sorry...but I did warn you...'

'You did.' He was smiling down at her. He wanted to tell her that she didn't need to apologise. That his toes would recover in no time and he'd actually enjoyed this impromptu—albeit unsuccessful—dance lesson.

And then he realised just *how* much he had enjoyed it.

How much he was loving the feel of this woman between his hands.

And time seemed to stop right about then because they were still holding each other's gazes and it was one

of those moments that was a tipping point and Lachlan knew exactly which way it could tip. He only needed to see the slightest hint of an invitation and he would be kissing this gorgeous, vibrant woman.

The romantic music was still filling the room but somehow they both heard another sound and it was only then that they both discovered they were being watched. How long had his mother, with her dressing gown tied tightly around her waist, been standing there in the open doors that led to the main hallway of the house?

Shocked, Lachlan moved swiftly to turn off the music. Flick was looking just as shocked, nervous even, as silence fell and rapidly deepened in the wake of the music being cut. It was Flick who had the courage to speak first, however.

'You came downstairs,' she said.

'Obviously,' Lady Josephine snapped. 'Seeing that you didn't answer your pager, I decided I'd have to find out for myself what was going on with all the lights on and that loud music.'

'Oh, no...' Flick looked horrified now. 'I must have left my pager in the kitchen.'

'Sorry, Mother,' Lachlan said.

Had she seen that he'd been seriously thinking about kissing her private nurse? Would that be enough, without the disturbance of the music, to use this as an excuse to fire Flick? That would send him back to square one in his attempt to make life easier for both of them just when he was starting to feel like his life was under better control?

'We didn't mean to disturb you,' he added, his gaze

sliding briefly sideways to catch Flick's. 'It won't happen again.'

'You've always managed to create a disturbance
without trying,' his mother said. But it was Flick she
was staring at. 'You can't dance,' she said. 'I've always
considered that an appalling lack in any young woman.'

Flick's huff of breath sounded more amused than
incredulous. 'Lachlan tells me that you used to be a
dance teacher,' she said. 'Maybe I've come to the right
place, then?'

Lady Josephine turned away but Lachlan was quite
sure he heard her muttered words.

'Maybe you have.'

It had been a real risk being that cheeky to her client
but, at the time, Flick hadn't given it a second thought.
As she went after Lady Josephine to offer help in getting back up the stairs, she realised that part of her
might have actually been hoping that she would get
fired on the spot.

Because she deserved to be?

If they hadn't been interrupted at that point in time,
Flick knew that she would have ended up kissing Lachlan McKendry. She might not want to be attracted to
this man but wishing it away was never going to work.
Worse, in that moment, she'd had the distinct impression
that Lachlan was equally attracted to her. And, when
he'd looked at her as he'd told his mother that it wasn't
going to happen again, she'd also realised that he didn't
want anything to be that disturbed—including her role
as Lady Josephine's carer.

It had felt like a tacit agreement that, yes, there was attraction there, but nothing was going to happen. And that was fine by her. But Lady Josephine was still obviously highly irritated by the incident, judging by her curt refusal of assistance from Flick and the speed with which she started going up the sweeping staircase. She stopped when she got to the landing, however, and Flick caught up with her as she clutched the bannister with one hand and put the other to the centre of her chest.

'What is it?' Flick asked instantly. 'Are you having trouble breathing?'

'No…it's my chest… Pain…'

Flick took hold of her arm. 'Sit down. Here, on the stairs.'

'What's going on?' Lachlan was walking out of the ballroom and had paused at the foot of the staircase. He came up the stairs two at a time when he saw Flick helping his mother to sit down.

'Chest pain,' she said quietly.

'Show me where,' Lachlan demanded. 'Does it go anywhere else? Like into your arm?'

Lady Josephine shook her head.

'How bad is the pain? On a scale of one to ten with one being no pain and ten being the worst you can think of?'

'…nine…'

'Right.' Lachlan scooped his mother into his arms.

'Put me *down*,' she demanded.

'Nope. I'm not about to let you go off to your room and die from a heart attack. I'm taking you to hospital.'

He looked back as he started down the stairs. 'Flick, could you go and grab Mother's GTN spray? And then come with us, please? There's no time to wait for an ambulance to get here from Cheltenham and I'll need someone else in the car.'

He didn't need to say that he might need help if this escalated into something as serious as cardiac arrest. 'Of course.'

'I do *not* want to go to hospital,' Lady Josephine said. 'You can't do this, Lachlan. I won't allow it.'

Lachlan shook his head. 'We're going to get you properly checked this time. And, Flick?'

She paused at the top of the stairs. She could see the real concern in Lachlan's face. There was no way his mother was going to persuade him to let her stay at home and she liked how much he obviously cared.

'What is it?'

'Could we take your car, please? There's not much of a back seat in mine.'

The back seat of the Volkswagen Beetle wasn't that much bigger than Lachlan's sports car but Flick was small enough to be able to sit beside Lady Josephine as they sped towards the nearest hospital. It made more sense for Lachlan to drive, anyway, seeing as he knew these narrow, country roads far better than she did. She kept her fingers on Lady Josephine's pulse, which was a little rapid but steady, and she was watching carefully for any signs of deterioration.

'Has your spray made any difference?'

'No.'

'We'll try another dose in a few minutes, then.' Being

unresponsive to the medication could mean that this was more than an episode of angina but Lady Josephine didn't seem to be showing any other signs that she could be suffering a heart attack. Her skin was warm and not clammy and she wasn't unduly distressed.

'You're not feeling like you might be sick, are you?' Flick asked.

'No. I've told you, I don't need to go to hospital. I'm in my dressing gown, for heaven's sake. How embarrassing is this?'

The triage nurse in the emergency department could see how embarrassed her new patient was. 'You're in exactly the right place, Mrs McKendry. Sorry, Lady McKendry. It's very important to get something like chest pain looked at. We're going to get you into a private cubicle now and get a monitor on to see what's happening to your heart.'

Apparently, there was nothing abnormal happening. Flick was standing at the foot of the bed as the consultant was talking quietly to Lachlan a short time later.

'There's no sign of any ST depression. Or anything else that would concern me on her twelve lead ECG. Your mother's in great shape for her age.'

'But she had chest pain after climbing stairs. She does suffer from angina.'

'I can't see any confirmation of that diagnosis in her notes. She did come in for an asthma attack a while back. Perhaps it's chest tightness that's being interpreted as pain?'

'That's possible.'

'If so, that doesn't seem to be a concern at the mo-

ment, either. Her oxygen saturation on room air is normal and she's not showing any signs of respiratory distress, apart from hyperventilating a bit when she first arrived.'

'I'll talk to her,' Lachlan said. 'Or maybe it would be better coming from you. You might be able to persuade her to have a proper investigation, like an exercise stress test.'

'I'll see what I can do. Oh…and thanks again for your lecture today. I found it extremely educational.'

Lady Josephine wasn't about to agree to any investigations. 'I'm absolutely fine. Take me home, Lachlan. Now, thank you.'

A nurse found a wheelchair to take Lady Josephine out to the car. Flick was astonished at the smile she offered Lachlan.

'Good to see you again,' she murmured. 'Give me a call sometime?'

'Friend of yours?' Flick asked as she pushed the wheelchair out of the cubicle. She'd been more than astonished by the blatant flirting of that nurse, if she was honest. She was aware of a nasty little flash of something that felt almost like jealousy.

'Never seen her before in my life.' Lachlan sounded bemused enough to be believable.

They'd parked her car illegally in one of the on-call doctors' car-parking slots in the ambulance bay but, because the consultant had recognised Lachlan as a visiting specialist, nobody had asked for it to be moved.

There was someone else waiting to use the parking

slot, though he didn't seem annoyed when he saw Lachlan opening the driver's door.

'Thanks, Josh,' he called. 'No time now but we really need to catch up soon.'

Lachlan shook his head as he shut his door. 'Weird,' he muttered. 'You'd think I'd been working here for years instead of it being my first visit to the ED.'

'First and last as far as I'm concerned,' his mother told him. She lapsed into silence after that for the trip home. She was sitting in the front passenger seat this time and Flick had insisted on being in the back.

'You'd be more squashed than an extra sardine,' she told Lachlan. 'You drive. That way we'll all get home faster. It's getting late and I'm sure your mother's very tired.'

She was tired herself but it only took looking away from the window to catch a glimpse of Lachlan's profile to give Flick the feeling that she wouldn't be falling asleep anytime soon tonight. Not if it was going to be as difficult as she suspected it would be to stop the whirl of thoughts clamouring to take priority in her head. That car crash of a dancing lesson, for example, and how Lachlan had made her laugh so much her knees had almost buckled. When had she last laughed like that?

Too long ago.

She was remembering, too, that look on his face of such deep concern for his mother. He cared so much and it broke her heart that his love did not seem to be reciprocated.

There were deeper thoughts that Flick knew were only waiting for solitude and darkness to surface and

take over completely. Like how delicious it had felt to have the touch of Lachlan's hands on her body.

And how disappointing it had been to have been so *almost* kissed...

CHAPTER FIVE

LISTENING TO 'THE BLUE DANUBE' as his silver Porsche ate up the miles between London and Gloucester was a choice that Lachlan would not have believed he would ever make but it was exactly what he needed after the action-packed day yesterday.

For future reference, it was useful to know just how much extra work it was to have a film crew in his operating theatre. It wasn't just the meticulous attention to guarding the sterility of the area, which meant that the cameras needed the same type of plastic covering that was in place on the overhead standing microscope that Lachlan would use for the intricate surgery needed to join nerves. There was also the need to explain every move he was making in layman's terms, even though they would probably only use a small clip of Dexter's actual nerve transfer surgery.

The initial incisions to access both the masseteric nerve and the buccal branch of the facial nerve were probably too gruesome to be seen by a potentially young or non-medical audience. Maybe they would choose to limit the coverage to what could be seen on the large

screen that showed the field Lachlan was viewing through the microscope as he used microsutures and fibrin glue to perform the coaptation of the nerve endings. Oh…he had remembered to explain that coaptation meant joining, hadn't he?

Lachlan let the music wash over the need to pick over everything he remembered about the surgery to search for anything he could have done better and he let go of it all after a brief mental review of the visit to Dexter this morning, which had also been filmed. He hadn't forgotten any necessary advice, he decided. He'd warned Dexter to avoid pressure to his cheek, exercise, lifting anything heavy and vigorous tooth brushing. He had his own doctors to watch over him until Lachlan saw him again, which meant he'd been free to move onto his next commitment, which was, coincidentally, another nerve transfer surgery he'd been invited to lead as a teaching demonstration at Gloucester General Hospital.

This afternoon, he was due to meet a team of orthopaedic and neurosurgeons and the head of paediatrics to discuss the case of a young boy who'd been left with nerve damage after breaking his collarbone that was seriously impacting his ability to use his arm.

At least he could use this short journey as a bit of time out. He'd slept well in his apartment last night so it had to have been the extra pressure of performing in front of cameras that had left him feeling so much more tired than usual. The enjoyment of feeling the power and responsiveness of this wonderful vehicle he was driving was also a boost and, with the delightful sound of the classical music surrounding him, Lachlan could

indulge for a while in what felt like the happiest place he could have found.

Except that wasn't quite true, was it? This music was reminding him of the sheer pleasure he'd found in having Flick in his arms the other night. A pleasure that he'd known was out of bounds. He hadn't needed his mother's arrival, just in time to make sure he didn't kiss Flick, to remind him of why she was there in the first place—and how desperately he needed her to stay there. The episode of angina, or asthma, or whatever it had been had given them all a bit of a fright but, on the positive side, it seemed that his mother now also re-alised how lucky they were to have Flick in the house.

Good grief...his mother was actually undertaking to teach Flick how to dance the waltz. Lachlan found himself smiling as he remembered the conversation that had taken place the day after that trip to the emergency department.

'What are you looking like that for, Felicity? It was you that said maybe you'd come to the right place, be-cause you found out I used to teach dance. It was also your idea that I should be getting some exercise and I'd rather be walking around in the ballroom than outside, getting rained on and dirty shoes.'

'I...um...guess it might be a useful thing to know how to do.'

'It's more than useful. It's simply good manners, as far as I'm concerned. Like knowing how to eat your soup correctly.'

The look Flick had sent in Lachlan's direction at that point had been priceless. She might as well have had a

bubble over her head like a cartoon character, saying 'There's a correct way to eat *soup*?'

Oh, yeah… They needed to have Felicity Stephens in that house. It was coming back to life. No… Lachlan couldn't remember it ever having the kind of life that seemed to be taking hold now. The kind that made him wish he'd already completed his afternoon appointment so that he could be heading home right now. Who knew—maybe Flick would encourage his mother to embrace life the way she did herself? To find some happiness, even?

Maybe the suggestion of getting another dog was worth thinking about as well? And if anyone could persuade his mother to take on a challenge like training a new pup, it would be Flick. After all, she'd practically goaded Lady Josephine into giving her dance lessons, hadn't she, and broken the barrier that had kept the older woman in her personal suite of rooms for months.

Lachlan's breath came out in a huff of laughter. How many times had she trodden on his mother's toes already?

No wonder London Locums considered her to be one of their best. Flick was more than simply an excellent nurse, she was capable of not only dealing with difficult patients but making real progress with their health issues. And she was absolutely professional at all times.

Well…almost all times. Perhaps dancing with your employer might be considered less than entirely professional but it wasn't as if she'd kissed him. She knew as well as he did that it would be crossing an unacceptable line.

What would his preferred choice really be, Lachlan mused as he turned off the motorway and took the route his sat nav was advising to get to Gloucester General Hospital—to keep Flick as a professional medical carer for his mother? Or to be free to kiss her senseless?

His sigh was resigned as he completed his journey and had to leave the cocoon of this glorious car and get back to the real world. He would choose both, of course, but, sadly, that wasn't an option.

'Hi,' he heard someone call. 'What are you doing out here?'

Lachlan was turning, his key in his hand so that he could press the control and double-check he'd locked his car. When he turned back, he couldn't see who the woman had been calling to and, oddly, she seemed to be looking at him. Was this going to turn into another one of those weird encounters like the ones he'd had in Cheltenham Central's emergency department the other evening?

'Hey… *Josh…?*'

Apparently it was.

'Oi!' the woman was shouting now. 'What's going on, Josh? Are you seriously just going to walk away from me?'

That did it. He'd had enough. He stopped and turned.

'What is it with people calling me *Josh*?' he demanded. 'It seems to happen everywhere I go around here. And who the hell are *you*?'

A very attractive woman, he realised as he spoke. She had wildly curly auburn hair and dark eyes and she looked…well, about as feisty as Flick. But she was

nothing like Flick, really, so noting her attraction was purely academic.

'My name's Stevie,' she told him. 'And I'm sorry I shouted at you like that but…but you look incredibly like a friend of mine. Someone who works here. I… thought he was ignoring me.'

'Ah…' Lachlan managed to find a hopefully polite smile. 'And this friend is called Josh, I take it?'

'Yes…'

'I'm Lachlan,' he said. 'Lachlan McKendry. If you work here, perhaps you can help? I'm heading for a meeting in the paediatric department.'

'Oh…of course. I've heard about you. You're the famous plastic surgeon.'

A random nurse in the car park knowing who he was was almost as disconcerting as being called by the wrong name. He didn't have the time to waste on something that was making the hairs prickle on the back of his neck, anyway. He turned towards the hospital buildings again.

'Wait…' Stevie sounded hesitant. 'I know this might sound totally crazy but…are you, by any chance, adopted?'

Lachlan could feel his jaw sagging. This was just getting weirder. 'Not that it's any of your business,' he said slowly. 'But, no, I'm not.'

'Sorry…it's just that you look so much like Josh, you could be brothers. Twins, even.'

That made him laugh but then he shook his head. 'Sounds like the stuff of fairy tales. If you'll excuse me, I don't want to be late for my meeting.'

'I know exactly where you need to be,' Stevie said. 'Follow me.'

She led him rapidly through hospital corridors and up flights of stairs but when she finally opened a door and held it for him, he found himself somewhere he couldn't have dreamed of expecting. He was on the roof of the hospital. This was getting beyond weird.

'What's going on…?'

'Wait here.' Stevie's voice suggested he would be wise to do what he was told. 'Trust me, please…there's someone you have to meet before you do anything else. He's the head of the paediatric department so it's who you've come here to see anyway, but…' She shook her head as though it was going to take too much time to explain. 'I'll be back in a few minutes and then you'll understand why this is so important.'

He could have simply ignored her instruction, followed her back into the stairwell and found his own way to the paediatric department but…there was something in her tone and body language that made him feel curiously on edge. As if something major was about to happen in his life. If nothing else, a few minutes in the fresh air might let him regain his balance and, as far as hospital roofs went, this was an interesting place. It seemed to have been taken over by raised garden beds that looked like they were full of vegetables. Some of the planters had sizeable trees in them and there were seats dotted around, giving the impression that this might be a place that hospital staff came for some time out. To have lunch, maybe?

He was still admiring the layout when Stevie reappeared with someone following her.

That was when weird became spooky.

Lachlan was watching a mirror image of himself walking towards him. Same height. Same hair. Same *nose*...

'Josh?' Stevie was looking up at her companion. 'This is Lachlan McKendry. Lachlan, this is Josh Stanmore. Um... I thought it might be a good idea if you two had a bit of time before your meeting.'

Lachlan couldn't say anything. Neither, apparently, could Josh, until he responded to Stevie asking whether he wanted her to stay. Seconds later, they were alone, still staring at each other, and Lachlan had the impression that Josh knew exactly how he was feeling. That maybe his world was spinning off its axis enough to make him feel that he was about to fall.

'Come...let's sit down.'

They went to one of the wooden benches between the gardens, sat down and then stared at each other again. As strangers, it should have been incredibly rude. Instead, it felt as natural as breathing.

'Where were you born?' Josh asked.

'Cheltenham.'

'Me, too. When?'

Lachlan named the year and month and day of his birth and watched colour drain from Josh's face. His words were no more than a whisper.

'Same...'

'I don't understand.'

'I think I might.' Josh closed his eyes and took a deep breath. 'I'm adopted.'

'But I'm not.' Lachlan shook his head. 'Why would my mother have given one of her babies up for adoption? My father told me once that they'd been trying to have a baby for years. That he was the happiest man in the world to finally have a son and heir. My mother would have done anything to keep him happy and surely giving him *two* sons would have been even better?' His head was spinning even faster now. 'The only way it could make sense was if she didn't know.'

Josh frowned. 'I don't understand. How could she not know she was pregnant with twins? They had pre-natal medicine and ultrasound back then.'

'Maybe she was told one of her twins had died. Maybe somebody *stole* you.'

Lachlan knew he was staring again but this was beyond huge. He had a *brother*. He could have had a companion for the whole of that long and lonely childhood. Someone to share the fear of being sent away to boarding school. Someone to help him build those secret places in the woods. Someone who could have made everything so much better. He had a lump in his throat that was impossible to swallow and his voice was raw.

'I'll find out,' he promised. He pulled his phone from his pocket. 'Give me your number and I'll get in touch as soon as I can.'

'Let's meet again.' Josh nodded. 'But not here. I'll give you my address as well. This is going to break the hospital grapevine as far as gossip goes so we'll need to decide how we're going to handle it.'

'But we have a meeting.' Lachlan checked his watch. 'It should have started five minutes ago.'

'I'll go and postpone it. Toby's surgery isn't urgent and I doubt that either of us would be able to focus right now so it would be a complete waste of time for everybody involved.'

It took only a minute to exchange details.

'Can you find your own way out?' Josh asked. 'It might be better if we're not seen together yet.'

'Agreed. It was lucky your girlfriend found me in the car park and brought me up here.'

'Stevie's just a good friend,' Josh said. 'But you're right. She's bought us some private time to get a handle on this and find out what actually happened. I guess your mother might be the only one who knows the truth.'

Lachlan could hear the grim note in his own voice. 'We'll soon find out.'

'One-forty over ninety.' Flick removed the earpieces of her stethoscope and hooked it around her neck. 'That's not bad, Lady Josephine. Your GP will be pleased to hear that your blood pressure's down a bit. Now, it's nearly time to check your blood sugar and—'

The interruption as the door of the sitting room burst open without warning gave both women a fright. Flick's immediate concern was for her patient's blood pressure but then she turned towards the door and that changed into concern for Lachlan.

He looked nothing like the confident man who was in control of his world that she'd met on the doorstep

when she'd arrived at this house but it wasn't that she was getting a glimpse of the man who was hidden beneath that image. Or maybe she was. This was Lachlan upset. Thrown off balance for some reason and… angry? His words were measured but, yes…they were coming from a place that was raw.

'I want…the *truth*…'

It was probably only Flick who could hear the raggedness of the breath that Lady Josephine sucked in. It was hardly surprising that the automatic defence of being acerbic was used.

'What on earth are you talking about, Lachlan? And what do you think you're doing, coming in here without being polite enough to even knock? The truth about *what*, exactly?'

'About why you let someone steal my brother.'

It was Flick who gasped this time. The other two people in the room were completely silent as they stared at each other. She shouldn't be here, Flick thought, in the middle of what was obviously a private family matter. But what if emotional stress was enough to bring on an asthma or angina attack for the woman whose health was her responsibility?

'Or was it something more than that?' Lachlan broke the silence. 'Did you give one of your babies away because you didn't want twins? Put him up for adoption?'

'Go away, Lachlan. I have absolutely no idea what you're talking about.'

'I should go…' Flick said quietly.

'Stay where you are,' Lady Josephine ordered. 'And

find my spray.' She put her hand on the middle of her chest as if she could feel pain.

If she was, it wasn't about to distract Lachlan.

'I met him today,' he said.

Flick could see the muscles in his neck move as he swallowed hard and she realised that Lady Josephine wasn't the only person she was worried about here. Lachlan was grappling with something so huge he was having trouble finding where to start. She wanted to go and stand beside him and offer support.

To hold his hand…?

'His name's Josh Stanmore,' Lachlan continued. 'Born in Cheltenham. On exactly the same day as me, but even before he told me that, there was no mistaking that we were twins. Probably identical twins. It was like…like meeting myself…'

No wonder he was looking so shocked, Flick thought. Her gaze sought the small red cannister that held the GTN spray, in case Lady Josephine's chest pain was genuine. It was on the medication tray beside the asthma inhaler.

'He told me he was adopted,' Lachlan added. 'But he'd never known he had a twin.'

'You can't blame me,' Lady Josephine snapped. 'I wasn't told it was twins.'

'I don't believe you,' Lachlan said. 'You must have known you were pregnant with more than one baby.'

'Oh, for heaven's sake, Lachlan. You're being dense.' His mother looked away, as if the view outside was of more interest. 'I was never pregnant. You were also adopted.'

.The silence this time was so deep Flick felt like she was falling into it. How appalling was this? She knew how much Lachlan cared about his mother. And he was only now finding out that she wasn't the woman who'd given birth to him? How much worse could this be?

Quite a lot, it seemed.

'Even if I had known it was twins, I wouldn't have taken you both.' Lady Josephine's voice rose. 'I didn't want *one* baby, let alone two. I only agreed to the adoption because I knew it was the only way to save my marriage. Your father wanted an heir much more than he wanted *me*.'

The sound Lady Josephine made as she dragged in a new breath could almost have been the start of a sob. It could also be the first sign of respiratory distress. Flick watched as another breath was taken, a shorter gasp this time, and she could definitely hear a wheezing sound. She stepped towards the tray and picked up the inhaler but her gaze shifted to Lachlan as she did so. She wanted him to know that she understood how awful this was for him to hear and that, if she didn't feel so incredibly helpless, she would do whatever she could to try and ease *his* pain.

He caught her gaze but not for long enough for any silent message to be exchanged. He stared at his mother again and, for a horrible moment, he looked like a small boy who was fighting not to burst into tears and a piece of Flick's heart broke at that point. She couldn't do anything about it, however. Lady Josephine was definitely having trouble breathing now and she was reaching towards the inhaler Flick had in her hand. She shook

the cannister, took the cap off and held it to the older woman's lips.

'Let all your breath out,' she instructed. 'I'll press the button when you start breathing in.'

She didn't see Lachlan leaving the room. She just heard the door slam shut behind him.

A minute later, though, she saw him again as a movement outside caught her peripheral vision. Lachlan was walking fast, heading towards the woodland that surrounded the garden. The squeeze on Flick's heart made her aware of just how worried she was for him. How lonely was it going to be for him trying to get his head around what he'd just learned?

But she had to turn back to the person she was employed to care for.

'That sounds better,' she said. 'But try and slow your breathing down. Like this…' She modelled taking a slow inward breath and then releasing it again. 'I'll count for you. Take a breath in—one…two…three… And now out again—one…two…three…'

Another glance through the window showed that Lachlan had vanished, presumably into the trees, and Flick's heart sank a little further. It wasn't that long before it would start getting dark, and he hadn't even put a warm coat on…

CHAPTER SIX

'HE'LL BE ALL RIGHT, lovey. He knows those woods like the back of his hand.'

'But it's dark. And cold.'

'I know.' Mrs Tillman wiped her hands on her apron as she sighed heavily. 'Such goings on. This was never the happiest house but this…this feels very different.' She headed back towards the oven. She was cooking Lachlan's favourite dinner of roast beef and Yorkshire pudding because she'd told Flick she didn't know what else she could do to try and help.

'Did you know he was adopted?' Flick asked.

Mrs Tillman shook her head. 'He was a toddler when me and Jack started work here. Maybe two years old? He had a string of nannies. I think Lady J. found a reason to get rid of them as soon as she knew her husband had started sleeping with them.'

'Oh, no…'

'How is Her Ladyship now?'

'She's upset. It took a while to get her asthma under control but it was definitely an emotionally triggered attack. I think she's telling the truth about not knowing

that Lachlan was a twin but… I don't know, it might have been better *not* to tell the truth about never wanting a child in the first place.'

'Aye…' Mrs Tillman sighed again. 'I'll take her up some dinner, though I don't expect she's hungry. Are you going to have something?'

'Later. I'll wait until Lachlan comes back. *If* he comes back…'

'He'll come back. He always did when he was a boy and got hungry enough. At least you'll be here when he does. I need to go and look after my Jack.'

'Of course. I can take Lady Josephine's dinner up, if you like.'

'Oh, thank you. To be honest, I'd like to be with my Jack right now.'

Mrs Tillman had been right in thinking that the food wouldn't be welcome, however.

'You need to eat,' Flick told Lady Josephine. 'Or it will be more difficult to control your blood sugar levels. I'll leave it here and come back later for a test.'

Sure enough, she found that Lady Josephine's BGL had dropped when she went back to find the dinner untouched. The insulin dose had to be adjusted and Flick wanted to check again before her patient retired for the night but she was told to go away and not to come back till morning so she had to hope that the pager would be used if she was needed before then.

What was more of a worry was that Lachlan still hadn't returned to the house. Flick found herself pacing and then standing to stare out of whatever windows she could find that gave her a view of the gardens and that

ominously dark woodland beyond. Finally, just after nine p.m., she saw the shadowy figure crossing the lawn and then heard the front door slam shut.

By the time she headed for the stairs, having wavered but then decided in favour of intruding at such a personal time, she heard another door slamming shut and knew it was Lachlan's bedroom on the other side of the first floor but Flick wasn't going to let that derail her decision. Instead, she headed for the kitchen, where the oven had long since been turned off.

It wasn't going to be hot roast beef and all the trimmings but the relief that Lachlan was safely back in the house was enough to make Flick realise she needed food and surely he did as well. She cut and buttered thick slices of homemade bread and made sandwiches with the beef. She looked at a jar of horseradish sauce in the fridge, which would have been a classic condiment for the beef, but then she spotted something else and, for the first time in hours, felt her lips curl in a tiny smile. She put a bottle of wine on the tray and then two glasses, which was possibly presumptuous but she'd made enough sandwiches for two people because, even if Lachlan didn't want to talk, it could make a big difference just having some company.

Knowing that someone cared…

The knock on his door was unexpected.

Unwelcome.

But surely his mother hadn't come to hurl any more verbal bombs about how he hadn't been wanted and had never actually belonged here?

'It's only me...'

The sound of Flick's voice through the door was almost equally unsettling because, for a horrible moment, Lachlan felt like he might really lose control and start crying or something. Because he could feel the edges of *that* feeling again—the happy/sad one—but this time it was the happy that was tipping the balance and, man... he could do with a hint of happy at the moment.

He opened the door to find Flick holding a huge tray, laden with plates and wine and...two glasses? It looked heavy and it was automatic to offer assistance by holding his hands out to take the tray. Flick seemed happy to let him take it, following him into his room as if it was an invitation to join him.

'I finally got hungry,' she told him. 'And I figured you'd be even hungrier after tramping around the countryside so I thought we could have a bit of a picnic.'

A picnic? A happy, summery sort of thing to do? The idea was crazy but it also made Lachlan almost smile as he put the tray down on a table near the windows.

'It's freezing in here.' Flick rubbed her arms and then stepped closer to the ornate fireplace on the other side of the room. 'Is it safe to light this?'

'I would think so. Tilly's husband looks after getting chimneys swept every year and it always used to be laid with kindling and a supply of wood every time I came home...came *here*,' he corrected himself. 'I can hardly call it "home" any more, can I?'

Flick ignored his bitter comment. She knelt in front of the fire, striking a match to ignite the screwed-up newspaper beneath the kindling. She wasn't wearing

her uniform now, or even the smart clothes she'd worn when she'd first come here. She had well-worn denim jeans on and a white shirt beneath a navy-blue cardigan that looked thick enough to be soft and warm. And… Lachlan took another look…

'What on earth have you got on your feet?'

'Ugg boots.' Flick didn't move, other than to blow on the baby flames to encourage their growth. 'They're an Aussie thing. Lined with sheepskin so they're perfect for English weather almost all year round but especially tonight.' She looked up at him. 'You must be freezing—you went out hours ago and you weren't even wearing a coat.'

The fact that she'd noticed what he'd been wearing, had watched him perhaps and then been worried about him, made something tighten hard in Lachlan's chest, even though he knew it wasn't physically possible for a heart to be squeezed. He was cold right through to his bones, though, he had to admit, so he crouched down beside Flick and held his hands out to the now cheerful flicker of flames.

'This is excellent. We can have our picnic right here.' Flick's smile was even more warming than those flames. 'No, don't move… I'll get the tray.'

She jumped up to fetch the tray before Lachlan could argue but he didn't want to move anyway. There was something very comforting about settling down properly on the hearth rug to watch the flicker of flames and soak in the warmth. Flick put the tray on the rug in front of him and then gathered some cushions from the nearby armchairs.

'Luxury,' she declared with a grin. 'Now, dig in.' She held the plate of chunky sandwiches towards him. 'I'll sort the wine. Also Australian…like my Ugg boots.'

Lachlan hadn't given food a thought as he'd roamed the woodland, trying to deal with an impossible maelstrom of thoughts and emotions, but as soon as he was holding that soft, fresh bread in his hands and got a whiff of the roast beef, he was suddenly starving. One bite in and he found he was having another one of those moments when it felt like tears were embarrassingly close.

'Tomato sauce…?'

'Mmm…' Flick passed him a glass of wine. And a smile. 'A bucket of it.' Her smile widened. 'Hey… it could be considered fine dining from where I come from and…and I knew you liked it.'

The navy blue of the cardigan Flick was wearing was pretty much the same colour as her eyes in the shadows caused by the flickering flames and the firelight was also making streaks in her blonde hair glow like sunshine, but it wasn't this woman's extraordinary beauty that was overwhelming Lachlan right now. It was because she was caring for him. And about him. And she knew the worst, because she'd been right there when he'd learned that horrible truth about the lie his life had been.

The comfort of the fire and food was helping as well. And the wine. Even more, it was that he could feel so comfortable simply being in the company of another person, without needing to make conversation or do

anything other than exchange an occasional glance or half-smile.

'I'll get rid of the tray,' Flick offered, when they'd cleared the plates and polished off the wine.

'No…don't move.' The smile Lachlan received told him that Flick was well aware he was echoing her earlier order to him. 'It's…um…nice to have someone to talk to.' Although he hadn't exactly done much talking, what he could see in Flick's eyes told him that she was ready to listen if he wanted to. And…maybe she was the only person in the world he *could* talk to right now. 'I think the occasion calls for dessert,' he added, hurriedly. 'How 'bout I find some ice cream?'

'A picnic wouldn't be complete without it.' Flick nodded.

'And, I don't know about you, but I suspect a day like today also calls for some more wine.'

Flick's nod was grave this time. 'I think so, too,' she murmured. Her gaze was still holding his. 'I'll just stay nice and warm here, shall I?'

'I think that's only fair. It was you who came up with the idea of the picnic, after all.' Lachlan took the wineglasses off the tray and put them down on the tiled hearth. 'I'll be right back.'

Flick could—and probably should—have gone to check on Lachlan's mother and do another blood glucose test but she knew she wouldn't be welcome and she was confident that the pager alarm would be used if something serious happened because that asthma attack today had been genuinely frightening for Lady Josephine. She also

knew that Lachlan needed her more right now. Not that he'd said anything about what had happened but that comment he'd made about it being nice to have someone to talk to made her feel the need to hang around a bit longer in case he *did* want to talk about it.

Thank goodness he was, at least, looking a little better after some food and warmth. He'd looked like a ghost when she'd arrived in this room and Flick had had to fight the urge to simply put the tray on the floor and take him into her arms and hold him tightly for as long as it took to start fixing what had been broken. Getting the fire going had been a welcome distraction to fighting that surprisingly powerful desire. Flick added another log or two to tap into the distraction that movement could provide but it didn't stop a distinct feeling of pleasure rippling through her body as Lachlan returned and closed his bedroom door behind him.

He'd been quick because he hadn't stopped to do anything other than collect the basic supplies. He held a tub of ice cream and two spoons in one hand and a bottle of red wine and a corkscrew in the other. Chocolate fudge ice cream, Flick noted as she peeled off the covering, which would be even more delicious with the rich, red wine Lachlan was opening.

There was something disconcertingly intimate about sharing the same tub of ice cream, taking turns to dip their spoons into the treat but sometimes mistiming it enough for the spoons to touch—which felt remarkably like it was their hands touching. Maybe that was what made Lachlan feel like he could finally talk about it.

'So many things make sense now,' he said quietly. 'I

knew from very early on that I had to do well at everything I tried because that was what my father noticed. An achievement or a school prize was when I would get hugged. Or be given whatever it was I had my heart set on. He gave me my first Porsche when I was made Dux in my last year at secondary school.'

'This is the boarding school you got sent to when you were only five years old?' Flick could feel the echo of her horror the first time he'd told her about that. She put her spoon down, having lost her appetite for dessert.

Lachlan shrugged. 'I wasn't the only kid that age.'

'But it must have been terrifying. And lonely.'

'Home was pretty lonely, too,' Lachlan said quietly. 'I think I knew all along that my mother didn't love me. I don't think she even liked me so it's no real surprise to learn that she didn't want me. I tried so hard but nothing ever made her really happy. She'd pretend she liked a picture I'd drawn for her, or the bluebells I'd picked in the woods but they disappeared instantly. I think she threw them away the minute I got taken away by my nanny.' He let his breath out in an ironic-sounding huff. 'They are just starting to come out again, those bluebells. Don't think I'll be picking any for Mother *this* year.'

He abandoned his spoon now to pick up his glass and empty it. When he picked up the bottle and offered Flick a refill as well, she simply nodded. She didn't trust herself to speak at the moment in case she interrupted Lachlan's thoughts by doing something stupid, like crying.

'I did a lot of thinking out there tonight,' he said.

'To be honest, it was more of a bombshell meeting Josh today than to finally find out that I was adopted.'

'I'll bet.' Flick was actually reaching out to take his hand before she realised what she was doing. She disguised the movement by shifting the unwanted ice-cream tub to the hearth. 'I can't imagine what it must have been like.'

'It was unnerving,' Lachlan admitted. 'Like looking into a slightly distorted mirror. Our voices sound exactly the same too and…and there was a moment when we both rubbed our forehead at exactly the same time… like this…' He used his middle finger to rub the centre of his hairline and he smiled wryly. 'We even used the same finger…'

'Wow…'

'And out there in the woods, I thought about how much fun we could have had as kids, building the secret places I made alone. I even went and sat in one for a while today. And I thought about how much better school would have been if I'd had someone to share it with. A brother. A *twin*. A best friend…'

'Oh… Lachlan…' This time Flick didn't stop herself from touching his hand. She wrapped her fingers around his and squeezed.

'I feel like I've had half of my life stolen. Half of myself, even. Is that a bit mad?'

'No…' Flick held his gaze. 'No, it's not.'

'I can't forgive my mother. Not that she *is* my mother.'

'If it's any comfort, she really didn't know that you were a twin. She was very upset.'

'She knew she never loved me.' Lachlan's voice was no more than a whisper. 'Or wanted me.'

Again, he drained the rest of his wine from his glass. Then he stared into the fire, which had burnt down to embers. Flick let go of his hand to lean forward and put another piece of wood into the fireplace and it was when she turned back that she saw a single tear rolling down Lachlan's face. Startled, she raised her gaze to catch his and she knew that she was seeing everything there was to see about Lachlan McKendry in that moment.

A man who was completely raw. Being torn apart by incredibly powerful emotions. And Flick knew, only too well, how devastating that could be. She moved quietly, close enough to put her arms around Lachlan because… well…because she needed to hold him as much as she suspected he needed to be held by another human.

Oh…the warmth of her.

The softness.

The murmur of her voice, even though the words made no sense.

He'd never let a woman see him cry. Ever. But she wasn't offering him pity. What he could feel in that embrace was the empathy of someone who understood this depth of pain. Someone who could see past anything superficial to what was important. Someone who could offer love because she had a heart that was as beautiful and real and unique as the rest of her.

Lachlan had no idea when it was that it tipped into something very different.

Escape?

A desire to abandon boundaries that had been put in place to protect a person who'd never felt any desire to protect him?

Or was it simply a surrender to an attraction that had been simmering from the first moment he'd laid eyes on Felicity Stephens and had only been fuelled beyond control by the intimacy of what had happened here this evening? In his bedroom, of all places, with the romance of flickering firelight and the probably unwise addition of a little too much alcohol.

Whatever the cause, it was happening. He'd raised his face from where it had been buried against Flick's shoulder and they were so close to each other their noses were merely a hair's breadth from touching. It could have been Flick who moved first—except it felt like she was melting rather than moving—and he moved his hand to cup her neck for support and then they were gazing at each other for a long, long moment as their breathing mingled and the only sound was the soft crackle of the fire. Silent questions were being asked and answered in that moment.

Do you want this as much as I do?

Yes…oh, God…yes…

We probably shouldn't…

Being professional was a big thing for Flick. He didn't want her doing something she might regret later.

It's one night…a night like no other will ever be… Maybe we both need it…

That was invitation enough to convince Lachlan. The feeling that maybe his distress had taken Flick back to a place where she had been in need of the kind of com-

fort she had unhesitatingly offered to him. And that, maybe, she hadn't had somebody there for her?

Whatever...

In slow motion, Lachlan brushed Flick's lips with his own—no more than a butterfly kiss. He saw her eyes close when he did it again and then he closed his own eyes as he let his lips settle against hers, gently feeling the shape of them, angling his head so that his mouth could capture more of that softness and heat that was enough to be spreading through his entire body. And then her lips opened beneath his and he could *taste* her and nothing on earth had ever cast a spell like this and desire became an almost desperate need as he deepened that kiss and let his tongue ask for permission to fulfil more of that need.

Minutes later, they were both fumbling with buttons. His shirt was undone a lot faster than his fingers could manage the tiny buttons on Flick's shirt but there was skin exposed to the firelight in a very short time and he'd never seen anything as enticing as the soft swell of the most perfect breasts in the world. Lachlan lost the power of rational thought as he hooked the edge of her bra to put his lips to that satin skin and his tongue to a nipple that was as hard as a stone. As hard as part of his own anatomy had already become. The tiny sound of need that came from Flick as he undid the fastening of her jeans was almost too much. He had to slow this down or something that was this good would be over too soon when it should last for ever, which was what this perfect woman deserved.

But as he moved to take a breath Flick reached for

him to open the zip on his trousers and she was touching him through the fabric, and it was clear that she didn't want this to slow down. Lachlan got to his knees and then his feet. He reached a hand out to Flick who took it, keeping her gaze locked on his as she did so. He pulled her to her feet but only let go to scoop her body into his arms. Then he turned and walked the few steps it took to get to his bed. He set Flick down gently onto her feet and took his sweet time to kiss her again. And then she stood there, completely still, as he carefully removed the rest of her clothing.

She was watching him as he couldn't resist a long look at her body, from head to toe and back again, but, unlike the first time he'd done that, this time she didn't seem to mind at all. She was waiting to capture his gaze as it returned to her face and there was the hint of a smile on her lips.

'Your turn,' she whispered…

CHAPTER SEVEN

'You look about as good as Lady J. does this morning.' Mrs Tillman was frowning as she looked up to see who was coming into the kitchen. 'And that's not a compliment, by the way. Coffee?'

'Oh, yes, please. I might need the whole pot. I didn't get much sleep last night.'

Flick combed her hair back with her fingers and then wound a band around the short ponytail she'd created as Mrs Tillman got milk from the fridge and a mug from a hook. She was hoping there was no hint showing on her face of *why* she hadn't slept much. She had crept back to her own room at some point before dawn and had even drifted into sleep for a brief period before the alarm on her phone had sounded.

Then she'd tapped the snooze function button on the screen at least twice. Not because she wanted to snatch a few minutes' more sleep but because she wanted to remember why her body felt like this. Revel in it, even. In that almost bruised feeling in places that hadn't been touched for so long they had been forgotten but the border between pain and pleasure was too blurred to define.

She was also weary in a way that wasn't due to a lack of sleep but the aftermath of the release of a surprising amount of tension that she hadn't even known she was living with. Probably because it had simply become part of her way of life. One of those things you learned to accept because they couldn't be changed.

Mrs Tillman put a mug of fragrant coffee in front of Flick and then shook her head.

'It's rattled everybody, this business. I saw young Lachlan out walking as soon as dawn broke.'

'Oh?' Flick couldn't control the sudden jump in her heart rate but she could crush that inappropriately fierce flash of disappointment. 'He's already had breakfast, then?'

What had she been expecting—that he would be waiting to see her? That she'd know, just by looking at him, that last night had been more meaningful than simply a one-off escape from overwhelming emotional upheaval? How ridiculous. It wasn't as if she would even want that to be the case.

'He said he'd pick something up later. He's back to London for the day.' Mrs Tillman was back at the sink, reaching for something on the windowsill. 'He left this for you. Maybe he knew you wouldn't have had a great night either.'

It was a small jam jar she was holding, with a tiny bunch of flowers in it.

'Or maybe he's scared that you won't want to hang around and work for Lady J. any longer with the family skeletons coming out. That he'll come home and find that you've packed your bags.'

'I'd never leave someone in the lurch, even if I did want to change positions.' But the idea that Lachlan was worried she might disappear made Flick smile as she buried her nose in the blooms. 'I love bluebells,' she said. 'They smell like the woods. And spring. And…'

And these ones made her realise that Lachlan had been thinking about her at the same time she had been lying in her bed, thinking about him. He'd given her something that had meaning, too, because he'd told her that he'd given his mother bunches of bluebells to try and win her love but she'd thrown them away. Flick was not going to throw these away.

'I'll take these to my room when I go upstairs,' she said aloud. Maybe she knew what else these flowers smelled of now. The start of something new? Not that she had any idea of what that something might be but she was again aware of how different her body felt this morning. That was certainly new.

And it was…unexpectedly nice…

More than nice. Lachlan was probably halfway to London already but this feeling gave her a connection that was not about to break, even if it was being stretched over that kind of considerable distance.

'I'd better head up now, in fact,' she added, picking up her coffee as well as the jam jar. 'I'm a bit worried that you think Lady Josephine's not looking well.'

He didn't really have anything urgent enough to require a trip to London but the pull towards St Bethel's Hospital and the Richmond International Clinic was too strong to ignore. Maybe he needed to reconnect with the

life he'd had only days ago, before it had been turned inside out. Some time in his modern apartment with the stunning view over the Thames would also make a welcome change from the sombre stone walls of his ancient family home and the woodland that surrounded it.

Family home…as if…

There was still a pull from that direction, though. Lachlan could feel it even as he soaked in the feeling of power beneath his hands and played with the boundaries of the permitted speed limits as he passed every other vehicle on the motorway. It was raining but his automatic wipers were maintaining perfect visibility and the way the car was stuck to the road with its built-in safety features gave him the confidence to push just a little further. The adrenaline rush was almost enough to banish the fatigue that was only to be expected after a totally sleepless night.

The tug of that pull to the house he'd left behind him was suddenly sharp and it was centred deep in his gut and…and it felt like desire.

Was that what this pull was all about? Flick…and the most amazing sex he'd ever had in his life?

It wasn't clear cut, though, was it? Their night together had been in his childhood home and it had only happened because he'd been completely thrown off balance by what had happened yesterday. To find he had a brother. To learn that his mother had never wanted him. It was no wonder that he'd sought comfort in someone's arms and the chance to escape reality briefly.

That didn't explain why he'd been drawn to the woods at first light this morning, mind you. Or why

he'd searched through the swathe of flowers to find the few that were open enough to give the scent he remembered so well from his childhood. Why had he wanted to do that so much? He'd told Flick the flowers had been one of the unwanted gifts he had given his mother. Was he so confident that she would understand that he was trying to thank her for her understanding? For being there? That she would recognise the symbol for what it was?

Yes…he was that confident. Nobody had ever touched him quite like that in his life—both physically and emotionally.

Felicity Stephens was an extraordinary woman. She might not be in his life for very long but he had to thank his lucky stars that she'd happened to be there last night, when he'd needed someone so badly. Not just anyone, either. Lachlan was quite sure that nobody else on earth could have made him feel like she had. As though he was truly worth caring about. As though *she* cared that much…

The text message on his phone came onto the dashboard screen as Lachlan slowed for the first set of traffic lights on the outskirts of the city.

Josh here. Don't know about you but I didn't get much sleep. How 'bout we meet again tonight? Here's my address—

Another great feature of this new car was the ability to answer a text verbally.

'Sure thing,' Lachlan dictated. 'I'm in the City for the day but should be back by seven p.m. See you then.'

Looking up from the screen, he caught a glimpse of the top of his face in the rear-view mirror. Good grief... how could he look this wrecked with just one night's sleep missed? The skin around the bottom of his eyes looked blue enough to be bruised—as if he'd been in some kind of fight.

How battered his spirit felt matched that notion as well, come to think of it.

It didn't occur to him to send a message to Tilly to let her know he wouldn't be back for dinner. Maybe he didn't want his mother to know where he was. It wasn't simply that it was none of her business. He didn't want the reminder that she didn't actually care—because she never had...

The rain had set in by early afternoon.

Lady Josephine looked as tired as Flick was feeling and she was in a very strange mood. Even one of her cutting comments would be preferable to the awful silence that filled the room as Flick went through the routine of checking and recording vital sign measurements. With the weather making the room as dingy and dismal as the atmosphere, it was obvious that something had to be done.

'Would you like me to bring you up some afternoon tea? And light the fire, perhaps?' Oh, that suggestion might not have been the best. It reminded Flick instantly of lighting the fire in Lachlan's room last night. And everything that had followed...

She cleared her throat. 'It's a bit of a dull afternoon, isn't it?' she added hastily.

Lady Josephine snorted. 'I thought it was a uniquely English attribute to resort to talking about the weather to avoid anything more awkward.'

Something in her tone suggested that she would rather be talking about the awkward things and Flick hesitated only a moment before putting both of her suggestions into action. Carrying the tray up from the kitchen a short time later, she was confident she was doing the right thing. Okay, the family's private business was not something she should get into, but it was affecting her patient enough to have potentially serious consequences—like that asthma attack yesterday—so, if Lady Josephine wanted to talk, it was actually part of Flick's job to listen.

Preferably without judgement, she reminded herself as she poured the tea and buttered one of Mrs Tillman's excellent cheese scones, although that might prove difficult. This involved Lachlan, after all, and she had shared his heartbreak yesterday in a way that made her far more involved than was strictly professional.

Professional boundaries didn't seem to be concerning Lady Josephine, either.

'I've been thinking,' she announced as Flick offered her the milk jug. 'You're about the size I used to be at your age. I'm too scrawny now, of course.'

'For what?'

'To wear my dresses.' Lady Josephine took a sip of her tea but pushed the plate with the scone aside, before looking up at Flick. 'You don't need to look so shocked.

I'm not suggesting some kind of macabre fashion show. I just thought…if you wore a dress for your next lesson, it might make a difference. You might understand what it is about dancing that's so…wonderful…'

'My next lesson?' It had been the last thing on Flick's mind today.

'You're not giving up already, are you? I'd thought better of you than that.'

'No, I'm not giving up.'

Yet. There had been an errant thought in the back of her head, however, that her position here might not be tenable after what had happened last night. Oh… and there it was again…that rush of sensation that was her body announcing that it was properly coming back to life again. Like pins and needles in your foot after it had gone to sleep, only this was less painful and far more pleasurable.

'Choose a dress then. For next time. Not today because I'm too tired.'

It occurred to Flick that Lady Josephine might be asking for an assurance that she wasn't about to be abandoned so she complied with the odd request. It was easy to find a dress that she knew she'd love to try on. A ripple of silk in the darkest blue, with diamantés covering the bodice and scattered across acres of fabric that made up the ballerina-length skirt. She held it against her body, still in its plastic cover, and knew it would make her look more beautiful than she possibly ever had. It was a real Cinderella moment that reminded her of how she'd felt when she'd decided to stay in this re-

markable old house—that she'd stepped into some kind
of fairy tale and was up for the role of being a princess.

And…oh…after last night there was no one else who
could be the prince other than Lachlan McKendry.

Flick had to close her eyes and take a very deep
breath to try and centre herself before she took the dress
back into the sitting room to show Lady Josephine,
whose nod advertised satisfaction at her choice, if not
approval.

'I won a national competition in that dress.'

'Shall I take it with me? I'd better try it on and make
sure it fits before we have that lesson.'

The older woman shrugged. 'If you like. You can
take the tray away, too.' She had turned to stare at the
fire. 'Have you spoken to Lachlan today?'

'Um…no. Not since yesterday evening.'

The look she received didn't suggest disapproval or
annoyance. Rather, it seemed like a request for information and Flick couldn't be anything less than honest.

'He's…upset. But…'

'But what?'

How much should she say? How much did Lady Josephine want to say? Flick could only follow her instincts
here and they were personal rather than professional.
She carefully draped the dress over the back of a chair
and sat down on the edge of it herself.

'I don't think he was totally surprised to learn he was
adopted,' she said quietly. 'He told me that he never really felt wanted.'

Flick could feel the ache of unshed tears. Last night,
Lachlan's tears had captured her heart.

And there was no getting away from the fact that his lovemaking had captured her body and soul.

How could she keep working for the woman who was responsible for what had happened to make Lachlan feel that he'd had half his life stolen? Who had never felt loved?

'He wasn't my son.' Lady Josephine's words were fierce, as if she was being forced to admit something against her will. 'My sons died. All of them...'

Flick's indrawn breath was a gasp. '*All* of them?'

'Three. There were three.' Lady Josephine wasn't looking at Flick as she spoke. 'The first one, William, lived for three months and I loved him with all my heart.' She shook her head. 'As much as I adored my husband, even though I knew he was never faithful.'

She closed her eyes and stopped talking but Flick couldn't break the silence. She knew there was something more to be said and that it was important that she hear it. She listened to the rain now pelting the windows, instead, and just waited. She needed another piece of this puzzle. She even had the odd thought that she was meant to be here. To hear this. To be able to help people who needed more than her nursing skills?

'My second baby lived for a day,' Lady Josephine said finally, so quietly her voice was almost a whisper. 'The third was born dead, a month before he was due, but I didn't cry that time. I didn't even care any more...'

'It was too painful, wasn't it?' Flick suggested gently. 'Loving a baby and losing him is the kind of pain nobody feels they could ever bear to go through again.'

She knew that. Dear Lord, she knew that too well.

She could almost feel the weight of an infant in her own arms who had never had the chance to take a breath. And maybe her knowledge of that pain came across as being as genuine as it was.

'I was glad—' Lady Josephine was watching her as she whispered '—that I didn't have to feel it again.'

'How long was it, after your last baby died, that you adopted Lachlan?'

Lady Josephine shrugged. 'I forget. A few weeks.' The breath she pulled in was wheezy. 'A couple of months, perhaps.' She had to take another breath after only a few words. 'It was Douglas who arranged everything…including the nannies.' She was reaching for her inhaler on the table. 'He made it easy for me to agree… Impossible not to.'

Flick got to her feet to help with the administration of the bronchodilator. Supporting Lady Josephine with her arm around the older woman's shoulders and her other hand holding the inhaler to press the top at just the right moment as a new breath was being taken felt like more than a simply professional touch.

It felt like a hug. An acknowledgement that her story had touched Flick on a very deep level even though she was so sympathetic to Lachlan's side of the same story. She could separate the strands to find herself alone but involved on both sides. Pulled in two directions, in fact, but it was easy to choose which one to focus on at this moment. She watched her patient carefully for signs that her respiratory distress was starting to ease but she decided another dose was necessary just a short time later.

'I'm going to give your doctor a call,' she said.

'That's two attacks in two days. You're under a lot of stress at the moment and it could be that you need something extra to help control things.'

Lady Josephine didn't put up an argument, which was an indication that her own life had been turned upside down as much as Lachlan's. The afternoon sped past with the doctor's visit, a new medical plan to be formulated and initiated, and new medications to be collected from the village pharmacy. It wasn't until much later that Flick had time to realise that perhaps Lachlan wasn't coming home tonight.

It was a shame, because she wanted a chance to tell him about that revealing conversation with his mother. It wasn't an excuse for the emotional damage done by the way he'd been raised. It might not lead to any kind of forgiveness, even, but it did provide a background that could at least offer a level of understanding. Flick was the right person to talk to him about it, as well, because she already understood.

She could imagine herself in Lady Josephine's position, with no escape from repeated grief that had left her too numb to be able to love that poor adopted baby. Fighting a depression that hadn't been recognised, let alone treated. Flick had been able to run from her grief and she'd kept running for years because it had been the perfect way to avoid loving anything enough for its loss to be painful. A job. A place. A person. Another baby would be unthinkable.

On the other hand, it might well be a good thing that Lachlan wasn't in the house tonight.

Because she was missing him too much already…?

* * *

It was when Flick was in the kitchen on an afternoon break the next day that she saw Lachlan again for the first time since their intimate night together.

Of course it was. This house might be the biggest Flick had ever lived in but most of her time with Lachlan had been in this one room. Talking time, anyway. Yesterday, she had been preoccupied with what silent messages might be communicated when they saw each other again but, now that it was happening, it was the last thing on Flick's mind. She was far more concerned about Lachlan's physical state.

'Are you okay? You look…'

'Wrecked. Yeah… I know.' Lachlan eyed the mug in front of Flick. 'Any more coffee in the pot?'

'You look like you need more than coffee.'

'You could be right. What's the best cure for a hangover?' Lachlan was rubbing his forehead in that gesture he'd told her he shared with his twin. 'I blame Josh,' he added. 'The whisky was his idea.' He sighed. 'I don't think I even had that much of it, mind you.'

'Headache?' Flick was taking in his pale skin and the circles under his eyes that looked dark enough to be bruises. 'I could find you some paracetamol. Have you had lunch yet?'

'I can't remember when I last ate. I was supposed to have dinner with Josh but he got the whisky out and we started talking and we didn't stop. We were up most of the night.'

So that was why he hadn't come home. Flick felt a wash of relief mix with her concern. He hadn't been

somewhere else in order to avoid her. He'd been with his twin brother, taking the first steps in an astonishing and unexpected new relationship. And he'd now had two nights in a row with very little sleep? No wonder he was looking so wrecked.

'I could cook something,' she offered. 'Bacon and eggs are supposed to be good for a hangover.'

· 'I'm not that hungry.' Lachlan took a tumbler from a cupboard and filled it with water at the sink. 'Maybe I just need to catch up on some sleep. Or get a bit of fresh air.' He drank half the water. 'Besides, Tilly wouldn't be happy if we messed up her clean kitchen bench. Where is she?'

'Upstairs. Playing Scrabble with your mother while I take a bit of a break. It was rather a long day yesterday what with getting the doctor out again.'

But Lachlan wasn't about to enquire after his mother's health. In fact, Flick had seen the shutters come down as soon as she'd mentioned her. She could almost feel barriers being hastily erected. Lachlan drained his glass and set it down.

'Yep,' he said. 'Fresh air is the cure, I'm sure of it.'

His words were cheerful. He straightened up as he turned towards the door. He even found a smile and that reminded Flick of the persona she'd first met in this man. The one that could hide the real Lachlan McKendry so well. And it hurt, far more than she might have anticipated, to find herself being shut out like this.

She didn't want to be shut out. She needed to find a way to punch a hole in the barriers before they got any more solid.

'Thanks for the bluebells,' she found herself saying. 'They have the most amazing scent. It fills up my whole bedroom.'

Okay…that did it. Lachlan paused and turned. Maybe it was the mention of the bluebells or, more likely, the reference to a bedroom but the tension Flick had expected to be between them was definitely here. Strong enough to be using up all the oxygen in the room, in fact. For a long moment, they simply stared at each other and she could see just how torn Lachlan was.

He wanted to say something…but didn't want to at the same time.

He wanted to leave…but didn't want to…

The tension increased to a point where it had to break. Flick opened her mouth to say something but couldn't find any words. Maybe she was looking torn herself because something in Lachlan's expression softened.

'They smell even better in the woods,' he said quietly. 'Come and see…'

Flick was already on her feet but had barely been aware of moving. 'How far does the signal for the pager work?' she asked. 'In case I'm needed.'

'Far enough.' Lachlan was turning away again. 'But, in any case, Tilly can cope. She doesn't miss much so I expect she'll see where we're going from the window. You did say you're on a break?'

She had said that.

And it felt right to go with Lachlan, to search in the boot room for a pair of wellies to cope with the damp ground after yesterday's rain and to follow him across

a lawn now bathed in spring sunshine, because he had become an integral part of why she felt needed here.

Flick was tangled up in Lachlan's story as well as his mother's now and…and there were threads being woven into her own story that were too important to ignore. Whatever else was happening here, her own life was changing enough to make her feel she was standing at a very significant crossroads. Her body had not only come back to life thanks to Lachlan's touch, she was aware of a connection that was even more powerful. If she chose to, she could fall in love with this man and that opened possibilities that were so big they were terrifying.

She should be scared, she realised. She should probably choose a different path to go on at this unexpected crossroads but she didn't, because this, too, felt right. If he was inviting her, she needed to walk further on the same path as Lachlan. Until she could see where it might be leading, at least, and whether her heart had healed enough to be able to go there. If she needed to, she knew that she could turn around. She'd know the moment it didn't feel right and that would be the time to change direction completely and run. She could do that, too.

She'd had plenty of practice, after all.

CHAPTER EIGHT

SUNLIGHT FILTERED INTO the woods, making the new leaves on oak trees a soft, green halo above dark trunks and the carpet of blue flowers a stunning contrast.

The scent was strong enough to make Lachlan feel lightheaded for a moment. Or maybe his head was just so full of tumbling thoughts and emotions it was spinning out, giving up trying to find something solid and safe as an anchor.

It was Flick who reminded him that he was actually within the best anchor that he'd ever had—in a place he had always loved.

'This is *so* amazing. I'm scared to walk on them—I don't want to squash any flowers.'

'There are tracks. Like this one.'

Without thinking, Lachlan held out his hand to guide Flick onto one of the many paths that the deer followed in this forest. A sideways glance gave him another glimpse of Flick's delight and he realised that the bluebells darkened by this dappled light were an almost perfect match for the shade of blue of her eyes. A squirrel scurried up a trunk just ahead of them and

Flick laughed, a joyous sound that—weirdly—brought the prickle of tears to the back of his eyes.

It was that sad/happy thing again. He probably should be letting go of Flick's hand by now but, instead, he found himself holding it a little tighter. And she didn't pull hers free.

'These are oak trees, yes?'

'Yes. They're the most common trees here but we also have chestnut and beech, ash and birch trees.'

'And squirrels. I love squirrels.'

'There are deer, as well. They keep these tracks open. I used to love seeing them. And hearing the woodpeckers or seeing owls.'

'This place is magic.' Flick's steps slowed as another swathe of bluebells appeared in front of them. 'I feel like I'm stepping into a fairy tale.' She was smiling up at him. 'And I think you were right.'

'About what?'

'Needing the fresh air. You're looking a bit better.'

He was feeling better, Lachlan realised. His head wasn't spinning any more. He was happy to be here. To be with Flick.

'This is home,' he told her quietly. 'When I think of my childhood home, it's not the house that comes to mind first. Or my parents. It's here, in these woods. Maybe it's the only part of my life that I feel I was lucky to have.'

That quirk of Flick's eyebrows was eloquent.

'Oh, I know how privileged I was to live like this and get the best education and opportunities. My life could

have been so different. It could have easily been Josh here instead of me and I wouldn't have chosen his life.'

'Why not?'

'When we were talking last night, I got the impression that his whole life had been difficult. When he was just a little kid—about three—the people that adopted him had their own baby. A "real" son, Josh called him. He wasn't wanted any longer. By the time he was five, his parents were talking about putting him up for adoption again.'

Flick gasped. 'That's so awful.'

'His grandmother thought so, too, so she took him to live with her and it caused a family rift that was never fixed. Josh felt like it was his fault. That he was being cared for but he wasn't really wanted. Like me...'

Flick was still holding his hand and now she squeezed his fingers. 'It's an unbelievable coincidence,' she said. 'That you were both adopted and you both end up being doctors but even more, that you both had a childhood that nobody should have.' Her eyes were shining with potential tears. 'You should have been kept together. And had a family who loved you both.'

Lachlan's smile was wry. 'It's no wonder we found we have something else in common too.'

'What's that?'

'Neither of us has ever wanted to settle down. The idea of making a family of our own is the stuff of nightmares. He's the same as me with women—any hint of something permanent being wanted and we're running for the hills.'

Flick was smiling but her gaze slid away from his

before he could read her expression. Her hand slid clear of his at the same time and she crouched quickly, as if she'd been waiting to touch the petals of the flowers at their feet, but Lachlan had the impression that she was deliberately creating distance between them.

He didn't like that. He wanted the closeness of the connection he'd discovered with this amazing woman. The closeness that meant he didn't have to hide anything about himself—even his tears. His night with Flick, on the day his world had imploded, felt like it had saved his life. Or at least his faith in humanity. He'd felt truly wanted for maybe the first time in his life. Truly cared for.

'I should head back,' Flick said as she stood up. 'I've had more of a break than I usually do.' She was still smiling as she turned. 'Thank you so much for showing me the bluebells.'

Lachlan wanted to take her hand again and hold her here a little longer. Instead, he walked beside her and tried to close the gap in a different way.

'What is it that makes *you* run, Flick?'

Her glance was startled. 'What do you mean?'

'The way you live. Never staying long in one place. Never settling…'

'Been there, done that.' Her tone was dismissive. 'Didn't really work out that well.'

This time, Lachlan didn't resist the urge to take her hand. He pulled her to a stop.

'Tell me,' he said softly. And then, when he could see her hesitation, he held her gaze as well as her hand. 'Please… You know more about me than anyone else on

the planet,' he added. 'But I don't know that much about you. Except that you can't dance very well.'

That made her smile. 'Hey... I'm getting lessons.'

He didn't want to even think about his mother, let alone ruin this moment by talking about her. He wanted to talk about Flick. To find out what was important to her. What she might consider to be home and whether it was about a place or a person. Perhaps she could see the questions in his eyes and how much he wanted the answers.

'I fell in love once.' She spoke slowly as she finally broke the silence. 'I married the man I loved—Patrick— and our life was perfect—right up until it all fell apart.'

Lachlan could see the depth of pain in her eyes.

'I lost our baby,' she said simply. 'Not that long before he was due to be born. And...that same week, Patrick got diagnosed with pancreatic cancer. I nursed him for a couple of months until he died and... I couldn't stay there any longer because it was too hard. I started moving and...and I guess I've never stopped. I've never wanted to stop because I might get caught by something. Or someone.' She dragged in a shaky breath. 'I could never survive loving and losing like that again.'

The woods around them were so quiet when Flick stopped speaking, Lachlan couldn't even hear a bird call. They were completely alone.

'We all have our stories,' Flick added softly. 'And real life is never a fairy tale so they don't always have happy endings, do they?'

Lachlan couldn't find any words to tell Flick how sorry he was that she'd suffered such tragedy. Or that if

it were possible he'd want to erase at least some of that pain that kept her running. Telling her that, one day, she might find that she *could* turn the page and start a new chapter in her life would be dismissing an experience that had been so unbearable it was clearly going to leave shadows in her eyes for as long as she lived. But what he could do was to fold her into his arms and hold her. To try and give her the kind of comfort she had given him when he'd needed it most.

To let her know that he cared.

He had no idea how long they stood there in the warmth of the sunbeam that had found this spot, breathing in the delicate scent of the flowers around them, hearing faint birdsong and feeling each other's heartbeats. However long it was, it wasn't enough, though. And it was rudely broken by the strident sound of Flick's pager that carried a reminder of the real world and its hardships and, in particular, a person Lachlan still wasn't ready to even think about, let alone forgive.

'Good to know it works out here, I guess,' Flick said, as she pulled away from his arms. 'That means I can come out here again and smell the flowers when I need a break.'

'They'll be here for weeks,' Lachlan promised. 'There's plenty of time.'

Flick opened her mouth as if she was going to say something but then closed it again, giving her head a tiny shake to indicate that she'd changed her mind.

'You're right,' she murmured as she started walking again. 'There's plenty of time.'

* * *

She should have told him when she'd had the chance, days and days ago now.

Lachlan needed to know that there'd been a reason his adoptive mother couldn't love him—that it was about *her* and not him. And the perfect moment to have told him was after he'd been holding her and she could feel how much her own sad story had touched him.

But…*oh*…the way it had felt being held in his arms like that…

She hadn't let anyone that close since Patrick had died. Never. She'd never let anyone care about her that much because she wasn't prepared to take the risk of caring about *them* that much.

If she'd tried to talk about his mother right then, she would have seen those shutters come down again and he would have pushed her away because he was nowhere near ready to hear what she needed to tell him. And not only would it have ruined a memory of something so beautiful it could bring tears to her eyes—being held like that in a fairy tale, bluebell wood, it would have broken a new level of trust between them which was something that would be impossible to build again.

Like hope, trust was a fragile thing when it was new-born.

A precious thing.

Something that was getting stronger with every passing day but that only made it harder to risk testing it by pushing boundaries. Lachlan didn't want to speak to his mother. Or to see her. If he knew that she was watching from her windows when he came and went from

the house, he gave no sign of it. Even now, as Lady Josephine waited for the few seconds it took for her blood glucose measurement to appear on the screen of the meter, her gaze was drifting towards the windows. She wanted to see Lachlan but she knew she had to wait for him to be ready, in the same way that Flick had known she had to wait for the right time to tell him what she knew about his mother.

Sometimes, the watching and waiting seemed like an exercise in frustration. Lachlan commuted to London on more than one occasion and stayed overnight and when he was in residence he was leaving the house early and giving frequent evening lectures and training sessions that kept him out until late most nights.

Flick always waited up for him when she knew he was coming home because she knew she'd get that look. Sometimes it came after he'd had a meal that Mrs Tillman had left to keep warm in the oven or after he'd done some preparation for the next day's work but sometimes it came the moment his gaze met hers—especially if he'd been away for a day or two. It was the look that was an invitation to go to his room. Or hers. It didn't matter as long as it had a bed and a door they could use to close off the rest of the world. It had never been supposed to have been more than a one-off source of comfort on the night that Lachlan had been so upset but it had happened again, that evening after he'd taken Flick to see the bluebells and it had still felt like a source of comfort that night—maybe for both of them.

Over the last ten days, however, it had morphed into something rather different. Something that still held an

element of comfort for people whose life experiences had led them to choose to face life alone but there were definitely new levels of physical pleasure being woven into their private time together and it was the kind of pleasure that could rapidly become addictive.

Flick would find herself holding her breath as she waited for that look and it was more need than desire that was stealing her ability to draw in more air. She was desperate for an invitation that was only becoming more and more irresistible as they got to know each other's bodies more and more intimately. How could it take no more than a glance to ignite a passion that could not only last for hours but get more intense every time?

She knew perfectly well that she was breaking rules. That having a sexual relationship with her employer was completely unprofessional but...she was hooked and it seemed like Lachlan was equally caught and it was just as unprofessional from his side of the equation, wasn't it? It was a shared guilt but there was also an unspoken but shared excuse that made it less of an issue. Lachlan had made it very clear that his relationships were only ever short-lived and he knew it was the same for Flick. That they would only have a short time together because he would head back to his London life soon enough and she would move on to another locum position.

Given the effort that Lady Josephine was putting into her own care since the shock of the confrontation with Lachlan, it seemed quite likely that a full-time carer would not be needed in this house for much longer. Lady Josephine's confession about her past had changed something that made Flick wonder if that had

been the first time she had ever spoken about the grief of losing her own babies and feeling unable to love her adopted son.

The shock of recognising how much damage had been done could have made the older woman withdraw even more into herself but, somehow, the opposite seemed to be happening. Was Lachlan's mother trying to find a way to make an apology? Or, at the very least, not be a burden?

Whatever it was, it was making a big difference. Lady Josephine was taking control of her own medications and monitoring, like performing her own finger prick tests to measure her level of blood glucose. Her use of the preventative medication for her asthma had meant she hadn't had another attack and she was exercising more and more. She was giving Flick dancing lessons in the ballroom almost every day. She was walking in the gardens and had even ventured into the woodland yesterday. There was a tiny vase on her table right now that had a few bluebells in it.

Flick would never see or smell these flowers again without being able to feel what it had been like to be in Lachlan's arms. As Lady Josephine recorded her BGL in her medical diary, Flick found herself reaching for the vase, so that she could pick it up and hold it close to her nose and soak in that gorgeous scent and it was at that moment that she realised she'd been very wrong about something. Two things, in fact.

She'd thought she'd know when it was time to run.

She'd thought she had a choice about whether or not she was going to fall in love with Lachlan McKendry.

But the rush of emotion as she breathed in the scent of being held in Lachlan's arms told her just how wrong she'd been. This wasn't just the scent of new beginnings for her. It was the scent of being cared for.

Being loved…

And returning love…

She knew, at that instant, that she was way past the point of no return on both her assumptions and she had no idea what she was going to do about it. She couldn't simply run and leave her patient before she knew she could look after herself. And she couldn't fall out of love, could she?

Perhaps Lady Josephine noticed the slight tremble in her fingers as she carefully put the vase down again.

'Lachlan used to bring me big bunches of bluebells when he was a little boy.'

'He told me that.' Flick met her gaze. She didn't say anything about how it had made Lachlan feel when his offerings had been rejected but there was a new level of trust between the two women and a growing ability to communicate by saying very little.

'I couldn't bear it,' the older woman added softly. 'They smelt like tears…'

Flick's heart was breaking for her. She had wanted to love her adopted son but she'd been pushed past the point of endurance and forced to find a safe place.

She was in desperate need of at least understanding, if forgiveness wasn't possible.

Flick had to hope the right moment to talk to Lachlan about this would present itself soon—in a way that would mean he wouldn't push her away and slam the

door. With the disturbing revelation of how deeply she was now involved—how deeply she was in love with Lachlan—the prospect of breaking that connection had just become a whole lot bigger. So huge, Flick felt a trickle of fear shimmy down her spine.

'He needs time,' she said aloud. 'I know how hard it is but… I think everybody needs more time to get their heads around it all.'

Including herself.

CHAPTER NINE

TONIGHT WAS ONE of the nights Lachlan had something to do to prepare for a training session at Gloucester General Hospital the next day.

'Has Tilly gone home already?'

'Yes…why? Are you hungry?'

'No. I ate in town. I had an appointment with a butcher. I don't think Tilly would be happy to have this in the fridge overnight so it's good that she's gone home.' He put down the two, large cool boxes. 'Want to see?'

'Sure.'

'It's for a workshop that's lined up for tomorrow. Advanced suturing. In particular, running subcuticular sutures.' Lachlan only met Flick's gaze briefly as he lifted out a small section of pig skin from the bags he was fitting into the fridge. He knew if he caught that gaze for too long, he'd forget all about anything he needed to do this evening because the only thing that would be filling his mind would be how soon he could get Flick alone—in his bedroom.

What had started unexpectedly in the confusion of

his world being upended had changed into something that he just couldn't get enough of. He couldn't call it 'Fun' exactly, because that was far too pale a word to come anywhere near describing what it was like to make love with Flick. It was the best thing that had ever happened to him and it had come when he'd needed it the most. A lifeline that he wasn't ready to let go of just yet. But, right now, it would have to wait and this was a good test to see if he could ignore the temptation.

Flick was peering at the skin. 'What's happened to it?'

'We gave it a nice, jagged laceration. The butcher found a metal tool that was perfect for the job and he was only too happy to help me prepare the samples. I've got some with nice, neat surgical incisions but what I really want to teach in the workshop is how you can make a wound as messy as this into a candidate for the suture technique that gives the best possible cosmetic result. I just need to check that it's going to work.' He opened his satchel to take out a suture kit.

Lachlan could feel Flick watching him as he set up a board to use on the kitchen table and he knew she was genuinely interested in what he was telling her. He liked that. He also liked the feeling of control he had right now because it gave him confidence that the strength of his desire for Flick wasn't going to end up being a problem. He'd be able to walk away when he needed to, just as he had done with every relationship he'd ever had with a woman.

'So, some people argue that tissue adhesive gives just as good, if not a better result but there are times when

glue isn't going to be enough to hold things together and this is a great technique to have up your sleeve.'

He picked up a needle with its attached thread. 'The secret is to decontaminate a wound very thoroughly and then make the edges straight.'

Flick was sitting on the edge of the chair beside him, leaning in to watch what he was doing. 'How do you do that? There are no straight edges at all.'

'Like this… I'm using a whip stitch and taking the smallest possible bites to bring the edges together.' Years of perfecting his skills enabled him to work swiftly and precisely. 'Then I'm going to use the scalpel and run it down one side of the line of stitching and then the other and…*voila*…' he lifted the thin, jagged segment of skin clear, leaving two straight clean edges.

'Okay, I'm impressed.'

'But wait…' Lachlan grinned at her. 'There's more.'

With a new suture, he anchored a stitch at one end of the laceration and then took tiny bites parallel to the wound, just under the surface of the skin. When he got to the other end, he anchored another knot into the deeper, dermal layer and buried it under the skin by taking the needle out a little way away from the end of the cut. When he snipped the thread, it retracted under the skin and all the suture material was completely invisible and the edges of the laceration were in perfect alignment.

'That would barely leave a scar at all in real skin, would it?'

'That's the plan. Doesn't work if there's too much tension, of course. Or on thin skin like an eyelid but it

has its place. I've got a good group coming tomorrow. GPs, surgeons and ED staff. Some nurses doing advanced training as well.'

'I started my nursing career in Emergency.' Flick sounded thoughtful. 'Maybe I should see if I can get my next locum gig in an ED. I miss this kind of stuff.'

'Why not a permanent job instead of a locum? That way, you could get to do some advanced training, maybe, and go to cool workshops like mine.'

He couldn't read her expression but it reminded him of when she'd stopped herself saying something that day he'd taken her to see the bluebells. As if she'd thought better of whatever it was she'd intended to say.

Was she wondering whether she might actually prefer to settle somewhere for a while? To stop running? It would be a good thing if she was because she deserved to start that new chapter in her life. One that might even make up for the sadness she'd had to live with.

There was certainly a hint of wariness in those gorgeous, blue eyes and her lips were parted, ready to speak. Or to kiss... This time, Lachlan caught her gaze and kept holding it until he saw that wariness replaced by desire as her eyes darkened and the tip of her tongue came out to touch her lips. In slow motion, perhaps because they were both savouring every heartbeat of the anticipation, they leaned closer. Until their lips were touching. Until the kiss stole any remnants of that control Lachlan had thought he'd had.

But it didn't matter.

He knew it would be there when he needed it again

and he didn't need it yet. Who wouldn't want to make the most of this while it lasted and who knew how long that might be?

The skills Lachlan had demonstrated when he'd been showing Flick the suture technique he intended teaching had been impressive.

The skills he demonstrated in her bed a short time later were even more impressive. Or maybe it didn't take that much skill when even the lightest touch of his hands on her body was enough to take Flick to a place where nothing else mattered. Where passion could explode with such power but so gently it was heart-breaking.

This wasn't the first time that Flick had felt a tear trickling down the side of her nose as she lay in Lachlan's arms as their breathing and heart rates slowly returned to normal and they came back to the real world, but it was the first time that she understood why this was so poignant.

It was because she was in love with Lachlan.

Because—even though she had told him she could never risk this kind of love when it came with the potential of devastating loss—it had happened anyway.

And she wanted this feeling for ever.

The feeling that she knew she could only ever have if she was in this man's arms.

And she knew it couldn't be for ever because he'd spelt it out, that day in the bluebell wood.

He's the same as me with women—any hint of some-

thing permanent being wanted and we're running for the hills...

The day that she should have told him what she knew about his mother. Flick's heart rate picked up again as she summoned enough courage to do what she should have done then.

'You asleep?' she asked softly.

'Not yet.' Lachlan's arms tightened around Flick. 'I should be. Can't believe how tiring this training programme is proving to be.'

'It's not as if it's the only thing you've got going on in your life. I'm not surprised it's hard work.'

'I feel like I'm pushing something very heavy uphill half the time. Life's just got too complicated. Too different.' With her cheek against Lachlan's chest, she could feel that his heart missed a beat. 'I've got a brother now. Real family and that's making me have to think about the future and that's not something I've ever done. Not in personal terms, anyway. Career, yes. Family, no. Because I didn't think I had a family.'

'But you do...' Flick's thoughts were threatening to run in a different direction. If Lachlan was starting to think about a future that included family, could that mean he might consider changing his stance when it came to relationships with women? With *her*?

'I had a meeting with Josh today. I'm doing a nerve transplant surgery on one of his patients—a two-year-old boy called Toby who's lost effective use of one arm after breaking his collarbone and doing some significant damage to the brachial plexus network of nerves. And—' Flick could hear a smile in his voice '—he re-

minded me that I'd suggested we have a night out for dinner, including his friend Stevie, some time. As a kind of "thank you" for the way she saved us from having to meet for the first time in front of a whole bunch of people.

'I've been wanting to take you out somewhere nice because you deserve a proper night off,' he added. 'So how 'bout it? Dinner at one of the best restaurants the Cotswolds has to offer?'

'Sounds fabulous,' Flick said. 'And…speaking of dinner, I need to tell you that your mother's decided to stop eating dinner in her room. She's going to come down and start using the dining room again. I think she's really hoping that you might join her one night.'

The silence from Lachlan was a warning that he didn't want to talk about this but Flick had to ignore it.

'There's something else I have to tell you. That I should have told you as soon as I knew but I was worried that you might think I was interfering or that it might be too much on top of everything else and you'd just leave. I… I didn't want you to leave…'

Oh, man…that was almost a confession that she was in love with him, wasn't it? She could feel how still Lachlan was and the odd tension in his muscles that was holding him like that.

'I told you that I lost my baby,' Flick said quietly. 'So I know how hard it was that your mother lost a baby. Not just one baby. Three of them. Three boys, one after the other. I think it must have been something genetic that caused it. She had her heart completely broken by the first death of the baby she'd loved and nurtured for

three months. By the time she had a very late miscarriage—like mine—with her third baby, she was past being able to grieve. And that was when your father arranged for your adoption. Can you imagine what it was like for her to be expected to become a loving mother to a child who wasn't her own—and at a time when she must have felt that life wasn't even worth living?'

Lachlan slipping his arm from beneath Flick's head as he sat up in her bed felt like her worst fears were about to come true. He was going to push her away and simply walk out. She bit her lip as she heard him blow out a stunned breath.

'Wow...' Lachlan was silent for a long moment as he tried to gather his thoughts. 'I never knew.' There was a fight going on in his head now. Or was it his heart? He could feel the yearning he'd had to be loved as a small boy and the pain of never feeling good enough battling with his empathy for someone who'd been through such a devastating experience.

'I feel sorry for her, of course,' he added, 'but I can't promise it's going to change how I feel about her. Or how I remember my childhood.' He shook his head. 'It's another thing I have in common with Josh in a way, isn't it? His adopted family had their "real" son after he was adopted. Mine had them before but the result's been remarkably similar, hasn't it? Two people who don't trust in family or want to risk trying to make their own.'

He didn't want to think about it any longer because this was yet another revelation that was shaking the foundations of his life. Lachlan needed a distraction. Fast.

'What's that?' he asked. 'Hanging on the back of your door?'

He hadn't noticed it when he'd pushed the door shut behind them. Why would he have when all he'd been able to think about had been Flick and what they were about to do. Every time, he wondered whether their love-making could possibly be as good as the last time and he was always astonished that it could actually be better. He knew exactly what kind of touch would elicit those delicious sounds of a need that matched his own and how to keep Flick teetering on the brink of paradise until she begged for release. Tonight, he'd even managed to time it so that they fell over the edge together, which was yet another new and amazing experience for Lachlan.

'It's a ball gown,' Flick told him. 'I haven't worn it yet, because I decided I needed to know how to dance a lot better first, but I got it out because I thought I might be able to wear it for my lesson tomorrow.'

Oh…this was the perfect distraction even if he was so tired it felt like he needed to sleep for a week. Lachlan didn't want to go back to his own room yet, though. He didn't want to be alone with his thoughts.

'Wear it now,' he said softly, bending down to kiss Flick's lips.

He saw her tongue come out to lick her bottom lip—as if she wanted to taste him again—and that created a flash of pleasure that was sharp enough to puncture the cloud of confused thoughts vying for time in his head.

His smile was intended to persuade her. 'Wear it for me,' he whispered.

He watched her getting out of the bed, taking the

dress from its plastic package and stepping into it. He got up himself, so that he could pull the zip up at the back. Knowing that she had no underwear on beneath those slippery ripples of fabric was arousing him all over again. This was certainly the best distraction ever.

'It fits,' Flick murmured. 'Your mother was right when she said I was the same size she used to be when she danced in competitions. She won something big wearing this dress.'

Okay...more distraction was needed. Lachlan hurriedly pulled on his jeans. He put his shirt on but couldn't waste time doing up any buttons.

'Come with me.' He took hold of Flick's hand without allowing her any time to protest but she didn't seem to mind. Both barefoot, they tiptoed along the hallway that went past his mother's bedroom and then raced silently down the stairs. When they reached the ballroom, Lachlan put on only as many of the small, side lights as it took to lift the darkness to a point where he could see the shimmer of the sparkles in Flick's dress and he put his phone in his pocket, so that only they would be able to hear the soft music.

And then they danced. Barefoot. Flick's hair was a tumble of classic 'bed hair' ruffled waves and he couldn't forget that she was naked beneath a dress that was even more gorgeously sparkly in this soft light. Lachlan was half-naked himself with his shirt unbuttoned and the sleeves rolled up. He was tired enough for this to feel as if it was part of a dream. Maybe that was why Flick felt so light in his arms and how she responded to his lead as if she'd been dancing her whole life.

They circled the parquet floor once and then again. There was no stepping on toes but, rather, a feeling of connection that was almost a continuation of their lovemaking.

It felt like flying.

It felt like falling at the same time.

Falling in love…?

The music ended almost as he had that thought and Lachlan could only stare at Flick, stunned by what had just hit him completely unexpectedly.

He saw the lines of concern appear on her face. 'You look *so* tired,' she whispered. 'You need to sleep.'

He did. Maybe, by some miracle, things would look different in the morning. He would have come back to his senses. But he couldn't go upstairs to his own room without saying something.

'You've learned to dance.' His words were soft. 'You are an amazing woman, Felicity Stephens. I hope you know that.'

There was a smile on her lips as she stood on tiptoe to place a soft kiss on his.

'I think it was the dress that made the difference. Only I need to take it off. This bodice is tight enough to be really uncomfortable.'

Lachlan couldn't help letting his gaze drop to the swell of her breasts over that beaded bodice but it only made him want Flick all over again. Made him want to somehow keep what they had for ever.

He swallowed hard. This was the kind of dangerous territory he'd always kept very well clear of.

'Goodnight, Flick,' he murmured. 'Sleep well.'

CHAPTER TEN

'I THINK WE'RE good to go.' Lachlan tapped the paper in front of him. 'I'm happy with these results of the repeat nerve function electrical test. It sets us up to use the classic approach to repairing the brachial plexus network.'

Josh looked up from the detailed result sheets they'd both been studying. 'That's where you use the distal branches of the spinal accessory nerve to neurotise the suprascapular nerve?'

'It is. I'll find the donor nerve first because that's easier than locating the suprascapular notch and nerve.'

'I'm looking forward to watching. You're not bothered that the gallery's going to be packed?'

'I'm getting used to things like that. I've been in London today, filming a follow-up appointment with a boy that's part of a medical documentary. I did a masseteric nerve transfer surgery to treat his facial paralysis a few weeks ago. It'll take months to get the full benefit but he's putting everything he has into retraining his muscles. We're just beginning to see the first

signs and he's so excited. It's the kind of thing I love most about my job.'

'It can't be easy flitting back and forth like that and then having a late night like this. No wonder you look done in.'

'Yeah.' Lachlan rubbed the back of his neck. 'I think I'll just crash in town tonight.'

'Come home with me?'

'Thanks, but I rather fancy a nice hotel with room service. Close enough to walk in and get some fresh air before the surgery tomorrow. I'm not getting enough exercise at the moment. My joints are making me feeling twice as old as I am.'

'As *we* are.' Josh smiled. 'I feel like that sometimes. I'm getting older way too fast.' His smile faded. 'Are things no better with your mother, then? Is that part of why you don't want to go home tonight?'

Lachlan shrugged. 'Maybe. I'm still trying to get my head around it all, you know?'

He didn't want to share the new information he had about Josephine McKendry with Josh yet. Not until he was sure about how he felt about it and he was too exhausted to go there right now. Or to think about how he was feeling about Flick, for that matter. He owed it to his small patient to be in the best possible form tomorrow morning and that meant pushing anything personal aside.

'There's a great hotel just a block or so away. I'll walk out with you and point you in the right direction.'

'Thanks, mate.'

A cleaner who was mopping the floor outside the

ground floor pharmacy did a double-take of the two identical men walking past him but neither Lachlan nor Josh were bothered. They were getting used to it, now. Getting used to the idea of being related, too.

Family.

One of the 'F' words that Lachlan had long considered against the rules, along with 'Full time' and 'Future'. The opposite of the acceptable 'Fun'.

Good Lord…had he really been that shallow such a short time ago?

He paused as the brothers stood outside the hospital but he wasn't taking any notice of the direction Josh was pointing in.

'Do you think it made it easier?' he asked, 'Knowing all along that you'd been adopted?'

'I think it made it worse,' Josh told him. 'I knew I was different. That I didn't belong, somehow, but I didn't know why until a "real" son came along and I wasn't wanted any more.'

Lachlan shook his head. 'I never knew and I think that was worse because I didn't belong either but I never knew why. Until I met you.'

And the truth had finally come out. How much worse would it have been if Flick hadn't been there at the start of all this? How much harder would it be when she'd moved on, possibly in the not so distant future? At least Lachlan could be thankful that he hadn't said anything about how he was feeling about her in the ballroom last night. If he had, she might have packed her bags already. She'd made it very clear why she lived a no-madic kind of life.

'I've never wanted to stop because I might get caught by something. Or someone...'

'I could never survive loving and losing like that again...'

'Real life is never a fairy tale...'

Josh's glance suggested he could guess that Lachlan's thoughts were straying. 'Life's got a bit crazy, hasn't it? For both of us.'

'You're not wrong there. I've got too many things changing too fast and I've never liked feeling that I'm not in control.' Lachlan let his breath out in a sigh. 'Ah, well...tomorrow's another day, huh? Show me again where the hotel is?'

Being taken out by Lachlan to have dinner with his brother and friend at one of the most prestigious, Michelin-starred restaurants in the area felt very much like they were on a double date. As if their secret, temporary relationship had just been elevated to a new level. Nothing with any promise of permanence, of course, but the way Lachlan's hands shaped Flick's shoulders as he helped her to shrug off her coat made her realise just how comfortable they were as a couple now. How easy it was to communicate with simply a touch or a glance.

Which was why Lachlan probably knew how startled she was to find herself with another version of him. For a while, she felt as awkward as Lachlan had clearly been the night before, when he'd finally agreed to join his mother for dinner in what seemed to be a first, tentative step on both their parts to move forward. Not that

they'd discussed anything personal but Flick, who'd also been invited to join them, had felt like the polite conversation was a cautious attempt to find common ground that could be built on later.

Being introduced to Josh and his friend Stevie as 'Felicity' made things even more awkward.

'Call me Flick,' she'd told them. 'I've only ever been called Felicity by the taxman or the police.'

'What were the police after you for?' Lachlan was smiling as he caught her gaze. 'No, don't tell me… I think I'd rather leave that to my imagination for a while.'

Oh…that smile. That rather intimate innuendo that came with his words made it seem like they'd been doing this for ever. Dating. Being out in public as a real couple.

And it felt so right that Flick found herself relaxing as drinks were ordered and menus perused. It didn't surprise her at all that both she and Lachlan chose the same starter of hay-smoked scallops.

'How's that lad doing?' Lachlan asked Josh. 'From the brachial plexus repair?'

'Very well…'

'I've been trying to get back to see him again but it's been full on.' Lachlan put down his fork although he'd barely tasted his food. 'Lectures here, surgeries there and I've had to dash up to London a couple of times as well.'

'Sounds stressful.' Josh sounded sympathetic.

'At least I don't have to worry about anything on the home front.' He raised his glass in Flick's direction. 'You're doing a fabulous job,' he told her. 'I'm not at

all surprised that London Locums considers you to be one of their very best nurses. I will be grateful to you for ever. For everything...'

Flick had to break that eye contact—before Lachlan could see just how much his praise and appreciation was melting her. How much she loved him... She stared at her plate, even closing her eyes for a heartbeat to try and regain control.

Josh's question about how long she'd been a locum nurse was a welcome direction to take her thoughts.

'Oh, years...' Flick found a smile for Lachlan's brother. 'I love the excitement of everything being new. Meeting new people, getting to know a new place. A new challenge...'

She stopped talking, her gaze shifting instantly to Lachlan as he made an odd sound of discomfort.

'It's a bit warm in here, isn't it?' Flick watched, concerned, as he rubbed his forehead in a familiar gesture that indicated stress. Then he pushed back his chair. 'Excuse me for a moment. I just need a bit of fresh air.'

Concern became a flash of alarm as Flick watched Lachlan head for a set of French doors near their table that led to a pretty courtyard garden with manicured hedges and strings of fairy lights. She pushed her plate away and had her hands on the table ready to push herself to her feet and go after Lachlan but Josh had moved first.

'I'll go,' he said.

She was still watching as Josh joined his brother outside and started talking to him. This was good. Josh was a doctor and, if Lachlan was unwell in any

way, he would be able to help better than Flick could. What was really worrying her, however, was the level of her concern.

She knew she had fallen in love with Lachlan McKendry. She hadn't quite realised until now just how profound her feelings were, though, had she? This wasn't just concern that someone she cared about might be unwell. This was a twinge of a fear that she'd had to face before—that the person she couldn't live without might be in danger…

Oh, boy…she might be in a bit of trouble here.

Catching a glance from Stevie only strengthened the instant connection she'd felt for this friend of Lachlan's brother with her gorgeously wild, red hair and big, genuine smile.

She wasn't the only one who was in love with a twin, was she?

Not that either of them wanted to say anything aloud. There was a note in that glance that was one of understanding. They both knew how the childhoods of these twins who'd been separated had shaped a remarkably similar attitude to whether they wanted a permanent relationship in their own lives. Flick could recognise things in Stevie's eyes that she was feeling herself. Like hope. And fear.

It was that fear that made her look outside again and then it suddenly became infinitely worse because she saw the moment when Lachlan became unsteady on his feet and then crumpled, clearly having lost consciousness. Josh caught his brother in time to stop him hitting his head on the flagstone terrace and Flick could

see him crouching to see if Lachlan was breathing by the time she'd run from the table and pushed open the French doors, Stevie on her heels.

'What can I do?' It was Stevie who spoke first as they got to the two men.

Flick's brain was frozen. With her experience in emergency departments, she should know exactly what to do but the fear was paralysing her now.

'Oh, my God...' she whispered, dropping to her knees beside Lachlan. She could actually feel the blood draining from her face. *'No...'*

She touched Lachlan's hand. Curled her own fingers around it and held it tightly, as if she could somehow share some of her own strength. Above her, Josh's words seemed faint—as if they were coming from a long way away.

'He's breathing. And he's got a good, steady pulse. He may have just fainted for whatever reason but I think we'd better call an ambulance.'

Flick was still clinging to Lachlan's hand as he regained consciousness before help arrived but he still seemed drowsy and his speech was slurred enough for the paramedics to be concerned. They helped him into the back of the ambulance to take an ECG and check vital signs like his blood pressure, blood glucose level and oxygen saturation. One of them asked how much alcohol he'd had but Josh was insistent that there was something more going on here and that scared Flick even more.

What was going on and how serious could it be?

Lachlan had picked up on a note in his brother's voice

and he was trying to sit up. 'Gotta go home…' he said. 'It's my mother…she's the one who's sick…'

'She's all right,' Flick reassured him. 'I just rang Mrs Tillman to tell her that I would be going to the hospital with you so I might be later than expected.'

But Lachlan was shaking his head. 'No need. I'm fine. And it's my mother you're employed to care for… not *me*… I don't need it… Can look after myself…'

He was pushing her away. Like she had feared he might when she'd been avoiding telling him what she'd learned about his mother's story. She knew how badly she didn't want to be pushed out of his life. How much it could hurt. But she'd had no idea, had she? This was hurting far more than Flick had ever imagined it could.

Especially now. When Lachlan was sick. Possibly afraid. When he most needed someone who cared to be by his side. And that person should be her but then Josh spoke.

'I'll go with Lachlan,' he said.

His gaze told her that he understood. That she wasn't to worry because he wasn't about to leave his brother alone even if Lachlan was so sure he could cope without anybody. And Josh had more right to be with Lachlan at a time like this, didn't he? He was family. Not just someone who'd been employed to care for his mother. Lachlan had said he didn't need her.

Perhaps he didn't want her, either…

CHAPTER ELEVEN

THERE'D BEEN A few things in Lachlan McKendry's thirty-six years on earth that had scared him enough to be memorable but this particular moment made every other occasion instantly insignificant.

'I'm sorry to have to give you this result, but it's AML.' David, the consultant and head of the haematology department, clearly knew he didn't have to elaborate on the diagnosis to the two other doctors in the room but perhaps he didn't realise that the third person present had medical knowledge. 'Acute myeloid leukaemia,' he added quietly, his gaze shifting to Flick.

Lachlan closed his eyes as he shifted in the bed, trying to find a more comfortable position. The local anaesthetic in his hip had worn off some time ago and a dull ache was making sure he didn't forget the bone marrow biopsy he'd had first thing this morning. Or why it had been necessary.

He heard Josh clear his throat. 'We kind of guessed it might be, last night,' he told David. 'When we added up his symptoms after that first blood count had come

through.' He was standing close to the bed. 'But I was still hoping we could be wrong.'

Lachlan could see a reflection of his own fear in Josh's eyes and he didn't want that, any more than he'd wanted his brother to stay with him after that first, worrying test result last night. He wasn't used to having someone who genuinely cared about what was happening to him because he'd never let anyone that close and…it made things harder. You had to worry about them, as well as yourself.

'A normal level of blasts—the immature white blood cells—should be less than five percent,' David said, breaking the sombre silence in the room. 'Yours are over twenty percent, Lachlan.'

Lachlan didn't want to look at Flick to see how she was taking the news. Because he was afraid she would look like Josh did? Or more afraid that she wouldn't— that she was only here out of politeness or perhaps, at best, friendship?

'Is there a genetic component?' he asked. 'Because, if there is, maybe Josh is at risk and he'd better get himself tested as well.'

'I did read about a case of identical twins getting diagnosed with AML a few days apart,' Josh said. 'Probably because I was up half the night, reading.' He offered Lachlan an apologetic smile. 'Concordant AML, it's called, but the good news is that they had a sibling who was an HLA match and they got a stem cell transplant, which has apparently cured them. They didn't even get any graft versus host disease.'

HLA. Human leukocyte antigens? Lachlan needed

to do a bit of reading himself and refresh everything he knew about haematology.

'A bone marrow/stem cell transplant, with or without chemotherapy, certainly offers the potential of a complete cure,' David nodded. 'But we're a wee way away from talking about that yet. What we need to focus on right now is some more tests to collect as much information as we can about the subtype and staging and then we'll be able to plan your chemotherapy regime, Lachlan. I'd like to start as soon as possible. Tomorrow, even.'

So, there it was.

This was real. And urgent. This wasn't just yet another revelation to add to the ones that had turned Lachlan's life inside out in recent weeks. They had merely been warning shots and now his life was actually imploding. Josh clearly wanted to believe he was going to have a positive outcome like the case he'd read about but there was also a distinct possibility that he was facing the end of his life.

And it was scaring the hell out of him.

And...he couldn't help looking at Flick now. He wanted nothing more than to be alone with her. For her to put her arms around him and hold him so tightly he could think about nothing more than how much he needed her.

How much he loved her... If he'd had any doubts at all about how he felt about this woman, the thought that he might not live much longer had just wiped them out completely. It was strange how it could focus the mind like a laser beam on what was actually important in life.

And that was people.

Love.

He'd learned to live without it. Avoid it. How ironic was it that he'd found two people who represented the best of what people and love could offer, just in the last few weeks? Which meant this was going to affect them as well.

Hurt them.

Neither of them deserved that but it was especially awful for Flick when she'd been through this before. If he'd been unsure of whether he would see how much she cared when he caught her gaze, those doubts had also evaporated completely. She looked easily as pale and sick as he was feeling himself. As if she was already hurting past the point of it being bearable—because she really did care about him.

Loved him, even—as much as he loved her?

He couldn't do this to her. Or to Josh. He could sense how much his brother wanted to be involved—how connected he was—but maybe the only way Lachlan could show how much *he* cared was to spare him the kind of pain that could well be on the way. The kind they all knew about, that came with either losing or not receiving the love they needed so much.

Lachlan deliberately shuttered his gaze as he held eye contact with Flick. An unspoken denial of how he felt about her. A non-verbal shove that was intended to tell her the opposite, in fact. That he didn't need her. Or want her.

And the message seemed to have got through because Flick appeared to shrink back. To gather herself

in some way that made her seem smaller and more vulnerable. Her voice sounded different, too. As though it was someone else that was speaking.

'I'm so sorry,' she said. 'But I can't do this again...'

Lachlan had already broken the eye contact but he could see her in his peripheral vision. And he could see the shock on Josh's face when she turned and walked out of the room.

He didn't feel shocked.

He felt...relieved... Surely it would be far better for her in the long run to be angry with him and get as far away as possible. He couldn't blame her for running. He'd do it himself, if he could.

History was not supposed to repeat itself. Not this kind of history, anyway, and especially not when you'd done everything possible to make absolutely sure it *couldn't* repeat itself.

Flick actually felt so physically sick she went into the nearest toilets and ran cold water to cup in her hands and splash onto her face.

Leukaemia.

Cancer.

Watching someone that you loved *this* much slip away from you and being unable to help. Having your heart break, again and again, into tiny shards that she now knew could make you bleed inside for years and years.

She couldn't do this again because she wouldn't survive.

Even now, as Flick left the shelter of the bathroom

and made her way to the front door of Cheltenham Central Hospital, she could feel the cracks widening in her heart already and the pain was enough to make her feel unsteady on her feet. She stopped again, beside a kiosk in the main entrance that sold magazines and newspapers.

'Are you all right, love?' The woman in the kiosk was leaning over the counter to peer at Flick.

'I'm…fine…'

Flick reached out towards a tall, rotating stand of magazines in the hope that it would provide support. But even as she touched it, she could feel it falling away and taking her with it.

And then everything went dark.

'Ah…there you are. Welcome back.'

'Where am I?'

'In the emergency department of Cheltenham Central. You passed out in our foyer and someone carried you in here a few minutes ago. What's your name?'

'Flick…'

'Pardon?' The young doctor was looking bemused.

'Officially, it's Felicity. Felicity Stephens.' The lights above her were very bright so Flick screwed up her eyes. Was that why she could suddenly see Lachlan in her mind? And hear his voice as he used her proper name?

'I'm so sorry, Felicity… I've had a rather difficult day and I suspect you might very well be the answer to my prayers.'

More than that. She could see that first glimpse of who Lachlan McKendry really was under that polished

and sophisticated exterior. The real man who was upstairs in this hospital and…and she couldn't afford to start thinking about him. Not if she was going to survive.

'But you prefer to be called Flick?' The junior ED medic was on top of things now. 'How old are you, Flick? And do you have any underlying medical conditions I should know about?'

'I'm thirty-two. And, no… I'm perfectly healthy. I'm just a bit stressed, that's all. And I skipped breakfast.'

'As a rule, perfectly healthy people don't faint and remain unconscious for a while. We'd like to run a few tests before we let you go, okay?'

'I need to get home. I'm a nurse. I have someone to look after.' Flick tried to sit up only to find her head was still spinning a little. And she didn't need to rush back to Lady Josephine. In fact, she'd been ordered not to.

I can look after myself, for heaven's sake. I should have been doing it years ago. Go and find what's happening with my…with Lachlan. Please… I need to know he's all right.'

'As a nurse, you'll know we have a protocol to try and identify the cause of unconsciousness.' The doctor was wrapping a tourniquet around her arm. 'We'll take some bloods, do a finger prick for your BGL and do an ECG. Any chance you could be pregnant?'

A huff of something like laughter came from Flick's throat. That would be the straw that broke the camel's back, wouldn't it?

'No chance,' she said. But there was a tiny voice at the back of her head, reminding her of that first time

she and Lachlan had made love. When emotions had been running so high that night in the wake of Lachlan learning not only that he'd been adopted but that his mother had never wanted him, protection hadn't crossed their minds. But it had only been the once and…and how long ago *had* that been?

The doctor must have seen the flash of alarm in her eyes.

'We'll do a urine dipstick as well, just to cover all the bases. It'll be quicker than the blood test.'

Quick was a relative term, of course. It was well over an hour before her doctor had the chance to come and talk to her again. By then, Flick had been given a sandwich and a cup of tea.

'I'm feeling absolutely fine now,' she told the doctor. 'It *was* just because I skipped breakfast. I won't do that again.'

'Have you noticed any other symptoms in the last couple of weeks? Nausea? Sore breasts? Can you remember when the first day of your last period was?'

The last time Flick could remember even thinking about her period had been when she'd taken her toiletries from her suitcase to put with what she was packing to bring to the Cotswolds and the trickle of fear that ran down her spine arrived at the same moment she realised that her last period had been while she'd still been in Australia.

That tiny alarm bell was there again but this time it was ringing loudly enough to drown out everything else. Flick could feel herself going pale—the way she had only last night, when she'd knelt beside Lachlan,

not knowing whether he was still breathing or not. That same reaction was an echo in her head as well, even as she could feel a welcome numbness sweeping in to protect her from trying to cope all at once with something that could have catastrophic repercussions in her life. Something she'd never thought she'd have to think about again.

No...

She didn't need this doctor to confirm the news she was warning her was coming but it was probably something that had to be done.

'I'm sorry if it's a shock for you,' the doctor said gently. 'But there's no mistake. You're definitely pregnant.'

CHAPTER TWELVE

'YOU DON'T HAVE to be here.' Lachlan avoided making any direct eye contact with Josh, who'd been sitting quietly beside his bed for some time now. 'I know I'm not exactly good company.'

It had been a hell of a day with so much happening as his specialists launched him into remission induction with the intention of killing all the AML cells in his blood. He'd started the first day of this frightening twist in his life with a surgical procedure to insert a central venous line just under his collarbone and, this afternoon, Lachlan had spent a couple of hours hooked up to a machine to undergo leukapheresis—a procedure that could rapidly reduce white blood cells counts to provide a head start to chemotherapy designed to achieve remission.

He had never felt this exhausted in his life. The intense medical procedures he'd undergone had been confronting on more than a physical level because he was being forced to face up to the reality of his situation and…it was terrifying.

As a form of escape that he hadn't been able to re-

sist today, Lachlan's thoughts had drifted frequently to catching something far more pleasant to focus on. Like his beloved woodland, with its current carpet of blue-bells, or the kitchen of his childhood with its warmth and the lingering aromas of comfort food. The problem with that, however, was that he couldn't think of anything pleasant that didn't include Flick and he was missing her so badly today, it was another level of pain all on its own.

He wanted her to be sitting where Josh was. He wanted her to know that he hadn't meant to hurt her when he'd sent her away. When he'd hurt her by telling her that he didn't need her. Had he really been so dismissive that he'd told her she'd only been employed to care for his mother? But he couldn't give in to the desire to see her again. Not when protecting her from this was perhaps the only way he could show how much he cared about her, even if she would never know.

He cared about Josh, too. More than it should be possible to care about someone he'd only met a matter of weeks ago. But then, he'd had that feeling that half of his life had been stolen—more than that—that he'd been missing half of himself. No wonder it felt so right to have Josh here. And so wrong, for the same reasons it would be wrong to ask Flick to go through this by his side. He knew, without anything being said, that Josh felt the same way about being reunited with his twin. He shouldn't have to go through this, either.

But Josh had other ideas.

'I want to be here.' His tone was a warning not to argue but Lachlan also had other ideas.

'You managed without me in your life for thirty-six years, Josh. It won't be that hard to get used to it again.'

'I don't want to get used to it. You're my brother. The only family I've got.'

'You might have to get used to it.' Lachlan tried a wry laugh but it came out embarrassingly close to a kind of strangled sob. 'Take a leaf out of Flick's book. She's managed to walk away, no problem.'

'Has she? Has she actually gone?'

'Well…she's still here—in the district, at least. Only until we can find another locum nurse. My housekeeper, Mrs Tillman, is sorting that mess out for me.'

Tilly had come to see him late this afternoon. Just a very brief visit, for no more than a minute or two, because she could see how tired Lachlan was and he could see how upset she was.

'You're not going to believe this,' he told Josh, 'but she says Josephine is upset about me. Crocodile tears, huh?'

'I doubt that. Sometimes it takes a shock for people to wake up and see what really matters.'

'Well… I've had a shock and…guess what? Nothing really matters.' Because it was never real, was it? He'd come as close as he ever had in the last few weeks to believing that he could trust the most important things in life, like family—and love—only to find he was about to lose them. Right now, that seemed worse than never having found them at all.

He'd managed alone for his whole life and he could manage this alone too. Especially because anyone else who was too close would only suffer along with him.

He knew that Josh was finding the discovery of family connection and the love it represented as significant as he was so he had to persuade his brother to back off and protect himself, even if he had to be cruel to be kind— like he had with Flick.

'Go away, Josh.' This time, Lachlan did make eye contact with his brother. 'Get on with your own life. Get over yourself and marry that nice girl with that astonishing hair.' He managed to find a smile although he couldn't hang on to it because he didn't want Josh to see his lips tremble. 'Go. Be happy for both of us...'

Lachlan desperately needed to sleep. Not simply because exhaustion demanded it but because it was the best way to escape, at least for a little while. But sleep wouldn't come, even long after Josh had gone.

He found himself going over and over their conversation. Had he been right, in suggesting that his mother had been shocked into realising that she did actually care about the adopted son she'd never thought she wanted? Had she pushed him away in the same way as he was pushing both Josh and Flick away from himself now, because he was afraid of the pain that could be experienced on both sides by leaning into having people caring about him? About how much worse it would be to know he had no future when he had people *he* cared deeply about?

He could almost begin to understand.

Begin to forgive...

But still the peace that sleep could bring eluded him. His thoughts drifted from his mother to Josh. From Josh to Flick. Disjointed thoughts, flashes of emotion

and—despite everything—a persistent longing, *hope* even, that refused to be dismissed. They were impressions and images, memories and feelings that all felt like pieces of a puzzle that had been tipped, haphazardly, all over a tabletop and were lying, completely jumbled up, in front of him.

Lachlan had no idea where to start to try and put them together but, in the moments as sleep finally stilled those thoughts, he had the feeling that the picture that puzzle would make might be just out of sight but it was imperative that he find out what it was.

Because it could be the most important thing he would ever see in his life and there was pressure building because he could be running out of time...

It was funny that you could be so numb you couldn't feel anything at all but you could still function well enough that nobody else could tell that your life had fallen apart. But, then, the people around her had enough on their minds already, didn't they?

Mrs Tillman overheard the tail end of a conversation with Julia at London Locums the next day when Flick said it might be necessary to line up some candidates to take over Lady Josephine's medical care, but if she disapproved of Flick abandoning the family in a time of crisis she didn't let it show.

'I've got some lovely cheese scones just out of the oven,' was all she said. 'Make sure you have one, won't you, with a cup of tea?'

'I'm really not hungry, thank you.'

'I'm not sure if Lady J. wants to come down for her

dinner tonight but it's in the oven for later. I'm off up to Cheltenham to see how our Lachlan's getting on. When we rang earlier, they said he was starting treatment already, poor lad. But that's a good thing, isn't it? Starting treatment early?'

Flick nodded. 'The sooner the better.'

Lady Josephine hadn't wanted to go downstairs for dinner.

'Unless you're eating something, Felicity?'

'I'm not really hungry.'

'Neither am I. But I can't really miss a meal, can I? Not if I'm taking proper care of myself.'

'You're doing very well,' Flick told her. 'Even with all this new upset, you haven't had an asthma attack or any chest pain and your blood glucose levels are a lot more stable than I would have expected.'

'I want to be able to take care of myself.' Lady Josephine took in a quick breath. 'I want to be able to take care of Lachlan, if he'll let me. I didn't do a very good job of that when he was a child, did I? Maybe I can make up for it, at least a little.' She wasn't looking at Flick as she spoke, she was staring out of her window at that view across the gardens towards the woods. 'I'm feeling older today,' she added softly. So softly Flick barely heard. 'And I'm lonely...'

She pretended not to have heard, in case commenting on the admission embarrassed Lady Josephine. 'I'll bring your dinner up on a tray,' she said. 'Maybe some for both of us. And, after that, maybe we could have a game of Scrabble?'

Lady Josephine caught her gaze then and her voice

was much stronger. 'I knew you were brave the first time I met you. Feisty. I liked that about you right from the start.' Her smile softened her face so that she looked like a very different woman from the one Flick had first met. 'You've changed something in this house,' she added. 'You've brought life back into it. Even some music and dancing and I don't want to lose that again. I want Lachlan to forgive me one day. Do you think that might be even possible?'

'He loves you,' Flick told her. 'That's why it hurt so much to be told he hadn't been wanted. But, I also think, if you love someone enough, then anything's possible.'

It was probably the thing that Lady Josephine had said that she might not have intended to have been over-heard that punctured the safe, numb cocoon Flick had wrapped around her heart.

I'm lonely...

The words came back in the middle of another sleepless night to echo in the silence of her room. More than echo—they resonated deep within Flick because she was lonely too. She had been ever since she'd lost Patrick but she'd never stayed still long enough to let herself think about it. She'd run away from the realisation just as effectively as she'd run from getting involved with someone. And, okay, she'd talked to Julia today about moving on from this position in the McKendry household but she couldn't run this time, could she?

Her hand moved to lie gently on top of her belly.

How could she run when she'd be taking something so precious away from someone she cared about so much?

There was nothing more precious than a baby.

A new life.

Something to live for.

Tears were streaming down Flick's cheeks now. If nothing else, Lachlan had the right to know that he was going to be a father. That, even if he didn't win this battle, there was a part of him who would still be in the world. Being cherished.

But, oh…the pain that was seeping in as the numbness lifted was unbearable. She'd have to pull herself together before she went to see Lachlan. He had more than enough to deal with without her making things worse.

Without knowing she was doing it, Mrs Tillman backed her up.

'The world hasn't ended, lovey,' she told Flick the next morning as she put a cup of coffee in front of her. 'Goodness me, I think Lachlan looked happier when I went to visit him than you do at the moment.'

'How was he feeling?'

'He said nothing hurt, he was just very, very tired. He'd had some extraordinary thing done to him where they take out all your blood and spin it around so fast all the cells separate and they take out the bad ones and then put all the blood back. I really didn't understand how they could do that. He's going to start on the chemotherapy next and I expect that will be harder. Are you going to visit him?'

Flick nodded. 'I'll ring and see if he's allowed visitors.'

Apparently, the only visiting hours allowed were mid-afternoon and early evening. Flick picked up her

car keys to head into town in the afternoon but ended up sitting in her car, having not even turned on the engine, as she tried, and failed, to decide how she was going to tell Lachlan what he needed to know and how he might react. When she tried, she failed not to let herself be totally overcome by fear. And grief. Old, remembered grief but worse—this new one that was so sharp it was threatening to shred her heart into ribbons.

She sat in her car for so long she could see that the sun was sinking below the canopy of the tallest trees in the woodlands as she walked from the garage back to the entrance to the house. Without thinking, she changed direction, her shoes crunching on the pebbled paths and then silent on the grass lawns as she made her way into the woods, retracing the path that Lachlan had taken her on when he'd introduced her to the magic of the bluebells.

The flowers were past their best now, weeks later, but there were still enough to be a soft haze of blue covering the ground between the dark trunks of the trees, lit up by shafts of sunshine that pushed their way through small branches and clouds of leaves. Flick found the exact spot that Lachlan had taken her to and she had to close her eyes and stand very still as the scent surrounded her and memories crowded in with the deep breath she took.

Like that first time in many years that she'd encountered this scent, when she'd buried her nose in those flowers in the jam jar that Lachlan had picked as a gift for her after they'd made love for the first time.

The night their baby had most likely been conceived…

The time Flick had realised that things were changing. That her body was coming back to life and, with the benefit of hindsight, that it *was* possible that she could risk her heart and fall in love again.

Opening her eyes, she could almost see Lachlan here with her as she remembered telling him about the baby she'd lost and how losing the man she loved as well had broken her too much to ever be able to put those pieces back together again. But then he'd held her and, while she might not have recognised it at the time, that had been when the distance between those broken pieces had begun to shrink.

Flick was barely aware of the tears still rolling slowly down her face as she stooped and picked a flower and then another. By the time she had three blooms between her fingers, she was remembering seeing a tiny bouquet like this on Lady Josephine's table and that had been the moment she'd realised that those pieces had been put back together. That she was totally in love with Lachlan and that she couldn't run away. She could hear an echo of Lady Josephine's words, too, about those flowers.

'They smelt like tears...'

But to Flick they still smelt like a new beginning. Still holding those few blooms, she wrapped her arms around herself as she took another deep breath, soaking in the scent.

And that reminded her of that night in the ballroom and the way Lachlan had been looking at her after that magical, barefoot dance together with Lachlan's shirt unbuttoned and her wearing that gloriously swirly blue dress.

You could only look at someone you loved like that.

He did love her, didn't he? Had he pushed her away because he was trying to protect her from the possibility of having to relive the devastation of losing Patrick? The experience she'd told him had been so unbearable she had learned to run from getting that close to anyone ever again?

But surely that was her choice to make?

What if the shoe had been on the other foot and she was the one who'd been given a scary diagnosis? How much worse would it be to face something like that without someone who cared by your side? She remembered how helpless it had made her feel not being able to change the outcome with Patrick but why hadn't she thought about the gift she'd given by being there with him for every possible moment and loving him until the very end?

Would she want Lachlan to be with her—to hold her in his arms—even if she knew he'd been through heartbreak like that before? Of course she would—but only if he wanted to be there and if he felt strong enough to stay, and that would have to be entirely his own choice. She would never have put pressure on him by asking.

That was what Lachlan was doing, she realised. He had given her a way out. A chance to run. The space to make that choice for herself. Flick brushed away the last tears on her face and could feel her strength gathering. Perhaps she'd already made that choice when she'd come here to a place that was always going to be filled with memories of this new love in her life. Or perhaps that should be simply a new life…

Along with the strength came a new resolution. Lachlan couldn't be allowed to assume that the worst was going to happen, either. Life was full of unexpected twists and turns. For heaven's sake, he'd discovered that he had an identical twin brother and it was already obvious that they had formed a strong bond. There was also a very real possibility that Josh could be a perfect match for a stem cell transplant and a complete cure for Lachlan. And it could be that she and Lachlan had a future ahead of them that they could dream about like any other couple in love.

If she was right, that was, and he was in love with her.

She had to find that out for sure, mind you, but she knew she'd know the moment she walked into that hospital room and caught his gaze because there were so many things they could say to each other without actually speaking any words. Flick found herself smiling as she crouched down again to pick a few more flowers to add to the ones in her hand. Maybe it was a bit of a cliché to take a bouquet as a gift when you went to visit someone in hospital but this was different.

It was personal.

Some couples had a special song that was deeply significant to them both. She and Lachlan McKendry had a flower…

Sometimes, success was not something that you could celebrate at all.

Who knew?

Lachlan lay in his bed, alone in his private hospital

room, feeling more alone than he had ever felt in his entire life. It had been another long day and he'd had doctors and nurses and technicians around him as they planned and then started a chemotherapy regime that would hopefully put him into remission in the shortest possible time, but now he was alone.

Because he'd been so successful in pushing the people that really mattered out of his life.

Visiting hours this afternoon had come and gone with nobody arriving. Evening hours had started a while back now and, again, there was nobody. He'd tried calling Josh a little while ago, with the intention of apologising for what he'd said last night, but his brother hadn't picked up. He hadn't even had a text message from Josh, which he couldn't really be surprised by since he'd told him to go away and get on with his own life. He didn't have any right to expect that Flick would front up, either, when he'd basically told her that she wasn't needed. Or wanted.

And these were good things, Lachlan tried to reassure himself. It was what he'd wanted, wasn't it? That he could handle this on his own. That he wouldn't drag anyone else along on what could potentially be a rough journey. The only downside of being left with nothing but his own thoughts to distract him was…well…he was thinking too much.

About what life had been like only a matter of weeks ago. About how his professional life had been exactly what he'd always dreamed of it being and the only major worries in his personal life had been that his mother had kept antagonising and then dismissing her carers and

that his current female companion had made the fatal mistake of wanting to talk about their 'future'. Good grief...he had to think for a moment before he could remember her name. Sharon? Cheryl? No... Shayna.

Lachlan sent a silent apology out into the universe but then he found his mouth twisting into a wry kind of smile. What wouldn't he give to be able to talk about a 'future' with someone now? Or 'family', which was another one of the 'F' words he'd believed he never wanted to apply to his own personal life. He could still count the hours since that final, dramatic twist in his life and the shock had stripped everything irrelevant away, leaving him with a perspective on life that was stunningly simple in its clarity.

The work that he loved so much mattered, of course. He could change lives and do amazing things for others but...what really mattered when you were faced with something *this* huge was who actually cared about *you* and not just about what you had done with your life.

How many times had he heard or read about people losing their battle with a terminal illness where there was comfort to be found in the simple sentence that they'd been surrounded by their friends and family.

More 'F' words. And what was even more ironic was that there was another one that simply wouldn't be silenced. One that he could feel, even more than he could hear echoing in the back of his head, especially when he was alone like this and when he closed his eyes.

Flick... Felicity... *Flick*...

Maybe he'd whispered her name out loud without

realising it but the last thing he'd expected to hear was her voice, unless that was also in his imagination?

'I'm here, Lachlan.'

His eyes flew open but, because he was lying down, the first thing he saw was a bunch of slightly bedraggled bluebells. They looked as if they were almost ready to drop their petals. As if their stalks had been clutched a little too tightly for a little too long. They were also the most beautiful things Lachlan had ever seen. Because he couldn't see them without remembering the way he'd held Flick in his arms that day in the woods. About the way she'd climbed into his heart and pulled the door closed behind her so that there was no way she would ever leave it.

No… Maybe that had been when the door had been pulled tightly shut but she had reached a space in his heart and soul well before that. When she'd seen him for exactly who he was—a man who'd been so damaged by never feeling loved—and she had taken him into *her* arms and he'd known that he could never truly give up on wanting to be loved.

He'd believed that he never wanted a family.

But the truth was the complete opposite. It had been the only thing he'd ever truly wanted.

Lachlan raised his eyes to meet Flick's and realised they were almost the same colour as the flowers she held in her hands. They were also shining very brightly with unshed tears.

'I had to come,' she said softly. 'And I'm not leaving you again. I love you too much to do that.'

'Oh…thank God,' Lachlan breathed. He couldn't

look away from those eyes. He wanted to soak in the love he could see there until it filled every cell in his body. 'I only told you to go because it was the only way I could think to show you how much I love *you*.'

'I can think of a much better way.' The tears were escaping from Flick's eyes but she was smiling.

Those bluebells somehow got scattered over the covers as Flick found space to squeeze in beside Lachlan on his bed so that they could just lie there and hold each other, their heads so close together on his pillows that their foreheads were touching.

'You're right.' Lachlan felt too weak to do anything other than accept Flick's gentle kiss but he could keep his arms around her and feel the way she was holding him. 'This is a much better way.'

'That's not what I meant.' He could feel Flick's breasts push against his arm as she took a deep breath. 'I've got something to tell you.'

'You just told me the most important thing you could ever say.' Not that Lachlan would ever tire of hearing her tell him how much she loved him. In fact, he needed to hear it again. 'But don't stop,' he added. 'Don't ever stop. I promise I won't, either. I love you, Flick. I love you *so* much.'

'I'm pregnant,' Flick whispered. 'You're going to be a father, Lachlan.'

Oh…*man*… He hadn't seen that coming. An 'F' word that hadn't even entered his head. One that eclipsed all others but included them, as well. Father. Family. *Future*…

A future that was more than worth fighting for.

'That's what I meant.' Flick's voice wobbled. 'We're going to win this battle. Because I need you. Our baby needs you.'

This was breaking her heart—in a good way.

That they wouldn't win the battle ahead of them was not going to be allowed any head space right now but what was making her heart full enough to burst was the realisation that *these* were exactly the kind of moments that mattered. That made life so worth living.

Flick hadn't been embracing moments like this in too long but she wasn't going to miss any more of them. She was going to make the most of every single one. Lachlan was still in a stunned silence. Or maybe he just needed to rest? Flick touched his face with a gentle stroke of her fingers.

'So, there I was, in the bluebells,' she said, so softly that only the man she loved could hear her words. 'And I'm thinking about you meeting our baby. Seeing his— or her—first smile and taking their first step. About taking them to school on their first day. Being part of a family. The way you and Josh should have been, with parents who loved you so much you'd always know how wanted you were.'

Flick could feel Lachlan's arm tighten around her. She could feel, rather than see, the tear that escaped his eye because she still had her forehead resting against his and her nose touching his. She was too close to see what the expression was in his eyes, but that didn't matter because she could feel exactly how he felt. She could feel them exchanging strength. Making silent vows to

do whatever it took to make sure they were both there to welcome that new life and nurture it with the kind of love they had found in each other.

'We'll celebrate everything,' she added. 'Birthdays and weddings. Christmas and…and…'

'Bluebells?'

'Yes…' A huff of laughter escaped Flick. 'We'll celebrate bluebell season. Every year.' She had her own tears escaping again now and she knew they were mingling with Lachlan's. 'I said something to your mother yesterday when she asked me if I thought it might be possible that you could forgive her one day.'

She paused for a heartbeat, worried that Lachlan might pull away at the reminder of past hurts, but, to her surprise, she felt his muscles soften a little.

'What was that?'

'That if you love someone enough, then anything's possible.'

'You make anything possible, Felicity Stephens,' Lachlan said quietly. 'You make life something that I never even imagined it could be. Not for me, anyway.'

Flick had to swallow hard. If only she could do the one thing Lachlan needed more than anything at this point in his life—give him the one thing that could mean he would be around to celebrate all the things that she was dreaming of sharing with him.

She probably couldn't, although she would get herself tested as a potential donor for a stem cell transplant, of course.

But maybe she wouldn't even need to do that.

They both heard the gentle tap on the door of Lach-

lan's hospital room. Flick didn't get off the bed, so she was still in Lachlan's arms as his twin brother came into the room. He wasn't alone. He was holding Stevie's hand as they came in and she had her arm around the shoulders of a young boy.

Josh's eyes widened as he took in that Lachlan and Flick were so closely entwined.

'We're interrupting something, aren't we? Maybe we should come back some other time?'

'No…it's okay.' Flick moved, sitting up and sliding her legs off the bed so she ended up just being perched on the side. As she pushed tousled hair off her face, she caught Stevie's gaze. The shared look was that of two women who were totally in love with the men they were with. A look of understanding. And joy. And…hope?

'Sorry I couldn't take your call before,' Josh was saying to Lachlan. 'We had a bit going on there for a while when Mattie here went AWOL.'

'Hi, Mattie.' Lachlan smiled at the serious-looking boy. 'I'm guessing that Stevie's your mum, yes?'

Mattie nodded. And then a smile broke out and lit up his face. 'And Josh's going to be my dad. And… and that means you're going to be my *uncle*.' He made an obvious effort to contain his excitement. 'I'm sorry that you're sick…'

Lachlan and Josh were looking at each other now and Flick could sense a similar kind of silent communication happening that she'd just shared with Stevie. Tears prickled at the back of her eyes as she realised that both these men, with a shared distrust of families and associated happiness, had found someone they could

love—who loved *them*—enough to change their lives. Something else they would have in common from now on? A bond that was creating another little miracle by giving them both an extended family. She touched her belly as she smiled at Mattie. This family was already growing…

'That is what we came here to tell you.' Josh put his hand on Mattie's shoulder as he smiled down at him. 'But it's not the only thing.'

'Josh's going to get himself tested.' Mattie looked as though he was bursting with pride. 'He's going to have a hole put into his *bones*.'

'Just one bone,' Stevie put in. She was looking just as proud of Josh as Mattie was. 'To see if he's a match.'

'He will be.' Mattie was beaming now. 'Josh says that nobody could be a better match than an identical twin and it's really lucky that he met you in time because it'll mean that you can hang around and be my uncle for ever.'

That made all the adults in the room laugh. Josh and Stevie were gazing at each other over Mattie's head. Flick turned to find Lachlan gazing at her and the laughter faded into something that wrapped itself around her heart so tightly she knew it was going to be there as long as she had breath in her body.

Lachlan was going to do everything he could to hang around for ever.

So he could be an uncle to Mattie.

And a brother to Josh.

Maybe even a son to Josephine McKendry.

But, most of all, he was going to be the man who loved *her*. The father of her baby. Her husband…?

'Hey…' Flick was still holding Lachlan's gaze. 'Did we forget something?'

'Yeah… I reckon.'

They were both smiling again as they spoke at exactly the same time. 'Will you marry me?'

They were both laughing as they spoke again, in unison.

'Yes…'

EPILOGUE

Nearly two years later...

THE BLUEBELL SEASON was at the peak of its glory in the woodlands of the McKendry family's Cotswold estate.

There were no small, lonely boys there, gathering a bouquet of the flowers to give to their mother.

There were no sad people there, either, quietly holding each other to share comfort or strength.

Instead, this patch of woodland, which was bathed in the amazing colour and scent of these iconic flowers, had a small and very select group of people, treading carefully when they moved to avoid squashing a single bloom as photographs were being taken to commemorate a wedding service that had just taken place in this magical setting. There were also two dogs who weren't being nearly as careful with the flowers.

'Come here, Cocoa,' Lady Josephine ordered. 'Just because the ceremony's over, it doesn't mean you can wreck all Jack's hard work.'

Tilly might have been delightedly working for many weeks on the wedding feast awaiting everybody back

at the house but her husband had also been busy and he'd constructed a wonderfully rustic arch from fallen branches he'd been collecting in the woods and had then decorated it with ivy and tiny, white roses from the gardens he'd nurtured for decades.

Flick had some of those roses in her wedding bouquet, as well. Along with a cloud of gypsophila and highlighted, of course, with what were now her favourite flowers on earth—the humble bluebell. The tiny lace flowers attached all over the silk chiffon skirt of her wedding dress matched the pattern of the lace bodice but there was nothing to detract from its simplicity. The dress had only spaghetti straps. Her shoes were white ballet slippers and she wore no veil—just a wreath of tiny, white flowers that nestled into her loose, tumble of shoulder length golden waves.

'I'd like one with all the boys this time.' The photographer was grinning. 'If you think you can cope with that, Lachlan?'

'Are you kidding? I've got toddling twins. I'm learning to cope with anything.' He ran to scoop up one of the boys, Liam, who was running after Cocoa, and then turned to try and see where his twin, Ben, had got to.

'I've got him,' Josh called.

'And I've got Lucky.' Mattie had his beloved, scruffy white dog in his arms. 'He's a boy too, isn't he?'

'Sure is.' Josh was trying to brush dirt off Ben's hands. 'Where do you want us?' he asked the photographer.

'Under the arch? No...that old log over there is much better. You sit in the middle, Mattie, and see if Lucky

will sit at your feet. We'll have Dad on one side, Uncle on the other and they can each hold a twin.'

It took a while to set the photograph up to his satisfaction but Flick was more than happy to stand and watch all the boys in her life as they laughed and tried to get close enough to make the photo work.

Stevie came to stand beside her and she was clearly loving this as much as Flick.

'How gorgeous is that?' Her smile was misty.

'We're outnumbered.' Flick shifted her gaze to the impressive roundness of Stevie's belly. 'Thank goodness you're having a girl.'

'If you'd waited a bit longer, she could have been a flower girl for you. How cute would that have been?'

'It feels like we waited too long already. It's been nearly two years.'

'I know. And I know Josh and I rushed off to the registry office in no time flat but that was for Mattie's benefit as much as anything. He needed to trust that us becoming a family was really going to happen. And it had to be just us because…well, you know…'

Flick nodded. 'Seems like for ever ago, thank goodness, but it was a rough few months, wasn't it? Especially getting to that hundred days after the stem cell transplant without any setbacks like infection.'

'Things were just getting manageable and then you went and had twins.'

Flick laughed. 'Who would have guessed that we had another surprise waiting in the wings? At least that was a happy one. And maybe that's why it hit me so suddenly and I fainted that day in the hospital.'

Her smile faded into something far more poignant as she let her gaze settle on her husband. 'Or maybe that was just the shock of thinking I could lose the love of my life…'

As if he felt her gaze on him, Lachlan looked up from where he was trying to prise Liam's fingers off one of his shirt buttons. The smile the two of them shared seemed to be the reason that Stevie had to brush a tear from beneath her eye.

'Josh always said that he was going to get a perfect result from being lucky enough to have a twin brother as a donor and look at him now—I reckon he *can* cope with anything at all. He's looking so well. And *so* happy…'

A peal of baby laughter came from the group on the log as Lucky leaned out of Mattie's arms to lick Liam's face.

'That's going to make a gorgeous photo.' Lady Josephine had come to stand beside Flick and Stevie. 'Just as well I put Cocoa back on her lead, though. She would have knocked them both over.'

The six-month-old chocolate Labrador had proved a valuable addition to the therapy that Lachlan's mother had been more than prepared to embrace as her contribution to the building of a new family. Now, nearly two years later, she was barely recognisable as the lonely, older woman who'd struggled with mental health issues for far too long. She was a beloved grandmother, not only to the twins but to Mattie as well. And Stevie was as much a part of this family as Lachlan's twin brother.

'It's a shame your mother wasn't up to travelling yet

after her hip surgery, Stevie. But Josh tells me you've almost got the cottage ready for her to move into.'

'Just a few final touches to make.' Stevie nodded. 'It all took far longer than we expected. The council can make you wait a long time for permission to do things to listed houses but it's all worked out perfectly in the end. Mum will have moved in by the time this one arrives—' she patted her belly '—and it was even better than the Big Brother programme for building a bond between Josh and Mattie as they tackled all their projects. I gave them matching leather tool belts that first Christmas we had together and they were both over the moon.'

The photographer had finished that shot. 'Let's have one more of the bride and groom,' he called. 'How 'bout you sit amongst the bluebells—or will that ruin your dress?'

Lachlan carried Liam towards his mother. 'Can you take him for a minute, Grandma?'

'Might be safer if someone else did.'

Lachlan's eyebrows rose. 'You're not feeling unwell, are you? Did you check your BGL this morning?'

'Of course I did. You know perfectly well my diabetes is under excellent control. I just happen to be holding a rather large and not particularly well-behaved young dog.'

'I'll take him.' Mattie had grown several inches in the last two years. 'I'm going to be a big brother soon, so I could kind of use the practice.'

Lachlan handed the toddler over. 'You'll be a fabulous big brother. Just like your dad.'

'How do you know I was born first?' Josh was grinning as he joined them.

'I was talking about how you met Mattie in the first place. Don't think you were born first, mate, but I guess that's something we'll never know.'

'Just as well. We need something to argue about.' Josh smiled down at Mattie as Lachlan took Flick's hand to lead her back to the photographer. 'How 'bout we take these wee fellows into the house? It's getting a bit colder.'

'That's where I'm heading.' Mrs Tillman was walking past. 'I need to see what's going on in my kitchen.'

'Let's all go.' Stevie smiled. 'I reckon our bride and groom might appreciate a quiet moment on their own when their photos are finally done.'

But they were actually getting a quiet moment already, as the photographer set up a longer distance shot and everybody else set off on the woodland track that would lead them back to the house.

Flick was watching them leave. Her mother-in-law, who she had such a special bond with, given how much they understood of each other's past lives. Her brother-in-law whom she loved anyway for being so like Lachlan and she could never thank him enough for making Lachlan's complete cure a possibility. She had to thank him for marrying Stevie, too, because the two women had become far more than sisters-in-law. They were best friends. And family. There were her two beloved sons as well, peering back over their uncle and cousin's shoulders, watching as they were taken temporarily out of sight of their parents.

And then Flick looked up at the person who was closest to her. Not just physically but a part of her heart and soul. The man she loved so much she'd had tears of joy on her face as they'd exchanged their vows, using their own twist on vows that hadn't lost their beauty by becoming so well known.

'You will feel no rain, because I will be your shelter...'

'You will feel no cold, because I will be your warmth...'

'You will never be lonely, because even when we're not together I will be with you, in your heart...'

'We are two people but we have one life before us.'

'I love you...'

She had tears shining in her eyes as she held Lachlan's gaze now.

'Do you remember the first time you brought me here to see the bluebells? Because you said they smelt even better in the woods?'

'How could I ever forget?' Lachlan's smile was as tender as the kiss he bent to place on Flick's lips. 'I was already in love with you—I just didn't realise it.'

'Do you remember what I said?'

'Tell me again.'

'That we all have our stories and real life isn't a fairy tale so they don't always have happy endings.'

'I remember.'

'But it's not true, is it? Not for us, anyway.' Flick's smile wobbled. 'The day I arrived here and we had some of Tilly's wonderful food in the kitchen and I was half-asleep from jet lag, I really did think I'd stepped into

some kind of fairy tale. And maybe it's been hard and it's not an ending but just a beginning but... I've never felt this happy in my life.'

'Neither have I.'

Lachlan kissed her again and it was so quiet in the woods they could hear the camera clicks of this moment being recorded for ever from the other side of the clearing. But they both felt as if they were totally alone together as they ended that kiss and smiled mistily at each other.

'Am I the prince?' Lachlan asked.

'I guess you have to be.' Flick nodded.

'That makes you my princess, doesn't it? Mind you, I already knew that, because...you know...you're wearing that gorgeous dress.'

'I am.'

'Are you going to be able to dance in that dress? Mother's expecting us to show off that perfect waltz we've been practising.'

'I know. I'd better hope I don't get nervous and stand on your toes like I did the first time.'

'I don't care if you do.' Lachlan swept Flick up into his arms, turning towards the photographer so that he could capture what had to look like pure joy, because that was exactly what it was. 'I love you, Mrs McKendry.'

'I love you, too, Mr McKendry.'

'Do you think it's time we went and found the rest of our family?'

'I do.'

'Maybe I'd better carry you. Just so you don't stand on my toes.'

Flick snuggled into his arms so that her head fitted into that delicious hollow just over his heart where she could feel it beating against her cheek.

'I think that's a very good idea...'

* * * * *

MILLS & BOON

Coming next month

RESCUING THE PARAMEDIC'S HEART
Emily Forbes

The lifeguard buggy pulled to a stop at the bottom of the metal stairs that led from the sand to the tower entrance and Poppy's jaw dropped as a lifeguard jumped out. Tall and muscular, tanned and fit.

Was that Ryder?

She managed to close her mouth as she watched him help his patient out of the buggy and up the stairs.

She hung back, out of the way, as Ryder got the man into the tower and onto the treatment plinth. Jet went to assist, instructing Bluey to keep an eye on the beach. Poppy stayed near the desk by the windows. The lifeguards had a job to do and she didn't want to be a nuisance but staying out of the way also gave her a chance to check Ryder out unobserved. She knew he hadn't noticed her, he was too focussed on his patient.

The last time she'd seen him there had been a hint of the man he would become, of the man waiting to emerge, but he'd still been a gangly teenager. He'd been tall but he'd yet to have a fast growth spurt or develop the muscle definition that would come with adulthood. But all traces of adolescence had disappeared now. Now there was no hiding the man. And no ignoring the feeling of warmth that was spreading through her belly and into her groin. Poppy leaned on the desk, taking the weight off her suddenly shaky legs.

Fortunately Ryder had his back to her and wouldn't be aware of her reaction but she was very aware of him.

He'd grown even taller and he'd definitely filled out. He'd developed muscles where he hadn't had them before. He wore only a pair of black boardshorts with 'Lifeguard' emblazoned across his hips and she had plenty of opportunity to admire the view of sculpted muscles and smooth, tanned skin. His shoulders

were broad, his biceps bulging, his waist narrow. He looked fit. He looked healthy. He looked magnificent.

She ran her gaze up the length of his spine and up his neck. She could see where the knobs of his vertebrae disappeared into his hair. He'd always had amazing hair, dark blond and thick, and at almost twenty-nine years of age it seemed he'd lost none of it.

Her gaze traced the line of his jaw. It was strong and square. He looked good, even better than she remembered, and she felt another rush of blood to her cheeks as her heart skittered in her chest.

Her hands gripped the edge of the desk as she observed him, keeping her fixed in place, and she wondered at the involuntary response. Was she stopping herself from crossing the room? While her rational mind might tell her that Ryder's unexpected appearance was of no consequence, it seemed her body had other ideas. Her palms were clammy and her mouth was dry and she suddenly felt like the sixteen-year-old schoolgirl she'd been when she'd last seen him.

When she had kissed him.

And he had kissed her back.

She knew from talking to her girlfriends that first kisses often weren't anywhere near as fabulous as they'd dreamed about but the kiss she and Ryder had shared had been everything she'd hoped for and more. It had been the biggest moment of her young life. It had changed her life.

She'd fallen in love.

First love.

She had only been a teenager but that hadn't made it any less real, any less all-encompassing, any less all-consuming.

And it hadn't made it any less painful when he'd walked out of her life.

Continue reading
RESCUING THE PARAMEDIC'S HEART
Emily Forbes

Available next month
www.millsandboon.co.uk

COMING SOON!

Also by Alison Roberts

The Paramedic's Unexpected Hero

Royal Christmas at Seattle General collection

Falling for the Secret Prince
Neurosurgeon's Christmas to Remember by Traci Douglass
The Bodyguard's Christmas Proposal by Charlotte Hawkes
The Princess's Christmas Baby by Louisa George

Twins Reunited on the Children's Ward miniseries

A Pup to Rescue Their Hearts
A Surgeon with a Secret

Available now

Discover more at millsandboon.co.uk.

Alison Roberts is a New Zealander, currently lucky enough to be living in the South of France. She is also lucky enough to write for the Mills & Boon Medical Romance line. A primary school teacher in a former life, she is now a qualified paramedic. She loves to travel and dance, drink champagne, and spend time with her daughter and her friends.